OVER MY HEAD

ALSO BY CHARLES DE LINT

Charles de Lint

OVER MY HEAD

WILDLINGS BOOK TWO

razOr
bill

RAZORBILL
an imprint of Penguin Canada

Published by the Penguin Group
Penguin Group (Canada), 90 Eglinton Avenue East, Suite 700, Toronto, Ontario, Canada M4P 2Y3

Penguin Group (USA) Inc., 375 Hudson Street, New York, New York 10014, U.S.A.
Penguin Books Ltd, 80 Strand, London WC2R 0RL, England
Penguin Ireland, 25 St Stephen's Green, Dublin 2, Ireland (a division of Penguin Books Ltd)
Penguin Group (Australia), 707 Collins Street, Melbourne, Victoria 3008, Australia
(a division of Pearson Australia Group Pty Ltd)
Penguin Books India Pvt Ltd, 11 Community Centre, Panchsheel Park, New Delhi – 110 017, India
Penguin Group (NZ), 67 Apollo Drive, Rosedale, Auckland 0632, New Zealand
(a division of Pearson New Zealand Ltd)
Penguin Books (South Africa) (Pty) Ltd, 24 Sturdee Avenue, Rosebank,
Johannesburg 2196, South Africa

Penguin Books Ltd, Registered Offices: 80 Strand, London WC2R 0RL, England

First published 2013

1 2 3 4 5 6 7 8 9 10 (RRD)

LIBRARY AND ARCHIVES CANADA CATALOGUING IN PUBLICATION

De Lint, Charles
Over my head / Charles de Lint.

(Wildlings ; bk. 2)

ISBN 978-0-670-06534-9

I. Title. II. Series: De Lint, Charles. Wildlings ; bk. 2.

PS8557.E44O94 2013   jC813'.54   C2013-901054-8

Visit the Penguin Canada website at **www.penguin.ca**

Special and corporate bulk purchase rates available; please see
www.penguin.ca/corporatesales or call 1-800-810-3104, ext. 2477.

ALWAYS LEARNING   PEARSON

FOR MELISSA,

FOR WELCOMES AND WONDERS

AND WICKED FAERIES, TOO

El sol sale para todos.
(The sun rises for everybody.)

CHAINGANG

I'm on my Harley, riding down the Pacific Coast Highway to Tiki Bay tonight. It's just an inlet, pretty much hidden from the highway, though it's got a small dirt parking lot. You can find some of the local surfers there, early mornings, late afternoons. Sometimes they party on the beach.

I'm already planning to break a few heads if I find they've been messing with my boy Lenny. He didn't tell me much on the phone. It was just:

"I need help, man."

"Where you at?"

"Tiki Bay."

And then he hung up. Or got cut off.

The parking lot's empty when I pull in. I shut down my bike and put it on its stand. Then I walk over to the rail and look down at the beach. I don't see Lenny, but this tall dude I don't know is looking back up at me.

I don't need my Wildling radar to tell me something's not right. The guy on the sand, he's some old-school Wildling—I can feel it all the way up here—and they never come looking for you unless there's trouble.

See, there's two kinds of us shapechangers, though the world only knows about the kids who got changed here in Santa Feliz. They think it's only kids. What they don't know is that there have been Wildlings since before there were people, and they come in all shapes and sizes and ages. Call themselves cousins. And there's all kinds of things I don't know about them—even someone like Auntie Min plays her cards close to her chest. I just know some of them are way older than anything else walking this world except maybe elephants and tortoises. And they're powerful. You just have to stand near one and the little *ping* of recognition that you normally get from another Wildling ratchets up, right off the board.

The fact that I can feel this guy all the way up where I'm standing means he's maybe the oldest cousin I've met so far. An elder. In my limited experience with elders, I know just one thing: nothing good's going to come out of meeting this guy.

I don't know what Lenny's got himself into, but I so don't need this. I'm still trying to play down my involvement with what happened to Josh a couple of weeks ago.

The trick to getting ahead in this world is staying off the radar so no one's paying attention to you. That means you avoid cops, news media, anything that's going to interfere with business. Riding cowboy's not the way to get that done.

Not like I'd ever turn my back on Lenny.

But I have a plan, see. Retire at twenty-five. Move to some Caribbean island. Kick back and enjoy life.

I was right on track, too, except the world keeps crapping on me.

Money isn't the problem. If I told you how much I have stashed away you'd call me a liar, but who cares? The money's still there and it's earning its keep. My money makes money. How're *your* investments doing?

Yeah, I deal drugs and I take bets. But don't cry to me about the poor kids whose lives I'm ruining. Nobody makes them buy dope or put their money down on some loser team that's never going to place. And why should I care about a bunch of suburban white kids who think wearing baggies and listening to rap makes them all gangsta?

Let them go a few days without food and all their little toys, with only jail time or a drive-by sitting in their future, and let's see how ghetto they really are.

Here's the three things you need to know about me:

First, I was always big for my age. By the time I was a teenager, I was the size of some big-ass wrestler. But you know, it's no different than a girl being born pretty. It's nothing I achieved on my own. It was just the draw of the cards.

Everybody's got things in their lives that they have no control over and I'm no different. It's not just my size. Or being Jason Washington's brother. He runs the Ocean Avenue Crips. Being J-Dog's brother gives me instant respect, but it's nothing I ever earned. I didn't choose to be born his brother, just like I didn't choose to become one of Santa Feliz's Wildlings, though I keep that one on the down low.

The second thing is, I don't take crap from anybody and I can back up those words. It's not just my size. That helps—no question—but everybody knows the Ocean Avers have my back. Though that comes with its own baggage.

The super-sized duffel bag stuffed to bursting with shit is my brother. J-Dog's crazy—no other way to put it. Comes from having been born a crack baby, I suppose. I don't know for sure, but it's as good a guess as any because, yeah, he's my brother, but the man's certifiable. Seriously. The only reason I didn't end up the same is Grandma put the fear of God into Momma when she was carrying me. No drugs. No booze. No turning tricks. The day after Momma put me in Grandma's arms, she went on a bender and died in some motel room of an overdose, probably with some guy's dick in her hand.

Grandma tried to keep J-Dog on the straight and narrow, but he's like a force of nature and there was nothing she could do with him. She tried with me, too, and I did a little better until I got jumped into the Ocean Avers. She was ready to take a belt to me that day, but what else was I supposed to do? Grandma couldn't look out for me on the street. I needed the other Avers to have my back.

Funny thing is, when I took the fall for J-Dog after he stole that car, she didn't give me any grief. She knew why I did it. J-Dog wasn't a kid anymore and I was only looking at juvie. He would've copped real jail time.

That's just the way we roll. Family sticks together. Ocean Avers stick together. J-Dog can put a crew of fifty on the street with one phone call, all armed to the teeth. So if I run into a problem I can't handle, I've got backup.

But I'm not much of a joiner. I've got a bunch of rules and J-Dog knows not to push me on them. I don't do strong-arm work and I keep mostly to myself. I don't party so much or throw my money around. I don't drink, I don't sample my own merchandise and I sure don't give a rat's ass about betting on some game. I've got a plan, remember? But somebody messes with the crew, I'll step up. The only place I draw a line is when the boys get bored and ride their choppers through Riverside

Kings' territory. I figure if you go looking for trouble with the RKs, you deserve to get your ass kicked.

The third thing is, I try to keep the gang life and my Wildling side separate. I wouldn't ask Wildlings to help out the Ocean Avers and I'm sure as hell not going to involve the gang in any kind of Wildling business if I can help it. Sure, I needed the gang to ride backup through the RKs' territory when I went to help Josh a couple of weeks back, but they didn't know dick about what was really going on.

Usually the only place the gang and Wildlings come together is with Lenny Mount. Lenny grew up next door to Grandma's so I've pretty much known him my whole life. He's not the smartest kid you're ever going to meet—I don't think he ever fully recovered from being thrown down the stairs by one of his stepdads when he was just a rug rat—but he's got a good heart. We got jumped into the Ocean Avers at the same time, and ever since his brother got taken out in a drive-by, I consider it my job to look out for him. That got to be important when he became a Wildling.

Most of us change at a traumatic moment. Me, I was on a date with a cute Mexican girl. Aina Para. We had dinner at a burger joint on Ocean Avenue, then I took her to a movie. I wasn't wearing my colours, wasn't even thinking about the gang. I met Aina at the Harley Davidson store in the ValentiCorp complex, and she didn't know anything about who I was except that my name was Theo and she liked my bike.

We had a nice time. I dropped her off at home, then rode my chopper down to the beach. I was sitting on my bike seat, looking out over the ocean—wondering about this life I'm in, how I still had a good few years to put in before I'd be on that

Caribbean beach—when I heard the sound of a low-rider pull into the parking lot behind me.

The rumble of its twin exhaust gave them away before I even turned around. Around here, only the Riverside Kings do that to their cars. When I did take a look, it was to see three of them walking toward me from a late-fifties Chevy Impala. Low on the ground, custom paint job. Sweet ride. They were all decked out in gang colours—headband, scarf hanging from a back pocket, the front guy's hoodie. I didn't need to see the colours to know who they were. All three were sleeved-out and necklaced with gang tats. The front guy's hands were empty, but his buddies were carrying baseball bats.

"Hey, *cabrón*," the lead guy said. "Nobody ever tell you to stay away from our chicas?"

It kind of pissed me off, how they'd ruined my mood, so I replied with one of the few bits of Spanish I knew: "*¡Chinga tu madre!*"

The enraged look on his face made me smile. He charged, his buddies in tow. I pulled out the tire iron I keep in a holster by my gas tank because you never know, right? But before I could use it, before they could reach me, something truly weird happened. My clothes got huge and collapsed on top of me.

I heard the clatter of the tire iron as it hit the pavement. I heard something squeak as I burrowed out of my clothes. And then I had a real WTF moment. Everything was wrong. My clothes hadn't gotten big, I'd shrunk. That squeak I'd heard had come from me because I made it again.

I was a frigging mouse and any moment one of those gangbangers was going to stomp me. Except they weren't looking down. They were looking at something on the other side of my bike and I thought they were going to crap their pants. Then they took off. They ran across the parking lot to their car like a bunch of little girls, leaving behind strips of rubber on the pavement as they peeled away.

I heard footsteps, then this old woman was hunkered down looking at me. Indian, Mexican, I don't know.

"Hey, little cousin," she said. "You want to be a real boy, you'd better start thinking of yourself as one."

It didn't make sense and it did all at the same time.

I knew what I was—what I'd become. A Wildling. It made sense that you just had to think yourself from one shape to the other. So I imagined myself the way I looked in the mirror, and just like that I was standing there in the parking lot, buck naked, towering over the old woman.

"Well now," she said as she stood up herself. "Aren't you a big boy."

"You have anything to do with this?" I said.

My hand opened and closed at my side, wanting the tire iron that was still on the ground. She didn't look like much, but I'd seen the faces of those Riverside Kings. I'd seen them run.

"What do you think?" she asked.

"I think you did something to scare the crap out of those bangers."

She didn't respond.

"So what did you do?" I asked.

"I showed them my real face. Now why don't you get dressed? That big old snake of yours is distracting me."

I laughed. I wasn't self-conscious—I couldn't care less about some old lady checking out my junk—but I did what she said because you never know when a cop is going to swing by on patrol. I'd never live it down if I got taken in for indecent exposure.

"Your real face, huh?" I said. "You going to show it to me?"

"You don't seem too perturbed about what's happened to you," the old lady said instead.

I shrugged. "I know who I am. Now I'm something else on top of it. It's not like I don't watch the news."

"You're an interesting boy," she said. "Do you want a few pointers about how to get by in your new life?"

"So you're the welcome wagon?"

"Hardly. I was just sitting there watching the tide and contemplating life when I heard the commotion and saw what happened. I know what you're going through. But maybe you don't care what an old lady's got to say. You wouldn't be the first. I won't be insulted if you just walk away right now." She waited a beat before she added, "Or we can talk."

"Show me what you've got," I told her.

That's how I met the old bag lady who calls herself Auntie Min. She says she's some kind of guardian spirit of Santa Feliz and I don't know about that. But she's got lots of mojo, no question. And she sure helped me through my first few days of being a Wildling.

Lenny Mount didn't have my luck.

His change happened when he was high as a kite, wandering along the side of the highway. I'm not sure what happened. Maybe he got too close to the cliffs and slipped. Maybe he decided he could fly. He never did explain.

But it turned out he *could* fly.

One moment he's just another kid, grew up in the Orchards like the rest of us ghetto kids. The next he's a seagull, riding the winds high above the shoreline where his clothes have fallen and the undertow's dragging them out to sea.

He was lucky. He could have changed back into a kid while he was still in the air. Instead he managed to land first. Whatever drugs he'd done had been washed from his system, so he knew enough to come looking for me, bare-assed and all.

Losing all your clothes happens to everybody the first time. You learn pretty fast how to be wearing them when you change back to your human shape. Don't know how it works. Don't much care. Just so long as it does.

Anyway, we have a clubhouse just outside of town, on the land side of the Pacific Coast Highway—not right on the highway, just back a little ways down a dirt road. It used to be some rich dude's ranch until he owed J-Dog a little too much money and signed the deed over. Now it belongs to the Ocean Avers.

It's got a guesthouse in back and that's my crib, my private space. Nobody just walks in. I've got AC and a sweet sound system, Blu-ray, big-ass TV, top-of-the-line computer, PlayStation. It's where, if I don't want to join the boys when they're partying, I can kick back and take it easy.

That's what I'm doing the night Lenny changed. Surfing the Net while some old black-and-white horror flick's on the flat-screen. I can hear the *boom-boom-boom* of the bass from the main building, but it's no more irritating than the sound of traffic out on the highway.

Then in comes Lenny not wearing a stitch of clothing and looking like the sky just fell down on his head.

I knew right away what had happened to him—Wildlings have a kind of radar in their heads that lets us recognize each other. Doesn't always work on people you know well, but Lenny could never keep anything from me and his bare ass was a big giveaway.

If I had him under my wing before, now I really needed to take care of him or he'd end up in some government lab or something. I gave him some ground rules. Lenny's not smart, like I already said, but he can follow orders.

Rule number one: no changing where anybody could see him.

Rule number two: no telling anybody about what had happened.

Rule number three: if something happened—he got the urge to change and couldn't fight it, or he got surprised into it—he had to stay put and call me right away, as soon as he could.

So that's why I'm here at Tiki Bay tonight.

I take another look around the parking lot. Nothing's changed. There's still just me and my bike. No sign of Lenny. No sign of his ride. But it's no coincidence that this elder Wildling is waiting for me on the sand.

If I were smart, I'd be calling for some backup, but who am I going to call? The Avers know dick-all about Wildlings—never mind the old-school cousins—and the only Wildlings I know have less of a clue about any of this than I do. And the thing is, I don't depend on anybody else for help. People come to *me* for that. I've always been the guy that fixes the problem, not the one that goes around crying about it.

So I take that tire iron from its holster and walk down the metal stairs to the beach, holding it loosely at my side. Ready, but not threatening.

That vibe from the stranger just gets stronger and stronger. By the time I'm standing in front of him the *ping*'s going full tilt in my head like a pinball machine that just hit the jackpot.

He's a tall dude—taller than me. I'm two-fifty on a six-foot-two frame and he's got a couple of inches on me, all long lines and wiry. Pale-skinned with jet hair, face chiselled like a cliff and just as still. It's funny. You don't see many of the elders with skin that pale. He's shirtless and barefoot, wearing only a dark cotton suit that's seen better days.

I don't say anything but my nose is working. I can smell him—musky and strong. I also get a faint whiff of Lenny. He's been here.

"I have a job for you," the guy says, like I work for him.

"Where's Lenny?" I ask.

"I need you to kill the boy with the mountain lion inside him," he says like I never spoke. "I don't care how he dies, just do it so it's clear he was killed by a human."

I know who he's talking about. Every Wildling and cousin from L.A. to the Mexican border would know.

"You want Josh dead," I tell him, "do it yourself. But you've got to know he won't be alone when you come for him."

Josh is a good kid, but everybody makes enemies. Thing I can't figure is why this old-school cousin wants him dead. Last time I heard, the elders all thought Josh was like the second coming.

"Don't try my patience, boy."

I can't tell if he's insulting me, or he's just calling me that because he's so much older than me. Doesn't really matter. First off, I don't do anybody's dirty work. Second thing, I like Josh. And only my grandma gets to call me "boy."

"Now you're just pissing me off," I say.

I move fast, bringing up the tire iron. I'm not planning to kill the guy. I'm just going to put a hurt on him.

But he's faster. And stronger.

He catches the tire iron as it's swinging toward him and plucks it out of my hand like he's dealing with some little kid. I'm too surprised to stop him from giving me a whack with the iron. If he'd wanted to, he could have bashed my head in. I know that. But I still feel like I've run headfirst into a wall.

I can't keep my balance and put out my hands to stop my fall. The sand doesn't feel right under my palms when I land on the beach. It gives too much. I brush away at it and there's Lenny's dead face looking up at me.

"You son of a bitch!" I yell.

I come up off the sand, done with playing around. But before I can even take a swing at him, he grabs me by my throat and lifts me from the sand. I dangle like a doll in his grip. My head's still ringing from the tire iron. Now I'm seeing stars and I can't breathe. But I can't get loose. Every time I try, he gives me a shake. Just before I black out he tosses me back on the sand.

I lie there wheezing. I've never run into anybody this strong before and I don't know what to do. I want to kill him for what he did to Lenny, but I play it smart and just lie there, catching my breath. Gathering my strength.

He hunkers down, sitting on his calves. There's still no emotion on his face. He doesn't say anything, just stares at me.

"I don't like repeating myself," he finally says. "Kill the boy and we're done. And make it look clean. Nothing that even hints at an animal attack or that cousins were ever involved. I'll give you a week. That should be time enough to do it right."

"Kill him yourself."

Something flickers in his eyes, then it's like I'm looking at a statue again.

"There's nothing I'd like better," he says, "but I have to stay out of this. The other cousins can't know I'm involved."

I try to keep him talking, hoping he'll lower his guard.

"What've you got against Josh?" I ask.

"It's not the boy himself. It's what they have planned for him. We need to disappear back into story and legend, not parade ourselves like cheap whores."

"Sure," I say. "I get it."

I make a show of moving slow as I sit up. Get my feet under me. But before I can lunge at him he reaches out and hits me at the base of my neck with the side of his hand. Just like that I lose all feeling in the right side of my body and fall face down onto the beach. I choke on a mouthful of sand.

"See that you do," he says, standing. "One week. If you don't have the job done by then, it'll be your grandmother lying here under the sand. Or that little Mexican girl that pals around with the boy. I know you like her."

Then he walks away. I struggle to get up. By the time I get my left arm under me and lever myself into a sitting position, he's gone. There's just me and dead Lenny left on the beach.

If I were human, I'd have to soldier through the physical pain. But I'm not. Wildlings aren't just stronger and faster than regular people. We heal quicker, too. It's just a matter of shifting from our animal shapes and back again. I guess the physics are the same as how we can shift our clothes with us and bring them back again.

Still don't care how it works. Just that it does.

I embrace the animal under my skin, then shift right back to my human shape. I look down at Lenny, his face bathed in the moonlight. You know how on TV you always see somebody closing the dead guy's eyes? I never got that till now. There's just something wrong about poor Lenny's dead stare.

I close his eyes and stand up. I pull out my phone and call J-Dog, tell him about Lenny's call, how I found Lenny murdered here at Tiki Bay. I don't mention the old-school cousin.

It's too early to figure out how I'm going to handle this, but I know one thing for sure. That dude's going to be dead by the end of the week. I don't care how hardcore he thinks he is.

Then I pull Lenny the rest of the way out of the sand and sit down beside him to wait for my brother.

MARINA

I'm at my dad's house watching a documentary on TV with my stepsisters Ria and Suelo when my sister Ampora walks in. I'm surprised to see her since she usually makes herself scarce when she knows I'm coming over. She frowns when she sees me sitting on the couch with the girls, but that's the most she can do. The first time I visited after the divorce she tore into me and Papá laid down the law. So now I mostly get the cold shoulder. She waits until school to give me the finger and mouth "*pocha*" when she can't avoid walking by me.

Ampora's a year younger than me. We look a lot alike—same crazy dark hair and trim build, same cheekbones and big brown eyes—but no one would ever mistake one of us for the other because of our fashion choices. I'm the surfer girl with the built-in tan, while she makes like she runs with the bandas. I don't know if she does or doesn't for real. She never wears gang colours and Papá would kill her if she got any tattoos.

She never comes over to my house. She and Mamá both feel the other betrayed them—Mamá by leaving Papá, Ampora by refusing to have anything to do with Mamá and me. I'll be honest. I used to come here in the hope that we could be close again, but I gave that up a long time ago. Now I just come for Papá, my stepmom, Elena, and the girls.

"Crap," she says, looking at me. "Is it Tuesday already?"

I feel the girls tense up on either side of me, but she doesn't go on and I keep my mouth shut, so that keeps the peace.

The documentary we're watching is about Wildlings. They just ran that old footage that everybody who lives here in Santa Feliz has seen a thousand times.

The grainy video, shot by a surveillance camera, shows a teenage boy crossing a parking lot, about to be swarmed by a half-dozen other kids. Halfway across the lot, he changes into a hawk—snap! Just like that. The film ends with him flying out of camera range. All that's left on the ground is a heap of clothes, a pair of running shoes and the other kids staring up into the sky with their mouths hanging open.

It's been a little over six months now since that happened, and to this day no one has any idea why some kids change while most don't, or why it's only happening to kids in Santa Feliz. There's all this talk—repeated in the documentary—about how there are no genetic markers, no sign of a virus or anomalies in the blood, which makes it impossible to predict or treat, or even develop a vaccine to prevent further occurrences. Blah blah blah. All most people living here really know is that every week or so some poor kid or another turns into a shapechanging freak. At least, those are the ones that we know about.

The male narrator's voice is low and ominous, trying to evoke fear. He speculates as to how many teenagers among our population of twenty thousand will be changed into Wildlings, how many already have and how one of them could be a seagull floating above the pier, a lizard on your garden wall or the kangaroo rat living in your garage.

I have all this stuff memorized by now—pretty much everybody in Santa Feliz does. I guess you'd think if you lived in the place where it was happening, you'd be sick of hearing about it, but reactions are pretty much evenly divided. The phenomenon captivates and excites people like my stepsisters, who can't hear enough about it. And then there are others who are terrified by it, wish it had never happened and want it all to just go away.

Or those like my sister, with her own blinkered view of the situation.

She slumps into a chair and looks at the screen. "Is this all that's on?"

"We like this," Suelo says.

Ria nods. "Yeah, Wildlings are cool."

Ampora laughs. "Come on. They're not even real."

My stepsisters look at me.

"Of course they're real," I tell them.

I mean, I should know, right?

"Oh, please," Ampora says. "That's exactly what they want you to think."

"Who's *they*?" Ria asks.

There's only one year's difference between my stepsisters, the same as Ampora and me. Unlike us, they get along just fine. Ria's eight and the youngest, which makes all of us want to protect her.

"You know," Ampora says, "the government. Big business. Whatever."

"What would be the point?" I ask.

I don't really want to be drawn into an argument, but this is just stupid.

"To keep us under control."

"Why would they want to control us? We're just another beach town. There's nothing special about us."

"Until now," Suelo says.

Ampora ignores her.

"We're the guinea pigs," she says. "They're running tests on us to see what they can get away with."

"By turning kids into Wildlings."

She shakes her head. "No, by making up a crisis. You just wait until the quarantine comes down and we're locked up tight. Under. Their. Control."

The sad thing is, she's not the only person who thinks like this. I know it's not true, but with people like Ampora it's impossible to change their minds. I don't really care what she thinks, but I don't like her scaring my stepsisters.

"Is that really going to happen?" Ria asks me.

I shake my head.

"God," Ampora says. "How can you be so naive?"

"I'm not being naive. No matter what you might want to believe, Wildlings are real—not a government conspiracy.

"Just look at the surveillance footage from the 7-Eleven," I go on. "That kid turns into a hawk. You can't fake that."

Ampora rolls her eyes. "Have you been to a movie lately?"

Before I can answer, my stepmother Elena comes out of the kitchen and fixes Ampora with a stern look.

"What did your Papá say about starting fights with Marina?" she asks.

I jump in before Ampora can. "It's okay," I say. "We're not fighting. We're just talking about Wildlings."

Elena crosses herself.

Oh, yeah. That's another reaction: the Wildlings are a curse that can be warded off with prayers and by burning candles to the saints. Elena's reaction isn't so different from how Mamá sees it, but she's not nearly as intense about it as Mamá.

There's footage running now on the TV of Congressman Householder being interviewed in his Washington office about the failure of his quarantine bill. Ampora points at the TV screen.

"There," she says. "It's guys like that who are behind this. Rich old white men."

Elena sighs and goes back into the kitchen. I don't like Householder any more than Ampora does. He's not even our representative, but I'll bet more people in Santa Feliz know who he is than they do the name of our own congresswoman. If you believe him, everything that's happening here is our fault and Santa Feliz should be sealed off before we start infecting the rest of the world.

"Well, he's not exactly brimming with compassion," I say.

"I could tell you what he's full of," she says.

I smile. "Are we actually agreeing on something?"

She pulls a face, gets up and stomps off to her room. The door slams shut. The girls and I enjoy the rest of the documentary in peace.

We're watching a dance competition with Elena when Papá finally gets home.

"I'm so sorry," he says when he comes through the door. "I tried to get away, but we really need to get this contract done and—"

"It's okay," I tell him. I put my arms around my stepsisters. "I've been having a great time."

"Elena said there was some trouble with Ampora?" Papá asks when he's driving me home.

I shake my head. "We were just talking about Wildlings. She thinks it's a big government conspiracy and I don't."

"Whatever the cause," Papá says, "it's a terrible thing to have happen to our young people. My heart goes out to the parents of those children who died in that laboratory."

"Do you really think Wildlings are a terrible thing?"

He gives me a sharp look before returning his attention to the road.

"You're as bad as the girls," he says, meaning Ria and Suelo. "They think it's wonderful, like those books that they've read a hundred times."

"The Animorphs," I say, referring to the girls' favourite series of books from back in the nineties, where superhero kids fight off an alien invasion by shifting into animals. Ria and Suelo can almost quote them word for word.

"It's not natural," Papá says.

"Maybe it's completely natural."

He frowns at me, then shakes his head.

"You really are as bad as the girls," he says.

"At least I'm not in denial about it, like Ampora."

"Ampora's stubborn—like her mother."

"Hey, she's my mother, too."

"You know what I mean."

I nod and look out the window. We drive under the I-405,

leaving the barrio behind. Going away from the barrio always gives me a funny feeling—like a big part of what makes me who I am has to be stripped away to become the gringa Mamá thinks I should be. But I can't turn into a good little gringa. It doesn't matter that I live on this side of the underpass, or even that I'm a Wildling now. I'll never stop being the Mexican girl whose roots are deep in the barrio. I don't care what Mamá or Ampora think.

I'd love to come out of the Wildling closet, but that's not going to happen any time soon. I glance at Papá. Neither he nor Elena would take it well. Mamá would go ballistic and have me in church and praying for forgiveness every moment that I wasn't in school. But I'd love to see the look on Ampora's face. And the girls would be in my corner. It would be so much fun to share the secret with them, but that can't ever happen.

I sigh.

"You all right, *mija?*" Papá asks.

I find a bright smile to give him. "I was just thinking of a history essay I have to do. I haven't even started the research."

A short but gentle lecture on the importance of doing well in school takes us all the way to the house I share with Mamá and my stepdad.

"I'm sorry I was late," Papá says as I start to get out of the car.

"I know."

I give him a big hug and stand at the end of our walk to watch him leave. I turn to go in and my phone rings. I check the display. For a moment, "Theo Washington" doesn't register. When it does, I press Talk.

"Chaingang," I say. "What's up?"

"We need to talk," he says.

"I'm listening."

"Not on the phone."

My pulse quickens. Something has to be wrong.

"I'm just getting home from my dad's place," I tell him. "And I'm still grounded, remember?"

"Can you sneak out later? I could meet you on the beach."

"This can't wait?"

There's a long moment of silence, then he says, "It's about Josh."

I stiffen as worry blossoms into full-out anxiety.

"Is he okay?"

"Yeah, so far," Chaingang says. "You sure you can't come?"

"Not for an hour or so. I'll get away as soon as I can."

"Call me when you're on your way," he says. "And sweetcheeks? Be careful. Make sure no one sees you once you're out of the house."

He cuts me off before I can tell him not to call me that.

I go into the house, trying to hide my worry. But it's hard. The last time Josh got into trouble we almost lost him for good.

It's almost four a.m. before I can sneak out. Mamá's had one of her restless nights and she's been up talking to the saints for ages. I've been taking catnaps, waking up every half hour or so to see if I can still hear the murmur of her voice. When I'm sure she's asleep, I put on my running gear and slip out of the house.

I'm not planning to actually go for a run—this is early, even for me. But it's a good excuse in case I get caught coming back inside. Officially, I got grounded for three weeks for staying out all night when Josh got kidnapped. Mamá thinks I was out looking for him, which she understands. She's only mad because

I didn't call. But the reason I didn't call was because that little adventure took us into some whole Wildling otherworld that kind of sits on top of the one we live in. Or maybe it's side by side.

I know. I'm still trying to get my head around it, too. But the point is, there was no cell reception, so I couldn't have called even if I'd thought of it. Trust me, when you're that far out of the normal world, calling your mom is pretty much the last thing on your mind.

And then, ever since the news about those murdered kids got out, Mamá's been more protective than ever.

So I'm grounded except for school, going to Papá's and my early morning runs. No band practice. No hitting the waves. Mamá knows I'd rather surf than run, so even though I get to stay in shape, not being able to catch a wave is a hard punishment. Running doesn't even come close.

We live less than a block from the ocean. I send Chaingang a text, then let my Wildling senses flood out as I jog down to the boardwalk. My running shoes are almost silent on the pavement. I can hear the wind in the palms and the siren call of the waves. The air is filled with the scents of eucalyptus and brine and a thousand other smells.

I stop at the boardwalk and look around. This early in the morning, even the treasure hunters with their metal detectors aren't out. The machines aren't smoothing the sand. There aren't any joggers or dog walkers or anybody. It's just me. I love being out when everybody else is asleep.

"Hey, Marina," a voice says from behind me. "Thanks for coming."

I just about jump out of my skin before I turn to look at Chaingang.

"How ...?" I begin, but I don't have to finish because I already know.

He didn't sneak up on me. He was already here in his Wildling mouse shape. He's probably been close by all night, waiting for my text. This has to be serious.

"No problem," I tell him. "What's up?"

"Let's talk by the surf," he says. "Less chance of anybody listening in."

"Will you stop being so mysterious!"

"I'm not being mysterious—just careful. Walk with me."

He grabs my hand and leads me to the shore, letting go when he sees he's got my attention and I'm staying with him. We walk along the water line. The waves wash in, erasing our footsteps almost as soon as we make them.

"Lenny Mount's dead," he finally says.

"Oh, I'm so sorry. He was the other Wildling in your gang?"

"Yeah."

"How did it happen?"

"He was killed."

I remember how Chaingang told me this had something to do with Josh, so I say the obvious: "Because he was a Wildling?"

Chaingang shakes his head. "No, because he knew me."

"I don't understand."

"Some old-school cousin killed him as an example."

I stop and he does, too, but he doesn't look at me. His gaze is out on the ocean, tracking the slow progress of a freighter.

"An example of what?" I ask.

Chaingang finally turns to me. There's something weird in

his eyes and it takes me a moment to figure out what it is. When I do, a chill goes up my spine.

He's scared.

Okay, this is Chaingang, so scared probably isn't the right word. I mean, normally nothing fazes him. But something's definitely got him spooked and I'm not sure I want to know what could do that.

"Here's the deal," Chaingang says. "Lenny was killed as an example of what'll happen to the people closest to me if I don't do what this guy says."

"You *talked* to the killer? And he's still walking around in one piece?"

"You don't get it," he says. "This guy's on a whole other level. He picked me up by the throat like I was some little kid. He could've killed me, too, right then and there, and I couldn't have done a damn thing to stop him."

"What does he want you to do?"

He looks away again. "He wants me to kill Josh."

My breath catches in my throat.

"Yeah," Chaingang goes on, "and it has to look like it was done by a human. Nothing to lead back to Wildlings or those old-school cousins. I've got a week to do the job. If it's not done, then he'll start in on my grandma and—other people close to me."

"This isn't making any sense."

"Tell me about it."

But when I start to think about it, I see a sick logic.

"You know what?" I say. "This must have something to do with how Auntie Min and some of the other cousins think Josh is some kind of chosen one."

Chaingang nods. "Poster boy for when the older cousins out themselves."

"Except some of those older cousins don't want that to happen."

Chaingang nods again. "One of them, for sure. And he doesn't want anyone to get the idea that Wildlings are involved. He was real serious about that."

For a long moment I can't speak.

"What—what are you going to do?" I finally manage to get out.

"I don't know. I've got a week to figure out who he is and then take him down. But I need your help."

"*My* help?"

His face closes down. "Hey, you don't want to get involved, no problem."

I put a hand on his arm.

"I didn't say that," I tell him. "It's just—what could *I* possibly do?"

"Well, we need to know who he is, what his weaknesses are—if he even has any. I thought you could talk to Auntie Min. See if you can find out who he is. But don't come right out and ask her. Just kind of ease up on it."

"You don't think she's mixed up in this, do you?"

"I don't know what to think," he says. "All I know is I don't trust anybody except for you and Josh. And we can't get him involved. Not yet, anyway."

"How can we not tell him?"

"Because he's liable to fly off the handle like he did when the ValentiCorp people grabbed him. Or he'll get all freaked and that'll be a giveaway. I figure this dude's watching me. That's why I need *you* to talk to Auntie Min. He can't see me going to her."

"Except ..."

"Yeah, I know," he says. "If he's watching me, then he's seen us together."

He actually gets a shy look, which might be the weirdest thing that's happened so far this morning.

He clears his throat. "I don't want him to figure out that I'm setting you up to warn Josh or any of the elders, so I was thinking we could pretend that we're—you know, seeing each other. On the sly."

"Like we're a secret couple?"

"I know. It's stupid."

"No, it's a good idea. But we'll have to sell it."

That catches him off guard.

"Sell it?" he says.

"You know." I step up close and put my arms around his neck. "Like this."

I stand on my tiptoes. He bends down and our lips meet.

I don't know where I got the nerve to do this. I guess it's because, for all his big, tough rep, I've always felt that he has a soft spot for me. That I can do this and he won't be rough or take advantage of me.

But I'm not expecting it to be so *nice*. No, scratch that. It's not nice, it's wonderful. His arms and chest are hard with muscle, but his lips are soft and by the time we break off I realize I've forgotten to breathe. But the best thing about it is the look in his eyes, so close to mine. I get the sense that he's drinking it all in, every moment, so that he'll never forget it.

I know I won't.

"That ..." I have to clear my throat. "That should work for whoever's watching."

"Yeah," Chaingang says. "It sure worked for me."

But then he seems to catch himself. He takes a step back, but one arm stays around my shoulders.

"We should go," he says.

His eyes say we shouldn't. His eyes say we should just lie down here together and forget the world. And I want to. Oh, I want to. But wonderful as that kiss was, I know we can't be together. He's a drug dealer and part of a gang. He's been to juvie and his brother runs the Ocean Avers. I don't want any part of that life.

But if he were to step away from it all ...

I don't let myself go there. You either embrace someone for who they are or you walk away. You don't try to change a person.

I just wish someone would tell my pulse that.

"What about your brother?" I ask, trying to think about something other than that amazing kiss. "What's he going to do?"

"J-Dog doesn't know anything more than me finding Lenny at Tiki Bay."

"You didn't tell him about the guy?"

"I can't. None of the Avers know about Lenny and me— that we're Wildlings. And they can't ever know about this guy. J-Dog's pretty much the toughest dude I know, and he's crazy enough to do pretty much anything, but that elder would take him down without even breaking a sweat. It's just us. You and me. We're on our own."

"We'll figure this out."

"I know. I knew I could count on you."

He walks me back to the boardwalk, arm still around my shoulders. I think he's put what happened between us out of his mind, but when we stop at the end of my street, he turns to me.

"Back there," he says. "That was nice."

I want to remind him that this is just a role we're playing, except then I'm back on my tiptoes and I give him a quick kiss.

"Later," I say.

Before he can react or say anything else, I set off for home at a jog.

When I get back into bed, I can't sleep. I think about this mysterious cousin and what he wants. I worry about Josh. I try to figure out how I'll sneak off to see Auntie Min.

But mostly I think about that long kiss at the water line and how good it felt to be in Chaingang's arms.

Theo, I tell myself.

From now on I'm going to call him Theo.

JOSH

I don't get girls. I mean I *really* don't get them.

Two weeks ago I had a girlfriend, but even that was complicated. Elzie was perfect. Cute, smart and a Wildling just like me. The first thing she told me was that she didn't want commitments. Then she hung out with me every day, like we were going steady, until she walked out of my life as suddenly as she came into it.

She did give me a choice: leave everything I know and go with her into an unspoiled otherworld that only Wildlings can find.

Or not.

I know why she stayed over there. That place was everything this world isn't, the way it must have been before people ever showed up. It's what she wants this world to be: no people and none of the crap that people need to survive, like houses and factories and roads and cars. But I have too many people I care about to abandon them all. So I abandoned her instead. I just let her go and came back here.

I still have no idea if I did the right thing. I know why I did it. I couldn't just walk out on Mom without any explanation. My father already did that, and I'm not going to be the same guy as him. But it's hard. I think about Elzie all the time. I just really really miss her. She was so free spirited and totally embraced her Wildling side. She showed me how to let out the mountain lion in me and appreciate the wild freedom it gave me. I haven't had that experience since I left the otherworld.

It's especially bad at night when there's nothing else to distract me. At least during the day I've got school to keep me busy, but that has its own pitfalls.

I don't know why I wasn't expecting it. Just because I survived being Tasered, kidnapped and then imprisoned for sick medical experimentation by a private corporation, doesn't mean the drama that is everyday life at Sunny Hill High School is going to take a vacation.

I'm not paying attention to it until it's too late. I'm just trying to fit myself back into my old world. My old life.

The elder Wildlings say it's impossible. I'm a member of the Mountain Lion Clan and that's who I am now. That's what my new life is, and they've got all kinds of ideas about what I'm supposed to do.

Turns out they're right—about me not being able to go back to my old life, I mean—but not for the reasons they gave me. The reason I can't get my old life back is because I totally messed up with my best friend Marina and, without her, all the things that were important to me don't mean very much anymore. Our friendship goes deeper than my relationship with Elzie. Marina and I have known each other forever, and up until a couple of weeks ago, I wouldn't have thought that anything could come between us.

But that changed after she lied to me. We said we'd put it behind us—and I'm trying—but what we really need to do is sit down and talk it out, and we haven't been able to do that yet. Since she's been grounded, I only see her at school and that's no place to have a serious, face-to-face, uninterrupted conversation. So we're left with a big disconnect. It all feels like small talk and surface friendliness, and I hate it.

I still hang with Desmond. We play in his garage, but the programmed drum beats we're using are no match for Marina's live playing. Des and I still go the skatepark. The beach. School. But everything seems ... smaller without her.

Without her. Without Elzie.

Mostly, the days just go by.

But meanwhile—and let me tell you, I didn't have a clue this was going on—Erik Gess had been building up a long slow rage aimed right at me.

Let's count the reasons he's so ticked off at me: I'm not white. He thinks I'm a drug dealer. He also thinks I'm a Wildling— thank you for that, Desmond. And then there's the fact that I made him look like a fool when he tried to jump me at lunch one day. He got suspended, I just got detention. That's got to hurt for the president of the Sunny Hill Purity Club and one of the stars of our school's track team.

I should point out that while the Sunny Hill Purity Club is associated with the national one, the national club is inclusive. It doesn't matter what colour your skin is. All you have to do is swear off drugs, alcohol and sex and you're golden. Not so much with our local version. Not only do I have it on good authority that they drink and smoke dope on the sly, they also have this whole whites-only thing. If you're Asian, Latino or black, don't even think of joining.

I've never had any interest in their club. I don't drink or take drugs, but I don't do celibacy. At least, I didn't until my girlfriend dumped me. No, that's not really fair. She wanted me to stay with her in that parallel otherworld we found ourselves in.

But I'm getting off track.

The point is, I've got a lot going on and I'm still trying to figure it out. If something's not right in front of me demanding attention, I don't think about it. Erik was still suspended when I got back to school, so he just wasn't on my radar anymore. That changed on his first day back.

I was still doing my detentions—I only had three more days of staying after school—so Desmond goes ahead to the skatepark, where I'll meet him later.

At least, that's the plan.

The problem is, a half mile from the school, a couple of guys from the track team come out of a lane onto the sidewalk to block my way. Kurt Stice and Hughie Jones. Wherever they are, Erik can never be that far away. I don't bother to turn around when I hear two more sets of footsteps coming up behind me. I know neither of them is Erik because I can already catch his scent coming from the lane Kurt and Hughie stepped out of. A moment later and there he is. He saunters around the corner of the adobe building looking very pleased with himself, and I realize that while I haven't been thinking about him, he's been obsessing about me.

I glance behind me. Allan Laramore and Christian Willert are standing there. All five of them are blue-eyed and blond—

which isn't hard to find in So-Cal—but it's like the junior branch of the Aryan Brotherhood has tracked me down.

"There's no place to run, Saunders," Erik says. "You're not going anywhere."

I turn back to him. "What do you want?"

"What do you think I want? You made me look like an asshole in front of the whole school. It's payback time."

"We don't have to do this."

He grins. "Oh, but we *do*. We're going to find out how tough you Wildlings really are."

"I'm not a Wildling."

That grin gets bigger. "Then I guess this is really going to hurt."

I have this long moment of clarity—or at least it feels long. I guess it's more like how time seems to slow down when you're in the middle of an accident. But I have all this time to think. I realize that I could probably take all five of them—without even having to shift into a mountain lion. The problem with that is, there goes any chance I have of salvaging a normal life. Nobody's going to believe I could take on all these guys by myself unless I *am* a Wildling.

So I take option two.

I let Allan and Christian grab me from behind. I struggle in their grip—but not like the mountain lion wants me to. It wants me to shred the pair. I only struggle enough to sell myself as being a kid, outnumbered and in trouble.

Then Erik hits me and I almost let the mountain lion go. It's not the pain of his fist in my face. It's the smarmy look of triumph on his. I want to wipe it off. The mountain lion wants to rip it off.

The next fist hits me in the stomach and I double over. Allan and Christian let me go and I fall down. I start to get up, but one of them kicks me in the back and I go down again. Then they all start kicking me and I realize this wasn't such a bright idea. If I didn't want a confrontation, I should have just taken off. I could have left them all behind in half a block.

But this—

Erik sits on my chest and starts pounding on my face.

"Hey, easy, man," I hear someone say. "You're going to kill him."

I don't have any choice. I have to let the mountain lion out now or he *is* going to kill me.

But before I can, I hear a car squeal to a halt right beside us. A door opens and a familiar voice yells, "FBI. Nobody move."

Except they all take off like scared rabbits. The mountain lion wants to chase them down and snap their necks, one by one. I just lie there on the pavement and try to breathe as I listen to them run off.

Something blocks the sun. I squint through swollen eyes to see Agent Solana bending down toward me. Agent Matteson is standing behind him. The last time I saw them was when they came by the house to tell me that the security guys from ValentiCorp were out on bail but I didn't need to worry about them. Part of their bail restrictions was that they weren't allowed back in Santa Feliz.

"Jesus Christ, kid," Matteson says. "You're a freaking mess."

Solana puts a hand behind me and gently helps me sit up.

"You—you should see the other guys."

It's hard to talk. My lips feel twice their normal size. My tongue finds a loose tooth.

"We did," Matteson says. "They didn't have a mark on them."

His lip twitches and I realize he's trying to make a joke.

"Why—are you guys—still following me?"

"We just happened to be driving by," Matteson says.

Yeah, right. But all I say is, "Lucky—for me."

"Yeah, no kidding. You must have really pissed those guys off."

"We need to get you to a hospital," Solana says. "And call in the locals. Can you identify any of your assailants?"

I shake my head. That hurts, too.

"No hospital," I say. "And no police."

"This is serious," Solana says. "Those boys could have killed you."

"Did—you ever go to high school?" I ask.

Solana nods.

"Remember how much everybody liked the kid who squealed?"

"This is heavy-duty bullying. Assault isn't the same as who stole somebody's pencil," Matteson says.

"No police," I repeat.

The agents exchange a look. Matteson sighs.

"There's not much we can do if he won't identify them," he says.

Solana nods. "But we're taking you to the hospital. You could have internal injuries."

I force myself to my feet and try not to sway. I hurt everywhere.

"I just got roughed up," I say. "You showed up right after it started. All I need to do is go home and lie down."

Solana glances at Matteson and shakes his head.

"I wouldn't say no to a ride home," I tell him before he can say anything.

Again they exchange a look.

"It's his call," Matteson finally says.

I accept Solana's help to the car.

When we're all inside, Matteson leans over the seat to look at where I'm slumped in a corner.

"Why did you let them beat you up?" he asks.

"It wasn't *my* idea."

"But with your abilities, you could have—"

"I keep telling you. I'm not a Wildling."

He studies me for a long moment.

"Yeah," he finally says. "I guess you're not."

"Seat belt," Solana says as Matteson pulls the car away from the curb.

I fumble with the clasp until it locks into place. I lean my head on the back of the seat and stare out the window. I can't remember ever hurting as much as I do right now. Under my skin I can feel the mountain lion's impatience. It wants to go hunting.

I close my eyes.

Mom's not home when they drop me off. I go in and grab some painkillers, then collapse on the couch. I manage to text Des to tell him that something's come up and I can't meet him, then I lie back. I know there's something about not falling asleep when you could have a concussion, but right now I don't care. The adrenaline rush that's been keeping me going has worn off and I need to crash. I wrap myself in Mom's TV blanket and let the painkillers take me away.

*

It feels like only minutes later when I wake to Mom hovering over me. The look on her face tells me I haven't magically healed while I was asleep. Then I remember. That only happens when you shift into your animal form and then back again.

"It's okay," I lie. "It looks way worse than it really is."

"What *happened*?"

"I got jumped by some guys after school."

For a moment her worry turns to puzzlement.

"I don't understand," she says. "Couldn't your—special abilities—protect you?"

"But that was the whole point. How better to prove that I'm not a Wildling?"

"And you think *this* was worth it?"

"It seemed like a good idea at the time."

"Who were these boys?"

I shake my head.

"Joshua Saunders. If you think I'm going to just stand back and let a bunch of thugs give my son a beating, you don't know me very well."

It takes me a lot longer to convince her than it did the FBI agents. And then I have to convince her that I don't need to go to emergency. She gets a bag of frozen peas from the freezer to hold against my mouth. I'd protest, but this is a better use for them. I never could stand the things.

By the time she stops grilling me, I'm exhausted. For one thing, it isn't easy talking around a bag of peas. She lets me go to bed, but I can still hear her grumbling to herself from where I lie. Then it all goes away as I fall asleep again.

*

Sometime in the middle of the night, I wake up from a jumble of weird, vivid dreams with the feeling that there's someone in my bedroom. It takes me a moment to get rid of the fog inside my head to focus on the figure sitting in my desk chair: Cory. He looks the same as he always does—like some street kid around my age, dark skinned, hair almost black—but he's one of those old-school animal people who've been around for a lot longer than the half-year or so that Wildlings have been appearing in Santa Feliz.

I have a bit of a love/hate thing going with him. He was the first to find and help me when I became a Wildling—so props for that—but deep down, I kind of blame him for it all having happened to me in the first place. Not fair—I know. But some things just don't make sense, they just are.

"You look like crap," he says.

"I haven't seen you for a couple of weeks," I say, "and that's how you start the conversation?"

"Well, you do."

I get more comfortable against the headboard, stuffing a couple of pillows behind me.

"I can't argue with that," I tell him. "What brings you around?"

He shrugs. "Nothing much." He waits a beat, then adds, "I hear Auntie Min's looking for you."

"She knows where to find me."

Cory nods. "I get how you're ticked off at all of us old-school cousins, but someone like Auntie Min—she's due some respect."

"I thought you were—how'd you put it? 'On my team.' That you weren't running errands for her anymore."

"I am on your team and I'm not running errands. I'm just relaying some information. Word around the cousins is that you're being disrespectful by not going to see her."

"First of all, I didn't know she was looking for me."

"You do now."

"Yeah," I say. "But as you can see, I'm kind of indisposed at the moment. And secondly, I thought being Mountain Lion Clan meant I wasn't expected to come running at everyone's beck and call. That it was a big deal."

"It is. But that's something you were born into. You didn't earn it. I'm coyote. My ancestors were right here watching raven pull the whole world out of that big black pot of his. But I still give someone like Auntie Min her props. That's how it is with our people."

I shake my head. "*Your* people, not mine. I don't owe you or her or any of you anything."

"You know it doesn't work that way. Do we have to have the whole conversation again about how this is who you are now and there's no going back?"

"See, that's where all of you are wrong," I say. "I may be a Wildling, but I'm not your people. I'm just a kid who had this mountain lion woken up inside him. Another roll of the dice and I might have gotten cancer instead. Your world, the things you people want, the expectations some of you have for me—none of it means anything, from where I'm standing."

"But—"

"No, I get it. I'm a Wildling. But that doesn't mean I have to be *your* definition of what that means."

Cory steeples his fingers, elbows on the arms of his chair, and looks at me.

"That's an interesting way to put it," he says.

"What's that supposed to mean?"

He grins. "Nothing. Everything. I just think that it might be instructional to find out what *their* definition of you actually is."

"I'm still not going to—"

He cuts me off with a wave of his hand. "It's cool. I've got this."

He's always done right by me, but I can't help the flash of suspicion I get. I hate that I've become the guy who has trouble trusting anyone. I guess that's what happens when you get burned enough. But I try not to let any of what I'm feeling show.

"Meanwhile," he says and gives me knowing look.

"What? Stay out of trouble?"

He laughs. "I'm coyote. That's not a piece of advice I'd ever give out. I'm just thinking that the next time somebody comes at you, you might want to get in a few licks of your own."

He's out of the chair and through the window, gone into the night before I can respond.

The next time I wake up, I'm not alone again. This time, I find Desmond sitting at my desk surfing the Net. It's daylight outside, so at least I can be pretty sure he didn't come through the window like my last visitor. He swivels the chair when he hears me move.

"I've seen you looking better, dude," he says.

"I've felt better."

He smiles, but there's no humour in it. "No shit. Who did this to you?"

"Gess and some of his buddies."

"And you just let them."

I don't want to go through the reasons all over again, but I do. Desmond shakes his head when I'm done.

"You know this isn't over, right?" he says.

"Of course it's over. Gess beat the crap out of me. He won. What else is he going to want?"

Desmond sighs. "Dude, now you're just playing dumb. He's going to be in your face every time you run into him in the hall. He'll want to go all public about putting the little black dude in his place. You know that. It's the way it works."

I sit up and swing my feet to the floor, wincing. Every part of me still hurts—maybe more than it did yesterday.

"Promise me you won't do anything," I say.

Desmond shakes his head. "I can't do that. And you better hope I get to Gess before Chaingang does."

Chaingang's built like a mountain and he's got no patience for idiots. He's also my friend, though given his status as an Ocean Aver, I don't really hang with him like I do with Desmond.

"Chaingang's not going to do anything," I say. "It's not like I'm in the gang."

"No, but you're both Wildlings and he told you he'd have your back. Bet that goes a lot deeper than gang loyalties."

"Crap."

I put my head in my hands. I'd kill for something to stop my head from throbbing.

"I didn't think of that," I add.

When Desmond doesn't answer, I look up to find him studying me with a puzzled look on his face.

"What?" I ask.

"I'm trying to figure out why you still look so messed up."

"Hello? Five guys jumped me?"

"Yeah, yeah. But I thought you Wildlings had some kind of magic healing powers. Didn't that guy in the lab with you have his leg come back"—he snaps his fingers— "just like that?"

"I have to change into the mountain lion and then back again for that to work."

"So why don't you?"

I sigh. "Because then I won't have a mark on me and everybody'll *know* something's weird with me."

Desmond shakes his head. "That is crazy, dude. Really. Listen to yourself."

"I'll heal up," I tell him. "Nothing's broken."

"Well, maybe this'll cheer you up," he says and swings the chair back around to the computer. "News feed says that the dude who ran the security at ValentiCorp got himself killed." He turns to look at me. "At least there's some justice in the world, right?"

I get a bad feeling. It's not that I care one way or another about Clint Gaillard. He wasn't the one experimenting on the kids that got taken like I did, but his Black Key Securities team did grab us and bring us in. When I think of what happened to those kids in there—what almost happened to me—it's hard to keep the mountain lion from roaring its rage. So I'm not sorry he's dead. But this feels ominous, like it could have repercussions.

"Does it say how he died?" I ask.

Desmond shakes his head. "The cops are being tight with the details." He gives me a once-over, then adds, "Your mom said you want to go to school today. Are you sure you're up for it?"

"Yeah. Just let me grab a shower and some more painkillers."

*

I was always the kid who kept his head down at school. You don't get noticed, you don't get into trouble. But now it seems like every couple of days I show up as the main attraction.

And now it's happening again. I'm the center of attention, with everybody hanging around outside the school talking about me, staring at my swollen and bruised face, whispering about Gess and me, and how the Feds happened by to break things up. I want to run and hide, but that's not an option. For once, this is exactly what I want: for everybody to look at the mess I am and really believe that I'm just some unlucky kid who got beat up. They're not thinking I'm a Wildling.

I walk up to the door and see Chaingang sitting in his usual place on a picnic table under the palms, shades hiding his eyes. He just shakes his head and looks away. I can't tell if he's disappointed or pissed off.

Desmond and I have almost reached the front door when it bangs open and I blink in surprise. Marina's standing there and I don't have to guess about her feelings. From the way she's glaring at me, she's furious.

"You and me," she says. "We need to talk."

"We've got class ..."

"Screw class. Right *now*, Saunders."

She stalks by without waiting to see if I'll follow. I look at Desmond and he shrugs.

"I've no idea, dude," he says.

Another glance at Chaingang shows a big smirk on his face. Great. Happy to amuse you.

Sighing, I set off after Marina.

"Maybe you should let me get this on my own," I tell Desmond when he falls in step beside me.

"Right, sure."

Marina's in Wildling mode, walking faster than a human could. It takes me a block to catch up to her. When I do, she stops abruptly, turns, then bangs the palm of her hand against my shoulder.

Wildlings are faster and stronger than human beings, but we're not invulnerable. I've got a bruise the size of a grapefruit and the colour of a plum under my T-shirt and when she hits it, I feel it. It's all I can do not to cry out with the pain. She doesn't even notice.

"How *could* you let this happen?" she says.

"Hey, it's not like I started it."

"Those guys could have killed you."

Her concern seems all ramped up out of perspective. I mean, guys get into fights all the time. Granted, I'm not usually one of them, but what do you do?

"It got out of hand," I tell her. "I thought I had it under control."

"But you didn't."

"No. I'm lucky those FBI agents are still following me around."

That stops her for a moment.

"They *are*?"

"Well, they claim they aren't, but how else could they show up just in the nick of time?"

Now she looks more worried than mad. I guess bringing up Matteson and Solana has calmed her down a little. And now that

I've got her on my own, without kids jostling by us in the halls, I figure it's a chance for us to talk a little bit.

"I know I screwed up," I tell her. "Before, I mean. The way I went all postal when I found out you were a Wildling and that you'd never told me."

She shakes her head. "No, you were right. I should have said something right away."

"Maybe. Probably. But I still had no right to get all pissy about when, or even if, you ever did."

She looks me right in the eye.

"You shouldn't have told me everything was okay when it's not," she says. "I know you don't trust me anymore."

"I was stupid. I do trust you."

She doesn't say anything.

"Come on, Marina. Can't we wind back to before all the crap? To when we were friends?"

"We are friends," she says.

"Then why does everything feel strained between us?"

She glances back in the direction of the school and sighs.

"It's complicated," she finally says.

"I don't get it. What's so complicated?"

She looks down at her feet. "Things just are."

I'm not sure what she means, but it feels like she's still hiding stuff from me. Maybe I don't trust her. Maybe it's too much to expect things to go back to how they were—not with everything that's happened since I first changed into a Wildling. I can't not be a Wildling and neither can Marina. This is what we are.

I shove my hands in my pockets.

"Okay," I tell her. "Whatever. I'll be cool about it. Just let me know when you want to talk."

She nods. I turn to go back to school, but as we walk away, she hooks her arm into mine and puts on her trademark swagger. How many times have we walked like this, her and Des and me? Me on one side, Des on the other.

So maybe we *can* get through this.

Chaingang lowers his sunglasses to look at us as we come up the walk to the front door. I smile at him, but he lifts his glasses back into place and looks away.

I can never read that guy.

The bell for the end of the period rings when we go through the door. Marina gives my arm a squeeze, unknowingly sending another shock of pain up that limb, and heads off to her locker. As I start for my own, Erik Gess steps in front of me, blocking my way. A couple of his buddies stand behind him. If I had hackles, they'd be standing up straight right now. As it is, the mountain lion in me wants to crush his face in its jaws and spit it out.

"You're in my space, Saunders," he says.

I remember what Desmond said this morning.

He's going to be in your face every time you run into him in the hall.

I *really* didn't think things through.

"What do you want now?" I ask.

He smirks. "Well, an apology would be good for starters."

"An apology for what?"

"Yeah," Desmond says, suddenly appearing beside me. "For what? For getting beat up by you and four other pussies because you don't have the balls to face him on your own?"

Marina is on my other side. I thought she was at her own locker, but obviously her Wildling hearing picked up on the trouble and she came back.

Erik looks from her to Desmond before his gaze finally settles on me again.

"Don't know that you picked the right bodyguards," he says, "but you're going to need them if you don't start showing a little respect to your betters ... *boy*."

I can hear the sharp intake of breath from thouse around us. It's not exactly like calling me a nigger, but when it's said like that, it's really pretty much the same thing.

Inside me, the mountain lion rumbles a warning growl. I'm pretty sure it wasn't audible, but Erik takes a step back and Marina takes a firm grip of my arm.

"Not in school," she says.

Erik backs up another step, but he's managed to hold on to his smirk.

"Better listen to your little *puta*," he says.

Marina holds me back as I start to lunge forward. But she's too far away to stop Desmond. Moving fast as a Wildling, he punches Erik in the face with enough force to knock him flat on his ass. Before Erik's friends can move in on us, the crowd suddenly disperses and we see Mr. Cairns, our English teacher, striding down the hall in our direction. Erik's friends wait a beat, then take off as well.

I can see Mr. Cairns assessing the situation as he draws near: my bruised face. Erik on the floor holding a hand to his nose from which blood is pouring. Desmond, me and Marina standing over Erik, with Marina holding me back. Desmond has his hand in his pocket, hiding his bloodied knuckles.

"Who's going to tell me what happened?" he asks.

Nobody talks. We stare anywhere except at him, giving each other quick glances.

"Somebody?"

"Erik tripped and fell," Marina finally says.

"Is this true, Erik?"

Erik's eyes are full of hate for us, but he nods. Mr. Cairns studies him for a long moment, then his gaze settles on me.

"And what happened to you?" he asks.

"A bunch of guys jumped me yesterday."

"On school grounds?"

"No, sir."

"And did one of these attackers happen to be Erik?"

"I didn't see who they were, sir. They jumped me from behind."

Mr. Cairns sighs.

"I should send you all to the office," he says. He gives us a last once-over, then sighs again. "Erik, go see the nurse. The rest of you, get to class."

"Yes, sir. Thank you, sir."

Mr. Cairns rolls his eyes. We scatter before he can change his mind.

"Nice one," I say to Desmond as we hurry down the hall.

"Come on, dude," he says. "I know you didn't want me to do anything, but the jerk was begging for it."

"I wasn't being sarcastic. I was two seconds away from ripping off his head. Literally."

"Sweet."

"No. That would have been a disaster."

"But we have to do something about him."

"Maybe I'll beat him up," Marina says. "That'll do wonders for his image."

Desmond and I look at her in surprise.

"What?" she says. "You don't think I'd love to do it?"

"Yeah," Desmond says. "But you're usually the voice of reason in our little gang. We are a gang again, right?"

Marina and I look at each other. I smile. The three of us against the world—like old times.

"Sure," she says. "The gang of three."

Des grins, happier than I've seen him in a long time. I have to admit, I'm feeling a little giddy myself.

"Maybe that should be our band name," he says. "Hey, here's my class. See you at lunch."

Marina and I both have history, so we continue down the hall to our own classroom. Just before we go in, she puts a hand on my arm.

"We still need to talk," she says.

"Absolutely."

"But we're good," she says.

She ducks into class before I can say anything back. Thank God she didn't squeeze my arm again.

CHAINGANG

I know Marina and Josh are just good friends, and I guess I'm happy for them that they're putting their differences aside, but I still feel pissed when I see them traipsing up the walk, smiling, her arm linked in his.

And you don't have to tell me. What happened with Marina last night was nice, but it didn't mean shit. We were just playing roles in case the crazy Wildling dude was spying on us. And even if we did feel something—I'm not saying I did, I'm just saying even if—it's not like anything could ever come of it. The last thing I want is for Marina to get jumped into the Avers. It's probably the last thing she wants, too.

But I'm still pissed.

So instead of hanging in my "office" for the day, I go to the student parking lot and get on my bike. Ten minutes later I'm on the Pacific Coast Highway, heading south. I stick to just a little over the speed limit so that some eager highway patrolman doesn't pull me over. Way I'm feeling right now, I might just take a swing at him, and that wouldn't end well. I go away again and it won't be to juvie.

Might be worth it, though, because I'm in the mood to hit something.

I tell myself to chill. I concentrate on the wind in my face and the sound of my wheels humming against the pavement. I think about retirement and getting away from all this crap. I'm miles away from Santa Feliz when I finally pull into a little parking lot overlooking a beach that's not much bigger. It's just a little sandy cove surrounded by cliffs. There are some surfers out in the water, waiting for a wave. It must be their jeeps in the parking lot.

I kill my engine and put the bike on its stand. Leaning on the metal rail, I time the beat of my heart to the rhythm of the waves. I finally feel the calmness—or I do until I hear footsteps approaching. I don't have to turn around. The wind's bringing me his scent.

"Week's not up yet," I say.

"I told you I want the boy dead," the guy says. "Not just roughed up."

Huh. So he thinks I sicced those skinhead wannabes on Josh. I can work with that. Especially since word around the school has it the FBI came along and broke things up. Gossip flies through the place like buckshot from a shotgun. My Wildling hearing picks up everything I want to hear and lots that I don't, but at least I've learned to filter out most of the crap.

"Yeah," I say, "and you also told me you wanted it to look like he'd been killed by humans. This was just a glitch. How was I supposed to know the Feds would come by when they did?"

"Now he's on his guard."

"I doubt it. But even if he is, it's not going to do him any good. And I've still got a week."

"Six days."

"So he'll be dead in six days."

I shrug like it's no big deal and stare out at the ocean. All I want is for him to buy this crap until I can get a line on him.

"Look at me," the guy says.

I take my time turning away from the railing.

"You think this is a joke?" he says. "Do you need another object lesson to show you just how serious I am?"

He doesn't have to mention Lenny by name for me to know what he's talking about. He probably never even bothered to learn Lenny's name.

"Oh, I know you're serious," I tell him.

I wish I'd thought to bring my sawed-off on this little jaunt. With a bit of luck, I might have had a chance to see how tough he is with a head full of buckshot.

I don't let anything show on my face, but he still says, "I know what you think you're doing."

"Yeah? What's that?"

"Stalling until you can figure out a way to take me down."

Smart dude. But I don't care how smart or fast or strong he is. There's always someone faster or stronger. Or smarter.

"You said you wanted nothing to make it look like Wildlings killed him," I say. "So you either let me do this my way or take the other option and do it yourself."

He nods. "Don't try to play me, boy. I've seen you tough kids come and go, and I'm still standing here."

"I'm real impressed."

He gives me a hard look, then turns and walks away. I lean against the rail and watch him go. He doesn't have wheels, so I figure he's got a shape that travels easily and fits in around here. Not a lot to go on, but it does narrow things down a bit.

What I really need is for Marina to get me a name from Auntie Min. Once I know who and what he is, we can start to plan out how he's going to die.

JOSH

Des is in a great mood at lunch, probably still riding the adrenaline rush of thumping Erik. He's full of plans for the band, the skatepark, hanging out. It's so infectious that I can't help but feel optimistic myself. Even Marina seems happy and relaxed, though I do catch her studying me from time to time with an expression I can't read. Her friend Julie joins us and it starts to feel like old times, like the whole Wildlings thing never happened and we're just a bunch of kids passing the time talking about music and good surfing beaches and the lame shows on TV. Julie teases Des and Marina, asking if they're going to the prom together. Des announces he might attend clown school next fall, then gets insulted when we all tell him that he could teach them more than he'd learn.

It's great. Other than being sore, everything is so normal. For the first time in longer than I can remember I feel like I'm living my life instead of just going through the motions.

After classes I do my detention, then we all meet up in front of the school. We're keeping a lookout for Erik and his pals, but they're nowhere in sight, which is a good thing. I don't need any more drama.

Marina has to go straight home, so Des and I walk with her. Julie's going to the library to study, which is interesting. She'd been hanging with the stoner crowd for a while, but it looks like she's getting serious about school again. We say goodbye to her and head off like we've done a million times before, the three of us just kicking along the sidewalk together.

But nothing in my life is ever simple anymore. We're only a few blocks away from the school when a familiar car pulls up beside us. The window rolls down and Agent Solana looks up at us from the passenger side.

"Got a minute, Saunders?"

"Not really," I tell him.

Agent Matteson leans across the seat. "We can do it here, or we can do it back at the office. Your choice."

"Seriously? I told you. I don't know who the guys were that jumped me."

The driver's side door opens and Matteson gets out. He puts his elbows on the roof of the car and studies me for a long moment.

"You still look like crap," he says.

That gets Des's back up. Marina stands frowning between us. I know she's trying to get a take on what the Feds want with me now, but good luck with that.

"Dude," Des says. "What do you think happens when a bunch of guys—"

"Yeah, yeah." Matteson makes a brushing-off gesture with his hand. "Just tell us where you were last night."

"You know where I was. You drove me home. Did I look like I was in any shape to do anything but collapse once I got inside?"

"You tell me."

"I just did."

But then I realize what's going on.

"This is about Clint Gaillard, isn't it?" I say. "The guy who was running security at ValentiCorp."

"What do you know about it?"

"Nothing. Des saw it on the news and told me he'd been killed."

Des nods and juts his chin in my direction. "The dude was still crashed when I came over to his place this morning."

"See?" I say.

"Yeah, but—" Matteson begins, except I cut him off.

"Look," I tell him. "I don't care one way or the other that he's dead, but I didn't kill him. What about those dead kids' parents? He's got to have pissed off people who are a lot more dangerous than I am."

"You tell me," Matteson says.

"Will you stop saying that? Why would you even think I had anything to do with it?"

"Good question," Matteson says. "Isn't it, Al?"

I look down at Solana. He shrugs.

"Coroner's report says he was torn apart by some kind of animal," Solana says. "They haven't got a line on just what kind, but they're working on it."

"And you think it's a Wildling."

"We're keeping an open mind," Matteson says.

"I keep telling you, I'm not a Wildling."

"Yeah, we get that. It's why a bunch of guys were able to beat you up as badly as they did yesterday. A kid like you wouldn't have a chance taking down a guy like Gaillard with his Seal training and everything."

"So why are you even asking me about it?"

"Just covering bases."

"Right," I say. "But the funny thing is, I've got a perfect alibi if I need one: you two keeping tabs on me. Did you see me leave the house last night?"

Matteson's eyebrows go up. "What makes you think we're following you?"

"Okay, play it that way," I tell him. "But I didn't do it, and I don't know who did."

"Good to know," Matteson says. "Thanks for your time."

He gets back into the car.

"Watch yourself," Solana says. "We don't always have your back."

Before I can ask him what he means, Matteson pulls the car away from the curb. I watch them go for a long moment. When I turn around I find Marina studying me with a considering look.

"What?" I say.

She shrugs. "Nothing. I've just never seen you so—I don't know. Forceful, I suppose."

"They're getting on my nerves. A lot of things have been getting on my nerves."

"I can see that. But the old Josh never mouthed off to cops like that. You're getting as bad as Des. Fighting, detention."

"Hey!" Des and I both say at the same time.

She grins and punches me lightly on the shoulder.

"Kidding," she says. "But," she adds in a more serious voice,

"I don't think those agents actually believe you were involved. It seemed more like they were giving you a heads-up."

"That doesn't make any sense."

"I know. That's what worries me. Because then you have to ask yourself, a heads-up about what?"

MARINA

I'm keeping secrets from Josh again and I don't like it. Especially not when we're all getting along so well again. But for now, I don't have any other choice. I know why Chaingang's worried. Just like him, I saw the video from the ValentiCorp labs with Josh killing that woman while he was in his mountain lion shape. If Josh thinks there's danger—especially any threat to the people he loves—he'll hunt this stranger down. I get it. I understand that need to protect your friends and family.

But if this old cousin's as powerful as Chaingang says he is, we need some serious intel before we go after him. First of all, we have to find out what his weaknesses are, and why he doesn't want any other Wildlings to know what he's up to. And we need to know why he wants Josh dead. Maybe some of the other elder cousins see Josh as some kind of chosen one, but killing Josh doesn't change the fact that there are all these other Wildlings running around out there—myself included.

So what's this guy going to do, just saying he *could* have Josh killed? Is he planning to kill everybody else next?

It's hard holding this new secret close to my chest as I'm walking home with Josh and Des. The pair of them are in such a good mood, laughing and joking. It's almost like old times. I'd so much rather just relax along with them for real instead of having to pretend. But neither of them seems to pick up on what I'm feeling.

"So, dude," Des says when we get to my house. "How much longer are you grounded?"

"Through the weekend. Five more days until I'm free."

"Bummer."

Especially since I need to get out and find Auntie Min as soon as I can. But I only nod in response.

"I know," I say. "First thing Monday morning, I'm hitting the waves."

"Can you have anybody over?" Josh asks.

"I suppose if you wanted to pray with us it would be okay."

Des's eyes go big. "Oh, come on. Seriously? I know your mom's big on the whole religion thing but ..."

His voice trails off when he sees me grinning.

"Gotcha, *dude*," I tell him. Then I turn to Josh. "It's probably not a good idea just yet. Seeing you is just going to remind her why she grounded me."

"And then she might add on a few days," he says.

"Probably not, but why take chances? I'm going crazy stuck at home day after day."

Josh looks sympathetic. "See you tomorrow, then."

Des lifts his hand for a fist bump, then dances back as I fake him out and try to punch him in the chest instead.

"Later," I tell them, grinning.

I start for the house and they head off to Des's place. When I get to my door, I pause and turn around. They're still laughing as I watch them get to the end of the block and turn the corner.

This is going to be hard. The sooner I get a better idea as to what's going on, the better. I am *not* going to keep this from Josh any longer than I have to—I don't care what Chaingang thinks.

Chaingang. Just thinking his name makes me remember that kiss.

No, I correct myself. If I'm going to go there, I have to call him Theo. When I think about kissing him, everything else just fades to background noise. I know I'm being stupid. Being with Theo isn't something I could ever make work. But I'd still like to kiss him again.

Mamá's in the kitchen making salsa. The air is filled with the scent of cilantro, chopped peppers and spices. I have to smile. She might want us to be good gringas, but that doesn't stop her from cooking the same traditional food she always has. Or from setting up her shrine to the saints in a corner of the living room. My stepfather doesn't mind. He loves Mamá's cooking, and I think he sees the religious artifacts more as art than objects of worship.

That makes me think of how different he and Mamá seemed when they first met, but they still made it work. Except he didn't have to give anything up. Mamá's the one who moved from the barrio to be with him. That's how it would have to be if Theo and I hooked up. I'd have to go to him—to the gang life.

"What's the matter?" Mamá asks.

I try to hide the guilt I'm feeling. "What makes you think something's the matter?"

"I'm your mother—how could I not know? What is it?"

"You mean besides being stuck in the house day after day?"

"Do we really need to have this discussion again?" she asks.

I shake my head.

"No, Mamá," I say because I know it's what she wants to hear. "But you asked me what was wrong. It's okay. I know I have to learn my lesson."

But that night I sneak out of the house again—not for another clandestine meeting with Theo, which is what I'd prefer, but to track down Auntie Min. My stepdad went to bed after the evening news, just as he always does, and Mamá followed not long after. I wait until my Wildling ears hear the steady breathing that tells me they're asleep before I finally slip outside.

It's not as late as it was when I went to meet Theo last night, but it's almost as quiet. The sound of the ocean calls to me over that of the distant traffic. I stand for a long moment, drinking in the dark stillness, my nostrils flaring. Then I remember this elder Wildling who wants Josh dead and I wonder where he is. Following Theo? Watching Josh? Watching me?

I don't sense anyone nearby, but Theo told me the man moves like a ghost, so he could be anywhere. I hate that. With my otter hidden under my skin, the dark of the night is one of the few times I feel completely free. I know I can shift to her sleek form and back again, and no one's the wiser. But the idea that someone might be out here spying on me creeps me out. At least when the FBI were skulking around, I could always tell where they were. But this guy ... he could be anywhere and I wouldn't know.

I move into the deeper shadows of the palm trees at the back of the yard and wait there awhile, weighing and measuring the night around me. I sift the air for scents, identifying each one before moving on to the next. I listen past the sound of the waves for anything that's even remotely out of place.

I can't hear or smell anything out of the ordinary. There's nothing moving. So finally I set off for the highway, keeping to unlit back streets where I can run at full speed and no one's going to notice a girl moving almost as fast as a car would in this neighbourhood.

It doesn't take me long to reach the overpass where Auntie Min has her camp. I slow down when I'm about a block away so that I can saunter casually through the makeshift village of cardboard shelters and trash. When I first came here, the other animal people wouldn't look at me, except with suspicion. Now it's only the homeless humans who ignore my presence. The cousins nod, some of them even smile. I don't see anyone who matches the description that Theo gave me. The real welcome comes when I reach the old sofa where Auntie Min is sitting.

I know now that her animal shape is some huge kind of moth, but she always reminds me more of a big old turtle or elephant that's been around forever. She looks about a hundred, but I'm not fooled into thinking she's some frail old bag lady. She's probably the most powerful of the elder cousins in this area, connected to the land and respected by the whole community. Why she lives like a homeless person, I have no idea.

She's propped up in the corner of her battered sofa. Lifting a hand when she sees me, her brown wrinkles deepen as her whole face smiles. She pats a cushion on the sofa beside her.

"Look who's finally come by to visit this old lady," she says. "I was sure it wouldn't take this long."

Back when we were rescuing Josh from ValentiCorp, Auntie

Min had offered to fill me in on the history of our people—Wildlings, cousins, the first people, whatever you want to call them—and I'd been wanting to take her up on it ever since. I'd felt a strong connection with her, and known right away that there was so much she could teach me. The trouble is, after I stayed out all that night, Mamá laid down stricter rules about where I can go and what I can do.

"I couldn't get away," I tell Auntie Min, "because I'm grounded."

She smiles. "Being grounded is a good thing. It emphasizes the connections we all share with the land and each other."

"Not that kind of grounded. My parents won't let me leave the house, except to go to school and visit my dad."

"That hardly seems fair. Does she not know the part you played in rescuing Josh?"

"She doesn't even know I'm a Wildling. I'm grounded for staying out all night."

"I see."

A sympathetic look crosses her face before her eyes brighten once more.

"Still, you're here now," she says. "What about this 'grounding' you were given?"

"I snuck out. I'm just so tired of being cooped up."

Auntie Min nods. "Of course. And it keeps you away from the grasshopper mouse, too, doesn't it?"

I can feel the flush rise up my neck until my cheeks are burning.

"How—how do you know about that?"

She laughs. "Oh, little otter. I know all the gossip of this land. If the birds don't tell me, then the little lizards will."

I see this as the perfect opportunity to turn the conversation away from personal embarrassment to what I really came for.

"So all the cousins answer to you?" I ask.

"It sounds so formal when you put it like that. The little cousins give me their respect and, in return, I help them with the various troubles that vex their lives."

"What do you mean when you say 'little cousins'?"

She shrugs. "We are all of equal stature in the eyes of the Thunders, but in the day-to-day goings-on of the world, some of the elder clans walk a little taller. But only because we have been here for that much longer."

"You mean cousins like Tomás and Cory?"

She smiles. "Cory comes from an elder clan, but he's still a pup. Tomás, however, is another matter. He has been a guiding force in the lands north of us for many many years."

"I guess you must know all the local elders," I say.

"There aren't many of us to know. At any given time, there are no more than a half-dozen at best in this area. Most of us tend to keep to ourselves and don't get involved in human affairs."

"I think I saw an elder the other day," I say, hoping she won't be able to tell that I'm lying to her. "He was this really tall guy wearing dark suit pants and jacket, but no shirt or shoes. He was pale-skinned, too, which I thought was weird since most of the older cousins I've seen so far are dark. And though I got a major vibe from him, I couldn't tell what his animal shape is."

"That comes with time and practice," Auntie Min says, but I can tell she's intrigued. "Where did you see this man?" she asks.

I make a vague wave with my hand.

"Down south," I say. "Around Tiki Bay. All the hardcore

surfers go there and I thought maybe he liked to ride the waves, too."

"Hmm."

"Do you know him?"

"I'm not sure," she says. "From your description, it sounds like Vincenzo of the Condor Clan, but that doesn't make sense. He has no love for the five-fingered beings. Truth is, he doesn't much care for his own people, either. You're more likely to find him in the middle of the Mohave or some other desolate place. And I think that I would have known if he were in Santa Feliz." She gives me a sharp look. "If you see him again, keep your distance. He has a special distaste for Wildlings and would be a formidable enemy."

"So these condors are pretty badass?"

Auntie Min shakes her head. "Don't mistake individuals for their clans. Yes, the people of the Condor Clan can be fearsome, but Vincenzo is something else again. He is one of the oldest and most powerful cousins I have met, and easily the most angry about our current state of affairs."

"You mean because he got outted," I say. "I don't mean just him," I add, "but all of you, now that the world knows about the Wildlings …"

Auntie Min sighs. "Yes, he faces the same risk of exposure that we all do. For an old cousin like him, that's an uncomfortable possibility. He's walked hidden among the five-fingered beings for centuries and would prefer to keep it that way. But most of us have seen how the wind blows. Better we introduce ourselves in our own time than be discovered and considered as yet one more threat to the security of the five-fingered beings.

"Which reminds me," she goes on, "have you spoken to Josh?"

"Sure. I see him at school every day."

"Could you tell him that I would like to speak to him?"

I nod. "But don't hold your breath. He's not ready to be your poster boy. He's just trying to keep his head down and get on with his life."

"Unfortunately, that choice might no longer be in his hands. As soon as he became a Wildling, destiny began making its own plans for him."

I know this spiel, and thankfully, she doesn't bother to repeat it. Josh is from the Mountain Lion Clan, one of the oldest and most respected of the cousin clans, which means the other cousins will listen to him. From the human perspective, he's a good kid with a mixed-race background. Some of the elder cousins like Auntie Min and Tomás think that makes him a perfect candidate to be their public face when they come out to the rest of the world. They need a friendly, uncomplicated kid like Josh to defuse the potential fallout when the world actually realizes what's what.

At the moment, everybody believes this is just something happening to kids in Santa Feliz. They have no idea that the animal people originate from the beginning of time and have been living hidden among them since day one. They also don't know about the pristine parallel world that exists side by side with the one we live in. Only the cousins do, and until we came along, only they had access to it.

Somehow, I don't think the cousins plan to share that information any time soon.

"I'll tell him" is all I say.

Auntie Min nods. Then she cocks her head and studies me for a long moment.

"What?" I finally have to ask.

"There was always a strong connection between you and Josh," she says, "and I was curious as to whether it had been broken. Now I see it is still there, but Theo is entwined in the pattern as well—much more than he was before."

"You can read the future?"

She laughs. "Of course not. But I can read patterns. I read it in the land and I read it in how we all interact with one another upon it. Everything is connected. But there are always surprises, even for one such as I, with all my centuries behind me. I find it interesting that you've chosen the grasshopper mouse over the mountain lion."

"I didn't say that."

"But you're with Theo."

I don't know how to explain the confusing mix of subterfuge and genuine emotion that's running through me right now. And even if I wanted to try, I couldn't. Not without giving away how Theo and I are trying to deal with this threat to Josh's life in a way that doesn't involve any of the other animal people.

"Josh made his choice first," I say instead. "He chose Elzie."

"But now Elzie is gone."

"I don't think Josh even knows I exist in that kind of way."

"Have you ever let him know how you feel?"

I shake my head. "But it doesn't matter, anyway. I'm not going to be the rebound girl."

"And you have Theo."

I don't know what I have, but I nod just to avoid discussing the topic any further.

Auntie Min tilts her head and looks at me as though she's reading my mind. "Hmm" is all she says.

"I should go," I tell her, getting up from the sofa.

"Come back when you can," Auntie Min says. "I have much to teach you about your new heritage—if you're still interested."

"I am. Honestly. As soon as things calm down a little."

Auntie Min smiles. "Outer tranquility first requires inner peace."

That sounds way too much like a fortune cookie, but I keep that thought to myself. I just give her another nod and set off back through the cardboard village and trash. I wait until I'm a block away before I pull out my phone and text Theo to tell him what I've learned. I half think he's going to want to meet up, but he doesn't respond.

I'm still trying to figure out how I feel about that after I've snuck back into the house and am lying in my bed.

I go over my conversation with Auntie Min again.

I haven't really chosen Theo over Josh. Or have I? I wasn't lying to Auntie Min about how Josh sees me as a pal, not a girl. I used to want to change that, but now I'm just confused.

Theo's in a gang. Who knows what his future's going to be? The victim of a drive-by? Or the perpetrator who gets caught and sent to jail?

Josh is the textbook definition of a great guy. Plus we love the same music and easygoing surf lifestyle. Okay, Josh manages to fall off a board more often than he stays on, but I can't even imagine Theo hitting the waves with me.

But he's such a great kisser ...

It's a long time before I finally fall asleep.

JOSH

Des keeps goofing around after we drop Marina off at her house, but then suddenly he gets serious.

"We need to come up with a plan to deal with Erik," he says.

It's such a nice day. Lots of sun, not too hot. I can hear the waves. I can *smell* the waves—or at least the brine in the water and the tangles of seaweed that are knotting in the tide at the shoreline. Movement catches the corner of my eye and I track a pelican across the sky, heading out to sea. Talking about Erik Gess is pretty much the last thing I feel like doing right now.

"You heard me, right?" Des says when I don't respond.

I nod without looking at him. "Sure."

"And?"

"You need to let it slide."

"Dude, you saw what happened after lunch. He's on your case and he's not going away until you put a stop to it."

"The way things stand right now, I don't see what I can do."

"Seriously? *Seriously?*"

I shake my head. "What do you want from me, Des? Should I track him down and beat the crap out of him?"

"Sounds good to me."

"Then what was the point of letting him and his goons beat me up?"

"You tell me."

I sigh. Now he's beginning to sound a little like Matteson.

"Look," I tell him. "I know how you feel about all of this. I know what you'd do if it was you who'd changed instead of me. But I don't want to be the public face of the Wildlings. I'd just screw it up."

"I'm not talking about going public."

"Then what do you think's going to happen if I take Erik down? Look at me. It's not like I was ever a threat even before I got beat up. And suddenly I can take him?" I shake my head. "I don't think so."

"You took him before—when he tried to jump you outside the lunchroom."

"Sure, but not like you want me to do now."

Des steps in front of me and pokes my chest with his finger. Why does everyone keep forgetting I'm bruised up?

"Okay," he says, "so you don't care about being on Erik's shit list. What about your friends?"

"Come on. Since when do *you* care about something like that?"

"I'm not talking about me," Des says. "Did you *hear* what he called Marina? Do you want to have her put up with that kind of crap? Dude!"

"I haven't forgotten."

I've been trying to—so I don't do something stupid. But the mountain lion under my skin sure hasn't forgotten. All it wants to do is tear off Erik's head. And when I see Erik's face in my mind's eye all *I* want to do is—

I take a calming breath.

"Fine," I say, stepping back from his finger. "So just saying I agree we need to do something about Erik. What did you have in mind?"

He grins. "A takedown—but get this. We do it in his own bedroom so that he knows nowhere is safe."

"I can change into a mountain lion, not a ninja."

"Whatever. You just need to show him that there are repercussions to being an asshole."

"And if he goes ahead and tells everybody anyway?" I ask.

"Dude, he's not going to tell anybody. And even if he did, who's going to believe him? You just need to get him on his own and explain the serious payback if he hassles you again. Then get out. You don't mark him, you don't trash the place. You let his own fear do the work for you."

"I could never sneak in without getting caught."

"I've been scoping out his place," Des says. "His room's on top of the garage and I'm pretty sure the stairs up to his room are right inside."

"When did you scope out the place? You were at school all afternoon."

Des shrugs. "I've been working on this since he first went to the principal crying about Wildlings." He cocks his head. "Look, if you don't want in, I'll do it myself."

Like I'm going to let him do this on his own.

"Okay," I tell him. "We'll swing by tonight. But we're just going to check it out."

"I told you, dude, I already—"

"I know. But I still want to see it myself."

Which is how come, just after midnight, Des and I are crouched in a jade hedge across the street from the Gess house.

It's a long stretch of California-style adobe, with a manicured lawn and palms out front. We just saw Erik go into the garage. A moment later the light goes on in the room above.

"See?" Des says.

I nod, but before I can say anything, I hear a rustle in the hedge and Cory's crouched down beside me. His eyes glow for a moment—like when you catch a cat or a dog in your headlights—then he moves his head out of the light. Des doesn't know he's there, so he jumps when Cory speaks.

"Tell me you're not doing what I think you're doing," Cory says.

Des almost falls out onto the sidewalk. He catches himself in time and glares at Cory.

"Jeez, dude," he says. "Maybe a little warning next time."

Cory ignores him. His gaze is fixed on mine.

"We're just scouting things out tonight," I tell him.

"Right."

But then Des launches into his explanation about why we have to do something about Erik before everything gets out of hand.

Cory's eyebrows go up, but Des doesn't have a Wildling's night sight and I doubt he sees.

"And ambushing him in his own home," Cory says. "That's not getting out of hand?"

"And you've got a better idea?"

"Sure. Let *me* deal with it. And that way the Feds won't find out you're involved."

"What are you talking about?" I ask.

Cory gives a nod down the road with his head. "Agent Solana's sitting in a car on the next block."

"Why are they following me? *How* are they following me?"

"The how's easy," Cory says. "He's tracking you through the GPS on your phone."

Des nods. "Spycraft 101, dude."

"So I should turn it off."

"No," Cory says. "That'll just tell him that you know about it—like a couple of weeks ago when you were trying to lose that other agent in the mall. Just leave it at home the next time you go out and don't want him to know."

"But I might need to make a call."

Cory shrugs. "So get a burner. You can even forward your calls to it if you have to."

"So are *you* following me, too?" I ask.

"Sure," Cory says with a grin. "But it's not so stalkerish as it sounds. I was coming by to talk to you. When I saw you heading out, I decided to tag along and see what you were up to."

"In other words, you were sneaking around."

"Hey, that's what coyotes do. Anyway, I was coming up to talk to you when I noticed Solana pull up. I figure he has to be using a GPS tracker. It's not like he's got our skills."

"*We* can track people like that?"

Cory taps the side of his nose. "You can if you've got the right nose."

I look in the direction where Cory pointed.

"What do they even want with me?" I say.

"I don't know. Why don't you ask him?"

"It's getting creepy. First they show up in time to save me from getting my ass hauled by Erik—"

"Sorry to disagree, dude," Des breaks in, "but they totally went to town on your ass."

I ignore him. "Which is like they're looking out for me, but then they stopped to hassle us when we were leaving school."

"What did they want?" Cory asks.

"To see if I had an alibi for when Clint Gaillard got killed." I see Cory trying to process the name and I add, "He was the guy who was running security at ValentiCorp."

Cory nods. "Oh, yeah. Him. I heard it looked like he'd been killed by a Wildling."

"Was he?" Des asks.

"Don't know. I'd have to see the body firsthand. But back to your little problem here. I'll handle the high school bully if you'll do something for me. Go talk to Auntie Min."

I shake my head, exasperated that no one wants to cut me a break. I just want a bit of down time before getting back into all this crap. Two weeks haven't been nearly enough.

"We've already had this conversation," I tell him through clenched teeth.

"I know. I'm not saying to do whatever she wants or even to agree with her. Just talk to her. Give her a little respect."

"Why do you even care?"

"Because she's got every damn bird, lizard and rat in Santa Feliz reminding me to ask you, and I'm sick of listening to them."

"You can understand regular animals?"

"I can if she sends them to me. So are we good with this deal?"

I sigh and close my eyes, trying to think. I've been intending to talk to Auntie Min at some point down the road, and I really don't want anything more to do with Erik, so I decide to tell Cory what he wants to hear.

"Sure," I say.

"Okay, then. It doesn't have to be tonight, but soon."

Before I can respond, Cory shifts into coyote shape and trots across the road. When he gets to the garage door, he goes through it like he just stepped through an illusion, not a real door.

"Holy Batman!" Des says. "How did he do that?"

My guess is he stepped momentarily into the otherworld, where there isn't a garage door, and stepped back out again once he was on the other side.

"Ninja coyote skills, I guess" is all I say. "Come on. Let's get out of here."

I know Des wants to hang around to see if we can tell what's happening inside, maybe talk with Cory when he comes back out, but I'm done. He hesitates as I push my way out of the hedge and start to walk away, but a moment later he's scrambling along after me.

"Hey, slow down," he says, looking back over his shoulder. "Do you want Solana's tracker to show you motoring along at the speed of a car?"

"Good point. Sorry."

"Nobody seems to be following us," he adds when he's facing front again.

"He doesn't have to."

"GPS. Right. Dude, this is so messed up."

"The Feds are just like the elders," I say. "They want something from me, but I can't figure out what it is."

"At least you can just ask Auntie Min. She seems pretty straight-up to me, in a roundabout kind of way."

He grins and I nod. You could say the same thing about Agents Solana and Matteson, but the truth is, I don't trust any of them.

"We both know what Auntie Min wants from me," I say.

"Poster boy," Des says with a smile in his voice.

I pretend I didn't hear him.

We wander out of Erik's neighbourhood and cross Ocean Avenue. There we turn south and head to where the pier juts out into the ocean. Our houses are just a few blocks past it. We're in no hurry and we've done this before, but usually Marina's with us as we take a late-night ramble through town. We all like it, but I think she likes it the best. The dark empty streets, the sound of the waves carrying farther than they ever do in the day.

I can't wait for her to not be grounded anymore. Not that it would make any difference for this kind of thing, but just seeing her at school's not enough. We need some normal time to get things back on track. We don't get to play music, we don't get to hang out or have movie marathons where Des pulls out all his old horror and kung fu movies. Nothing's the same and I miss her—how we used to be.

I hunch my shoulders and keep on walking. We're almost at the parking lot when I first hear the rumble of an engine. I've heard that particular engine before. Everybody in Santa Feliz knows the sound of Trucho Salazar's red and yellow '48 Hudson with its flamed paint job and pimped exhaust. People stopped complaining about it a long time ago because Trucho is Fat Boy Zaragoza's lieutenant, and Fat Boy runs the Riverside Kings. People who talk out of turn about them tend to have bad things happen.

They don't usually cause trouble on this side of the Pacific Coast Highway, but that doesn't stop them from cruising through. I think they do it to piss off the Ocean Avers. Some of the younger Kings—the ones that can be bothered—even attend Sunny Hill High.

Des doesn't hear the car yet. We could take off, but we're out in the open and he can't run like I can. They'd spot him. Maybe they'd do nothing, but you never know with the gangs—and that includes the Ocean Avers as well as the Kings.

There's no way I'd leave him behind.

"Just look at the ground," I tell him. "Keep walking and don't look around."

"Why?" he asks, but then he hears it, too. "Oh, dude. We are *so* screwed."

"They'll probably just drive by."

Except they don't. A moment later, the Hudson pulls up beside us.

"Hey, *putos*," a voice calls from the car. "How come you're not holding hands?"

Crap.

Des turns to me. "Dude, tell me you're not going to let them beat us up."

CHAINGANG

Here's how I roll: I run into a problem, I deal with it. End of story. So this crap with the dude who killed Lenny is really getting under my skin.

Maybe it wouldn't be so bad if I didn't come back from my ride to find J-Dog with his panties in such a twist. As soon as I see the state he's worked himself into, I realize I shouldn't have even tried going to school. I should have stayed at the clubhouse to ride herd on him because now he's had the whole day to fix his hate on the Riverside Kings for killing Lenny.

Now, if the RKs really had anything to do with it, I'd be the first to saddle up and lay some hurt down in the barrio. But I know for a fact they didn't. Trouble is, I can't explain how I know. J-Dog doesn't know I'm a Wildling—none of the gang does—and I can't talk about the psycho killer without something bad happening to Grandma or Marina. What I do know is that an all-out war with the Kings isn't going to solve anything. The only thing a war will do is make my job that much harder.

After a couple of hours of intense arguing, I finally manage to talk him out of retaliating, or at least convince him to wait for a bit to see how it plays out. Hopefully that will buy me enough time to sort out this kill-Josh shit.

It's almost sundown and I step outside to watch the last rays leak from the sky on the horizon. There's a good breeze coming from the hills behind me. I'm thinking of texting Marina when I hear the front door of the main ranch house bang open and there's J-Dog with a sawed-off shotgun dangling from one hand.

"Where the hell are you going with that?" I ask.

"It's no big deal, bro. I just ain't waiting to lay some retribution on the Kings."

"Yeah, it is. We've just been through why that would be a bad idea."

I see that look come into his eyes. It's like crazy just comes sliding out from somewhere in his brain and settles there.

"You trying to stop me?" he asks.

His voice is low and dangerous, and it doesn't matter anymore that I'm his brother.

"Depends," I say, keeping my voice calm. "If that's what it takes to stop you from dragging us into an all-out gang war, then yeah."

"You saw what they did to Lenny," he says, but the fires are banking a little in his eyes.

I can't believe we have to go through all of this again.

"Jesus, will you think for a moment," I say. "You don't even know for sure that it was the Kings. If they had done it, they'd have laid claim by now. Something's not right. They're not that stupid. And we shouldn't be, either."

"Are you saying I'm stupid?"

The crazy starts to shine a little brighter again.

I sigh. So far, we've had this conversation in front of a half-dozen of the boys. He needs to keep face. I get that.

"Let's you and me take a little walk," I say. "Have us a quiet word."

"It's not going to change anything."

"Hey, I know that. But hear me out."

I head off to the junkyard behind my crib. Used to be a nice field, but we've been here a couple of years now. Guys buy a ride for parts and the leftover pieces just pile up back here. Cars, vans, but mostly bikes in various states of disrepair. Some Jap bikes, but it's mostly old Harleys and Indians.

I don't look back as I go, but I don't have to. I can imagine the shrug J-Dog would give the guys. Now I can hear his footsteps in the dirt. I settle on the bumper of an old Ford truck—'46, maybe '47. I can't tell them apart the way I can bikes.

"So talk," J-Dog says when he reaches me.

I shake a smoke loose from a pack I snagged in the club-house earlier. I don't smoke, but I learned in juvie that cigarettes almost always ease tension. I don't mean the actual nicotine. It's more the ritual of offering the other guy a smoke, sharing a light.

I stick one in my mouth. J-Dog hesitates a moment when I hold the pack up to him. He sighs and takes the cigarette from me. Pulling his Zippo from his pocket, he lights his own, then mine. He takes a long drag before he sits beside me and leans the shotgun up against the bumper.

We don't say anything until we finish the smokes.

"So you're set on this," I finally say.

J-Dog shrugs. "What am I supposed to do? Only the Kings'd have the *cojones* to pull this kind of crap. We're not talking about some asshole taking a joyride through our territory. They *killed* Lenny, man. The thing I can't get around is why the hell you're not leading this run against him."

Now that I've got him away from the others, I can level with him a little.

"I can tell you for a fact they didn't do it," I say.

He turns to give me a sharp look. "You know who did?"

"Yeah, but this guy's so far out of our league, it'd be like going up against a rocket launcher with nothing but a straw and a spitball."

J-Dog's eyes darken.

"You *knew*," he says, his voice soft and dangerous, "and you kept it to yourself?"

I nod. "Because it's not gang business."

"You saying Lenny wasn't an Ocean Aver?"

I didn't want to be telling him any of this, but I don't see a choice. There's either going to be a gang war, or J-Dog's going to aim the gang at the old-school Wildling freak. If that happens, I don't think anybody will be walking away.

"No, bro," I tell him. "I'm just saying that's not all he was."

"You going to start making sense any time soon?"

"Lenny was a Wildling."

"Yeah, right."

"Him dying had nothing to do with the Avers," I go on. "It was a message to me."

J-Dog doesn't say anything for a long moment.

"This dude was sending you a personal message?" he finally asks.

I nod.

"And killing Lenny was the message?" He studies me like

he's trying to look inside my head before he adds, "Anything else you want to tell me?"

I know what he's thinking. He's waiting for me to spell it out, but I'm not going there.

"This is Wildlings business," I say instead. "Stay out of it."

His features go still and that light starts to glimmer in his eyes.

"Lenny was one of us," he says. There's steel in his voice. "You're one of us. That *makes* it my business."

I shake my head. "Play this one smart, Jason. Let me deal with it."

"That right, *Theodore*? You want me to roll over and play dead for you?"

"I said be smart. This guy could break you in two without even trying."

"That a fact?" J-Dog gets to his feet. "And I suppose you can take me, too?"

I stand up so I don't have to look up at him. Soon as I'm on my feet he takes a swing at me. I catch his fist without even thinking and hold it. The veins pop out on his forehead as he strains to push through, but I won't give. His left hand comes in for a kidney punch and I grab that one, too.

"I don't know if I can or I can't," I tell him. "But why would I want to?"

J-Dog's not as big as me, but he's always been that much stronger, that much faster. Then I became a Wildling and everything changed, except he didn't know it and I never had to put it to the test until now. He puts all he's got into breaking loose and he can't move an inch.

"Okay, then," he says.

He goes slack, smiles, like he's giving in. But I know better.

As soon as I let go, he comes at me. This time I pop him one. I try not to hit him too hard, but it still flings him back onto the hood of the truck. He slides toward the ground. His eyes aren't completely focused, but his hand still reaches for where he set down the shotgun. I kick it out of his reach. He goes all the way down until he's sitting on his ass in the dirt, glaring at me. I know he's just waiting for his moment. First chance he gets, he'll be on me.

"Don't do this," I say. "I'm still an Aver and you're still the boss. But I've got other responsibilities now. You need me to back you up, I'm there to back you up. But not in this. I've got to deal with Lenny's killer on my own. He finds out you or anybody knows and more people close to me are going to start turning up dead, starting with Grandma."

The crazy in his eyes goes hot.

"You're just letting this freak—"

"I'm not letting anything, bro. All I know is he's so much stronger than me I might as well walk up and let him put a bullet in my head. I can't take him down. But I'm working on getting an edge. I don't need to be distracted by a war with the Kings. And I don't need to guard my back against my own brother because you think I won some pissing match. You understand?"

The crazy goes down a few notches. Now he's just angry, and maybe it's not at me.

"Can I get up?" he says.

I sigh and offer him a hand. Before he can pull himself up, I jerk him to his feet. He tries to stay cool, but I can see his eyes widen a fraction. He's starting to get an idea now of just how fast and strong I am.

"I need you on my side," I tell him, "and the best way you can help right now is to lay off the Kings and give me some space. If I figure out a way you can do more, trust me, I'll ask."

He takes a steadying breath.

"Okay," he says. "I get it. But why don't we just shoot him? Get him in a crossfire and he goes down, end of story."

"Honestly, I don't know if bullets are going to do the trick."

"Come on. Didn't some Wildling girl get herself shot dead with a .22 a couple of weeks ago?"

"Yeah. But this guy's something else again. I don't know what he is, but if he even suspects I'm playing him, he'll be going after Grandma, and then you, and there's not a damn thing I can do to stop him. Yet."

"You've got a plan?"

"First I need some intel and I'm working on that. And Jason? Nobody can know—about any of this."

"I get it."

J-Dog dusts himself off. He gives me a glance as he retrieves his shotgun. I act like it's no big deal, but I'm watching him carefully. He makes a point of picking it up by the barrel, keeping his fingers away from the trigger guard.

"What about the boys?" he asks.

I know what he means. If we step out where they can see us and he calls off the strike against the Kings, he loses face.

"We get back where they can see us," I say, "you just tell me that I better come up with some real proof, then give me a shot in the head to make your point."

He grins.

"With your fist, not that," I add, pointing at the gun.

"Hey, I'm not going to shoot my own little brother. But I *am* going to enjoy this."

And he does. I ride his fist and let myself fall, but the truth is, my head's ringing and I see a few stars before I get up off the ground. J-Dog's already walking back to the clubhouse, shotgun tapping against his leg. The other guys look away. The last thing anybody wants to do is get involved in one of our arguments.

Now it's my turn to dust off my jeans. I stand there and watch the guys file into the clubhouse.

I want to be out doing something, but I don't know where to turn. I need to talk to Marina, see what she's learned from Auntie Min, but I have to wait for her to call me. In the end, I go back into my crib to catch some shut-eye. Once things start moving, I might not get the chance again for a while.

Patience is something else I learned in juvie.

I can tell by the sound of the birds outside that it's almost dawn when my door opens. I don't have to use my nose to know it's J-Dog. Nobody else would just walk into my crib except for Lenny, and Lenny's dead. I sit up on the couch where I've been sleeping. J-Dog's holding my cellphone in his hand. It must've fallen out of my pocket when he punched me. No wonder I haven't heard from Marina.

J-Dog sits on the coffee table, right in front of me.

"Who's Vincenzo?" he asks.

"Don't have a clue."

He tosses me the phone. "This girl thinks he's our guy—she one of your people?" he asks when I don't say anything.

I sigh. "You know how when you get busted, you don't give up any names, you just do your time?"

He nods. He's probably thinking of how I took the fall for him on that carjacking and saved him from going to a real prison instead of my going to juvie.

"It's like that," I tell him. "So whatever you see or hear—you and me—that's as far as it goes."

"Okay."

There's no crazy in his eyes, but they're focused sharply on me.

"So what kind of Wildling are you?" he asks.

He frowns when I don't answer.

"Okay," he says again. "Can you at least tell me what you're planning to do now? I can't have your back if I don't know where you're at."

"I'm going to get in touch with this guy named Cory—he knows all the old-school Wildlings."

J-Dog's brow goes up. "Say what?"

"There were animal people around long before kids started changing here," I tell him. "Probably right back to the beginning of time."

"You're shitting me."

I shake my head.

"So where's this Cory hang out?"

"I can't contact him directly—don't even know how. I'll get Marina to do that." I tap my phone as I speak so he knows who I'm talking about. "Vincenzo—if that's the guy—he's keeping sharp tabs on me. He can't see me talking to any of his people."

"Who are also your people."

I shrug. "It's like anything else. You're tight with some, others—not so much."

"I still want a shot at this guy."

"If I can make that happen, you'll get one."

"What's he want from you?" J-Dog asks.

I knew this was coming and I don't quite know how to field it. I settle for, "He wants me to kill a friend and make it look like it was done by a regular human. He doesn't want any blowback on him."

"But you're not going to do it."

J-Dog knows me well. But I've been thinking on this and I give him an honest answer.

"I don't want to," I tell him, "but if it comes down to my friend or Grandma, I don't really have a choice, do I?"

J-Dog nods. He gets up and gives me a serious look.

"We'll just have to make sure it doesn't come to that," he says.

Then he gives my shoulder a light punch and heads for the door. I send a text to Marina asking her to get hold of Cory to see what he can tell us. I hesitate a moment, then add she can tell him whatever she wants, just make sure he knows to keep his mouth shut.

I have this weird urge to flirt with her—no, it's more than that. I want to tell her how I'm feeling.

Crap. I don't want to come across like a wuss. Before I can change my mind, I just press Send.

I grab a shower. I don't have any appetite, but I eat breakfast anyway. I might be needing the fuel. Then I head for school.

JOSH

Normally the Riverside Kings don't start trouble in this part of town. But it's late and let's face it, walking along on our own this time of night, Des and I are like a couple of sitting ducks just waiting for someone to take a shot. When I turn to the car, I see Trucho behind the wheel. I recognize two of the others from Sunny Hill: Lil' Puppet, who's riding shotgun, and Gordo Lopez—no relation to Marina—directly behind Trucho. There's somebody else in the back on the driver's side, but I can't make out their features.

They've all got shaved heads and serious ink. Happily, I don't see any weapons. Yet.

"What happened to your face?" Trucho asks.

"I got beat up."

He grins. "Or maybe some rough sex with your boyfriend here?"

The other guys laugh.

"Hey, I know him," Lil' Puppet says. "He's Chaingang's bitch."

Gordo nods. "The kid from the news—the one that can change into a tiger or something."

"That right?" Trucho says, his gaze locked on me.

I shake my head, for all the good it's going to do. I can feel Des's tension beside me and I know that however this turns out, it's not going to be good. Mostly because I can't see us getting out of this in one piece without calling up the strength and speed of the mountain lion under my skin. I'm pretty sure I'll be able to take them, but nobody's going to buy that I used my supposed kung fu. That'll stamp out that rumour pretty quick.

"I don't think you're telling the truth," Trucho says.

Talking under my breath, I tell Des, "As soon as the fight starts, just take off."

"Hey, I'm not going to—"

"Just do it," I tell him. "I don't want to have to think about which one is you when this starts."

"What're you whispering about?" Trucho wants to know.

I fix my gaze on Des until he finally nods.

"Okay," Trucho says. "That how you want to play it?"

His door opens. His running shoes are quiet on the pavement as he steps out onto the street. The passenger door opens and Lil' Puppet comes around the car. Gordo starts to get out as well, but Trucho waves him back.

"We got this," he says.

I'm so sick of all these tough guys who think they can just walk all over you. Erik and his stupid posse of wannabes. The RKs here in front of me. Trucho in particular, with his macho swagger.

I plan to take him down first, then Lil' Puppet. If either of the guys in the back gets out of the car, they'll go down, too.

The mountain lion under my skin purrs with anticipation, but I hold him in check. I'm not going to start this. If Trucho wants to go to the hospital, he has to make the move.

His hand goes in the pocket of his vest and comes out with a knife. He flicks it open, grins at me, looking for the fear in my eyes. It's my turn to smile when he realizes I'm not scared of him.

I won't say I'm not nervous, but really, what can he do to me? I know I'm faster and stronger than him and it's not like he's holding a gun.

"Don't do this," I tell him. "It's not too late to get back in your car and drive away."

But before he can respond, we hear a vehicle coming fast down Ocean Avenue, heading in our direction. A moment later it squeals to a stop in front of Trucho's Hudson, high beams blinding us all. With the light in my eyes I can't see any better than the rest of them, but my nose catches Agent Solana's scent as soon as he steps out of the car. Then he comes into the light carrying a serious-looking pump action shotgun, barrel over his shoulder, finger on the trigger.

"Dude," Des says from beside me. "When did he get so badass?"

"Okay, *cholos*," Solana tells the Kings. "Time to pack it up."

"You know who I am?" Trucho says.

Oh, he doesn't like this, everything spinning out of his control.

"Do I look like I care?" Solana asks. "Now beat it."

"You're just some cop. What are you going to do—shoot us?"

"I'm off duty," Solana tells him.

Then he adds something in rapid-fire Spanish. I catch the words "cartel" and "Solís."

Trucho sneers at him. "Bullshit."

Solana drops his shotgun into a firing position.

"Try me," he says and jacks a shell into the chamber.

I can tell Des is in heaven. It's like he got dropped into one of his favourite action movies. But something feels off to me. Solana's a cop. FBI. What's he doing running around threatening to shoot people? The Kings might be low-life gangbangers, but they still have civil rights.

The mountain lion is pulling in all the scents. There's a lot of fear in the air—mostly from the Kings—and especially from the guy in the back seat with Gordo. Then I realize it's not a guy.

"Okay," Trucho says. "Okay. We're gone."

"Lose the knife," Solana says as Trucho starts to turn back to the car.

Trucho opens his hand and the weapon clatters onto the pavement.

"Now go," Solana says.

"No," I say.

Everybody turns in my direction.

"Dude," Des says.

I nod toward the car. "They've got somebody in there who doesn't want to be with them."

"Hey, we're going," Trucho says. "We don't want to cause any trouble."

Now he says that.

Solana doesn't ask me how I know. He just says, "Everybody out of the car. Now! Hands in the air where I can see them."

"Hey, come on," Trucho tries.

Solana aims his shotgun at the front of the Hudson.

"The warning shot's going through your engine," he tells Trucho. "The second one's for you."

Trucho glares, but he lifts his hands.

"Do what he says," he says. "Everybody out."

Lil' Puppet's already got his arms up. Gordo comes out, moving slowly, so as not to spook Solana. He joins the other two, hands raised. Finally, the fourth door opens and a teenage girl steps out onto the pavement.

"Marina?" Des says.

She looks like Marina, but the scent's wrong.

"No," I tell him. "That's her sister Ampora."

She comes around the car with her hands in the air.

"Ampora Lopez?" Solana asks. When she nods, he tells her she can lower her hands. "Are you all right?" he adds. "Did anybody hurt you?"

She shakes her head.

"Were these men holding you against your will?" Solana asks.

"Hey, we're just friends," Trucho breaks in. "Out for a ride, man. Nothing heavy."

"Was I talking to *you*?" Solana asks. He turns his attention back to Ampora. "Ms.?"

"It's true," she says, looking at the ground. "We were out for a ride. But now I just want to go home."

This is bad. No matter what happens, the Kings are going to come after Ampora, maybe her whole family. That's how the bandas get away with what they do. Nobody stands up to them because they know the hurt's going to fall down upon their friends and family, not just themselves.

Solana knows it, too.

"Well, this complicates everything," he says. "Now what am I going to do with you?"

"Hey, no, we're cool, *ese*," Trucho says. "You don't have to worry about us."

"Let me have a word with him," I say.

Trucho gives me a WTF look, but Solana only raises an eyebrow and smiles.

"Go for it," he says.

"I'll walk you to your car," I tell Trucho as I close the distance between us.

Trucho glares at me. His gaze flicks to Solana, who keeps the shotgun aimed right at him.

"Okay," he says.

"Back seat," I say as he starts to get in behind the wheel.

"You kidding me?"

"Do it," Solana tells him.

"Okay, okay. I'm doing it."

He gets in the back. When he starts to scoot over to make room for me I lean in and grab his shoulder.

"I know what you're thinking," I say. "First chance you get, you're going for payback. But I'm here to tell you that anything happens to Ampora, her family—hell, to anybody I know—and I'll make it my personal crusade to take you apart."

"You think I'm—"

I knew before I started this that he'd have to be convinced. So I close my hand on his shoulder and squeeze until the bone snaps under my fingers. He cries out and tries to get away, but he can't move. His squirming only makes the pain worse. I feel a little sick, but I don't know what else to do.

"You loco piece of—" he says.

He breaks off when I push my face right against his. I let a little of the lion out for him to see. The pissed-off eyes. A bit of teeth. Now I can feel him shaking under my hand.

"So we're clear?" I ask.

He gives a quick, scared nod.

"Because if you're not, we can finish this now."

"No, no. It's clear."

"Don't think I can't find you," I tell him. "It doesn't matter where or how far away you hide, anything happens to the people under my protection and they're never going to find all the pieces of you to put in one coffin."

I'm probably laying it on a little thick—comes from all those movie nights at Des's place—but Trucho's not in a position to be critical. I can tell he's buying it. How long it will hold depends on him. Once I'm not in front of him and the shoulder's been looked after, maybe he'll start to feel brave again.

"This goes for your whole gang," I tell him. "Anything happens, you take the weight. Understand?"

I give his broken shoulder another squeeze and his eyes water with the pain.

"Yeah, yeah, ease up," he says. "I get it."

I step back from the car. It's at that moment I realize that I can't hide from what I am. I can't let jerks like Erik beat on me because they're not going to go away. They're just going to beat on somebody else. Same with these bandas losers. I've got to use what I've got sitting under my skin to do the Spider-Man thing and take responsibility for what's messed up around me. But I'm going to do it on my own terms.

"Trucho wants one of you to drive," I tell Lil' Puppet and Gordo. "I think he needs to go to the hospital."

Lil' Puppet takes a step toward me, but stops when Solana swings his shotgun.

"This isn't done," Lil' Puppet says.

"Check with Trucho," I tell him. "I think it is."

I rejoin Des and the others as Lil' Puppet and Gordo get into the Hudson. They retreat from Solana's car and peel off, heading back to the barrio. I turn to Ampora and she punches me in the shoulder as hard as she can. What's with all the abuse this poor shoulder is taking? I stagger back a step, but catch her fist as she takes a second swing. I'm careful not to hurt her. But instead I've freaked her out with how strong I am.

I give her a little push away and take a step back myself.

"Dude!" Des says to her. "What's your problem? We just saved your ass."

She turns to glare at him. "I'm dead now—don't you get it? They were just going to rough me up a little, but now I'm dead. I've got a family. Two little sisters. They're going to come after us all."

"I can assure you—" Solana starts.

She cuts him off. "And what kind of a cop are you? I heard what you said to Trucho, so what are you, dirty or clean?"

"What did you say?" I ask Solana.

"He said he's a hit man for the Solís Cartel," Ampora says.

Even I've heard of them. According to the news reports, they run better than half the dope from Juaréz up here to So-Cal.

"Well, he's not," I tell her. "He just said that to throw them."

I hope.

"And you!" she starts, but I don't let her finish.

"No," I tell her. "Maybe other people buy into your hot-headed chica bullshit, but we know better."

"What makes you—oh, so that's what Marina says about me?"

"Marina doesn't have to say anything. All I have to do is see you at school, always walking around with a chip on your shoulder. Everybody gets it. You don't like anybody."

"You don't know anything about me."

I nod. "And I don't need to. I just need to know why the Kings are after you."

"It doesn't matter."

I look at Solana and he just shrugs.

"Okay," I say. "Don't tell us. We're going to take you home and I'll watch your place tonight to make sure the Kings leave you alone."

"And tomorrow night?" she asks. "And the night after?"

"Let's just take this one step at a time," I tell her. I turn to Solana to add, "Do you mind giving us a lift?"

"No problem."

I can't shake the feeling that he seems a little self-satisfied with how all this went down tonight, but now's not the time to get into it.

Des touches my shoulder. "Dude, I can't stay out all night," he says, regret in his eyes.

"I'll give him a ride home after," Solana says.

"It's not that I don't want to," Des tells me.

"It's cool," I say.

We all pile into Solana's car, Des taking shotgun, Ampora and me in the back. She's quiet and sullen for the whole drive to her house. She doesn't say a word until Solana drops us off and we're standing on the curb watching his tail lights disappear down the street.

She juts her chin toward me. "So all those stories about you," she says, "are you trying to tell me they're true?"

"You know how you don't want to talk to me about whatever beef the Kings have with you?"

She nods.

"Well, I don't feel like talking to you, either. Just go inside. I'll keep watch tonight, and tomorrow morning, we'll take your sisters to their school."

She frowns at me, but doesn't move. I'm surprised at how much she looks like Marina. I'd never really noticed it before. I suppose I can see it now because she's standing so still, right in front of me. When they're moving, they inhabit their bodies so differently. Marina is loose, comfortable in her skin. Ampora carries a tightness, like she's pulling away from the world instead of living in it. But if you were to put them together and take away Marina's skateboarder gear and Ampora's gangsta chic, the resemblance would be uncanny.

But while she might look like Marina, that doesn't mean I'm inclined to share any secrets with her.

"Look, I get it," I tell her because she still seems to be waiting for me to say something. "We're not friends. We don't have to be friends for me to do this."

"Then why are you doing it?"

If this were one of Des's movies I'm sure the script would have me come out with something witty and cool. But it's not. It's just real life and I'm just me. So I stick with the truth.

"Because somebody has to stand up to those shitheads. Go on in. You'll be safe."

She nods, but she still doesn't go inside. Instead she points to the playground down the block.

"My kid sisters play there," she says. "Lots of the little kids in the neighbourhood do. It was a safe place, you know?"

I nod to show I'm listening.

"Last week the bangers started coming around. They'll pull up in their fancy cars and all the little boys go crazy seeing those sweet rides. The bangers start struttin' their lies, talking about how jumping into the RKs will put these kids on top, make them special. All the other losers will be working their asses off for nothing, but not them. Side with the Kings and they'll have everything they want. Money, girls, parties, custom rides. *Familia.*"

"It's an old story," I say. "You seem to buy it."

That earns me another glare. "These kids are seven, eight, nine years old. The Kings are passing out *joints*. My sisters come home and ask why I don't have an RK for a boyfriend."

"I didn't say it was right."

"Damn straight it isn't right," Ampora says. "And I went over and told them to haul ass or I was going to call the cops."

My eyebrows go up at that. Nobody calls the cops—especially not in the barrio.

"What *else* was I supposed to do?" she asks. "*¡Híjola!* The bandas aren't going to listen to me. Not unless I've got a loaded gun pointed at their head. I *had* to threaten them with the cops."

"So tonight ... you weren't hanging with them by choice?"

"They said I needed a lesson about what it means to cross them."

"And you're mad because we pulled you out of that situation? They could have killed you. They love making examples of people."

She shakes her head. "They would have just roughed me up—made sure I understood what getting in their way meant. And so long as I kept my head down, everything would have been okay. But now ... my sisters ... my parents ..."

"And would you have?" I ask. "Kept your head down?"

"I ..."

But she can't answer. She doesn't have to. I already know. I might not know her very well, but Marina's talked about her enough. Ampora doesn't back off.

"So it's better this way," I tell her.

"How's it better? What can *you* do? Maybe I should be talking to whoever messed *you* up because somebody sure gave you a beating."

Only because I let them, but I'm not going to tell her that.

"No," she goes on, "you're just a kid that all these paranoid people think is a Wildling, and having some weird-ass cop in your corner isn't going to help. The bandas will eat you both and spit you out."

"He's a real cop."

"Yeah, but Wildlings aren't real, so where does that leave you?"

I raise my eyebrows.

"Oh, come on. Anybody with half a brain knows it's just some government scam to keep us down. And even if you *could* turn into a bird or a rat or whatever—how's that help with the bandas? The Kings'll just shut you down."

"Trucho didn't seem to think so."

I don't want to get into a pissing contest with her, but I can't stop myself from bringing it up. She didn't see what I did— nobody saw it except for Trucho—but she knows I did or said something to make him shut up and have Lil' Puppet drive them away. In *his* custom Hudson that only *he* ever drives.

"Yeah," she says. "What was up with that? You must have something big on him."

"You should go inside."

"But you haven't told me anything. I told you."

"I know. And I appreciate it. It's going to help me figure out how to make the Kings stay away."

"Uh-uh," she says. "You don't get to leave me hanging."

"Maybe not. But you haven't earned enough of my trust for me to tell you anything more."

She glares at me for one long moment.

Then it's "Fuck you, Saunders," and she stalks up the dirt driveway to her house.

Nice.

I have to admire her spirit even if I don't like her. But that isn't going to stop me from making sure she and her family stay safe.

There's not much cover on her street. Just a few scraggly palms, one of which is on her next door neighbour's lawn. I sit down under it, out of sight of her neighbour's windows, and call my mom to explain why I'm not home. She doesn't like it, but when I explain the situation, she doesn't argue. She just tells me to be careful.

"And Josh?" she adds before I can hang up. "You're not going to let *these* guys beat you up, too, are you?"

"No, Mom."

Next I text Des to make sure he got home okay. I start to put my phone away, but it vibrates with an incoming call.

"Dude," Des says as soon as I answer. "Is everything cool?"

"Yeah, it's quiet. I think the only danger I'm in is if Ampora decides to come outside and bust my chops again. That girl throws a mean punch."

Des laughs. "I guess the tough chica gene runs in the Lopez family."

It's true. Marina doesn't take crap from anybody.

"Could you send Marina a message?" I ask Des. "Fill her in on what's happening."

"Sure. You're actually staying there all night?"

"Yeah, but I don't think anything's going to happen. Ampora's worried about her sisters, so I'm going to see them safe to school before heading to Sunny Hill with her."

"Which is why you want Marina to know *before* you show up at school with her sister."

"Pretty much."

"And then what are you going to do?" Des asks. "Because this problem isn't going away."

"I know. We'll have to figure something out. Maybe Chaingang can give us some advice."

"Or Cory," Des says. "Have you heard from him yet? I'm dying to know what he did to Erik."

That reminds me. I promised Cory I'd go talk to Auntie Min, which I really don't have time for right now. How do things get so complicated this fast?

"Cory's got his own clock," I tell Des. "You never know when or where he'll show up. I'll see you tomorrow."

"Dude," Des says and he hangs up.

I stash the phone in my pocket and stand up. I'm thinking of taking a walk around Ampora's house just to get the lay of the land. But then I see headlights turn onto the street, moving slowly in my direction.

MARINA

So I wake to a text from Theo, but no matter how I look at it, it's all business. He thanks me for talking to Auntie Min, wonders if I can get in touch with Cory to see what we can get from him. Do I know how to contact Cory? Can I talk to him?

I try to read between the lines, but there's nothing there. It's like we never kissed. Like it didn't mean anything. I end up feeling stupid, like one of the women in Mamá's telanovelas who are always mooning over some guy or another.

Then my morning gets more complicated when I read the email from Des.

Ampora? Josh is guarding my father's house to protect them all from the Kings?

What's wrong with this picture? Just everything.

And then I realize that Josh getting Des to keep me in the loop is his way of letting me know that it's okay between us. That he trusts me and wants to keep me involved and in his life, even if that means he has to let me know he's with Ampora because he knows exactly how I feel about my sister from hell.

Except, if I'm reading Des's email right, Suelo and Ria are also in danger. As are Papá and Elena.

What the hell has Ampora done *now*?

And of course, while Josh is being so open with me again, I'm sitting here holding another big fat secret from him. I have to tell him. Except what if Theo's right and it just sets Josh off?

I'm feeling so miserable that I almost snap at Mamá when she pops her head into my bedroom to see if I'm awake. But I stop myself in time.

"Is everything all right, *mija*?" she asks.

I nod and pretend to rub sleep from my eyes.

"I'm just trying to wake up."

She studies me for a moment, then decides to take me at my word. As soon as she leaves, I return Theo's text. I tell him I'll try to track down Cory. I press Send before I write something stupid like that I miss him or something. I don't even know if I do. I don't know what I'm feeling right now.

I rush through a shower and breakfast, grab my stuff for school, then I'm out the door. On the way to Des's place I check for a text from Theo, but he hasn't responded yet. By the time Des steps out of his house, I'm waiting for him on the street out front.

"Dude!" he says when he sees me. "Did you check your messages?"

"That's why I'm here. What happened with Ampora?"

He tells me the story as we walk to school, and I can't stop interrupting with questions. It all seems so ridiculous. What were they even thinking to go off and stalk Erik like that? And why's Agent Solana tracking Josh's phone? Then there's this whole business with Cory.

"You should have seen it," Des says. "He went right through that garage door like some kind of ninja ghost."

"What did he do once he got in?"

Des shrugs. "I don't know. Maybe he ate him. Big bad wolf steps up and Little Red Riding Erik is no more."

"Cory's a coyote, not a wolf, and can I just say *ew*?"

"Really, dude? After what he did to Josh? After what he called you?"

"You don't kill somebody for that."

He gives another shrug. "Well, I wouldn't miss him."

"Where do the Kings come into all of this?"

"That happened when we were walking home from Erik's."

I nod when he starts to talk about hearing Trucho Salazar's pimped-out Hudson. Everybody knows the sound of that stupid car.

"You should have seen Josh," Des says. "I figure we're dead, but he's ready to take them all on by himself. He tells me to run—like I'm going to leave him—but then Agent Solana shows up and we find out that your sister's in the car."

"*Hanging* with them?"

It seems hard to believe, considering how Ampora's so down on the gangs. Sure, she dresses like some skanky gangsta chica, but she's no more a member of the RKs than I am. I always figured it was just something she did to look tough and show people not to mess with her.

"No," Des says. "It looked like they were—who knows what they were planning to do, but she didn't want to be there, and Josh just went all fierce on Trucho. I don't know what he said to him, but dude, those bangers just took off."

I shake my head. This isn't good. I can't believe Ampora would have gotten involved with the Kings, no matter what the reason. She should have been thinking of how this would put Suelo and Ria in danger. But that's Ampora for you. She doesn't think about anybody but herself. She never thinks about consequences.

"So Agent Solana drove you over to Ampora's house?" I ask.

Des nods. "We let them off and then the cop drove me home. I would have stayed, but, you know. If my parents ever caught me, I'd be grounded just like you. I can't believe Josh's mom is cool with him staying out all night."

"She knows he can take care of himself."

"But still ..."

"She also knows he wouldn't do it unless it was important," I add.

It makes me a little jealous. Mamá and Papá would go ballistic if they ever learned the truth about what I've got under my skin. Elena would be sad and I don't know about my stepdad. He's actually pretty open-minded and cool. But it wouldn't make any difference. Mamá would have me in a convent so fast in a last-ditch effort to save my soul.

We've reached Sunny Hill. I look to the picnic tables under the palm and eucalyptus trees, but Theo's not sitting in his usual spot. I know he also skipped most of yesterday.

"What's up with Chaingang?" Des asks when he sees where I'm looking.

I shake my head. "No idea."

The first bell rings. Five minutes until homeroom. I'm tempted to skip myself and go looking for Cory, but Des would insist on coming along, and if I haven't told Josh about the guy that's gunning for him, I'm sure not about to tell Des first.

"We better get moving," I say and start for the door.

On the way to our lockers, a light-skinned Mexican kid

pretends to shoot me with a finger gun, then blows me a kiss as he walks away. Des turns to watch him go, then looks at me.

"Oh crap," he says. "Do you know who that was?"

"Not by name," I tell him, "but I know who he runs with."

The Riverside Kings.

I feel a little sick. So not only did Ampora put the rest of the family in danger, she brought it outside of the barrio as well. And if they're threatening me, they might go after Mamá and my stepdad, too.

If Ampora was in front of me right now, I think I might actually punch her in the face like she deserves.

"Marina?" Des says.

I find a wry smile.

"It's okay," I tell him. "We'll get this worked out."

He gives me a doubtful look.

"Come on," I say. "We're going to be late for homeroom."

JOSH

When I see that car coming toward me, my first thought is that the Kings are making their play. I start to slip behind the trunk of the palm where I plan to wait and see what happens, but then I realize the vehicle's not tricked-out enough to be a bandas car. A moment later I recognize Solana behind the wheel. I step out from under the palm and walk to the street. He pulls in across from Ampora's house and lowers his window.

"Everything quiet?" he asks.

His voice is pitched low, but my Wildling senses let me hear him easily, even over the low murmur of the car engine. I nod.

"Let's talk," he says.

Even though he's saved my butt twice in as many days, I'm not sure I can trust him. But I'd like to know what he really wants from me, so I give him another nod and cross the street. He kills the engine as I go around the front of the car and slide into the passenger's seat. I twist around with my back to the door so that I can look at him.

"So let's talk," I say.

"What do you want to talk about?"

Cops and psychiatrists—they're all the same. They want you to do the talking. But I'm not playing that game tonight.

"How about we start with who are *you*, really?" I say. "Why are you still following me around?"

He holds both palms open between us like he's got nothing to hide.

"I'm just what you see," he says.

I shake my head. "No, you're more than just a cop and I know you're not a shapechanger."

Solana smiles and his eyebrows go up. "Yeah? How do you know that?"

"Hey, I can just get out of the car right now," I tell him. "I don't have to put up with this."

"Fair enough."

He leans back in his seat and looks out the front windshield.

"I grew up in Santo del Vado Viejo," he says after a moment of contemplation. "In the barrio. But my best friend lived just west of town on the Kikimi rez in the foothills of the mountains. I spent pretty much every weekend out there. My parents didn't mind because it kept me away from the bandas."

He smiles, still looking out the windshield, but I'm guessing he's looking a million miles away into the past.

"Man, I wanted to be an Indian," he says. "Jimmy—my friend Jimmy Morago—he was training in the Warrior Society and I got to train right alongside him. But I could only go so far because I wasn't Kikimi." Solana turns to look at me. "Lots of tribes have a Warrior Society, but the Kikimi have two. One follows the warrior's path like you'd expect, but the other society, they're all shaman. They protect the tribe's spiritual well-being, guarding against the monsters that are always circling around, looking for an opening."

"What do you mean by monsters?" I have to ask.

"They're skinwalkers," he says. "Shapechangers."

I don't know what any of this is supposed to mean, but I think I see where it's going.

"You mean Wildlings," I say.

He shakes his head. "No, the monsters literally have to put on the skin of whatever they want to change into. They can even put on the skin of a dead person and become that person—or at least, look just like them."

I guess he mistakes the look of distaste on my face for disbelief.

"You've seen kids turn into animals," he says, "and you have a problem with this?"

"No, it's just—you know—pretty sick."

"That's why the Kikimi call them monsters. They'll do anything to feed on the souls of the People—that's what Kikimi means in their own language."

"Where do they even come from?"

Solana sighs. "See, what they are isn't even the worst of it. The monsters are made by black witches who kidnap and rape young girls, then take their babies and raise them into these amoral creatures."

"Okay, that's *really* sick."

"I know. That's what Jimmy was training to fight against, and I so wanted to be fighting right at his side, but the big mysteries of the shaman's Warrior Society are only for people born to the tribe. I got to be with Jimmy until it was time for his vision quest, and then I was cut out."

I try to imagine being told I couldn't hang with Des anymore and can't.

"What did you do?" I ask.

"There was nothing I *could* do. But Ramon—that's Jimmy uncle and the main shaman out on the rez—he knew I was hurting. He took me aside the night Jimmy was going on his quest and told me to meet him at this abandoned ranch in the north part of the rez. He said my people had their own mystery traditions and it was time I learned about them."

His gaze goes distant again as his memories pull him back in time. I take the opportunity to do a quick check of the street and the area around Ampora's house. Everything's still quiet.

"So did you go?" I ask when I look back at him.

He nods. "Sure. It was strange. Out back of the ranch house there was a campfire with all these dark-haired, dark-skinned old men sitting around it. They were Mexicans, but they had more Toltec in them than Spanish, if you know what I mean."

I shake my head.

"Indian blood," he explains. "Back in the day, everybody would claim their ancestors were Spanish because the Europeans looked down on Indians even more than they did Mexicans. Most of us have Indian blood, but it doesn't seem to matter so much anymore, except how the tone of your skin will probably always make a difference. The lighter you are, the easier you fit in.

"Anyway, it ran strong in these guys. They were lean and wiry—a tough-looking crew—and even though I trusted Ramon, my heart still sank a little when he just introduced me to them and then walked away."

"Jeez," I say, knowing how I'd feel.

Solana smiles. "Sorry, I'm falling into storytelling mode. I start thinking about those days and old habits come back. Really, it wasn't so bad as all that. They were a tough old crew, but they treated me well. There was only one other kid there and he had a few years on me. He'd been studying with them for three years by the time I got there."

"Studying what? And who were they?"

Solana gives me another smile. "Mysteries. In the barrio people call them *los tíos*—the uncles. Some people dismiss them as a bunch of old men who sit around drinking mescal tea, but they're really warriors—just like the Kikimi shaman.

"The Toltecs believed that everyone has a parasite living inside their minds—a thing that tells you lies and then feeds on the fear that the lies bring. *Los tíos* believe that too, but they also know that sometimes the parasite can break free and then they have to deal with it, just like the Kikimi do their monsters.

"The parasite inside yourself—each person has to handle that on their own. But it takes a specialized knowledge to deal with the ones that run free. And then there's the parasite that lives inside the dream of the world—you really don't want to face that if you're not prepared."

"You're losing me," I tell him. "What's this dream of the world?"

"According to the Toltecs," Solana says, "everybody walking around is really asleep. The dream they live in is *this* world—where everything is a certain agreed-upon way because that's what we're all brought up to believe from the time we're kids. All those individual dreams create a bigger dream, which becomes the dream of the world. It's kind of like Jung's idea of a shared subconscious, except hardly anybody wakes up from it. Those who do become warriors like *los tíos*. And their world is far more complex than ours."

"So that's what you did? You studied with them and—what? Woke up?"

Solana shakes his head. "I did study with them, but maybe I was too deeply asleep because I just couldn't get it. It never felt real to me. With the Kikimi, what I loved was the physical training. There was some of that with *los tíos*, but also a lot more woo woo stuff. Like, they'd talk about this place called Aztlán, which is one of the worlds that lies invisible next to this one."

I give him a sharp look. Is he talking about the otherworld that the cousins took us to? But he takes something else from my face.

"Yeah, I know," he says. "And they say that *los tíos* can become hawks, or that they can put their souls in the body of a hawk, and that's how they know so much, because they can be anywhere and see everything."

"They turn into hawks," I repeat to make sure I heard him right. "Like Wildlings."

"I don't know. *I* never saw any of them change into a hawk— or any other animal, for that matter. I saw nothing to make me believe the world is anything other than what it seems. In the end, I became a cop instead, because that way I could actually see the results of what I was doing. Catch the bad guy and put him away."

He falls quiet again.

"Why are you telling me all of this?" I ask.

"Because once kids started turning into birds and animals here in Santa Feliz, I realized that maybe *los tíos* weren't so woo woo after all. If Wildlings can exist, then maybe those spiritual dangers are real, too. Maybe the only way to get through it is to wake up."

I nod, but I say, "I still don't see what it has to do with me."

"Once I saw what was happening here," Solana says, "I went back to talk to *los tíos*. They told me to find you—the boy that becomes a mountain lion."

"I've told you a million times, I'm not a—"

Solana waves away my protest. "Say whatever you want, but it doesn't change what we both know is true."

"Just because some bunch of old guys—"

Solana cuts me off. "*They're* the ones who told me to find you and help protect you until you wake up. So that's what I'm going to do, whether you like it or not."

I rub my face with my hands. I can't believe this. If it wasn't bad enough already that the cousins think I'm some charismatic emissary for their cause, now I've got a bunch of Mexican mystics, who can maybe turn into hawks, also convinced that I'm supposed to save the world. Or at least wake it up.

"What happens if I don't?" I ask.

"Don't what?"

"Save the world. Wake it up. Whatever it is that these guys think I'll do. What if they've got the wrong guy?"

"They don't."

"How can you be so sure?"

"Because the more I get to know you, the more I understand why you were chosen."

Considering all the weird stuff Solana's been telling me, I don't suppose there's any point in continuing to deny what's under my skin. But what he and everybody else doesn't understand is that it was purely random. When whatever it was shuffled the deck, some people turned into birds or otters. I pulled the card that says mountain lion. Lucky me, one of the major arcana of the animal people.

"I wasn't chosen," I say. "It just happened, that's all."

"Do you really believe that?"

That's when I realize that there's no point to this conversation. Nothing that I say will change his mind about my so-called destiny.

I open the door, half-expecting him to stop me. But he doesn't.

"I need to think about this," I tell him.

But I'm just being polite. It's say that or tell him I think he's as deluded as the rest of them.

"I understand," he says.

No, you don't, I think. You don't have a clue.

But I get out and nod, then shut the door. He waits until I'm back under the palm in the yard beside Ampora's house, then he starts up the car and pulls away. He's probably only going around the block or something, but I don't care, so long as I don't have to listen to him anymore.

But it doesn't matter. The things he told me keep running through my head for the rest of the night.

I'm standing at the end of the driveway when the front door opens and Ampora comes out with her sisters. Their dad left for work earlier, but I made myself scarce when he came out. Ampora makes the girls wait by the door while she comes over to me. Her sisters are so cute. They look like twins—just like Marina and Ampora do. I give them a wave and Ampora frowns at me.

"I didn't think you'd still be here," she says.

She's looked out the window from time to time throughout the night, so I know that's a lie, but I don't call her on it.

"I told you I would," I tell her.

"Right. I forgot. You're the big hero."

I don't bother responding to that.

"At least you didn't get beat up again," she adds.

"Funny."

"No, I'm serious. Someone really went to town on you. What makes you think it'll be any different when the Kings come down on you?"

"It'll be different," I tell her. "Trust me."

She makes a dismissive sound. "Why should I?" she goes on. "And I don't know why you're here. I don't need your help."

"I know *you* don't. I'm just here to make sure nothing happens to your sisters."

"So what are you—a boy scout looking for another merit badge? Or maybe you think it'll score you some points with your BFF Marina?"

God, she's a bitch. "Let's go," I tell her. "Otherwise the girls will be late."

"And what about after school?" Ampora asks. "What about tomorrow, and the day after that, and the week after that? Are you planning to play bodyguard for the rest of their lives?"

"Hey, I know it's not a perfect solution. I have to figure something out. But today I'm just concentrating on getting your sisters safely to school. Can we agree on that much?"

She shrugs. "Whatever."

She makes a beckoning motion with her hand and the girls

skip down the driveway to join us. I sit on my haunches so that I'm closer to their height.

"Hi," I tell them. "I'm Josh—a friend of your sister Marina."

They tell me their names, then Suelo tilts her ear to her shoulder and asks, "Are you her boyfriend?"

Ria punches her lightly and they both giggle.

I smile and shake my head.

"Are you Ampora's boyfriend?" Ria asks, and they giggle some more.

"I don't think Ampora likes me very much," I tell them.

"Don't feel bad," Ria tells me.

Suelo nods. "Ampora doesn't like anybody much."

"Except us," Ria tells me. "People in families don't have to like each other, but she really likes us."

The mountain lion in me senses Ampora's tension, but I don't look in her direction.

"Of course she would," I tell the girls. "Who wouldn't like you?"

That makes them giggle some more.

Ampora clears her throat. "Let's get a move on."

When I stand up, Ria takes my hand. I glance at Ampora to make sure it's not going to set her off, but she only rolls her eyes and doesn't comment. She takes Suelo's hand and we set off the few blocks to the girls' school.

The girls chatter happily the whole way and it makes me more determined than ever to make sure nothing happens to them. I see so much of Marina's good nature in them. Marina was just like this when I first met her, even though her parents had just gotten divorced and she was still missing the sister who now hated her.

When we get to the school I see a couple of gang members hanging by a car a half-block away. They're not wearing colours, but their tattooed arms and necks make their allegiances obvious. I point them out to Ampora and see her jaw clench.

"I'll wait for you here," I say.

Ampora nods and takes the girls into the school. My Wildling hearing lets me eavesdrop on her warning them not to go anywhere with anybody except for her. They're to wait near a teacher after school until she can come back to pick them up.

I keep a watchful eye on the bandas while she's talking, but they don't appear to be paying any attention to us.

"So now I suppose you're going to walk *me* to school?" Ampora says when she rejoins me. "Aren't you afraid of what people will say when we show up together?"

I'm sure it's the other way around: she's afraid of what *her* friends will say.

"I can walk a little behind you, if it makes you feel better," I tell her.

She makes an exasperated sound. "Do whatever you want."

"What about those guys?" I ask, nodding to the pair by the car.

"They won't dare go in the school."

"Maybe I should talk to them anyway."

"Don't make things worse," Ampora says.

She turns on her heel and walks away before I can respond. It doesn't take much to catch up to her.

"Can I ask you something about Mexican culture?" I say.

"Like I could get you to shut up."

"Have you ever heard of *los tíos*?"

She shakes her head. "What are they—one of your stupid surf bands?"

"No, they're supposed to be some kind of Mexican mystery society."

"I've never heard of them."

We walk along in silence for a couple of blocks.

"I could ask my father about them," she says suddenly. "Do they have something to do with the gangs?"

"No, it's just part of another problem I'm working on."

She gives me a glance. "I always thought you were just this quiet guy with bad taste in music and friends."

"And now?"

"Now I just think you're messed up."

We walk the rest of the way to Sunny Hill without talking. I stop when we're a half-block from the front door. It seems quiet. I don't see any bangers. I don't see Chaingang in his usual spot, either.

"Looks clear," I say.

"Yeah, so?"

"So go ahead to school."

"You're not coming?" she asks.

I shake my head. "I'm going home to grab a shower and a change of clothes. Maybe catch a couple hours' sleep."

She studies me for a moment, then shrugs and heads off to school. I go home to do just what I said.

I'm napping on the couch when my phone wakes me. I look at the screen. Des.

"Aren't you supposed to be in school?" I say.

"Dude, I could say the same thing about you."

He's talking really quietly.

"Where are you?" I ask.

"Boys' can. I just wanted to give you a heads-up. You know Juan Ruiz?"

"Name's not ringing a bell."

"Mexican kid. He hangs with Gordo and those guys."

I sit up straight. In other words, he runs with the Kings.

"What happened?" I ask.

"Nothing, yet. But when Marina and I came into school this morning he made a little gun with his fingers and pretended he was shooting her."

"Crap."

"Yeah. So what are we going to do about it? It's starting to get out of hand, dude."

"I know. Can you keep an eye on Marina till I get to school?"

"Sure," he says. "What are you going to be doing?"

"Trying to figure something out."

I cut the connection and lay my phone on the coffee table. I want to talk to Chaingang, but I don't have his number and he wasn't at school when I dropped Ampora off. Come to think of it, he wasn't there for most of yesterday, either. That means I have to track him down the hard way.

I grab an apple from the kitchen, then get my bike out of the garage.

CHAINGANG

It's not like I'm doing much of anything when the knock comes on my door. I'm just staring at a blank TV screen, waiting for Marina to call, trying to figure some way out of this mess. But it still ticks me off.

I know it's not J-Dog. He'd just walk right in, make himself at home like he always does. Anybody else ... well, I can't think of anybody I feel like seeing right now, so I let it ride. Whoever's there should get the hint and take a hike.

The knock comes again and I ignore it again.

Then a third time—louder.

I get up off the couch and cross the room. I fling the door open, but the "What the hell do you want?" dies in my throat.

It's Josh standing there. He still looks like crap, face bruised and swollen. But there's something different in his eyes. They narrow when he sees I'm pissed off, but he doesn't back off one step.

"I need some advice," he says, jumping right in. "About gangs. Specifically, the Riverside Kings."

"Say what?"

This, I wasn't expecting. As soon as I saw him standing there,

I figured maybe he'd found out about Vincenzo and was ready to tear me a strip for keeping it from him.

"Look," he says, "I've got a problem with the Kings, but I'm not asking for your help."

"Good, because—"

"But I need to talk to someone high enough up in the gang who can call off this bullshit. Can you give me a name?"

"Back up, bro," I tell him. "I don't have a clue what you're talking about."

His hands clench into fists, but he doesn't raise them.

"What's not to understand?" he says. "I need somebody in the Kings with some clout, but I don't know where to start. I don't think I could even get in to talk to Fat Boy—he's their top dog, right?—so I'm looking for somebody a little further down the food chain."

Well, at least this'll get my mind off my own problems, I think as I step aside.

"You might as well come in," I tell him, opening the door a little wider.

I motion toward the couch and he sits down.

"You want a beer?" I ask.

He shakes his head. I get one for myself. It's early for me, but I have the feeling I'm going to need it.

"Okay." I settle on the other end of the couch. "So what's this all about?"

Josh sighs, impatience written all over his face. "You know, I tried to do the right thing," he says. "I let Erik and his posse have a go at me and I didn't tear them apart like I could have. I just played the part of an ordinary kid. But they wouldn't let it go. They're still on me at school, so Des and I went over to Erik's house last night."

I toast him with my beer bottle. "I can get behind that. Give him a little righteous payback."

"That was Des's idea, but I was just going along to check things out—see if something would come to me that wouldn't make things worse.

"I took the beating," he continues, "and I wasn't ready to have that pain go to waste by showing him my Wildling side anyway. But then Cory came along ..."

He tells me about Auntie Min's message and how the coyote kid just ghosted right through Erik's closed garage door. Damned cousins. There's so much they aren't telling us.

But all I say is, "So you're going to bend over and be their chosen one?"

"I only agreed to talk to her so that Cory would get off my back."

"You remember what I told you. Go along with them and all you'll be is a puppet with their hand up your ass."

"Nice."

"I'm only saying, bro."

"Anyway," he goes on, "Des and I head for home, but—"

"Back up," I say. "What did Cory do to Erik?"

"I don't know. I haven't talked to him yet."

"Okay, so you and Des are walking ..."

"And we hear Trucho Salazar's old Hudson."

I frown. Trucho thinks it's real funny riding through Ocean Avers territory with that pimp-mobile of his. One of these days, I'm going to rip a tailpipe off his ride and shove it down his throat.

"I know where this is going," I say.

But when Josh continues, I realize I only guessed a part of the story.

"The Feds are still tailing you?" I say.

"Cory thinks they're using the GPS on my phone."

"So they know you're here."

Josh shakes his head. "I left my phone at home."

I let him go on until he gets to the part about the girl.

"Ampora," I repeat. "Marina's sister? Riding with the Kings?"

"Yes. But it's not like you think."

Up to that moment, it's been interesting, and I feel for what Josh is going through. But as soon as he tells me that Ampora is involved with the Kings, it's like a red mist clouds my eyes. That's way too close to Marina. If I had Trucho in front of me right now, I'd be doing more than shoving a tailpipe down his throat. If he so much as breathes in the direction of Marina, I'll take him apart, piece by piece.

I realize I'm squeezing my beer bottle so hard I'm going to shatter it and cut my hand all to crap. I put it down on the coffee table with exaggerated care.

"They are walking dead men," I tell him. "And as for Ampora, bro, I'm going to—"

"I've been trying to tell you—it's not her fault," Josh says.

I'm only half-listening as he finishes his story, explaining what Ampora did to get on the wrong side of the Kings, what he did to Trucho, how he watched Ampora's house all night and walked the kid sisters to school with her this morning.

I get up from the couch. "Okay," I tell him. "Now we go finish the job."

"No, wait," Josh says, getting up as well.

"You don't get it," I say. "The Kings are freaks when it comes to this kind of crap. That little bitch Ampora has no idea what she's done. You diss them and they don't just go after you, they go after the whole family. You want Marina to get popped in a drive-by?"

But like he did at my door coming in, Josh looks pissed and he doesn't back down.

"You think I don't *know* that?" he says. "But if *you* get involved, that's going to start a war between your gang and the Kings, and a lot more people are going to get hurt. I just need to talk to somebody—stop this before it goes too far."

I shake my head. "Nobody in the Kings is going to listen to you. They'll take you down before you can say word one."

Josh's eyes narrow and the small muscles in his jaw pulse as he clenches his teeth. "Then I'll *make* them listen," he growls under his breath.

Damn, he's going all hardcore. He actually thinks he can make it happen. This is why I didn't want to tell him about Vincenzo.

"Seriously, man," he says. "Give me a name. You must know who's got some influence in the Kings."

It'll be a complete waste of effort. But the whole time we've been arguing, I've been running names through my head.

"Maybe I do," I say.

I pick up my phone from the coffee table and punch in the numbers for the Harley store out at the ValentiCorp complex.

"Is Aina there?" I ask when someone answers.

I haven't seen Aina Para since we had our one and only date—the night I got changed into a Wildling. I didn't know at the time that her brother was Chico Para, one of Fat Boy's lieutenants, just like she didn't know I rode with the Avers. She's not involved with the gang life except for that one connection, and it's not like you get to choose your family.

I don't know if she understands why I never called her again, or if she's pissed, but I'm hoping she'll at least listen.

"Hello?" she says when she comes on the line.

"Don't hang up," I tell her. "It's Theo Washington. Maybe I'm the last guy you'd ever want to hear from—I don't know—but I need a favour that's going to save some lives."

There's a long silence. I know she hasn't hung up because I can hear her breathing.

"What kind of a favour?" she finally asks.

"I need a sit down with your brother."

"Oh boy."

"I'm not going in with any animosity," I lie. "There's just a thing that's come up with some friends of mine and we're hoping to clear it up with someone who might actually listen."

"You know I've got nothing to do with any of that, right?"

"Of course I know that. It's why you didn't hear from me again. I ..."

It's a little hard getting into this with Josh sitting there listening, but I owe her this much.

"I asked you out because I thought we could just be Theo and Aina," I tell her. "I didn't know who your brother was, and I wasn't planning on introducing you to mine."

"Just so you know, I gave my brother hell when I heard that he told you to back off."

I wonder what else those bangers came back with. Did they talk about how I'd vanished right in front of them, or did whatever Auntie Min show them just make them keep their mouths shut, period?

"I don't blame him," I say. "I might have done the same thing if I had a sister and I found out she was seeing somebody in a gang."

"You mean the wrong gang."

"No, pretty much any gang."

"Huh. Nothing about you's the way it seems, is it?"

"Just trying to keep it real."

"I'll give Chico a call. Can I get back to you at this number?"

"We'll be waiting. And Aina? I owe you one."

"Maybe I'll call you on that someday, *Theo*," she says and I hear the smile in her voice before she breaks the connection.

Josh doesn't have to ask how it went. With his Wildling ears, he heard both sides of the conversation.

"Old girlfriend?" he asks.

I shrug. "Never got the chance to find out."

I make myself sit down when all I want to do is get on my bike and go finish the job Josh started on Trucho. It takes me a few moments before I trust myself not to smash something, and then I realize Josh has been sitting there studying me.

"What?" I say.

"You ever think of going back?" he asks.

"Back where?"

"To that otherworld."

"Bro, it's so not my scene. I don't even have a clue how it works. But say I tried and by some fluke I got over there. What if I couldn't get back? I know the place has got something going for it, but it's too weird for me. I like my pleasures and I want to know my enemies."

He nods. "I get it."

"Have *you* tried?" I ask.

"No, but I don't think it's hard. I'll bet it's like changing to your Wildling shape. You will it to happen and it does."

"I guess your girlfriend's still over there," I say.

"I don't know. She's not my girlfriend—I mean, not anymore, right?"

My phone rings and I don't have to answer him.

"Aina?"

"I need you to be on the level," she says. "I don't want you to be setting my brother up. I know he's ... what he is. But he's still my brother."

"Girl," I tell her, "I know all about messed-up brothers. Trust me on that. We just want to talk to Chico."

Unless he won't call off the dogs on Marina and her family, and then all bets are off. But I don't tell her that.

"You know where Casa Raphael is?" she asks.

"The taquería up on South Shore Drive."

"That's the place. He said to meet him there in half an hour. And Theo? He said to come alone."

"I can't do that. It's not me that needs to talk to Chico, but my friend. I'm just facilitating."

She laughs. I guess she thinks that's a big word for a banger.

"Who's your friend?" she asks.

I give Josh an apologetic shrug as I say, "Just a high school kid."

"What? Does he know what you're getting him into?"

"It's more like he's getting me into it."

There's a long pause. "You're going to have to tell me all about this when it's over," she says, flirtation plain in her voice.

"Sure."

"Don't think I won't hold you to it."

Crap.

"I guess I need to tell you something," I say. "You know it's been a while since that night. I'm seeing somebody now."

Josh gives me a surprised look. There's another moment's silence on the other end of the line.

"Are all the Ocean Avers like you?" she asks. "Because I've got to tell you, the bandas don't think like gentlemen."

I'm not sure how to respond to that, so I keep it short. "No, it's just me."

She goes quiet again, then finally says, "I still want to hear the story."

"You got it. Thanks, Aina."

I close my phone.

"Let's saddle up," I tell Josh. "How'd you get here?"

"No, man. I'm doing this on my own. I can ride over there on my bike."

"You won't even make it halfway in that neighbourhood. I'm *coming*," I tell him as I stand up.

"Fine. But not as an Ocean Aver."

"I—"

The look on his face shows me he's dead serious.

"Okay," I tell him. "But you're riding with me."

We get as far as my Harley before J-Dog steps out of the clubhouse and comes sauntering over to us.

Perfect. I've just finished talking him out of a run on the Kings and here I am, maybe starting a war with them myself.

"What's up?" J-Dog asks.

"Nothing much, bro," I tell him. "Just a little personal business."

He gives Josh a once-over.

"Like we were talking about before?" he asks.

"You got it."

He gives Josh another long look, then tips a finger against his brow and turns back to the clubhouse. The handle of a pistol's sticking up out of the back of his jeans.

"What was that about?" Josh asks in a quiet voice.

"That's my brother J-Dog," I tell him, "so who the fuck knows?"

"My bike'll be okay here while we're gone?" Josh asks as he climbs on the Harley behind me.

I turn to look at him. "You're kidding, right? Who's going to mess with a bicycle outside of our clubhouse?"

"Somebody in the gang?"

"Only if they've got a death wish, bro."

I kick the Harley to life and the rumble of the big engine between my legs soothes me like pretty much nothing else can.

Except then I get a picture of Marina in my head.

There's nothing happening there for you, I tell myself.

I give the throttle some gas and the rear tire spits dirt as we pull out onto the highway.

MARINA

The lunch bell goes and it looks like Josh still hasn't shown up at school. A hard knot of worry settles in my stomach. I head outside and see that Theo hasn't shown up either. Even if he were there, I don't know what I'd do. It's way too easy to start stupid rumours in this school.

"Don't worry about Josh," Des says when he catches up with me outside.

"Yes, but—"

"Dude. He's working on the problem even as we speak."

"And you know this because?"

"I called him between classes."

I start to take my phone out, but he shakes his head.

"I already tried," Des says, "but he's not answering now. My guess? He left his phone at home so that the cops can't track him."

We're walking across the field toward the bleachers. Julie's already up in our usual spot. She waves and I wave back. I'm happy to have reconnected with her, but right now I wish she wasn't here because we can't talk about Wildling business in front of her.

"Track him doing what?" I ask Des before we get to the bleachers.

"Whatever it is he's got planned to get the Kings to back off."

I roll my eyes. "No, seriously."

"I am being serious."

This is worse than I thought.

"They're going to kill him."

"Chill, dude," Des says. "This is Josh we're talking about. If they get stupid, they're the ones who'll be going to the hospital."

"Des, they've got *guns!*"

I can't believe the things he comes out with. I know it's not really his fault—it's just the way he is. But sometimes ...

I turn away before I give him a well-deserved whack and then I see *her* across the football field, leaning against the chain-link fence with a couple of her friends like she doesn't have a care in the world.

Ampora.

I'm usually pretty good at keeping my temper, but my anxiety and frustration with Des have put me in a weak moment. Just seeing her now makes me go a little crazy. I think about the banger threatening me this morning, Ampora putting my family in danger, Josh up to who knows what kind of trouble ...

This is all her fault.

I set off across the field, ignoring Des and Julie as they call after me.

"Don't do this!" Des yells, hurrying to catch up.

I move a little faster. Not Wildling fast, which would give me away, but fast enough to leave him behind. Ampora watches me approach with the usual look of disdain in her eyes, but for once she doesn't make one of her snarky comments. One of the two girls leaning on the fence with her takes up the slack.

"Hey, *pocha*," she says. "You see a welcome sign anywhere around here?"

I can't remember her real name, but people call her Sushi or Shooshi or something equally stupid. I make a point of ignoring Ampora and all her judgmental friends unless it absolutely can't be avoided. Then I take the high ground and try to be civil. Usually.

Not today.

"*Shut* it!" I yell at her.

Before she can respond I have Ampora by the front of her jacket and I bang her up against the fence. The chain-link shivers a long way in either direction from the force of the blow. It takes her by surprise, but her eyes widen more when she tries to break my grip and she can't budge me. Her friends on both sides of me are pulling at my arms, but they can't move me, either.

My face is right in Ampora's.

"How could you?" I shout. "How could you let whatever stupid crap you're into blow back on the girls?"

"Hey, you need to—"

"No." I give her a shake. "*You* need to make this right. Whatever it takes, you need to do it."

"Marina," Des says from beside me. I feel his hand on my shoulder. "This isn't the time or place."

He's right. I know he's right. But I just want to shake her until I've rattled some sense into her. And then I want to hit her. But I let her go.

She gives me a shove and I don't budge even an inch. She can't hide her renewed surprise, but it quickly morphs into a glare.

"There wouldn't even be a problem if it wasn't for *your* stupid boyfriend," she says.

"Josh isn't my boyfriend."

"Yeah, but you wish."

"You don't know anything about me."

She rolls her eyes. "Oh, please. Like you don't go all mushy-eyed at the mention of his name."

"I've got a boyfriend," I tell her, "and it isn't Josh."

I don't know why I said that. It's not like there's anything really happening with Theo.

"What *do* you call your vibrator?" Sushi or Shooshi or whatever the hell her name is taunts.

Ampora and I both turn and tell her to shut up at the same time. Then Ampora pokes me in the chest with a stiff finger.

"Just tell him to back off," she says. "I can handle this."

"Because so far you've really had it under control."

"Yeah, well, whatever he does is only going to make things worse." She cocks her head, then adds, "You know, I never saw the upside of the Kings coming after the family. If I'm lucky, maybe they'll at least get rid of you before I get them to back off."

I draw back my fist.

"Marina," Des says before I punch her, his voice low but urgent.

I know why he's worrying. If I hit her too hard I could crush all the bones in her face. I wouldn't mind seeing how that turns out and that thought takes all the air out of me. How did I get to this point?

I give her a shove and she staggers back against the fence.

"Fix this," I tell her. "Whatever you did, fix it."

Then I turn away.

"Dude, that girl is a piece of work," Des says as we walk back across the field to the bleachers. "What's her beef with you anyway? Lots of people get divorced, but you don't see their kids blaming each other."

Josh and I have talked about this, but I've never really explained it to Des. I guess there are a lot of reasons for that, but mostly it's because Josh's parents split up, too.

"She's mad because I went with Mamá," I tell him.

"Yeah, so? She stayed with your dad and you're not pissed off with her, right?"

I shake my head.

"Then what gives with her?"

"Mamá's the one who left," I tell him. "She had an affair and Papá couldn't forgive her."

"Man, that's harsh. So your stepdad—was he the one your mom ...?"

I shake my head. "No, it was another guy from the neighbourhood. It was pretty much a one-night stand, but that was enough to break them up. She met my stepdad a year or so after she moved out. I went with her because she was so messed up I was afraid she'd do something even more stupid."

"Like what?"

"Oh, I don't know, but why do you think she got so religious? She's trying to get at least God to forgive her. Ampora and Papá never will."

Julie meets us at the bottom of the bleachers.

"What was *that* all about?" she asks as we start to climb up to the top.

"Family crap," I tell her.

"Yeah, well you were fierce. I don't think I've ever seen you that pissed off."

I half expect Des to jump in, but he just listens as I give Julie a heavily edited rundown of what's been going on. She's never liked my sister and that's the only part she focuses on.

What do you know? Maybe Des is actually learning some discretion.

"Hey," he says, pointing to where we left Ampora and her friends. "What's going on over there?"

"Isn't that Mr. Goss?" Julie asks.

I nod. My heart sinks as I see the gym teacher walk Ampora back across the field.

Something's happened. I just know it. The Kings have hurt Suelo or Ria and the office has sent Mr. Goss to tell Ampora. I strain to use the otter's ears to hear what they're saying, but they're far away, and there's too much noise on the field for me to make it out.

When they get to the bottom of the bleachers Mr. Goss jabs a finger in my direction.

"You too, Lopez," he says.

I look at him in confusion. Me too, what?

"Get down here!" he calls up.

I exchange glances with Des and Julie. Julie touches my arm.

"Now!" Mr. Goss says.

Oh, God. It has to be the girls.

I think I'm going to throw up. But I get to my feet and make my reluctant way down the bleachers to where he's waiting for me with Ampora.

I'm not mad at her anymore.

I'm too filled with dread to be anything but numb.

JOSH

Mom would kill me if she could see me riding on the back of Chaingang's Harley. She'd be even madder if she knew why we're heading into the barrio. She gets that I need to protect Marina's family. It's not something she likes, but she respects it.

I don't like it, either.

No, that's not entirely true. The mountain lion inside me is almost purring at the thought of getting the chance to take a few of those bangers down. But that's a last resort. What I really want is to negotiate a truce without anybody getting hurt.

Chaingang just laughs when I tell him that as we leave his gang's clubhouse and are cruising down Ocean Avenue.

"Why's that so funny?" I ask him.

With our Wildling hearing we have no problem under-standing each other, even over the roar of the motorcycle and the wind in our ears.

"Because the Kings are all loco," he says. "There's no negotiating with them."

"Then why are you even taking me to this meeting?"

"They'll go after Marina and her family. I don't know why *you're* going, but *I'm* going to break some heads."

"You told your friend Aina that we were just going to talk, and you told me that you weren't coming as an Ocean Aver."

"I say a lot of things I don't mean."

"I need to try talking first," I tell him.

"Sure, bro. It's all your show until they make it into something else. Shouldn't take too long for that to happen."

So I've got a bad feeling about this as we finally pull off South Shore Drive into the dirt parking lot beside Casa Raphael. A half-dozen cars are parked in the lot. Most are the custom, pimped rides that the Kings prefer, but there's also a real beater of a pickup truck. Chaingang pulls in beside the pickup.

"Now that's a nice ride," he says.

He's looking at the pickup. The only thing that seems to be holding its rusted panels together is a thick coating of encrusted mud and dirt.

"You're kidding, right?" I say.

"Come on, bro. It's a classic fifties Ford. J-Dog would know the year."

I want to say, no, it's an old beat-up excuse of a truck that looks even worse than it is beside all these cool custom rides. Instead I just shrug and turn to look at the restaurant.

Casa Raphael doesn't try to get the tourist trade. It looks like a bunker: a long one-storey adobe building with a tar-and-gravel roof. There's some dead grass along the verge between the building and the parking lots, with a pair of raggedy palms out front, facing South Shore. A few ratty agave plants and cacti complete the landscaping. The neon sign doesn't even have a name. It just reads "Taquería." A cracked wooden oval sign over the door says "Casa Raphael" in chalky, peeling turquoise paint.

"You sure you want to go through with this?" Chaingang asks.

I turn to look at him. "No. But I've got to do something."

"Be cool," he says. "We'll just play it by ear. I try not to over-think crap like this, myself."

I nod in agreement. What else am I going to do? Tell him no, let's just get out of here? How's that going to help the Lopez family? But I can't shake the bad feeling I got when we first pulled into the parking lot.

Chaingang leads the way to the door. When we step inside, it's like one of those old westerns. The place goes still and everybody turns to look at us. They're all Kings with their tattoos and hard faces, except for one old Mexican guy sitting by the window who looks to be a hundred years old. He's wearing faded jeans, cowboy boots and a checked flannel shirt, all of which set him apart even more from the bangers in their fancy running shoes, baggy T's and pants.

The decor's what you'd expect. Old Formica tables, battered wooden chairs. Nobody seems to be eating, except for the old guy, who's got a plate of enchiladas on the table in front of him. Everybody else is just waiting. Eight or nine of them are sitting around at various tables. The Wildling in me tells me there are two more behind us on either side of the door.

"Chico," Chaingang says to a guy sitting by himself in the middle of the long room.

He's got a shaved head covered in tats, which run down his neck and under his T-shirt until they emerge again in tattooed sleeves that cover both arms. Even the backs of his hands are tattooed. He gives us a big grin, showing off a gold-capped front tooth, but his dark eyes don't hold any humour.

"Chaingang Washington," Chico says. "Nice of you to come down to our part of town. Is this what you'd call slumming?"

"I'm just here for a conversation."

"You were supposed to come alone."

Chaingang jerks a thumb in my direction. "Josh here's the one who wants the conversation. I just came along to give him a lift."

"So he's not under your protection? He doesn't ride with you?"

"Josh doesn't need anybody's protection."

The dark eyes settle on me.

"That so?" Chico says. "Then who fucked up your face, boy?"

Before I can answer, Chaingang cuts in. "A word of advice. You really don't want to piss him off."

Chico's gaze flits to Chaingang, then back to me. But now he's studying me. I guess he's trying to figure out what he's missing, or if Chaingang's just yanking him.

"So you're a tough guy," Chico says.

"I didn't come to talk about that," I tell him. "I came to talk about the Lopez family."

"Yeah? So talk."

"I want to know what it would take for you to leave them alone."

"Me, I got no beef with them," Chico says. "Trucho—now that's another matter."

"Trucho and I came to our own agreement last night," I tell him.

I see a considering look come into Chico's eyes.

"That was *you* with the hit man from the Solís Cartel?"

"He's not with the cartel. He's an FBI agent. But none of that matters—"

Chico holds up a hand, cutting me off.

"I need to check you for a wire," he says.

I glance at Chaingang and he gives me an almost imperceptible nod.

"Sure," I say. "Do your thing."

Someone comes up behind me, but Chico holds up his hand again.

"No pat down," he tells me. "Strip."

I don't bother to look at Chaingang this time. I just pull off my T-shirt and drop my cargos to the floor.

"Man, somebody really did a number on the little rat," Chico says as he takes in the bruises that cover my body.

A couple of the Kings snicker.

I shrug. "Have you seen enough?"

I'm not planning to take off my boxers, I don't care who Chico thinks he is.

"Sure, sure," Chico says. Then he adds, "So what're you doing with the FBI? We don't get mixed up with federal crap."

Yeah, I think as I pull up my pants. Like the drug trade doesn't cross state lines.

"He's just a guy I know," I tell him.

"So talking about him—is that supposed to scare me? Is that why you brought him up?"

"Actually, you brought him up."

I pull my T-shirt back on.

"Are you dissing me, boy?" Chico says.

I sigh. "That's twice you've called me 'boy,'" I tell him. "You know my name. Use it."

"Or what?"

I realize I have to change my approach. It's not that I'm so prideful, or that I haven't been called worse. It's just becoming clear that unless I do something drastic, this thug is never going to take me seriously. If it were just me, I'd walk away. But Marina and her family are at stake here and that's a whole other ball game.

I look at Chaingang. "I don't have time for this," I tell him. "Would you mind waiting outside?"

"Josh ..."

I ignore the warning in his eyes. I know what he's trying to tell me. Be cool. Don't shift in front of civilians.

"Would you just *do* it?" I say, unable to keep the edge from my voice.

I don't know what he sees in my face, but he gives a slow nod and turns toward the door. I wait until I hear it close behind him, then I walk up to Chico's table. I think about all those action movies I've watched with Des and I feel stupid trying to play the part of one of their tough guy heroes. But it worked with Trucho and I need to do something to get Chico to actually listen.

"Okay," I tell him. "We've established that I'm not wearing a wire, you don't like black people, and somebody beat me up recently. Is that about it?"

He gives me the easy grin that still doesn't reach his eyes and spreads his hands.

"Come on, amigo," he says. "What makes you think I don't like—"

"I asked you, is that *it?*"

Those hard eyes of his go harder still.

"There's eleven of us," he says, "and you just sent the only chance you had to survive a fight with us out the door. Is this really how you want to play it ... boy?"

I give him a smile that I'm not really feeling. Inside, I'm

starting to feel nauseous. Only two things are keeping me standing: the thought of what'll happen to Marina and her family, and the mountain lion that's swelling under my skin, just aching to be let loose.

"Here's what I want," I tell him. "You leave the Lopez family alone. Period. Got it?"

"Or else what?"

"Or else I break the bunch of you into pieces, starting with you. And I won't stop like I did with Trucho last night. They're going to need body bags to drag you out of here by the time I'm done."

I hold his gaze until he suddenly laughs and leans back in his chair.

"Heh!" he says. "You really mean it. You've either got the biggest *cojones* of any kid I've ever met, or you're pure loco. Which is it ..." He waits a long beat before he finishes with "Josh?"

But I'm done playing nice. I know I can't back down now that I've started.

"You didn't answer my question," I say. "Will you leave them alone?"

"It's not up to me, kid. It's up to Fat Boy."

"Then will you give him my message?"

Chico shakes his head. "You really don't want to pull this crap with Fat Boy. He chews up little boys like you for breakfast and spits out the bones."

"He won't find that as easy as he thinks."

"You know, you need to be taught some respect, kid," Chico says. "We're not just a bunch of *cholos* running around like we don't have a clue. You come against one of us, then you come up against us all. That's something you maybe should have thought about before you walked in here."

"Will you give him my message?" I repeat.

Chico gives me another shake of his head. "Fat Boy does whatever he wants and we do what he tells us. I'm not going to him with some crap like this."

"Then I guess I have to make *you* the message," I say.

He gives me another smile, but this one goes all the way up to his eyes.

"Oh, *ese*," he says, "you know you're not walking out of here in one piece—right?"

I know what I have to do. I have to make him know that I'm serious, just the way I did with Trucho last night. As I start for him, he makes a motion with his hand. I don't know what it means until it suddenly feels like I've been punched in the back.

No, not punched.

The sound is like a clap of thunder in this enclosed space.

I've been shot.

It's like when the goons from ValentiCorp Tazed me. Everything slows way down, but it's moving too fast at the same time. The impact lifts me off my feet and slams me against Chico's table. The bullet goes right through me. Blood sprays out of the sudden hole in my chest where the bullet bursts out.

The shock hits me first. Stuns me. My ears ring.

Then comes the pain.

I can feel everything shutting down inside and a great black wave is flooding my head.

The table tilts when I hit it and follows me down to the floor.

I try to suck in air, but my lungs are filling with blood.

I sprawl on the floor.

The edge of the table lands on my back and the impact makes me spew blood out of my mouth.

I remember Chaingang warning me: *The Kings are all loco. There's no negotiating with them.*

I should have listened to him.

Then in the flooding dark I hear Chico say, "This is how you send a message ... boy."

CHAINGANG

Some have it and some don't. Some people can lay down the law with one look and there's no arguing. J-Dog can be like that—with the gang, no question, if not always with me. Grandma, every damn time. Hell, I'm twice her size and she could probably still give me a licking.

But Josh having that something?

If you'd asked me before today, I'd have had to laugh. He's a good kid, no question, but a leader? Sorry, that would be a big *no*.

But today. When we're standing in Casa Raphael—and he has to look *up* at me fercrissakes—I see the determination in his eyes. Back at my crib when he came to my door, I saw a foreshadowing of this iron will, but nothing like this.

Don't get me wrong. He doesn't scare me. The only thing that scares me is getting attached to people because then you're at their mercy. They can be taken away or can turn their backs on you. Just walk out of your life all on their own.

Seeing Josh like this ... now I get why the elders want him so badly. Why they *need* him to step up before everything goes to hell between the humans and us. Just look at him: Wildling, multiracial, raised by a single mom, a genuine true-blue guy with

more than a bit of steel in him. The kind of kid who'll stand up
to scrutiny while they run the show from the shadows.

So while my gut tells me that leaving him alone with the
Kings is the last thing I should do, the Wildling in me says to
let him call the shots here. And it's not because his mountain
lion is so much bigger than the mouse in me. It's because there's
something in who he is now that's bigger than I'll ever be.
Josh standing in front of me in Casa Raphael with that big old
mountain lion under his skin commands my respect.

So I walk out of the taquería.

But listen up, I'm not stupid. I don't trust the Kings because
I've yet to meet one that isn't a little nuts.

So I walk over to my bike and grab the crowbar I keep
sheathed along the bottom of the tank. I return to the door and
stand there, listening, ready. Except when it happens, I'm way
too late to do shit.

At the sound of the gunshot I slam through the door. The
crowbar comes down on the gunman's arm so hard that the
doctors are never going to be able to put all those bone shards
back together. I tap the fool on his head with the crowbar as he's
falling, and snatch his gun out of the air. Then I'm facing the
room in a crouch, ready for anything.

Anything, except for what I see.

Jesus, Josh.

He's sprawled on the floor in front of Chico, the table lying
half on him, and there's blood spurting everywhere. The banger
I took out is unconscious on the floor beside me. There's dead
silence. The rest of the Kings all have handguns and a couple of
shotguns pointed at me. All except for Chico. He's just sitting

there with this shit-eating grin, Josh at his feet, the kid no longer breathing.

I point the gun at Chico and I hear the sudden shuffle of the other Kings as they get ready to blow me away.

"Hold up," Chico says to his men. "We don't want a war with the Ocean Avers over this."

"Oh, you've got a bigger problem than that," I tell him.

His eyebrows raise in a mocking look and I decide that's where I'll shoot him. Right between those cocky eyebrows and the grin.

"Killing my man here," I tell him, "you've just bought every Riverside King a death sentence."

Chico shakes his head. "What? You're going to kill all of us? I give the word, you're not even walking out of this room, *ese*."

I don't bother answering. He doesn't know what he's facing. I'm fast enough that I can probably take out half of them before they finally get me. And I'll start with Chico.

Except I never get the chance.

MARINA

I ask Mr. Goss why we're going to the office but he just barks "No talking!" at me like we're in gym class. We make the rest of the trek from the bleachers to the office in silence. Ampora is fuming at my side and I can't figure out why she isn't worried about the girls like I am. I'm going to die if someone doesn't tell me something soon.

When we get to the office we're told to sit in the row of chairs across from the counter. Ampora waits until I sit down, then leaves an empty chair between us. The school secretary, Mrs. O'Shay, looks at us from behind the counter with a sad look in her eyes and the weight of my worry feels like it's going to crush me.

"Why won't they tell us anything?" I whisper to Ampora when Mr. Goss leaves.

Ampora turns to look at me. "Are you really that stupid?"

I give her a blank look in return. Why isn't she worried?

"Just let nothing have happened to the girls," I say.

There's finally a flash of worry in Ampora's eyes, but no sympathy in her voice.

"We're here," she says, "because you went loco on me out on the football field and somebody squealed."

"Is that all?"

I could almost hug her, I feel so relieved.

"I don't know about you," she says, "but if I get suspended my ass is grass. Papá is going to be so pissed off, and of course he's going to blame me, even though you're the one who started it."

I'm barely listening to her. The girls are okay. For that I'll happily trade a suspension, Mamá's disappointment and my probably being grounded for the rest of my life.

"Girls," Mrs. O'Shay says. "Principal Hayden will see you now."

She motions toward his office door.

"I am so not taking the fall for this," Ampora whispers to me as we walk into the principal's office.

Principal Hayden sits with his fingers steepled, elbows on his desk. He watches us come in and nods toward the chairs on the other side of his desk. We wait, but he doesn't say a word. He just watches us. Now that I know that this has nothing to do with my sisters, I'm content to wait it out. My Wildling nature has taught me patience, but I'm surprised that Ampora's just as ready to wait him out as I am. The hardest thing for me is to keep from smiling because Des has copied this pose a hundred times in the past.

"I know what you think," he finally says. "Anybody over twenty-five doesn't have a clue. But just because we don't say something, it doesn't mean we're blind to what's going on."

He falls silent again, this time giving us an expectant look.

"Is there a point to this?" Ampora asks before I can speak.

He nods. "Families are supposed to look out for each other."

"I don't see how that's school business," Ampora says.

"It becomes school business when verbal sparring escalates to physical confrontations."

I clear my throat. "Ampora had nothing to do with it," I tell him. "I'm the one who got angry and started pushing her around."

"I repeat," Principal Hayden says. "Do you really think we're unaware of what's been going on between the two of you?"

I shoot Ampora a quick look. She's got her hard face on—the angry mask she wears to keep the world at bay. I'm so familiar with that mask—and so sick of it—but I've long since given up trying to get through to her that we're not enemies. I didn't reject her and Papá. I left with Mamá because *she* needed me more. But Ampora never even tried to understand.

"It's no big deal," I tell Principal Hayden before Ampora can make this worse for us. "It's just—you know. Sister stuff. We don't take it seriously."

"And is that how you feel about it, too?" he asks Ampora.

She shrugs. "Sure," she says. "Let's go with that."

Principal Hayden sighs. "You know school policy about fighting on campus?"

"We weren't really fighting," I say quickly. "I know I gave her a push, but honestly, it was no big deal. And she didn't do anything."

"Except call you names every time the two of you pass in the hallway."

"She doesn't mean anything by it."

"I can speak for myself," Ampora says.

Principal Hayden nods. "So give me your take on it."

She looks at me, the ever-present anger smouldering in her eyes.

"I don't mean anything by it," she says.

"I don't see it that way," Principal Hayden says. He waits a beat to let that sink in, then goes on. "The report I received of what happened on the football field tells me it was more than a mere argument and a push. You know we have a zero-tolerance policy in this school."

He gives us each a stern look, so we nod. Thankfully, Ampora keeps her mouth shut. I'm starting to get a little scared now. Sure, I'm relieved that this isn't about the Kings going after our little sisters, but I've been grounded for two weeks now and I was really looking forward to getting my freedom back. That's never going to happen now.

"I should suspend you both," he says.

"But I didn't do anything," Ampora protests.

"Not this time," he agrees. "But your ongoing harassment of your sister hasn't gone unnoticed, young lady. Some might think that she had good cause to finally strike back, even though school policy doesn't agree."

"This sucks," Ampora mutters under her breath.

I hope Principal Hayden didn't hear her—I certainly did—but like he said, he's not clueless. It's easy to read what she's thinking.

"But I'll consider not suspending you if you'll both do something for me," he goes on. "I want you to go to the guidance office and talk to Ms. Chandra about what's going on between the two of you. Starting at lunch tomorrow."

"You can't make us do that," Ampora says.

"That's absolutely correct," he agrees. "I could just give you both a three-day suspension."

I can sense all the air going out of Ampora and she slumps in her seat.

"Fine," she says. "I'll go see the shrink."

"Marina?" he asks.

I nod. "Yes sir. I'll go tomorrow."

"Excellent. Let's get this business between you cleared up. You can go to class now. Mrs. O'Shay will give you hall passes."

"This is such bullshit," Ampora says when we leave the office.

"It's better than a suspension."

She turns to me. "You know what? I *like* school. The only thing wrong with it is that no matter how much I try to avoid it, I still end up having to see your stupid face at least once a day."

Then she walks away.

Nice.

JOSH

I feel light as air. Like I'm floating out of my body. The pain is gone and it's so calm drifting here. Everything's dark but it's a welcoming dark. The kind that feels like a warm bed, late on a Sunday morning when there's no reason to get up. If I just let myself go, I'll sink through the bed, deep into the ground, the ghost of a Wildling boy disappearing into the dirt, all the way down through the bedrock until whatever it is that makes me who I am is one more part of everything that is.

From far away I can hear voices—Chaingang and Chico—but I can't make out what they're saying. I just know they're angry. I don't know why. Words don't seem important anymore, it's so peaceful here.

But thinking of Chaingang brings me back to what's happening to me.

I'm dying.

Now the darkness feels like goop, like I'm swimming through mud. There's a burn in my chest where the calm was just a moment ago.

Where the bullet went through me.

Which is why I'm dying.

I think of Marina and Desmond, how I never got to say goodbye to them, or to my mom, or *anybody*.

And then that makes me think of Elzie and the last place I saw her.

I guess I should have stayed over there with her. That otherworld is looking pretty good right now: So-Cal without pollution or Kings or any of the other crap we've got here, starting with somebody blowing a hole through my chest. I remember Elzie and me play-chasing each other in our Wildling shapes, she the sleek jaguarundi and me the mountain lion. I remember us all sitting around the campfire with Cory and Rico—

Another memory pops into my head: Rico in the lab with me, missing a leg because the research freaks cut it off. But when he shifted into a snake and then back to his human form, he had both legs again ...

The mountain lion roars somewhere in the darkness. A bright heat spreads through me like a fever.

Rico.

Didn't have a leg and then he did. By switching shapes. Wham—bam. Just like that.

The mountain lion roars again.

Remembering what Rico did, I decide to set the lion free.

I mean, what have I got to lose?

It's all slow-mo again, but still flashes at lightning speed. It happens so fast that I don't have time to think about what I'm doing. I just do it.

I shift into the mountain lion's shape. Sudden light flares in my eyes. My claws dig into the floor as I shrug off the weight of the table and suck in a deep lungful of air. Then I shift again, remembering to bring what I was wearing back with me.

Nobody has time to react as I take two quick steps to where Chico is sitting. I pluck him up from his chair, grabbing him by the neck, and turn so that his body is between me and the rest of the Riverside Kings. Chico struggles in my grip until I give him a hard shake.

The fever's still burning in me and everything's a little blurry. The mountain lion is right in my throat, growling deep in my chest.

"My turn," I snarl in Chico's ear. "What do I pull off first? An arm? A leg?"

He's making gagging sounds. The other Kings are pointing handguns and shotguns at me, their eyes wide with shock. Chaingang looks surprised, too, but a slow smile spreads across his face.

I set Chico's feet on the ground. Before he can pull away, I grab his arm and twist it up behind his back. I grip his left shoulder with my free hand. He'd collapse if I weren't holding him upright. He gasps for air.

"Wait, wait!" he wheezes.

"Like you waited before you had me shot?"

"No, no! It was a mistake."

"Doubtful," I tell him.

"No, no. I swear I—"

"Shut up! The real mistake was having one of your boys shoot me when all I was trying to do was talk it out. But now we've run out of options. Talking didn't help. And getting shot *hurt*—a lot more than this." I yank his arm up a little and he cries out.

I see a guy huddled on the floor near Chaingang, just coming to, moaning and clutching an arm that dangles at a wrong angle. Chaingang's got a tire iron in one hand, a gun in the other.

"*Madre de Dios*," Chico says in a strained voice. "You should be dead. What *are* you?"

"The guy you shouldn't have pissed off."

The mountain lion wants to stop toying with him. It wants to just snap his neck and then deal with the rest of them. I pretty much want the same thing, only I'm not sure I have the stomach for it. But I don't know what else to do. If I let them go, they'll come after me. Then they'll go after Ampora and her family. They'll go after *Marina*.

I'm not letting that happen.

I look to Chaingang, but I don't find any help there. I realize he's waiting for me to make the next decision. The problem is, I only see two options and neither of them is all that great.

Either I let the mountain lion loose to kill a bunch of gangbangers, which puts their deaths on my conscience. I still have nightmares about the woman I killed back at the ValentiCorp labs.

Or I let the Kings go and nothing changes. The Lopez family will still have a death sentence hanging over their heads.

They'll come after me, too. After my mom and Chaingang because he's here with me. For all I know, I've already started a war between the Kings and the Ocean Avers.

This so sucks.

All I wanted was for them to leave us alone. Why does that have to be so complicated?

The Kings are starting to get restless. They're looking from one to the other, getting brave again. A few moments ago, they were wide-eyed and making the sign of the cross. Now I can see they're almost forgetting what just happened and I don't blame them. I'm freaked about it, too—I think I was pretty much dead for a moment before shifting to the mountain lion brought me back. It's so much easier to just believe none of it happened.

Chico struggles a bit—testing me—and I jerk his arm up again.

"Enough of this!" a new voice says.

I turn just enough to keep the Kings in view while I glance behind me. It's the old man. He's standing up from his table, glaring at us.

Maybe I'm making the Kings a little nervous, but they're not shy when it comes to tearing into this guy.

"Piss off, you stinkin' asshole," one of them shouts.

Like all the bandas, the shouter's tatted up, big crown on one side of his neck, a cross on the other. He's wearing baggy jeans and a sleeveless T-shirt with a brown stingy-brim fedora. I'm betting there are tats on his head as well.

The old man stares the banger down and asks, "Do you kiss your mother with that mouth?"

Fedora says something in Spanish and lifts his gun.

"You got a name, old man," he adds, "so I can find your grave to piss on it?"

"You don't need to know my name," the old man says. "All you need to know is that I'm from Halcón Pueblo."

And with those words, something weird happens. I feel Chico stiffen in my grip. Fedora lowers his gun. *All* the bangers lower their weapons and stare at the floor.

"*Pardon, tío,*" Fedora says. "I didn't know."

Chaingang and I just look at each other, thinking WTF? I reach out with all my senses, looking for that *ping* that lets me know he's a Wildling. I don't get anything.

The old man nods. "You will all go now. But you will do as the young man said and leave his people alone. There will be no reprisals for what happened here today. Your weapons stay here."

"Not so fast," Chaingang says. "These ass-wipes shot Josh."

The old man's eyebrows go up. "So I saw. But he seems fine to me now."

The bandas have put their weapons on various tables and are moving toward the door. A couple of them hoist up the guy Chaingang took down. Chaingang keeps looking from them to the old man, plainly unhappy that he's not getting to take any retribution.

"These men are not the immediate danger," the old man tells him. "The danger that you should be worried about comes from your *own* kind."

Chaingang shakes his head. "The Ocean Avers would never—"

The old man cuts him off. "I didn't say your affiliation. I said your *kind*." Then he turns to me and adds, "I would appreciate it if you would let Chico go as well."

I meet his gaze for a long moment before I give Chico a shove away from me. Chico doesn't even turn in my direction. He only has eyes for the old man.

"I will give your message to Fat Boy," he says. "There will be no problems. I swear."

The old man gives him a slight nod and Chico scurries out the door after the other gang members. I hear their cars starting up, the crunch of tires on the dirt as they leave the parking lot.

Chaingang's gaze never leaves the old man. He's obviously pissed. He lifts the gun he's holding, points it at him.

"So what's your deal?" he asks. "Are you some kind of bandas godfather? I caught the bit about the pueblo. *Halcón*—that means hawk, right?"

I start and look at the old man in a new light.

"You—you're one of *los tíos*," I say, remembering what Solana told me about them, how they can turn into hawks or see through hawks' eyes or something.

"The uncles?" Chaingang repeats, still pointing his gun at the old man. "I don't care if you call yourselves the aunties. I just need to know what's going on here."

"No, it's cool," I say. "Put down your gun. Agent Solana told me about them. They're like these warrior shaman."

That makes the old man smile.

"Yes," he says with a chuckle, "we are very fierce."

He stands there smiling, just this skinny old guy, but something in his eyes says he's not really joking. Still, I find myself smiling back at him.

"So are you here to help me?" I ask.

"I'm here to eat my enchiladas. The floor show was just a bonus."

He turns and reaches into a dusty backpack on the floor by his table, pulling out a piece of cloth. When he tosses it to me I realize it's a T-shirt.

"You might want to change what you're wearing," he says. "The *policía* don't take kindly to people walking around the way you are."

I look down at my chest. My shirt's a mess, drenched with blood, and there's a big hole in it where the bullet tore through. But at least I shifted back *with* my clothes.

As I peel off my shirt, Chaingang finally lowers the gun. He looks at it for a moment, then lays it on a table. I'm mesmerized by my own bare chest. There's not even a scar. But there's blood all over the floor. A *lot* of blood. I stare at it with a morbid fascination, my senses flooded with its metallic smell.

My blood.

"So now what?" Chaingang asks. "You here to do some kind of Yoda thing?"

That pulls me out of the little trance I fell into. I drop my bloody shirt into the pool of blood on the floor and put on the one the old man threw over to me. I guess it was white once. Now it's greyed from age and use. But it's clean. I can smell the detergent on it. Lemon. I focus on that instead of the blood.

When I look up, I see the old man shake his head in response to Chaingang's question.

"I told you, I'm here to eat my enchiladas," he says. "And you should go. You have bigger problems than some boys playing at being gangsters."

I think about all those guns the Kings had, about getting shot by one of them. That seems a little more serious to me than boys playing around.

"We will speak again," the old man says to me, "but you have other challenges to face before that time comes."

"Nuh-uh," Chaingang says before I can respond. "You're not pulling that crap on us—the mysterious old guy who knows more than he's saying. If you've got something to say, no games. Tell us now."

The old man gives him a mild look. "And if I don't?"

Chaingang's mouth opens, but then he just shakes his head.

Yeah, I think. Maybe it's not such a good idea to push our luck with a guy who could send all those Kings running away like a bunch of little girls.

"Why can't you tell us now?" I ask anyway.

He smiles. "Because until you have faced your challenges, I won't know if you're the right one."

"Right one for *what?*"

He studies me for a moment.

"I will tell you this," he says. "You are only as weak as you think you are. Expect to be defeated and you will be."

"Seriously?" Chaingang says. "That's all you got?"

But the old man doesn't answer. He sits down at his table and goes back to his enchiladas as if we're no longer here.

"I could find better advice in a fortune cookie," Chaingang mutters.

The old man continues to ignore us.

Chaingang and I exchange glances. I see the frustration on his face. But then he shrugs and starts for the door. He steps outside. I follow him to the door but I stop and turn back.

"Um—thanks, I guess," I tell the old man.

Still nothing. He lifts a forkful of enchilada to his mouth and chews.

"Will you at least tell me your name?" I try.

That has him lift his head.

"Sometimes I answer to Goyo," he says. "You can call me Tío Goyo."

And returns to his meal once more.

I wait a beat longer before I finally follow Chaingang outside to the hot parking lot. All the cars are gone, though there's still a little dust in the air. The only vehicles left are Chaingang's Harley and that rusted pickup that must belong to Tío Goyo. Then my gaze is drawn across the street to where a tall, dark-haired man is standing, looking our way.

At first I think he's just some resident of the barrio, out for a stroll. He must have stopped to watch all the Kings come tumbling out of the taquería and peel away in their cars. But he doesn't look Mexican—his skin's really pale, for one thing—and though people don't always have a lot of money around here, they dress better than this. He's wearing a shabby black suit with no shirt under the jacket and he's barefoot.

I'd think he's just some homeless guy, except I'm getting a serious Wildling *ping* from him. I got nothing like that from the old man inside the taquería and Tío Goyo's obviously got some kind of powerful mojo going on. But this stranger is really rocking the Wildling vibe, and there's something in the way he's looking at us that makes my skin crawl.

"Chaingang?" I say.

Chaingang nods before I can finish.

"Yeah, I see him, bro," he says.

MARINA

The afternoon drags. It's one of those days that seem to go on forever, which isn't helped by the endless circle of my thoughts. Between worrying about Josh and my little sisters, and this business with Ampora, I can't get my brain to shut up. And then I have the joy of how, in between each class, Juan Ruiz makes a point of letting me see him make a gun shape with his fingers and pretend to shoot me.

Just before last class he comes up behind me.

"After school, *pocha*," he says.

He's right in my ear. There's nothing I'd like better than to turn around and punch him right in the smirk that I know is there. But I know it's the last thing I should do. If I get caught fighting again, it won't be a trip to Ms. Chandra's office. Principal Hayden will have no choice but to suspend me.

And you know what? I'd deserve it.

So I clench my fists, hold my tongue and let him slip away into the crowded hall.

I'm also getting a little worried about how I can't seem to keep my temper in check lately. I goof around with Des and Josh all the time, giving them a push or a tap on the shoulder. That's not new. What's new is my wanting to do some serious damage to people like Juan and my sister Ampora.

Where is this coming from?

Sea otters aren't particularly aggressive animals, so far as I know. I should ask the Wildlings who come to my blog if they've noticed anything like this in themselves. The Wildlings I know aren't exactly a great barometer to judge anything against. Theo's always been a tough guy, getting into scraps. But then I think of Josh. He's never been like that. Except, ever since he became a Wildling, he's been a lot more aggressive. Maybe it's just the situations he's been in that have made him that way.

I have a flash from that video monitor we saw the night he escaped from ValentiCorp.

Josh as a mountain lion, killing that researcher.

But now Des says he's facing off with the Kings ...

God, what if people like Congressman Householder are right? What if we *are* dangerous?

Great. Something else to worry about.

"Hey!"

I turn to find Julie and Des coming down the hall toward me.

"So what happened?" Julie asks.

"Yeah," Des says. "Did you get busted for your girl-on-girl with Ampora out on the football field?"

I start to raise a fist to give him a punch, then realize what I'm doing.

What is *wrong* with me? Okay, so I usually give him a whack when he comes out with something like that, but *why* is that my response? Because it's not that far a stretch from joke-punching Des to wanting to have a serious go at Ampora or Juan.

I let my hand fall to my side and just nod instead.

"But he let us off with a warning," I tell him. "And we have to go see Ms. Chandra to work out our issues with each other."

"Dude," Des says with sympathy. "I'd rather have the suspension."

"I wouldn't," Julie says. She's sympathetic, too, but I can also see the worry in her eyes. "What's going on?" she adds.

"It's too long a story," I tell her. "We all have to get to class."

Julie nods. "I'll catch up with you after school."

I think of Juan's warning and his finger gun. He and the rest of the Kings are going to be waiting for me just off school property. Waiting for me and Ampora. And they won't just be making pretend guns with their fingers.

Do I really want Julie caught up in that as well?

"You know what?" I say. "I'm ready to cut class. Let's hang in the library and catch up."

Des raises his eyebrows.

"Oh, come on," I tell him. "I've skipped school before."

"To go surfing, yeah. But this? I don't know, Lopez. Fighting. Going to the office. Cutting class. Dude, between you and Josh, I'm seriously losing my bad boy cred around here."

Julie and I look at each other and smile.

She reaches up and puts her index finger under his chin. "I hate to break it to you," Julie tells him, "but no one ever saw you as a bad boy."

He puts a hand over his heart. "Just for that, I'm going to class. You two can gossip without me."

Julie makes kiss-kiss noises as he leaves.

"So dish," she says as we head for the library. "I know you and Ampora have never been tight, but you've always taken the high road before today."

I sigh as I walk along beside her, trying to figure out what to tell her. We hurry because the halls are emptying and we don't want to get caught out here without a pass. But when we turn the corner to the library, I stop dead in my tracks. It takes Julie a second longer, then she stops, too.

"Oh, crap," she says.

No kidding.

Erik Gess is standing between us and the library door. He looks a mess. His eyes are puffed, his face flushed, his clothes dishevelled, and he's got a serious case of bed hair. But it's the wild-eyed way he's looking at us that makes me check his hands to see if he's turned into some gun-toting whack-job. The fact that they're clenched into fists at his thighs, empty, doesn't instill a lot of confidence that he's operating with a full load. Not with that crazed look in his eyes. But maybe it means I have a chance of subduing him without anybody else getting hurt.

Of course, doing that is going to totally blow my cover.

I know the kids at school have gossiped themselves into thinking Josh knows some kind of kung fu, but no way am I going to convince anybody that I do, too.

Everybody's going to know that I'm a Wildling.

CHAINGANG

Damn. I see Vincenzo as soon as I step out the door and figure, this is it. He's tired of waiting on me and he's making his own play. Why the hell did I leave that gun inside?

Josh moves to my side. He glances at me and I guess he sees something in my face.

"Do you know that guy?" he asks.

"No."

It's not a complete lie. I don't know the first thing about Vincenzo, except that he's stronger than hell and he wants Josh dead. But I don't *know* him. I don't want to know him. I just want him dead.

Fat chance that's going to happen any time soon.

But that doesn't mean I'm just going to roll over for him.

I don't have the gun. I'm still holding my crowbar, but it didn't help me all that much the last time. The only difference is, now I know how fast and strong he is. Maybe I can work with that. Use that speed of his against him. Psyche him out, get him to commit, then hit him hard from a direction he's not expecting.

Times like this, I wish my Wildling aspect were more along the lines of Josh's. A little mouse? Not so scary. A big freaking mountain lion? *Now* we're talking.

"So why's he looking at us like that?" Josh asks. "Do you think he's with the bandas?"

"I doubt it. And besides, Chico gave his word."

"And how much stock can we put in that?"

"Not a hell of a lot, I suppose."

I've got to tell Josh what's really going down, but this definitely isn't the time or place. Not with Vincenzo standing there across the street, giving us the evil eye. He can probably hear every word we're saying.

Beside me, Josh is still studying Vincenzo.

"He must be one of the real old cousins," Josh says. "I've never felt the Wildling vibe so strong."

"I hear you, bro."

I don't know why Vincenzo's making such a big production out of it. If he's here to finish this, he should just do it. Me? I wouldn't be showboating. I'd step up and do the dirty deed— wham, bam, that's all she wrote—and then I'd be gone. Playing games is for chumps.

But I guess he figures he's got all the odds on his side, so he can do whatever the hell he wants.

When he steps off the curb, I tighten my grip on the crowbar. I want to tell Josh to take off while he can. But the truth is, I'm going to need that mountain lion under his skin if either of us is going to get out of this alive.

I turn to tell him to change right now, screw the consequences, but before I can get the words out, I notice a black SUV coming down South Shore Drive, slowing as it approaches Casa Raphael. Vincenzo waits for it to go by, except it doesn't. It turns into the parking lot.

The windows are tinted, so I can't see inside. I doubt it's any of the Kings coming back for a rematch. It's too soon for that and the only use they have for a vehicle like this is to boost it and take it to some chop shop. Then the window rolls down and I see it's one of the FBI agents who've been dogging Josh's ass. Beside him is the other.

Matteson and Solana.

"How did *they* find me?" Josh says to me before they get out of the car. "I didn't tell anybody where I was going and I left my phone at home."

They're Feds, I think. They're probably using a satellite feed. But I don't tell him that. Right now I don't care how they found him. I'm more interested in what Vincenzo is up to, but when I look back to the street he's gone.

The Feds get out of their car. The white guy stays by it, leaning on the hood. His partner walks toward us.

"I've been trying to reach you all afternoon," Solana says to Josh.

"Yeah, I forgot my phone when I left the house this morning," Josh says.

"Uh-huh."

"How did you know I'd be here?"

Solana doesn't answer right away. He just looks over at the telephone wires crossing South Shore. On a far pole, a red-tailed hawk is perched.

"Educated guess," he says.

I think about the guy inside the taquería who said he's from some hawk pueblo and give Solana a sharp look. Just what the hell's going on here?

"You're looking better than the last time I saw you," he says. "A couple of days ago I wanted to take you to the hospital, but look at you now."

I noticed that, too. When the shift from his Wildling shape and back saved his life, it also healed every scabbed cut and bruise he'd been wearing before. Until this moment, I hadn't realized how that might be a problem. Solana just seems curious, but I don't like the way his partner is studying Josh. I can almost see the cogs of his mind turning as he tries to figure it out.

"I heal fast," Josh says.

Solana nods. "I guess you do."

"Well, here I am," Josh tells him, not hiding the edge in his voice. "What did you want?"

I'm kind of surprised. Josh is a good kid. He doesn't have the experience of being on the wrong side of the cops for as long as I have, so I'd expect him to at least be polite and a little nervous. Instead he sounds irritated and he isn't trying to hide it.

The Fed seems surprised by Josh's attitude, too, but he tries not to show it.

"The name Rod Harper mean anything to you?" he asks.

Josh shakes his head. "Who's he?"

"One of the Black Key Securities guards who was working at ValentiCorp when you got snatched. He's turned up dead—just like his boss."

I've been trying to figure where Vincenzo got to—you have to be subtle about that kind of thing around cops. Keep looking around yourself while they're talking to you? The suspicion alarm goes up a notch. But the mention of Black Key draws my attention back to them.

"Will you get off my back? You really think *I* did it?" Josh says.

Matteson steps away from the SUV.

"A little less attitude, kid," he tells Josh.

Solana holds up a hand. "I've got this, Paul. Nobody's thinking you're good for it," he adds, directing his attention back to Josh. "You're not even on the radar."

"Then why are you telling me about it?"

"Use your head," Solana says. "Maybe the Sheriff's office isn't looking at you—and I know our office isn't—but that doesn't mean the surviving members of that Black Key team aren't going to consider you."

"Oh, come on. *Seriously?*"

But he doesn't look like he's joking and neither does his partner.

"Okay," Josh says. "So you're serious. What am I supposed to do about it?"

"Be careful?" Solana says.

Josh nods. "And you came all the way out here to tell me that?"

"Well, I would've called but you ..."

He lets the words trail off.

"I left my phone at home," Josh finishes.

"We're just saying, maybe you consider lying low," Solana says. "Stick close to home. Don't go anywhere by yourself for a while—not even to school."

Josh is shaking his head halfway through what Solana's telling him.

"Look, I appreciate your letting me know," he says, "and I'll keep an eye out for these guys, but I'm not going to just stick my head in the sand until this all goes away."

"Try thinking straight," Matteson tells him. "These Black Key guys trained as soldiers. They're ex-marines and Seals. If they're hunting you, you'll never even see them coming."

Josh nods. "Oh, yeah, and my house is like a fortress that they couldn't get into, right?"

Matteson frowns. "Listen, kid. I don't appreciate your pissy—"

Josh holds up a hand. "I'm not mouthing off. And I'm grateful for the heads-up. I'm just pointing out that the only way I could be safe is if I was in some little holding cell with an army of guards protecting me. That's not living. And how long would I be stuck there?"

"You're not going to change a damn thing, are you?"

Josh shakes his head. "But I promise I'll be extra careful."

The Feds exchange looks. They're like an old married couple who don't have to talk to communicate. Matteson lifts an eyebrow and Solana shrugs.

"Okay," Matteson says. "But can I have a word in private with you, Josh?"

He walks away, to the other side of the car. Josh hesitates. He gives me a look, then shrugs and follows after. He knows as well as I do that my Wildling hearing will let me follow the conversation.

I do another quick scan for Vincenzo. Still nothing. Not knowing what he's up to is making me more nervous than seeing him standing there across the street did.

"Do you know who you're running with?" Matteson asks

when Josh joins him. "His brother runs the local Crips and he's got a rap sheet."

"I know."

"You're not doing yourself any favours hanging around with a guy like that."

"I don't know about that other stuff," Josh says. "I just know he's my friend."

"Who takes you for a little ride into the River Kings' turf? Come on, kid. You're just lucky you haven't run into any of the bangers yet. Friends don't put friends into situations like this."

Josh just shrugs.

"Jesus, kid," Matteson says. "I'm trying to do you a favour here. Don't you think you've seen enough trouble with that ValentiCorp business? You really want to get caught up in gang crap now?"

I keep scanning for Vincenzo while I listen to them. Then I become aware of Solana and realize that I wasn't being as subtle as I'd like to think I was.

"Expecting someone?" he asks.

"Well, you know. I don't really have the home-ground advantage around here."

Solana nods. "What *are* you doing here?"

That's when it occurs to me that the Feds might decide to take a walk into the taquería, and then we're *really* going to be hip deep in crap.

"We're supposed to meet a guy with a board Josh is looking to buy. But he's late. Maybe you scared him off."

I see Josh's head go up and know he's listening to us at the same time as he's listening to Matteson, who's now listing off all the crimes I'm suspected of having committed. It's an interesting list. Most of the stuff is pure bullshit. I figure he's just making crap up to scare Josh off.

"And you were planning to haul a board back on this bike of yours?" Solana is saying.

"And that's weird because?" I ask.

Solana's getting irritated with me.

"Why'd you come here?" he calls over to Josh.

"To buy a board," Josh replies. "Guy was supposed to show up with a vintage Dogtown, but we've been waiting for an hour now. Looks like he's a no-show."

"A board?" Solana repeats.

Josh nods. "Yeah, a skateboard. Why?"

"No reason."

Solana turns back to me. I give him an innocent look that he doesn't buy.

"I need to roll," I tell him. "You got anything else you want to discuss?"

They wind it down quickly after that.

"Agent Matteson doesn't like you," Josh says as we watch the SUV pull out of the lot.

"You think?"

Josh doesn't answer. Instead he looks back at the taquería. Disbelief washes over his features and he looks kind of innocent, like he used to.

"What was I even thinking?" he says. "Do you know anybody else as stupid as me?"

It wasn't the brightest move, letting all the Kings see his Wildling shape, but it's not like he had a choice.

"It worked out okay, bro" is all I say.

"If Tío Goyo hadn't stepped up," he says, "I think I would have killed them all."

"Or at least the ones I didn't."

He looks at me. "And that doesn't bother you?"

"Should it?" I ask him. "Someone comes after me and mine, I've got only two words for them: no mercy."

"And you don't think about them? They don't haunt you?

I shake my head.

"I do," he says. "That woman in the lab? I think about her all the time."

"Do you think about what she was going to do to you? What she already did to those other kids? Do you think any of that ever kept *her* up at night?"

He shakes his head. "But I'm still not sure that gave me the right to take her life."

There's not much I can say, so I give the area another quick scan. Still no sign of Vincenzo. But that doesn't mean anything.

"Are we done here?" I ask.

Josh gives a slow nod.

"You sure?" I ask. "You don't want to stick around to see if that guy shows up with the vintage board?"

That gets me a twitch of a smile.

I straddle my bike and start it up. I love the sound of that engine, deep and throaty.

"Get on," I tell him. "We need to talk. Nobody will be able to hear us over the sound of this, especially if we're moving."

"Who do you think is listening?"

"Would you just get on."

"Okay, okay," he says. "But I need to get back to school to meet Ampora, so we can pick up her sisters."

"Nobody's gunning for them anymore," I say as we pull out onto South Shore.

"Unless they didn't get the memo."

"There's that, bro. So tell me. What's the deal with these hawk uncles?"

"I'm not really sure," Josh says. Then he tells me about his conversation with Solana earlier this morning outside of Ampora's house.

"You buy any of that?" I ask when he finishes.

"You saw how the Kings reacted to Tío Goyo."

"I guess. But shaman warriors, bro? What's going to show up next? A bunch of zombies? Maybe a vampire? Gotta tell ya. I'm not rocking the Creature Feature vibe."

"If we can exist—Wildlings, I mean—who's to say what else is out there?"

Vincenzo for one, I think, but I don't say that. I was going to bring Josh into the loop about Vincenzo, but I've changed my mind. First I want to see what Marina was able to find out from Cory. Maybe I can take the sucker down before I have to tell Josh about him.

"I don't get any kind of a Wildling vibe from Solana," I say.

"Me neither."

"So what is he?"

"What he says he is, I guess," Josh says. "A guy who's seen a little deeper under the skin of the world than most people have."

"I don't trust him."

"I think I do."

"Be careful with that, bro."

"I'm more worried about these ValentiCorp guards. If they're really after me, what's to stop one of them from coming after me with a sniper rifle?"

"One thing at a time," I tell him. "Check in with Ampora. Make sure things are cool with her little sisters. We can hook up later and do some brainstorming."

"I appreciate—you know. Everything."

I think to myself, are you really going to appreciate me when Vincenzo gets his way?

But all I say is, "I told you a long time ago that I'd have your back."

As we approach Sunny Hill, there's still an hour before classes end for the day, so Josh asks me to let him off a block away. He looks around when he gets off the bike, his gaze going high, scanning the telephone poles and trees—for hawks, I guess. I look for Vincenzo. Neither of us sees what we're looking for.

"You sure you don't want some backup?" I ask. "In case the local yokels haven't got their new orders from Fat Boy yet?"

"No, I think I can handle some kids."

You're just a kid, I think, except I'm beginning to understand that he's a lot more than that.

I just nod. "Later, bro."

I ride a couple more blocks, then pull over into an alley to send Marina a text. I kill the engine under the shade of a jacaranda tree and put the bike on its stand, but before I can get off, Vincenzo is beside me. He shows up out of nowhere. One minute I'm alone, the next big ugly's in my face.

"The boy is still alive," he says.

Right to the point, no small talk. But that's fine with me. The less time I have to be around this freak, the happier I am.

"Look," I tell Vincenzo. "I did the best I could. I led him into an ambush and the Kings freakin' killed him."

That earns me a frown. "Do you take me for a fool? I saw him walk out of the taquería with you."

"Yeah, well, the dying part didn't take."

"I don't find this amusing."

"And you think I do? I'm stuck between making sure some innocent kid gets offed or you killing my family. The last thing I want to do is piss you off."

He studies me for a long moment, then gives a slow nod.

"Tell me what happened," he says.

"There's not much to tell. One of the bangers shot him point blank, blew a hole in him the size of a fist. He goes down and there's blood everywhere. Then he changes into a lion and gets back up and the bangers are out of that place like the devil's on their ass."

He's nodding as I talk.

"I saw them come streaming out of the taquería. But how did the boy survive? Are you sure he was dead?"

"Not dead enough, apparently, but man, you don't just get up and walk away after getting hit the way he did. I heard him take his last breath. I heard his heart stop. But then he gets up all the same. I've never seen anything like it."

He's still nodding. "But there was no blood on him—on his shirt—when he came out with you."

"Yeah, we made some old guy in there give us a shirt."

"What old man?"

"How would I know? Just some old guy eating lunch. Go

look for yourself. There's no way they've cleaned that place up already."

"This complicates everything," Vincenzo says.

"Look, you want me to keep going after the kid, I will."

"Let me think on it first."

"And the deadline?"

"Everything is on hold. I'll get back to you."

"Yeah, but my family?"

"They're all right for now. Unless I find out you've been lying."

And then he's gone again. But I know the trick he's using. He didn't just vanish. He stepped into the otherworld—the same one we ended up in when we did that frontal assault on ValentiCorp. I still haven't figured out how to make the sidestep into it, but then, I haven't been trying. Now I'm thinking that might be a useful trick to have hidden up my sleeve.

My phone's still in my hand, the screen blank. I wake it up and send a one-word text to Marina: *Cory?*

JOSH

"Josh?"

Though he seems familiar, I can't quite place the clean-cut guy approaching the low adobe wall where I'm sitting. I've been waiting for school to finish so that I can go collect Ampora, amusing myself by trying to figure out if the hawk on the telephone pole is one of *los tíos*, a Wildling, or just an everyday hawk.

The guy coming toward me's not much older than I am, but he's decked out like an old man: chinos, golf shirt, loafers, hair trimmed short.

"It's Danny," he says, reaching out his right hand. "Danny Reed."

Even with the name, it takes me a moment to recall that this is Elzie's friend. Ex-friend. The one who sold out. The last time I saw him, he looked like a beach bum with dreads and raggedy clothes. No, scratch that. The last time I saw him, he turned into some kind of antelope and the FBI captured him. Except the whole thing was faked so that he could go undercover and finger Wildlings for the FBI. Elzie wouldn't say much about his betrayal, but I know it cut her deeply.

I deliberately ignore the extended hand. "I don't know what kind of bullshit you're selling," I tell him, "but I'm not interested."

"Look, I screwed up. I get that. Elzie was right. Nothing's going to be changed from the inside."

"It's not me you should be apologizing to."

"I get that, too, but I can't find her. It's like she dropped right out of the world."

Which is exactly what happened, but I'm not about to tell him that. The last thing we need is for the government to know about the pristine world sitting sideways from our own. A whole new world of natural resources they'd just plunder and spoil.

"I can't help you," I tell him. "I haven't seen her for a couple of weeks."

"Crap. Because that's not the only thing I need to talk to her about."

I look away, across the street.

"This other thing concerns all Wildlings," Danny says.

"I already told you, I'm not interested in anyth—"

"Yeah, yeah. You're all protective of her—I get that. I do. But you need to listen to me."

I stand up and point two fingers toward his eyes. "No, *you* listen to me. Get the hell out of here."

"You've heard about the Black Key Securities guys that are being killed?" he says as I start to turn away.

That stops me.

"What about them?" I ask.

"This isn't in the news, but they've found a third body, just like the others, torn up like they were killed by some kind of animal." He waits a beat, then adds, "Or a Wildling."

"I still don't get—"

"Let me finish—then you can walk away. That's not all. Some of the other men who were part of the same team have turned themselves in to protective custody, and this whole business is going to blow up in our faces."

"What do you mean by *our?*"

I wonder how much the FBI knows about what really happened down there in the ValentiCorp labs. Do they know I killed the head researcher?

"*Our*, as in you and me and every other Wildling. You know about Congressman Householder's little crusade against us?"

"I'm not an idiot."

He gives me a look that says he's not so sure of that. "Well, he's using these latest murders to get back on his soapbox. He's even claiming those kids you found were killed by Wildlings. He knows the quarantine is never going to fly, so now he's pushing for containment camps. He wants us all pulled out of the general population so that the government can contain the danger we represent."

"Can they actually do that?"

"They can do whatever they want—haven't you figured that out yet? The old air force base is going to become our own Guantánamo Bay. On the plus side, our Bureau Chief is pushing for voluntary Wildling registration, same as before. He says the only ones that are going to be 'contained' are those whose animal shapes are deemed too dangerous to be allowed to run around unchecked."

That would be me for sure.

"How would they even find us?" I ask. "There's no test that proves whether or not you're a Wildling."

Except then I remember who I'm talking to. I hope he's not wearing a wire.

"You're going to finger us for the FBI," I say.

"Hell, no. You think I'm crazy? I learned my lesson."

"Yeah, right."

"I don't care what you believe," he tells me, "but don't kid yourself. I won't be helping them, but it won't be hard for them to find others who will. A bunch of kids turned themselves in and they got all buddy-buddy with them. If Householder gets his way, anybody they nab who didn't voluntarily register will automatically go to the holding camp. Lindel—the Bureau Chief—is hoping to pre-empt Householder from bringing in this containment legislation because we know that's going to set off every Wildling in Santa Feliz. Lindel doesn't want the headache of trying to police the mess that'll turn into."

"What do think is going to happen?" I ask. "That all the Wildling kids are going to storm government offices? Get real."

"Look," he says. "You know and I know that's not going to happen. But the government doesn't see it like that. They see someone with power, they figure they're going to use it. Because that's what the government would do."

And I thought dealing with the Kings was a big enough problem all on its own.

Thinking of the Kings reminds me of the time. School's out and I need to get there.

"I've got to go," I tell Danny.

"Right. If you see Elzie, tell her what I said, and pass the word to the other Wildlings, too."

I nod. But not before I check with Solana. And for sure not before I get to the school.

I don't bother to watch what Danny does. I just take off for Sunny Hill.

MARINA

I'm still trying to figure out how to get Julie out of the way so that I can deal with Erik when Erik starts shuffling down the hall toward us. I step in front of Julie so that he has to come at me first. But he doesn't attack. I don't think he was ever a threat. As he gets closer I can see that the crazy look in his eyes isn't I'm-going-to-kill-you crazy, but scared crazy.

"Look," he says. "I'm sorry—okay? Tell the guy I came and said I was sorry. Tell him to just leave me alone now."

The *guy*? What guy?

Then I remember Des telling me about what he and Josh were up to last night. How Cory went into Erik's house ...

"What happened to you?" I say.

"I—I ..."

God, he's a mess. And when was the last time Erik was at a loss for words?

Julie touches my back of my arm.

"You're not actually talking to him, are you?" she asks.

"Look at him," I say. "He's not going to hurt anybody."

"Who cares? It's Erik Gess. Whatever happened to him, he deserved it."

But I shake my head. "We need to get him out of the hall before someone sees him."

Erik's just standing there, staring off into space while we're talking. Ignoring Julie's advice, I grab his shoulder and steer him toward the door of the girls' restroom. Erik doesn't offer any resistance.

"Make sure no one comes in," I tell Julie.

"Again, why?" she says.

Because I want to find out what he knows about Wildlings, but how am I supposed to say that without starting a whole new round of questions I don't want to answer?

"I just want to find out what happened to him," I say.

"This makes no sense at all," Julie tells me, but she holds up a hand before I can say anything. "It's cool. I'll keep a lookout. Just be quick about it."

I open the door and give Erik a little push. He walks in docilely enough. Julie slips in behind us and stays by the door. I give Erik another push toward the sinks.

"Let's get you cleaned up," I tell him.

I wet some paper towels and wipe his face and arms while he just stands there. He's got bruises and little cuts all over his arms. He looks like he's been out mountain-climbing or something, and the mountain won.

"Can I borrow your hairbrush?" I ask Julie.

"Seriously? You want me to get Gess-cooties on my brush?"

"I don't have one with me."

Julie makes a so-grossed-out face, but digs her brush out of her backpack and tosses it over.

"I'm going to have to get that sterilized now," she mutters. "Maybe I should buy a new one."

I tune her out and concentrate on dealing with Erik's bed hair. There's not much I can do about the condition of his clothes. But I get him to straighten his shirt and brush some of the dirt off his pants. It helps compose him, but he's still not the Erik Gess I know and dislike. His eyes are too haunted.

"Tell me what happened," I say.

He leans against a sink and runs a hand through his hair. It's an oddly tender gesture for a guy like Erik, who's more likely to strut than look vulnerable.

"I was over at Jonesy's place," he finally says. "We were just chilling with a few beers and some fatties, you know? There were some girls there and I guess I made out with a couple of them. But I didn't get wasted or anything."

I nod to show I'm listening and try to keep the irritation off my face. This is the Sunny Hill Purity Club. They've all sworn vows of abstinence. The national organization would be on their case so fast if they ever knew. I glance at Julie and she puts her finger into her mouth and pretends to barf.

"And then what?" I ask.

"I went home. Went up to my room." His eyes are starting to do that skittering thing that you see in crackheads, looking everywhere for some threat that isn't there. "And then—then he came in."

"Who came in?" I prompt when he doesn't go on.

"I don't *know*." He rubs his face. "I don't even know that it was real. He walked right through my closed door like it wasn't even there ... this guy ... this guy ..." His gaze locks onto mine. "He didn't even have a face. There was like this dog's head where his should have been, but it wasn't a mask. It was real. So freaking real. I guess I was way more wasted than I thought I was."

So it *was* Cory. I remember Josh telling me how he had this trick where he could wear his coyote features in place of his own, but still walk around like a man.

"What did he do?" I ask.

Erik peers at me as though he's seeing me for the first time.

"Why do you care? Why are you even listening to this? It's all got to be bullshit."

I nod. "Except look at yourself."

He turns to the mirror. Even with his hair brushed, face washed, he looks a mess. There's no quick fix for the condition of his clothes and the bruising and cuts on his arms.

"*Something* had to have happened to leave you looking like that," I say.

He puts his back to the mirror, shaking his head.

"No way," he says. "No way any of that was real."

"So what do you *imagine* happened?" I ask.

"I ... I ..."

He keeps shaking his head.

"Try," I tell him. "You must remember something."

He gives a slow nod. "I remember the dude coming through my closed door, looking like some half-assed dog-boy. He grabbed me and then we were somewhere else—like in the mountains somewhere. It's just all rocks and dirt. He lets go of me, but then he gives me a shove and I fall down on the rocks.

"'I don't like people like you,' the dog guy says. Then he says, 'You think you own the world, but everything you do proves you're not even fit to live in it. Why don't you think about that for a while.'

"And then he just disappears and I'm left alone up on this

freaking mountain and there's nothing for as far as I can see in every direction. I was there for hours. I tried climbing down, but I kept running into dead ends—cliffs where the rock just fell away for what looked like miles."

By the door, Julie's completely entranced by what he's saying, but I'm feeling a little sick to my stomach. Cory took him into the otherworld. What's to stop Erik from blabbing about it to everyone? That beautiful place is going to be ruined.

"So how'd you get here?" I ask.

"I—I don't know. I remember the dude finally came back—like, one moment I'm sitting on a rock by myself, cold and starving, and the next, he's standing in front of me and he's asking me what I've learned and I tell him I just want to go home. He looks at me for a long time, then he finally nods.

"'Think you can stop treating people like crap?' he asks me. He tells me to apologize to all these people I made so miserable.

"And I said, 'Yeah, sure, anything,' and he pushes me off the rock I'm sitting on, but when I land, it's on the sidewalk outside school."

When he falls silent again, I say, "So then—what? You decide to come in and apologize to *me*?"

He nods quickly. "Just keep that dog-faced dude away from me."

"I don't know any dog-faced people," I tell him.

"But—"

"Seriously?" Julie says from the door. "Guy walking around with a dog's head on his shoulders? Face it, moron. Someone spiked whatever you were smoking or drinking last night and you've just been tripping ever since."

He looks to me and I nod.

"But not about being an asshole," I tell him, "and apologizing to the people you treat like dirt is still a pretty good idea."

I guess whatever he experienced has really had an impact on him because instead of bristling and then lashing out, he just looks at the floor.

"I said I was sorry," he says.

"Yeah, you did."

I look at my phone to get the time.

"You'd better hole up in the boys' restroom until the bell rings," I tell him. "Then I'd go home and maybe think twice about getting that high again."

He doesn't respond, so I pull him away from the sinks and give him a little push toward the door. Julie circles around him and joins me in the main part of the restroom. She heads to the counter holding the sinks and turns to face the stalls, then hoists her butt up on the counter.

"Okay," Julie says when the door closes behind Erik. "On a scale of zero to weird, that was right off the scale."

"No kidding."

"And you, *mi amiga*, are having a seriously messed-up day."

"Tell me about it."

She smiles and shakes her head. "No, you tell me."

So I hop up to sit beside her, and she lets me vent about Ampora's latest effort in her unending quest to make my life miserable.

"I can deal with her messing with me," I finish, "but putting my little sisters in danger—that's just unacceptable."

Julie nods. "What are you going to do?"

"I honestly don't know."

So far as I see, there's only one thing I *can* do to protect my family, and that means involving Theo, which makes for a whole new set of problems. It's also not fair. If I don't think I can be with him because of his gang affiliation, how can I just use him and his gang the first time I run into trouble?

It's so messed up. I can't stop thinking about him. But I don't want to have a lead role in some romantic tragedy. I've already had the starring role in an unrequited love story. I just want what other couples have.

"Earth to Marina," Julie says.

I sit up with a start.

"Where did you just go?" she asks.

"I ..."

It's funny. Julie and I used to hang out all the time, but we kind of drifted apart last year. We never looked like we'd have much in common in the first place. She's a tall green-eyed blonde who has the best balance on a board of anyone I know that isn't a Wildling, while I'm always going to be the tomboy barrio girl.

She started hanging more with the stoner crowd, listening to jam bands like Phish and whatever the latest incarnation of the Dead happens to be, while I remained the surfer girl with my board and my Dick Dale tapes. We'd still surf together from time to time, but away from the swells, we just didn't have as much in common anymore.

And then I suddenly had a secret I couldn't share with her: I became a Wildling. Josh and Des never picked up on it, but Julie could tell something was different. She just didn't know what. That really made me pull back from our friendship.

Anyway, ever since that night a few weeks ago when I got Julie to cover for me while I was out looking for Josh, we've been seeing more of each other. It helps that she's given up smoking her big fatties—because she realized she wants to go to university, she told me, and weed and studying don't really go hand in hand. She's stopped hanging out in the stoner pit at the far end of the football field, and we're study partners again.

But I still feel guilty about keeping my Wildling aspect from her. So when she asks what I'm thinking about, I can't just blow her off. I've missed her and I don't want to push her away again, even if I still have to keep some secrets.

"I'm seeing somebody," I tell her. "Sort of. It's complicated."

Her eyebrows go way up. "What about Josh?"

"I've dated other guys before."

"Yeah. Except right at this moment, you're single, he's single. It's finally the perfect time."

"This new guy's pretty special," I tell her.

"So who is he?"

"I can't tell anyone—that's part of why it's complicated. It would really mess things up if people found out."

Julie pulls a face. "Tell me you're not talking about a teacher, because *ew*."

"God no! But there could be serious repercussions."

"You're *killing* me here."

"I'm really sorry. But it's not just my secret."

"He's an older guy, isn't he?" she says. "God, he isn't *married* is he?"

"Where do you come up with this stuff?" I ask her. Then, because I know I have to give her something, I add, "He's a great kisser."

"Better than Josh?"

"I never kissed Josh—not in that way."

"So how long have you been going out with this mystery man?" she asks.

"Not that long. I don't even know that we're exactly going out—actually, that's more of the complicated part. He's probably not good for me, and while I know he likes me, he's probably worried about how I'll fit in with his crowd."

She gives me a considering look, but then the bell finally goes and I hop down from the counter.

"I have to get outside," I say. "I know she doesn't seem to care, but I can't let Ampora face the Kings on her own."

"Yeah, well sister, you're sure not going to have to face them on *your* own," Julie says.

I start to shake my head—there's no way I'm letting her get mixed up in this—but she puts a finger to my lips.

"Don't even try," she says.

I'm torn between wanting to argue with her and getting outside. I settle on dealing with the Kings first and we head out into the crowded hallway. Before we reach the front door, Des has fallen into step beside us.

I turn to him. "You know you don't have to do this."

"Good one," he says.

My phone vibrates as we push through the front doors. I glance down to see a one-word text from Theo: *Cory?*

I thumb a quick response—*Later*—and stow my phone away because I can already see Ampora across the street, shouting at the half-dozen Kings who are waiting for us there.

I guess this is the point where the world finds out I'm a Wildling.

I pick up my pace, which leaves Julie and Des struggling to keep up. Juan looks up at my approach and laughs.

"Nice," he says, switching to English. "It's the bitch's sister."

"<I speak Spanish, asshole,>" I tell him in my mother tongue.

"<Yeah, lying on your back with your legs spread wide.>"

I take a step forward, fists clenched, but Ampora gives me a push.

"<Go away,>" she tells me. "<I don't need your help with these little jerks.>" Then she looks over my shoulder and adds, "<Oh, great. Here comes your boyfriend.>"

My heart skips a beat and I turn around, but it's only Josh jogging down the block toward us.

That stops me. How did I get to "it's only Josh" so fast? Just a few weeks ago, he was always on my mind.

But then Juan grabs me by my shirt and hauls me so close to him that we're only inches apart and I don't have time to think about anything except for how this has gotten way out of hand.

"<Say goodbye to your pretty face,>" he says and I hear the *snickt* of his switchblade opening.

CHAINGANG

I frown at Marina's quick response. What the hell is "later" supposed to mean? We need to get moving *now*, while we've still got a chance. She's just getting out of school so ...

I get a picture in my head of her in her surfer shorts and a T, the swing in her walk. I think about all the days I sat there on my picnic table and watched her come and go from school— glowing like she just caught a wave. Maybe *later*'s exactly where we should be at because right now I'm tempted to drive up to Sunny Hill, swing her onto the back of my Harley and take off— screw what anybody's got to say about it. Just drive until we get someplace where nobody knows us, where we can just be the two of us without any of the crap in our lives.

Yeah, like that's ever going to happen.

I shove the phone in my pocket, but before I can start up my bike I hear a giggle coming from the branches of the jacaranda tree high above me. Peering up through the foliage, I see a little kid sitting up there, brown skinned and dressed for the beach in a baggy T and raggedy jeans cut off at mid-calf. I can't tell if it's a boy or a girl. I just see big eyes in a long narrow face, which seems strange for a child. Her face is framed by long curls that are matting into dreads as thick as his—her?—skinny little arms.

"What's so funny?" I ask.

The kid laughs and points down at me. "You are. How'd you get so big with that little cousin skin of yours?"

"What? How would you know—"

"—What kind of cousin you are? How could I *not* know? It's like the difference between land and sea—you know what *that* is, right?"

This kid has a hell of a vocabulary, and he doesn't give me a chance to answer. "You just *know*, little mouse."

Now I realize I'm getting a Wildling *ping* from the kid. I'd been feeling it all along, but I assumed it was just some Vincenzo residue. But the kid's definitely sending out a vibe—and it's not one I've felt before. It's not fresh, like Josh or Marina's, but it doesn't have the gravitas of the older cousins like Vincenzo or Auntie Min.

"Name's Theo," I say. "Not 'little mouse.'"

"What's wrong with mice? They crunch so nicely between your teeth—though maybe that's a rude thing to say to a mouse."

The trouble with Wildlings is, you can't tell what kind they are just by looking at them—or at least I can't—yet. This kid apparently has no problem. But the point here is that maybe this is just a Wildling kid fooling around, or maybe it's something a lot more dangerous. I need to know which. Another complication, or a possible ally?

"Okay, little boy," I say, leaning on the little. "What exactly do you want from me?"

"Little *boy*? What makes you think I'm some stupid *boy*?"

I hold up my hands, palms toward her, and make a note to myself that she's got gender issues.

"My bad," I tell her. "I'm just a stupid boy—what do I know?"

"Nothing."

"Apparently. Do you have a name?"

"Everybody has a name."

"Uh-huh. And what's yours?"

"Well, it's not Big Stupid."

I sigh. "Is there a point to your sitting up there yanking my chain? Because hey, I can just go."

She drops from her perch, bouncing from branch to branch, until she lands on the front wheel of my Harley, where she balances like a monkey. Her size startles me. It wasn't so obvious when she was up in the tree, but right in my face like this, I see she's no bigger than a toddler. If she tops three feet in height, I'd be surprised.

"How'd you get mixed up in Condor business?" she asks.

"The tall dude I was just talking to being the condor?"

She nods.

"Wasn't my choice. He just showed up out of nowhere and started leaning on me."

"In the old days, we'd just snap his neck and throw his body down some big deep hole."

"Uh-huh."

"We would."

"I tried. But it turns out he's a lot stronger and faster than me."

She cocks her head and studies me for a long moment.

"My name's Donalita," she finally says.

"And I'm still Theo."

"I know *that*. What are we going to do now?"

"What do you mean 'we,' *kemo sabe*?"

That earns me a blank look. Guess she never watches reruns of *The Lone Ranger*.

"What I'm trying to say," I explain, "is that I've got things to do that don't include having a kid tag along—no offence."

"But I want to see how your story goes. I could be a big help. I know all kinds of things."

"I'm sure you do. But if people see me hanging around with you, robbing the cradle's the *nicest* thing they're going to say."

"You mean I look too young?" she asks.

"That's putting it mildly."

"Well, how's this?"

I'm looking right at her, but I still don't see it happen. One moment she's this toddler, perched on my tire, the next she's a teenage girl standing with her legs on either side of the wheel, head cocked, laughter in her eyes. She's still skinny, but now she's about as tall as me.

"How—how the hell did you do that?"

"It's a secret."

I give a slow nod. "Yeah, I can see how it would be."

She gives my shoulder a friendly push. "I'm kidding. Lots of the cousins can do this, though it's mostly the tricksier ones."

"The tricksier ones," I repeat, still trying to get my head around what I just saw.

"Sure. You know. Like coyotes and crows and hares and such."

"So what do you really look like?" I ask. "I mean, do you even have one real face?"

Again, it happens too fast for me to see, but now there's a coatimundi sitting on my handlebars, looking at me with her white nose and bandit face, the plume of her ringed tail rising straight up behind her. Then she's the teenage girl again.

"So you're a coati," I say.

"Maybe. Or maybe that's another trick."

"Oh-kay."

She gives my shoulder another push. "Don't look so worried. With me helping you out, everything's going to be great."

"And you're helping me because ...?"

"I don't like the Condor Clan."

"Even though you can just snap their necks and then throw their bodies down some big deep hole."

"Maybe I exaggerated that part a little."

"Did you now?"

She shrugs.

"So what've you got against the condors?" I ask.

"They're mean and ugly and ... and ..."

"Stupid?"

She shakes her head. "They're stupid but not *stupid* stupid. The problem with them is that they're oh-so-very clever. And scary. If Vincenzo died, I'd laugh and dance and sing for days and days and days."

"What did he do to you?" I ask. "Be straight with me now."

All the good humour leaves her features. Her eyes go flat and hard.

"He killed my little sister. We'd been together forever—from before you people came here and built all your roads and houses— but he just snapped Luisa's neck like she meant nothing. Except she did mean something. She meant everything to me."

I lay a hand on her shoulder and give it a squeeze.

"I'm sorry," I tell her.

"Me too."

"Why'd he kill her?" I ask.

"He found out that she took her boyfriend into *el entre*. Her *human* boyfriend. He killed them both."

"El *where?*"

"You know—the world on the other side of this world."

I give a slow nod. "And that's Vincenzo's job, to keep it a secret?" I ask. "Something he does for the elders? Or is he just a cruel bastard on his own initiative?"

She gives me an odd look, then says, "We don't have the same hierarchies as the five-fingered beings do. There aren't any police or bosses or anything."

"Then what gives him the right to go around doing what he does?"

"Nobody can stop him."

"Right."

"But there's always somebody stronger," she says. "We just have to find that somebody and get them to kill him."

"I'm down with that. But I'd rather deal with him myself."

She grins. "You see? That's why I *like* you. You're not scared of some stupid old condor."

"Oh, I'm scared of him," I tell her. "But that won't stop me from trying to figure out a way to take him down. Nobody threatens my friends and family and gets to brag about it."

The corners of her mouth droop. "At least your family's still alive."

"Yeah, but for how long?" I think about that handy ability of hers. "So can you take any shape?" I ask. "Like, could you be a bear or something like that? Something big enough to take him on?"

She tilts her head back and forth as she answers. "I could look like a bear, but I wouldn't smell like a bear and I'd only be as strong as I normally am."

Makes sense that she can't do more or she wouldn't be here now, looking for me to help her. She'd already have done it herself.

"Got any ideas on how we can deal with him?" I try. "Beyond finding somebody bigger and stronger to do the job for us?"

"I thought *you* were going to figure that out," she says and grins at me expectantly.

Which puts me back to square one.

"Well, at least we've got a little breathing room," I say.

"Because of what Vincenzo told you?"

I nod. "Yeah. He said everything's on hold until he figures a few things out."

"So this would be the perfect time for him to make his move," she says.

Damn. Why did that not even occur to me?

"What does he want you to do?" she asks.

"Kill the Great White Hope of the elders, except he's not all that white, and he doesn't want any part of whatever they've got planned. Doesn't seem to make any difference to Vincenzo, though. He just wants the kid gone."

Her eyes go wide. "Do you mean the new boy from the Mountain Lion Clan?"

"Yeah. His name's Josh."

"You have to tell the elders."

I shake my head. "Can't. If I do that, Vincenzo starts killing the people I care about, starting with my grandma."

"Oh, this is bad," she says. "This is so very bad."

"Got that right. She's a great old lady."

"No, I mean, yes, but no, I was talking about that new boy—Josh."

"Why? What exactly do they have planned for him?"

"I don't know. I just know that he's the last of you new cousins to be born."

"There haven't been any others?" I say. "Really? I just thought kids had finally wised up and learned how to lay low."

"No, he's the last. That's got to mean something—right? Like why ever it was happening stopped because they finally got it right. Whatever *right* is." She frowns. "I'm sorry. That doesn't mean that you're—"

I wave a hand before she can finish. "It's okay. I get that I'm not part of the big picture."

"And being Mountain Lion Clan," Donalita adds. "That's a pretty big deal."

"Yeah? And why's that?"

She shrugs. "It just *is*. It's what everybody says."

So she doesn't know, either. If I had a filing cabinet in my head labelled "weird-ass crap I need to figure out," it just got a little fatter. Maybe it's time I got more serious about getting up to speed.

"So these everybodies," I say. "Do you think any of them know more than the others?"

"You mean about your friend?"

"Sure. But while we're at it, about Vincenzo, too. What's he get if Josh is dead, and why doesn't he want anybody to know he's behind it?"

"We could ask Auntie Min."

I shake my head. "Somebody who isn't an elder."

"You don't trust Auntie Min?" she asks, eyebrows raised.

"How about Cory?" I say, ignoring her question. "Do you know how to get in touch with him?"

"Cory? But he's coyote."

"Yeah, so?"

"They're the tricksiest of us all."

"Again—so what? If I'm going to trust you, why wouldn't I trust him?"

"Because he's killed people."

I think about her telling me how she'd like to throw Vincenzo into a pit and dance on his grave, but all I ask is, "And you wouldn't? If you had Vincenzo dead to rights, you're telling me you wouldn't pull the trigger?"

"I ..."

She gets such a pained look on her face that I feel bad. She's a sweet kid—even if she's probably a few centuries older than me.

"You know," I tell her, "that wasn't fair. But the point is, if Cory's killed people, that doesn't automatically make him bad. Maybe they deserved it. Maybe he had no other choice."

She studies me for a moment, then smiles.

"You're not really a Big Stupid, are you?" she says.

I can't help but laugh. "How the hell would I know?"

She steps around to the back of the bike and climbs on behind me.

"Let's go talk to Cory," she says.

JOSH

When I come around the corner, I see Ampora, Marina, Des and Julie facing off a half-dozen Kings across the street from the school. Juan grabs Marina and I sprint at Wildling speed—I don't care who sees me.

I straight-arm Juan and he goes stumbling, falling onto his back in the weeds and dirt. Marina takes a step toward him, but I put out my arm to stop her.

"Let me deal with this," I tell her.

"But—"

"Lookee, lookee," one of the other Kings says to me. "It's Chaingang's bitch."

"Yeah," another puts in. "It's so cute the way he got rid of his dreads. Guess he wants to look just like his boyfriend."

They all laugh. I recognize Gordo and Lil' Puppet from the other night when I shattered Trucho's shoulder. Then there's the guy they call Tiny, who's kind of like the Kings' version of Chaingang, except he's even bigger and he's got such a mean streak that everyone at school gives him a wide berth. I don't know the guy who just spoke or the skinny one standing beside him.

Juan gets up from the dirt, an open switchblade in his hand.

"Yeah, well," he says to me. "Chaingang isn't here, is he, *ese?*"

"You need to call Fat Joe, right now," I say.

"And you need to shut your mouth. I'm not calling the boss on the say-so of some little ass-licker."

"Then call Chico."

I see the confusion on the faces of Ampora and my friends. They think I'm nuts. But they weren't at the taquería.

"You on drugs?" Juan says. "I'm not calling nobody."

"Okay," I tell him. "Then this is on you. I'll make sure not to break your jaw so that when you're talking to your boss from your hospital bed, you can tell him we don't have a deal anymore."

He steps closer, threatening me with the knife. "What the hell are you talking about?"

I don't budge.

"You ready to start a war?" I ask him. "Because that's what you're doing here."

Juan flicks the knife toward where Marina and the others are standing.

"And is this your army, *ese?*" he asks. "It's going to be a short war."

"I don't need an army," I tell him.

"Maybe you should listen to him," Gordo says.

"Yeah," Lil' Puppet adds. "Doctors say Trucho might never be able to use his arm again."

I see the momentary uncertainty in Juan's eyes as he tries to match what his friends are telling him to the kid he sees standing in front of him.

"That was you?" he asks.

I don't bother answering. I'm trying to be calm about this so that it doesn't escalate into what happened at the taquería. But Juan's not ready to lose face.

"You think you can take me?" he asks.

I still don't respond. When he moves, it's fast and I'm not expecting it. The switchblade slashes at me and I dance back, but not quickly enough. The tip of the blade opens a shallow cut across my stomach. The sudden scent of my own blood again tears away my pretence of calm. My gaze fills with a film of red anger.

Before I realize what I'm doing, I grab his arm as the blade comes back for a second slash. With a hard snap of my wrist I break the bones in his forearm. The switchblade falls from his limp grip and goes clattering along the pavement. I give Juan another shove and he cries out with pain when he lands on his broken arm.

For a long moment nobody moves, then Tiny charges me.

"Audience," I hear Marina say.

She's speaking softly, but the word cuts through my rage and I understand the warning. She means that we've got an audience of students gathering to watch the fight from a safe distance. So instead of tearing into Tiny the way I want to, I dart up close. Before his big hands can grab me, I punch him in the solar plexus with all my Wildling strength.

His hands land on me, but they have no strength. He drops to his knees, making a weird wheezing sound as he tries to breathe. Then his eyes roll up and I step out of the way before he can fall on me. He hits the ground hard enough that I swear I feel a tremor from the impact.

"Hey!" I hear someone yell out.

I glance over my shoulder to see a teacher running from the

school. We're off school property, so there's not much he can do except call the police. I really don't need that headache on top of everything else.

I turn to face the remaining Kings and point a finger at Lil' Puppet.

"Call Fat Boy," I say. "Tell him to fix this or you're *all* going down."

"Hey, man—"

I cut him off. "Just tell him. I didn't want this and I didn't start it. But I'll damn well finish it if I have to."

"Dude!" Des starts. "What *happened* today?"

I ignore him to ask Ampora, "You told your sisters not to leave the school until you got there, right?"

She's staring at me wide-eyed, but manages a nod.

"Go get them," I tell her. "Now."

"Dude," Des tries again.

I shake my head. "Later," I say. "The skatepark."

Then I take off.

I don't put on my full Wildling speed, but I'm motoring fast enough that no one's going to catch up to me. The remaining Kings take off and I hear the teacher yelling at them to stop, but they're not stupid. The teacher isn't going to chase after them— not with Juan and Tiny to take care of.

I'm around the corner and out of sight in moments, not even winded. I just hope Marina and the others got away clean.

I look down at my shirt. The switchblade only nicked me— it's not even worth doing the mountain lion switch to deal with it—but now there's blood on this T-shirt. If I keep this up I'm going to be going through clothes faster than a Valley girl.

I'm about to head for the skatepark when I catch a glimpse

of a tall barefoot man in a shabby dark suit as he turns down a side street ahead of me.

He reminds me of the guy who was standing across the street watching when Chaingang and I came out of the taquería. That man also looked like some homeless guy, except the Wildling vibe coming from him was so strong I knew he was one of the old cousins. The man I just saw has disappeared too quickly for me to get a take on him. But he sure looked like the same guy.

With all that's going on these days, seeing him twice in one afternoon seems like too much of a coincidence. I cross the street and break into a quick jog to catch up with him. I don't even reach the corner before I hear a piercing shriek, and then there's a big bird dropping from the sky, hurtling right for my face. I throw up my arms, but it doesn't attack. It just skims by. I turn to see it rise higher and realize it's a hawk. A red-tailed hawk.

That was just weird.

I watch for a moment as it circles above me, then I set off for the corner again. Again the hawk drops screeching from the sky, cutting me off. This time, it lands on a newspaper box and stares at me.

There's no Wildling buzz, but I know this is no ordinary hawk. It's not hard to figure out what it's doing here.

Guess *los tíos* don't want me to follow that guy.

"Okay," I tell the bird. "I get the message."

Across the street is a lawn of brown grass and dust. Beyond the lawn, a woman stands on her porch looking at me. I don't know what she makes of all this. The hawk in my face, me talking to it.

I don't stick around to find out. Instead I go back the way I came, heading for the skatepark once more. I look back over my shoulder and the hawk lifts into the air, satisfied that it's done its job.

Now I've got something else to add to my list of things I need to talk about with Solana.

MARINA

As Josh runs off, I have long enough to think that I barely even know him anymore, but then I realize that whatever's going on with him is going to have to wait. Right now we need to clear out of here ourselves before Mr. Sanchez reaches us. The Kings that Josh didn't put out of commission have already bolted.

"Did you see him take down Tiny?" Des is saying. "I mean, one punch, dude."

I can tell he wants to get into a blow-by-blow of what we just saw. But if he's forgotten where we are, I haven't. I give him a little push.

"Run," I tell him.

Ampora's still staring after Josh, so I grab her arm and get her moving. I guess she's still so surprised at how Josh handled the Kings that she doesn't even protest. She just lets me lead her away at a quick jog. Des and Julie fall in behind. By the time Mr. Sanchez reaches the place where we were, there's only Tiny and Juan left behind, and he's too busy looking after them to come chasing after us.

We get to the mall and turn right, heading for the barrio, when Ampora finally shakes my hand loose. We've all slowed down to a walk now. I wait for Ampora to tear into me like she usually does, but when she speaks, it's not to put me down.

"Did you see his face?" she says. "And his arms? There were *no* bruises on him—not like this morning."

I know she's talking about Josh.

"He—heals fast, I guess," I say.

But she's already speaking again and not even listening to me.

"And where'd he learn how to fight like that?" she asks.

"Jiu-jitsu," Des says. "The dude's an expert."

"No kidding," Julie says. "Where'd he study? I thought he was only into skateboarding and surf music."

I suppose that's all the reminder Ampora needs. She stops suddenly and we all follow suit.

"You don't have to come with me," she says.

"It's okay," I start to tell her.

She shakes her head and interrupts me. "What I mean is, I'm going to get the girls and I don't want any of you to come with me—okay?"

Then she stalks off, her back stiff.

"Bitch," Julie mutters.

I nod in agreement. "Yeah, no kidding. Where does she get off? All of this is her fault because she got involved with the Kings. Jumping into a gang is the last straw. Did she ever think of what might happen when she decides to blow them off the way she does everything else?"

Des clears his throat.

"What?" I ask.

"Dude, I thought you knew," he says.

"Knew what?"

"The reason the Kings want to hang your sister up by her heels. She found out that they were starting to sell dope at that park near your dad's house, so she went over there and told them to pack up and get out or she was going to call the cops."

I feel the blood drain out of my face.

"My little sisters play there," I say in a small voice.

"Exactly, dude. Josh said that's what set her off."

I'm about to puke, so I sit down on the curb, clutching my stomach. Julie and Des join me on either side.

"I was so mean to her," I say. "I never gave her a chance to explain."

Julie touches my arm. "She doesn't exactly brim with goodwill."

"It doesn't matter. This means she's not the bad guy. She never was. *I'm* the bad guy."

"You could never be the bad guy," Des says, patting the top of my head.

I push his hand off. "I *attacked* her on the football field."

"Well, that *did* happen."

"I was just so mad."

"I should have told you," Des says. "But I thought you knew."

"I didn't. I have to go apologize to her."

"Nuh-uh," Julie says. "You have to go home. You're still grounded, aren't you?"

"Yeah, but—"

"Do you want your mother to add another couple of weeks?" Julie stands up and offers me a hand. "Come on. I'll walk with you."

I let her pull me to my feet, but I still feel like I might throw up.

"Are you coming?" I ask Des.

He shakes his head as he stands. "I'm going to go catch up with Josh at the skatepark."

"Call and tell me if there's anything important I should know."

"You got it, dude," he says. "I won't screw up again."

"You didn't screw up," I tell him. "I screwed up." I hold up a hand as both he and Julie start to protest. "No, it's true. It doesn't matter whether I knew or not, I still should never have lit into her like that at lunchtime."

Des taps my shoulder with a light fist.

"Shit happens, dude," he says. "Welcome to my world."

"You can apologize to her at school tomorrow," Julie says to me.

Des smiles. "Or you can save it for when the two of you go to your session with Ms. Chandra."

"That's not funny," I tell him.

"Come on," he says with that goofy grin of his. "It's kinda funny."

I aim a punch at him, but he steps back, still grinning. I can't help it, I have to give him a weak smile back. The sick feeling doesn't go away, but the tightness in my chest lets up and it's a little easier to breathe.

"I'll text you later," he says. "After I've talked to Josh. See ya, dude," he adds, pointing a finger at Julie.

Then he sets off.

Julie shakes her head. "I don't know if he's the nicest guy I know, or the goofiest."

"A little of both," I tell her as we start walking to my house.

Julie nods. "And yet he would have taken on those Kings for you, no question."

"Between Des and Josh, I don't know who has the stronger moral core."

"Hmm."

She has a dreamy look in her eyes that makes me shake my head.

"Don't even *think* about it," I tell her. "His girlfriends never last more than a few weeks."

"Maybe he just hasn't met the right girl. I've always thought he was cute."

I roll my eyes, but I keep the conversation on the possibilities of her and Des because the longer we talk about that, the less time there'll be for me to have to evade her questions about what else is going on.

At one point, I pull out my phone, but there's still no text from Theo. I'd definitely sneak out of the house if I thought I could see him tonight.

But first, he has to call me back.

CHAINGANG

"Pull in here," Donalita finally says as we come up on the north side parking lot by the pier.

We've been riding in what seems like aimless circles for twenty minutes. She's been yipping and squealing every time we've turned a corner or gone over a bump. It was getting to the point where I couldn't tell whether she was making sure we weren't being followed, or just enjoying the ride. But when I asked, all she said was, "Keep going. Cory likes to move around."

Now I follow her direction and pull into the lot. It's a weekday, but it's hot, so the lot's almost two-thirds full. I park under a palm and put the Harley on its kickstand after Donalita hops off. I sit for a moment longer, doing a quick security check.

Between the parking lot and the beach are a half-dozen picnic tables strung out in a row along the boardwalk, palms towering above them. Cory's sitting at one of the tables talking to a kid who looks vaguely familiar, but I can't place him. In a town this size, everyone who's not a tourist looks at least a bit familiar.

There are kids at the other tables, more on the beach. Surfers out in the water with their boards waiting for waves that aren't coming in this weather. A volleyball game happening down on the sand.

There's no sign of Vincenzo. I check the sky for condors, but it's clear blue except for the odd seagull, so he's not spying from up there. Not seeing him doesn't ease the bad feeling in the pit of my gut. You can be damned sure that all bets are off if he sees me in Donalita's company and talking to Cory. He'll be going after Grandma and J-Dog and Marina.

That thought sends a jolt into my chest, but I'm here and committed now.

"Who's the kid?" I ask Donalita, nodding with my chin at Cory's table.

She shrugs. "Somebody with a problem that he hopes Cory can solve. It's Cory's way of making up for all the troubles his ancestors made, back in the long ago."

"What kind of trouble?"

"Oh, you know. Silly Coyote always means well, but he can't help screwing things up. Brought the five-fingered beings fire, sure, but he also brought death—that kind of thing."

I can't tell if she's putting me on or not.

"I thought those were just stories," I say.

"We're all stories," she tells me. "Some people just have bigger stories than the rest of us—and that's not always a good thing. It's never healthy to catch the attention of one of the old cousins like Vincenzo."

I'm not sure if she means me or Josh. All I know is I hope Cory can tell me something that'll give me an edge on the creep.

I swing my leg off my bike, but Donalita puts a hand on my chest before I can step away.

"Hold up, cowboy," she says. "You don't go interrupting something like this."

"Like what?"

She taps her ear. "Mousey mousey. Why don't you listen in and find out?"

The first thing Auntie Min taught me after my change was how to put a filter on the storm of scents and sounds that my Wildling senses throw at me. Without that filter, the barrage would be overwhelming. Over time I've learned to fine-tune what I take in—a conversation across the street, a woman's perfume from the other side of a room—and ignore everything else.

So I focus on what's going down between Cory and the kid. It's not so much like tuning to a radio station, as zooming in with a telephoto lens, except the lens in this case is my ears.

"—don't want to shift back only to find out that I've killed somebody, you know?" the kid's saying.

"I hear you," Cory tells him.

"I've got a little brother. What's to stop him from wandering into my bedroom looking for me, except I've shifted in my sleep and now there's a viper waiting under the sheets, ready to take a chomp out of him?"

"So you dream of changing?" Cory asks. "And that's when it happens?"

The kid nods.

"There are ways to control a dream," Cory tells him.

I tune them out and turn to Donalita.

"So Cory's what?" I ask. "A therapist for these kids?"

"Oh-so-strange as it seems, he's pretty good at figuring out their problems."

I roll my eyes.

"Well *you're* going to see him, aren't you?" she says.

"Point."

It's another five minutes before the kid leaves and I can walk over to Cory's table. Donalita's at my side until we're under the palm, then she gives Cory a wave and scurries up the rough trunk with a Wildling's speed. I doubt anybody else even noticed. Looking up into the mess of dead vegetation under the huge palm fronds, I see she's shifted to her coatimundi shape and has curled up, fast asleep.

Cory smiles when my gaze returns to him. "So you've met Donalita."

I nod as I sit across the table from him.

"This kind of thing keeping you busy?" I ask.

"Busy enough."

"How do they find you? How do they even know about you?"

"Word of mouth," he says. "And sometimes I find them. But before you ask, I can't solve their problems for them. All I can do is steer them on a course where they can figure it out for themselves, and most of them do."

"That's actually pretty cool," I tell him.

He smiles. "Not too touchy-feely for you?"

I shrug.

"So what can I do for you?" he asks. "Unless this is a social call ..."

"No, I ..."

It's funny. I came here to see what he can tell me about Vincenzo, but what comes out of my mouth is, "Have you ever heard of a bunch of guys who call themselves *los tíos*? I think they hang out at a place called Halcón Pueblo, though I couldn't tell you where that is."

He gives me a curious look and nods. "Sure, but it's been a while."

"What do you know about them? Are they cool or what?"

"They're a mystic order—sort of like warrior priests, except they're not trying to point you to salvation. Instead they're trying to get people to wake up to their full potential in the here and now so that they can protect the world from evil spirits."

My heart sinks a little. So ... space cadets.

"Evil spirits," I repeat, not trying to hide the scepticism in my voice.

"It's a big world," Cory says, "with more going on in it than you or I could ever understand."

"Fair enough," I tell him.

I don't want to argue—not when I'm coming to him for a favour. And the Wildling thing is bigger and stranger than anything I could have imagined, so I guess anything's possible.

"What makes you ask about them?" Cory says.

"I was just curious. I couldn't get a take on the one I met. He didn't have a Wildling vibe, but there was definitely something going on that you wouldn't call human."

"I've never really sat down with one of them, but I've felt that vibe. They keep to themselves—big on the secrets, if you know what I mean. Story is, they can see through the eyes of hawks. Some people even say they can turn into hawks, but I've never seen it and I've been around a while. About the only thing I know for sure is they don't have cousin blood."

"Huh."

"Where did you run into him?" Cory asks.

"That's the weird thing. I was in the middle of a face-down with a gang of Kings and he just stepped up and shut them down with a few words. Never seen anything like it. He wasn't particularly forthcoming afterward, but Josh knew who he was. Or at least, *what* he was."

"Whoa—back up. What were you and Josh doing facing down a bunch of Kings?"

I hesitate, taking a moment to check around us. When I still see no sign of Vincenzo, I fill Cory in. I go right back to getting that phone call from Lenny, to Vincenzo bracing me in the alley just before I met Donalita. The only thing I leave out is that kiss Marina and I shared. He cocks his head when I talk about Marina, the way a dog does when it's trying to figure out what you're saying, but in this case, it's like he's trying to figure out what I'm *not* saying.

None of your business, I want to tell him, but I don't.

"I need to know how to take him down," I say instead. "Before somebody else gets hurt."

Cory nods. "We need to talk to Auntie Min."

"No!"

The word comes out harsher than I meant. Truth is, it was a gut reaction and I didn't even think about it.

"But she—"

"No elders. None of the older cousins."

"But why *not*?"

"I don't trust any of them."

"I hate to break this to you," he tells me, "but *I'm* one of the older cousins."

"Yeah, but you're different. More importantly, Josh trusts you."

"But if Josh is starting to show dominant—"

"No. Elders. Period."

Cory sighs. "Look, Vincenzo is before my time. I've only *heard* of him and none of it is good. If he's after Josh and *los tíos* are sniffing around—don't you see that this is getting too big for us to deal with? Bigger than anything *Josh* could deal with?"

"You didn't see Josh in the taquería. He got shot in the back, for Christ's sake—the bullet blew out half his chest—but then he did a quick change back and forth, and just got up again, ready to take on the whole gang. And he would have done it, too, if that other guy hadn't sent them all packing."

Cory nods. "I hear you."

"Do you really? Because from where I sit, I'm thinking not so much. All you want to do is go running to Auntie Min."

I hear a snicker from above, where Donalita's still cuddled up in the palm tree, but Cory ignores her.

"Let's look at it from another perspective," he says, his voice mild. "Do you know how many kids have become Wildlings here in Santa Feliz?"

"I don't see what—"

"Humour me."

"Okay," I tell him.

I try to do a mental count, but how would I know?

"No idea," I admit.

"Me neither," he says. "But you've got to figure maybe seventy or eighty—that sound about right?"

"If you say so."

"Now ... how many have changed since Josh?"

"How am I supposed to know that?"

"None," Cory says.

"None?"

I've heard that twice today now and it still doesn't seem right.

"It's true as the sky," Donalita calls down in a singsong voice.

I look up to see she's changed back to a small girl. Holding on to the trunk with one hand, with her feet in the nest of dead leaves, she's swaying back and forth. She waves and grins when she sees me looking. I turn back to Cory.

"Now, you can come up with all kinds of theories about why that is," Cory goes on, "but the one I'm hearing most is that whoever was changing the kids stopped with Josh because they finally got it right. They got what they wanted."

"You mean the elders."

He shakes his head. "No. Or at least, none that you've met and no one's taking credit or even being suspected of doing it. We're as much in the dark as anyone."

"True-true-true," Donalita calls down.

"So what is it that they got?" I ask. "What were they shooting for?"

"No idea," Cory says. "All I know is that all the other kids who got changed are little cousins. None of you come from one of the big old tribes ... except for Josh."

I give him a considering look.

"So you're siding with the elders," I say. "You think Josh should become their figurehead—the poster boy for the Wildlings."

He shakes his head. "I'm on the fence about that. I don't think it's necessarily a bad thing, but it has to be Josh's choice. No one ever followed a reluctant leader."

"Then why go to Auntie Min with this?"

"Auntie Min's got a lot of insight. If we give her all this new information, she'll probably be able to see something that we can't. From what you've told me, it sounds like Josh needs way more support and protection than you or I can give."

He's probably right, I think.

"I guess that makes sense," I say. "But it still has to be Josh's decision."

JOSH

Now that I'm paying attention, I see that no matter where I go, there's always a hawk perched somewhere nearby. I never see them following me, but as I make my way to the skatepark, there's always one in sight. It'll be perched on top of a light post, maybe up in a palm, a eucalyptus, or on the rooftop of a building. Once I know to look, they're easy to spot.

When I get to the skatepark, sure enough, there's another one on a hydro pole across the street. Or maybe they've all been the same one. It doesn't really matter. I ignore the bird and drop onto a bench to watch the skateboarders. There's the usual gang practicing tricks and showing off. My attention keeps coming back to a girl I don't know in a tank top and Daisy Dukes, her long dark hair in a ponytail. She's pushing hard, totally focused, riding the kicker to see how much air she can put between the ramp and her board.

The whole time I've been watching, it's like she's in the zone and can do no wrong.

I know just what she's feeling. That microsecond when she's airborne and grabbing the tail of her board feels like it lasts forever. Like she's some high-flying bird. When she comes down, her balance is perfect as she rushes up the other slope of the kicker.

Watching her makes me wish I'd brought my own board. It's like seeing a great band. My fingers always get twitchy, wanting a guitar in my hands.

There sure hasn't been time for music lately. But before I can get too down about that, Des drops onto the bench beside me and offers me his fist.

"Dude," he says. "Way to stick it to the Kings."

I don't share Des's excitement, but I bump his fist anyway.

He checks out the blood on my shirt. "How's the cut?"

"It's nothing."

He grins. "Those Kings can't say the same thing, dude."

"I'd rather we didn't have to fight in the first place," I tell him.

"Well, sure," he says. "Nobody goes looking for trouble. But when it shows up, that's the way to deal with it, hard and fast."

"This isn't an action movie—it's my life."

He shakes his head. "Now it's both. So what happened this afternoon? Did you actually work out some kind of deal with the Kings?"

"I thought I had."

I tell him about going to the taquería with Chaingang. By the time I get to where I'm shot, he's bouncing on the bench.

"Oh man, oh *man*," he says. "The guy just *shot* you? What did it feel like?"

"What do you think? It hurt like freaking hell. Now let me finish."

When I'm finally done, he leans back on the bench, shaking his head.

"Dude ..." is all he can manage.

"I know."

"This is ..." He turns to me. "I get it now. It's not a movie. We don't get to leave it behind in the theatre."

"'Fraid not."

"Nothing's going to be the same anymore, is it?"

I give him a weak smile. "Way to sum it up."

"And you've gone public."

"Yeah. Well, just with the Kings so far, but there's no way it'll stop there."

"What are you going to do?" he asks.

"No clue. I keep wishing I could just dump the whole mess in somebody else's lap and have them tell me what to do."

"In that case, what about one of the elders—like Auntie Min or Cory? Or even these hawk uncle guys?"

My gaze goes to the hawk, still on its hydro pole perch, before it returns to Des.

"Everybody's got their own agenda," I tell him. "I don't think any of them are all that concerned about what it means to me."

"Well, dude," he says, "I don't know if it helps, but I'm not going to turn around to be the surprise villain near the end of this movie of yours."

"Thanks. It helps."

"Maybe you should talk to Marina about it," he says. "She always says she's the smart one in our crew."

"She must be. You don't see any of this crap blowing back on her, and she's been a Wildling for a lot longer than me."

He nods. "Except right now she's messed up because she didn't know that this time around, Ampora was on the side of the good guys."

I raise an eyebrow.

"Oh, she tore into her something fierce at lunch," Des says. "Had her in a choke-hold up against the fence along the football field. I think she might have really laid a beating on her if I hadn't been able to talk her out of it."

"But Ampora was trying to help the kids at the park. A stupid move, but she meant well."

Des nods. "Yeah, except no one told Marina about that. She thought Ampora was running with the Kings. I've never seen her that mad."

"It's because we're Wildlings," I find myself saying. "We're tapping into primal impulses."

"You mean like, you're Hulking-out?"

"God, I hope not. But more and more, hitting somebody just seems to be the only solution."

"Some people deserve to be hit."

"Maybe, but you can see how quickly it can escalate, just by what happened with me and the Kings."

"It's not your fault they're assholes."

"No, but there must have been a high road I could have taken."

"Like you did with Gess? That turned out *so* well."

That reminds me of how the last time I saw Cory, he was going into Erik's house to deal with him.

"Have you seen Erik?" I asked. "Do you know what happened to him?"

He shakes his head. "If I ever see him again, it'll be too soon. I hope Cory took him to the top of some cliff and dropped him into the ocean."

"You don't mean that."

Des turns to give me a serious look.

"Dude," he says, "I totally do."

We fall silent for a while until Des nods with his chin to the latest girl on the kickers.

"Damn, she's good," he says.

I nod, happy to be distracted. "Do you know who she is?"

"Her name's Sandy Mounts—Justine's cousin. She's just here for a week, apparently, because her dad had to go on a business trip. Her mother's not in the picture."

"How do you know all that?"

"Come on, dude. Cute girl like her? How could I not find out all I can?"

But I don't answer. I'm looking past the kicker where Sandy's rolled to a stop beside another girl. I look past the other skaters, too, all the way to the street on the far side of the park, where a line of custom cars is pulling up to the curb, one after the other. Classic machines with crazy paint jobs. Low-riders, chopped coupes, you name it. Rides that sweet around here only mean one thing: the Riverside Kings. Des's gaze follows mine.

"Oh, crap," he says. "Does that mean what I think it does?"

I don't bother answering. I just get up from the bench and start walking across the park toward them.

"Hey, wait up!" Des calls.

"Just stay back," I say when he catches up to me. "I don't need to be worrying about you while I deal with this."

I know he wants to argue, but for once he just does as I ask. Maybe he finally gets how serious this is. I don't want to make him feel useless, but I really need to be able to focus on having no distractions while I'm dealing with the Kings.

All around me the kids are stopping and getting off their

boards to stare. Most of them are checking out the Kings, but a few of them are looking at me. As I pass Sandy, I hear her say to her cousin, "What's going on?"

"Don't get involved," the other girl tells her. "This is gang crap."

"But where's the other gang? Are they after us?"

"No, they're after him."

I don't have to look to know that she's pointing at me. Guess I've already got a reputation.

MARINA

By the time we get to my house, Julie might as well be planning her wedding and how many babies she and Des are going to have. It's ridiculous, but it's also kind of cute, and I gave up trying to tell her why it would never work out blocks ago. And who knows? I could be wrong. It's not like I haven't already shown pretty much a complete lack of good judgment today. The best thing about Julie fixating on all of this is that listening to her keeps me out of my own head.

Or at least as much as anything can.

Still, nothing lasts. All too soon we're at the end of my walkway, Julie's saying goodbye, and I'm left standing there alone on the pavement with all the day's failures piled up on me. The huge muddle they make in my head isn't helped at all by the yo-yo of emotions I've been tangled up in all day.

I feel awful about how I treated Ampora. I'm also worried, and a little upset, that Theo hasn't called. But overwhelming as it's been for me, I find myself thinking about Josh and all he's had to deal with. If it's this overwhelming for me, how does he cope with everything going on in his life? Because let's face it: he's been living in the middle of some weird nightmare circus. Cops, kidnappings, our screwed-up friendship, losing Elzie, pressure from the elders, this whole mess with the Riverside Kings. And he doesn't even know about Vincenzo.

That stupid rogue elder brings me back to Theo. Okay, so we're only pretending to have a secret affair to throw off Vincenzo, but I know it's more than that. I know Theo feels something for me—the same way I feel something for him. Sure, it's complicated, but couldn't we at least talk about it? Instead all he does is send me a one-word question. All business, nothing personal. Maybe that's his way of saying that he doesn't want anything remotely serious. So many guys are like that—just want to hook you and then the challenge is over. Except we barely even got started.

And I don't believe it.

Or is it just that I don't want to believe it?

If we're going to be fair, I wasn't much better in the communication department, sending back my own one-word, all-business text because I had to rush out to save Ampora's ass. Not that she appreciated it. But I can't even be mad at *her* because she was trying to do the right thing and I was the one who assumed otherwise. I didn't stop to ask first. I just tore into her.

I'm usually pretty good at dealing with things, but not today. I can't even grab my board and let the waves clear my head because I'm still grounded. Plus I miss the otter in me. It's like that part of me that I so loved has been cut out and tossed away. The only thing that seems to be left is to crawl into bed and pull the covers over my head.

I open the door quietly. I can hear Mamá in the kitchen getting dinner ready, so I close it behind me just as quietly.

"Marina?" Mamá calls from the kitchen.

There's no sneaking by her. You'd think she had Wildling hearing.

"I'm home," I call back.

She steps into sight, then walks down the hall to where I'm standing and touches my hair.

"How was your day?" she asks.

"Oh, you know—the usual. I have to go study."

I feel like the lie is written all over my face, so I duck and head through the living room before she can ask me anything else. Before I can get to my bedroom, I find myself pausing by Mamá's shrine to the Virgin and *los santos*. My gaze moves away from the paintings, votive candles and Mamá's beads to a small framed photograph hanging just to the right of an image of Our Lady of Guadalupe. It's an old picture from better times: Ampora and I can't be much more than seven or eight. Mamá's sitting in a plastic lawn chair in our old backyard with the two of us standing on either side, big smiles all around. We were happy because everything hadn't unravelled yet. Mamá hadn't had her affair, Ampora didn't hate us, and I hadn't become a Wildling.

I want to ask the painting of the Virgin of Guadalupe why it all had to happen, but there's no point. They never answer. Not the Virgin, not *los santos* and for sure not God himself. They're too busy amusing themselves by turning our lives into telanovelas, and I'm left looking at a picture of what used to be.

But that's not really fair—and not even entirely true. I love my stepmother Elena and I adore Ria and Suelo. I can't imagine a world in which they don't exist. But I miss the family I had in that picture. I feel horrible for how I treated Ampora. And I miss the old days, when Mamá knew how to have fun. We would do such silly things and laugh for hours. Now Mamá's always sad and Ampora hates everything I say or do. What happened today will only make it worse. I don't care what Principal Hayden thinks. Going to talk to the guidance counsellor isn't going to solve anything.

I sigh and start to turn away only to find Mamá standing in the doorway, watching me with a concerned look in her eyes.

"*Mija*," she says. "What's the matter?"

There's no point in pretending that there's nothing wrong. Not with me standing here in front of her shrine. When has she ever found me like this? Try never.

But what do I tell her? That her daughter's a Wildling? That she might be falling for a guy who's in a motorcycle gang and he's also a Wildling?

I might as well stick a knife in her chest because I don't know which would horrify her more.

So I take the easy way out.

"What do you do when you find out you've misjudged somebody?" I ask her. "When you've told them off, except then you find out that they didn't deserve it?"

"You apologize."

"What if you're pretty sure they won't care?"

"If you are me," she says with a sad smile, "you pray to the Virgin and *los santos* that the ones you have wronged will eventually listen to you and see that your apology is sincere. You can't force anyone to forgive you. But first you must say those words to them. You must tell them that you're sorry."

I give her a glum nod. I know she's thinking of Papá and Ampora and how, even after all these years, they have yet to forgive her.

"Talk to me," Mamá says. "It hurts me to see you in such a state."

"It's Ampora."

"Ah."

"No, it's not like you think. She didn't do anything this time. It was me. I was the—" Bitch, I almost say, but this is Mamá and we're in front of her shrine. So instead I only say, "I was the one in the wrong."

"What did you do?" Mamá asks, her voice careful, as though she's not entirely sure she wants to know.

Explaining takes a while and there's only so much I can share. I tell her this: how Ampora stood up to the Kings to protect Ria and Suelo and the other children in our old neighbourhood; how that brought the wrath of the Kings down on Ampora, and through her, on all of us, her whole family; how I hadn't been aware of her altruistic motives and got mad at her for putting us all in danger. Yelled at her, pushed her up against a fence. Almost hit her.

I don't mention Theo—the last thing she needs to think is that I'm interested in a boy and, God forbid, one that's in a gang. And of course I don't tell her any of the Wildling business. But I do say that Josh managed to defuse the confrontation with the Kings.

Mamá makes the sign of the cross. She didn't only live in East Riversea with Papá and us. She grew up in a barrio in Mexico. She knows firsthand how the bandas impact the lives of everyone around them. There's no avoiding their presence. All you can do is duck your head and hope they don't notice you. What you don't ever do is report them to the authorities.

"*Josh* put an end to it?" she asks, clearly perplexed that this could happen.

I nod.

"But he's such a small boy. How could he stand up to them?"

"I don't know."

That's true—I really don't know how yet.

"But he can be very persuasive," I add.

Mamá is quiet for a moment. She looks at her shrine. The Virgin with her dusky skin. *Los santos*. The votive candles and her beads. I don't see whatever it is that she sees, but the images seem to strengthen her.

"You must have had an angel watching over all of you. Your sister has been difficult for a long time now," she finally says. "Ever since the divorce. I know she's been hard on you and some might say that this is something she brought on herself. But *mija*, we both know what you did was wrong, if understandable. And if she will not accept your apology, you cannot make her."

"But what do I *do*?"

"You could ask Our Lady to help Ampora see that you're truly repentant."

Like *that's* ever going to happen, is my first thought. But as I look on the kind features of Our Lady of Guadalupe, I remember how I always loved going to church when I was young. I didn't turn my back on it until Mamá betrayed the family and then turned so fervently to religion when there was no one else she could ask for the forgiveness she craved.

Today I understand her a little more than I ever have. It's so hard to have done something wrong but know that you'll be dismissed when you try to accept responsibility for what you've done and make things right. When the people you've hurt won't even let you *try* to make things right.

I don't really believe praying can make it better. I don't even see it making me feel any better. But it would make Mamá feel better.

"Maybe I'll try it," I tell her.

I search her face before I kneel down. But there's no triumph in her features, no sense that she feels she's finally won me back into the fold. There's only sympathy for what I'm going through.

She kneels beside me.

"I will pray with you," she says.

"I'd like that," I tell her, and I'm surprised to realize that I actually mean it.

The sense of well-being I get in sharing this moment with Mamá doesn't last. How could it? The little girl I once was—the one who went to church with wide eyes and true faith—she doesn't exist anymore. There's only me, and I've already had too many disappointments in my life to believe that invisible spirits in the great beyond look out for us down here.

After a while I get up. I make the sign of the cross—more out of respect for Mamá than what her shrine symbolizes—and go to my room. I drop my backpack on the floor, walk to my window, then back to the door. When I realize I'm pacing, I force myself to sit down at my desk. There I shuffle books and paper around in a meaningless pattern before I finally turn on my computer.

I'm not in the mood to work on my blog—not even to answer comments it might have gotten—but if I don't do something to get out of my own head, I think I'll go crazy.

I consider doing a short post to ask my readers if they've

noticed themselves having a shorter fuse, getting more aggressive recently, but I know that's a bad idea as soon as it comes to mind. The authorities probably follow blogs as part of their general info-gathering and who wants them to read anything like that?

Instead of writing, I look through the new comments. I'm only half paying attention when I come across a post saying that Congressman Householder is coming to town to speak at a "Humanity for Humans!" rally. I click on the link, which brings me to a picture of his hateful face urging everyone to attend and stand up for their rights as human beings.

This is so awful it literally makes my skin crawl.

CHAINGANG

My phone rings before we can head off to look for Josh. The caller ID shows me it's J-Dog.

"What's up, bro?" I ask.

"Where are you?" he asks.

I tell him.

"So you're not part of whatever's going down at the skatepark?"

"What's going down at the skatepark?"

"Oh, nothing much," he says. "Just a goddamn army of Mexican car freaks having some kind of powwow on *our* turf, and your little animal boy's right in the middle of it."

Across the table from me, Cory sits up straighter. He's not missing a word.

"Let me get this straight," I say into the phone. "You're telling me that the Kings have Josh cornered in the skatepark?"

"Dwight says right now it's more like they're talking something out," J-Dog says. "Josh and Fat Boy. The other Kings are standing around, keeping watch."

Dwight's one of ours. An Ocean Aver who likes skateboarding, but also uses the opportunity to deal to the other skateboarders when they're looking for some weed. His own little niche market, I guess. But one day, one of those kids is going to get too whacked-out to do their trick on the board, and you know Dwight won't have their back then. Avers don't mix business and pleasure.

"What I want to know is," J-Dog goes on, "is this your personal business or should we be saddling up because, I've gotta tell you, I'm in the mood to bust a few heads."

"It's personal." I tell him. "I'll go deal with it."

As I stow my phone, I see Cory giving me a measuring look.

"That was your brother?" he asks.

I nod.

"And he knows about Josh?"

"It wasn't planned. He just found out about me, then Josh came by my crib and J-Dog figured it out. It's cool. He's not going to tell anybody."

"But—"

"I've got to motor."

Cory stands up when I do. "I'm coming with you."

I shake my head.

"No, man," I tell him. "I took enough of a chance coming here as it is. Vincenzo was pretty clear what would happen if I talked to any of you. Cruising through town with you on the back of my bike is just begging for trouble."

"Don't worry about that," Cory says.

"Yeah? It's not your ..."

My voice trails off as Cory does that Donalita thing and changes from the Indian kid he normally looks like to a long-haired surfer dude.

"Ohhh-kay ..."

I look around us. Almost stranger than the change in his appearance is that no one even noticed. Cory smiles as though he knows exactly what's going through my head.

"People see what they expect to see," he says.

"If you say so."

But it's still giving me the creeps, Cory's voice coming from this surfer.

Donalita scampers down the tree and perches on the picnic table.

"And if you're worried about your grandmother," she says, "I'll watch out for her."

I make myself look away from Cory and focus on her. "And when she wants to know who you are?"

Donalita grins. "I'll tell her I'm your girlfriend."

"Like *hell* you will."

She laughs. "Don't worry. I can be good."

"And what are you going to do if Vincenzo shows up?"

"I'll teach her the tricks a coati-girl has for hiding."

I don't have time for this. If Fat Boy himself is having the meeting with Josh, it's serious. I need to have been on my way ten minutes ago. I search Donalita's face. I don't know that I actually trust her, or that I want to trust her, but I take a little comfort in the idea of someone watching Grandma's back.

"You have a phone?" I ask her as I walk to my Harley.

"Sure."

I rattle off my number. "You call me if anything seems off. *Anything.*"

"Aye aye," she says and throws me a salute.

"This isn't a time for goofing off."

"Don't worry," Cory says. "She can be more serious than you think."

She flashes me a toothy smile but the teeth aren't a girl's anymore. They're sharp and pointed, and there seem to be an awful lot of them.

"Okay, then," I say.

I start up the bike. Cory hops on the back and I take off for the skateboard park.

JOSH

Fat Boy's name isn't ironic, except in that his bulk isn't so much fat as muscle. The guy's huge, covered in tattoos, and he just seems to get bigger and bigger the closer I get. Bigger than either Tiny or Chaingang, that's for sure. And there's not going to be any taking him down by surprise like I was able to do with Tiny. Fat Boy might be smoking a joint, but his eyes are bright and alert, fixed on me with the unblinking intensity of a snake.

And of course he's not alone, not with that entourage of classic cars. Three or four bandas spill out of each one. By the time I've reached where he's standing, they're about thirty-five strong, each one a little colder-eyed than the next. But at least none are carrying weapons that I can see, and most of them stay near their cars. Only a handful have joined Fat Boy, one of them being Chico Para, the head guy from the taquería. He's the only one not looking at me. Instead he seems focused on something very interesting on the pavement at his feet.

I'm a little surprised that they came out in such numbers since I know they're only here to deal with me. The way Fat Boy's staring me down, he probably figures he can do it all on his own without even breaking a sweat. But I guess the gang has to make a show of strength because on this side of Rio Grande Drive, they're intruding on Ocean Avers' territory. With so many Kings here, the Avers would have to come out in full force, and that's not likely since the bandas are here for me and—my relationship with Chaingang notwithstanding—whatever happens to me isn't gang business.

When I reach Fat Boy I look him right in the eye—or at least I try to. The effect's a little lost since he's so much bigger than me that I have to look up. A lot. I half expect the hawk who's been watching from the telephone pole across the street to come swooping down to stop me, but he remains where he is.

Fat Boy looks amused at the way I marched right up to him, and that's not good. He needs to take me seriously or this is never going to end.

"You didn't bring enough men," I tell him.

That takes the mocking look out of his eyes.

"Listen, you little shit," he starts, but I cut him off.

"Seriously," I say. "There was a point where I would have let you save face, but you didn't keep your men in line. So I need to draw the line right here, where everybody can see."

Oh, he doesn't like that at all.

"Let's get something straight, *pendejo*," he says. "The only reason I'm talking to you instead of tearing you a new asshole is because Don Goyo asked me to make peace with you."

I can't help it. I glance at the telephone pole again, but the hawk's not there anymore.

"Bullshit," I tell Fat Boy. "You don't make peace by having your goons jump my friends after school or by showing up here in force."

"Don't push it," he says.

Chico's still not looking at me, but a skinny little guy with a scarred face and mean eyes gives me a glare. His tats cover every inch of exposed skin: haloed saints and a crucifix vying for space with strippers, snakes and barbed wire. I've always liked ink, but this seems like overkill.

"Let me take him down, boss," he says. "Teach the punk some respect."

Fat Boy holds up his hand and the guy shuts up. Then Fat Boy fixes his gaze on me. I can see he's making an effort to keep his own temper. It's not something I suppose he has to do often, and it's obvious he doesn't like it.

"Don Goyo says—" he starts, but I cut him off.

"I don't care what the uncles say or do. This is between *me* and *you*. And your word's no good to me anymore."

Now he can barely hold back his anger.

"I never gave you my word," he says through gritted teeth. "And if you keep this up, I never will."

"Bring it on," I tell him.

"Look at the kitten," a stranger's voice says from behind me. "Just itching to pop his claws."

"So fierce," a second voice says.

"Such a fool," adds a third, and this one I recognize. It's Tío Goyo. "He fights a battle already won while the war goes on around him."

This weird sensation comes over me as I hear those voices. All of a sudden it's like I have a map in my head and on it I can place every living creature in the park and along the streets. Des and the visiting girl, Sandy. Her cousin Justine and the other skateboarders. The three hawk uncles and all the Riverside Kings. Even every damn ground squirrel and bird in the skatepark, from the gulls and crows feeding around the garbage can to a pelican flying overhead. But no hawks.

Of course not, I think as I turn to face *los tíos*. That's because they're standing right here.

And they're probably responsible for putting this creepy GPS kind of feeling in my head.

The two guys standing on either side of Tío Goyo look like they're cut from the same cloth as he is: old, wiry desert rats, dark-skinned and sharp-eyed. I'm hyper-aware of Fat Boy and his gang behind me, but this sensory overload in my head is really freaking me out.

"What did you do to me?" I ask.

Tío Goyo's eyebrows go up.

"In my head," I say. "What did you put in my head? It's like I've turned into a human GPS."

One of the other old guys snickers.

"We didn't do anything," Tío Goyo says. "The more you assert your authority, the more changes will come to how you perceive the world and how it perceives you."

"What are you talking about?"

"Perhaps," Tío Goyo says, "you should finish your business with Señor Zaragoza first."

It takes me a moment to realize he's talking about Fat Boy. When I turn around, whatever machismo I had going for me has drained away. I don't feel like a powerful mountain lion, ready and able to tear into some human punks. The reality of the moment settles into me instead: I'm just some half-assed school kid who's trying to intimidate a big scary Mexican gang leader.

"Have you assured Josh," Tío Goyo asks Fat Boy, "that you

will honour a truce that guarantees the safety of his friends and family?"

Fat Boy shakes his head. "The little *pendejo* wouldn't shut up long enough for me to tell him."

"But now it's all settled?"

"Of course, Don Goyo."

Tío Goyo turns to me. "Does this satisfy you, Josh?"

I have to clear my throat before I can speak.

"If you're going to leave us alone," I say, "why were your guys waiting for my friends after school?"

Fat Boy frowns. I don't think he's going to answer, then Tío Goyo says, "The boy has a point, Señor Zaragoza."

I don't know what kind of a hold *los tíos* have over the Kings, but clearly, it's strong. I know Fat Boy would rather just beat the crap out of me, but instead he forces an apologetic smile that never quite reaches his eyes.

"We didn't get word to them in time," he says in a mild voice. "It won't happen again."

"So we're in agreement, Josh?" Tío Goyo says. "The Kings will leave you and yours alone and you'll extend the same courtesy to them?"

The skinny guy beside Fat Boy snorts.

"You have something you wish to add, Señor Delgado?" Tío Goyo asks him.

Delgado immediately ducks his head. "No, Don Goyo."

Fat Boy gives Delgado a casual smack with the back of his hand and the skinny guy staggers a couple of steps sideways. Then Fat Boy makes a fist and extends it to me. I give Tío Goyo a questioning look. When he nods, I bump fists with Fat Boy.

"We're done here," Fat Boy says.

I nod. I'm not really sure what's going on—why the Kings are so deferential to *los tíos*—but the bandas return to their cars and I'm left standing with three old men who don't give off a Wildling vibe, but seem just as powerful as the Wildling elders all the same. I watch the Kings—with my eyes and with the new sensory input in my head—as they get into their cars and drive away.

"How do I turn it off?" I ask Tío Goyo when the gang's gone. "This thing in my head."

He shrugs. "I assume you had a similar dilemma when you first changed? All your senses seemed too strong?"

"Yeah."

When he doesn't explain any more, I realize what he doesn't feel he has to spell out: learn for yourself how to dial it down. Great.

I look past the uncles. We're still getting a lot of curious looks from the kids in the park, but with the show—such as it was— over, they're starting to go back to what they were doing before the Kings arrived. Des is walking in our direction, but he stops when that girl Sandy asks him something. I turn back to *los tíos*.

"So which of you was the hawk following me?" I ask.

Tío Goyo dismisses my question with a wave of his hand.

"I want you to meet my friends," he says, "Benardo and Marcos. They wished to see your progress firsthand."

"You know I have no idea what you're talking about, right?"

"And yet," Tío Marcos says, "you are embracing your responsibilities."

Tío Benardo nods. "Though you might want to temper your enthusiasm with a little forethought. Brute force isn't always the answer."

"This isn't helping," I tell them.

"What they mean," Tío Goyo says, "is that forcing your will on others won't necessarily solve your problems. Someone else will always come around to test your right to rule."

The other two uncles nod.

"You mean the way I was trying to make the Kings leave us alone? I *tried* talking to them first and you saw where that got me."

"Consider the *tone* of that conversation you were having," Tío Goyo says. "You attract more bees with honey than with vinegar."

"But you're doing well," Tío Benardo says.

"Oh, yes," Tío Marcos agrees. "So long as you remember that *you* are in charge, not the lion under your skin. The lion only chooses between two courses of action: attack or retreat. Your choices aren't so limited."

"So you're saying *I* should back off some—communicate better," I say.

All three of them nod.

"Though you'll still run into the odd mad dog," Tío Benardo adds, "and when you do—"

"Those you have to put down hard," Tío Goyo finishes.

The tracking device in my head has been aware of Des approaching. I turn when he calls my name and *los tíos* choose that moment to leave.

"Hey, wait!" I call after them.

They're not Wildlings, but they're capable of the same deceptive speed that we have. In seconds, they're out of the park.

"Dude," Des says when he reaches me, "did you just make Fat Boy and his whole crew stand down?"

I shake my head. "Honestly? I don't really know what happened. But they're going to leave us alone."

Des grins. "Well, it looked golden from where I was standing. You weren't giving an inch. Who were those old Mexican dudes?"

"*Los tíos.* They're the real reason the Kings backed off. I told you about the one I met at the restaurant."

Des nods. "I wonder whose uncles they are?"

"I don't know. I think that's just what they're called. *Los tíos.* The uncles."

Des takes my arm.

"Come on," he says. "Sandy wants to meet you."

I don't have to look in her direction. The tracker in my head shows me that she and her cousin are already approaching us.

"I don't have time," I tell him. "I need to make sure Ampora and her sisters are okay and let them know that they're not going to have any more trouble from the Kings."

"Dude, this girl's hot."

I know she is, but I don't need any more complications in my life—especially not from someone who's only attracted to me because I'm tough and stood up to the Kings.

"Later," I tell him. "Distract them for me—would you?"

"Seriously?"

"Later," I repeat.

I head off before they can reach us.

CHAINGANG

By the time we get there, it's all over. There aren't any Kings at the skatepark, and there's no Josh. All I see is a bunch of kids hanging out on the benches and practicing their skills.

Cory gets off the back of my bike, but I keep my seat. I don't expect to stay long. I see Dwight and wave him over, but then Des leaves a couple of cute girls he's been talking to and jogs over before Dwight can reach me. I wave Dwight back since you can never tell what's going to come out of Des's mouth. If it has anything to do with Wildling business, I don't want Dwight to hear.

"Cory, dude," Des says as he gets close enough. "You've got to tell me. Erik never showed at school and ever since we left you last night I've been dying to know what you did to him."

Cory and I exchange glances. He still looks like the surfer dude he changed into so how come Des knows who he is?

"You can recognize me?" Cory asks.

Des laughs. "Why wouldn't I? I'm not a stoner."

I start checking the area for any sign of Vincenzo.

"This is interesting," Cory says.

"No, it's not," I tell him. "If Vincenzo spots us, my

being with you is going to blow up in my face. Maybe he already has."

Des gives me a confused look. "Dude, *what* are you talking about?"

"No, it's just him," Cory says. "I've seen this before. It's rare, but some five-fingered beings just see through the illusion."

"What illusion?"

"And if Vincenzo is one of the rare ones?" I ask.

"He's not. Cousins can't see the difference. If he was close enough, he could smell me, but he's not."

"Um, standing right here, guys," Des says, waving his hand in the air then tapping his chest. "What are you two talking about?"

Cory shrugs. "Nothing much. As for Erik, I just explained the logic of good manners and what happens to those who don't have them."

That's enough to distract Des.

"So you didn't, like, eat him or something?"

"No, I didn't eat him."

Des looks thoroughly bummed and I understand. I learned back in grade school that the one thing you don't ever do is back down. You might get the crap kicked out of you, but you don't command any respect by rolling over. I get what Josh was trying to do, but with guys like Erik Gess, you have to put them down right from the start or they never go away.

"What happened here?" I ask.

Des fills us in and I'm left with more questions than answers.

"He just talked to Fat Boy," I say, "and then the bangers all left? This whole business with the Kings—it's done?"

"That's what Josh told me."

There's got to be more to this. Fat Boy never backs down.

"What did he say to them?" I ask.

"Don't know, dude. I was too far away to hear. I would have been right there with him, watching his back," he adds, "but Josh insisted he do it on his own."

"Yeah, he's growing bigger balls all right."

Des nods. "Is it true—what happened at that restaurant this afternoon? Some dude shot him and he just got up again?"

"Pretty much. But it wasn't easy on him. I'll bet it hurt like hell."

"These older Mexican men you saw," Cory says. "They weren't part of the gang?"

Des shakes his head. "Josh called them the uncles and says they pretty much defused the whole sitch."

That's the second time today, I think. What's in it for them?

"So what's their game?" I ask Cory.

"At the moment?" he says. "Keeping Josh safe, it seems."

"I don't trust them."

Cory smiles. "From my experience, you don't trust anybody."

I don't take offence. You can't be offended by the truth.

"You know," I say, "I never got Donalita's number."

"I rest my case," Cory says.

"Who's Donalita?" Des asks. "Man, I am so out of the loop."

I don't bother to respond to either of them.

"Josh say where he was going?" I ask.

"To tell Ampora that everything's settled now."

I nod. "Okay. That should keep him out of trouble. Cory, why don't you set up a meet with the old lady? Meanwhile I'm going to check up on my grandma. Text me the where and when, and I'll track down Josh, see if I can convince him to come talk to her."

Des grins. "With your grandma?"

"Ha ha."

"I'm serious, dude. I don't have a clue about half of what you two are saying," Des says.

"Tell Josh he owes me the meeting with Auntie Min," Cory says to me.

"Will do."

Des looks at me and says, "Let me give you my digits and I'll take yours."

Des waits for me to rattle off my phone number and tells me his, then says, "I can find Josh. Shoot me a text and I'll make sure he shows up."

I can't help it. My eyebrows go up in a question.

"Dude," Des says, "I've got this. I know Auntie Min—she's cool, and I'll tell him that. Josh'll meet with her on my say-so."

Cory looks to me and I just shrug. It's his call.

"Someone should fill Marina in while we're at it," I say.

"I'll text her," Des says before I can offer to do it myself. "I already told her about what went down earlier."

I open my mouth, but close it before the protest comes out. It's probably better if nobody knows I have her cell number.

"Later," I tell them and start up my bike.

Grandma's house is in Orangewood—that's the part of Santa Feliz where the tourists never come. There's nothing pretty about it. Just a lot of adobe and clapboard houses with dirt yards, scraggly trees and more junked cars in the lanes than ones that actually run. J-Dog and I tried moving her out years ago, but she won't budge. She won't turn her back on us—family doesn't do that, not around here—but she'll, and I quote, "be damned if I'll let you spend one penny of that blood money on me."

She lives off her pension and the groceries we sneak in. Since she doesn't throw them out, I figure she's opinionated, but not stupid. She knows she can't survive on her pension alone.

When I get to her house I find the two of them drinking iced tea on her front porch. So much for Donalita staying invisible. She's still looking like a skinny teenage girl, dressed like she might have come from the skatepark I just left. Grandma's not much bigger than her, but you only need to exchange a few words with her to know that she stands tall.

Donalita raises a glass to me in a toast as I come up the walk.

I nod at her and bend over to give Grandma a kiss before I settle in one of the other lawn chairs.

"Donalita tells me you're her Big Brother," Grandma says.

The way she says the words I can see the caps. I shoot Donalita a dirty look.

"I didn't know boys could mentor girls in that program," Grandma goes on.

"It's not an official program," I say. "She just calls it that. I'm looking out for her is all. She's got nobody else."

"You better not be taking her anywhere near your brother and those friends of yours."

"No, ma'am."

She fixes me with that look of hers that can read any lie.

"See that it stays that way," she says. "You're not so big that I still couldn't give you a licking."

I am, and we both know it, but all I say is, "Yes, ma'am."

Donalita snickers and Grandma smiles at her.

Great, like I need them colluding on me. But since they're getting along so well ...

"I was hoping maybe you could look after Donalita for a few hours," I say. "Just while I take care of some business."

Grandma's smile disappears.

"It's not like you think," I say. "Some friends of mine are in trouble and I want to help them clear things up."

"This have anything to do with your brother?"

"No, ma'am."

She gives me that look again.

"Well," she says, "I'm going to consider the fact that you have friends outside that gang as a step in the right direction. What kind of trouble are we talking about here?"

"Somebody's trying to hurt them."

Grandma sighs. "I suppose it would be a waste of time to ask if maybe just one time you let the police handle something like this? It's their job, after all."

"Not in this case."

Grandma shakes her head. She turns to Donalita and says, "You're still young enough to break any bad habits you might have, so let me just tell you, never get too stubborn for your own good."

Donalita lays her small smooth hand on Grandma's wrinkled one.

"This time he's right," she says. "I'm one of the people he's helping and I can tell you for a fact that there's nothing the police can do to help."

"What have you got this poor girl mixed up in?" Grandma demands of me.

Donalita answers while I'm still trying to come up with what to say.

"Theo didn't start anything," she says. "He's just going to fix it."

"Do I want to know more?" Grandma asks.

"Probably not," I say.

"But it's dangerous?"

I don't answer, but for Grandma, that's answer enough.

"I never thought I'd be saying this," she tells me, "but if it starts looking bad, you call your brother."

"I will. I need to go now."

When I stand up, she does, too.

"Come give your grandmother a hug first. You stay safe," she adds, talking into my shoulder as I hold her. I love this old lady more than life itself.

I step back and there's Donalita looking expectant.

"What?" she says. "No hug for me?"

I ruffle her hair.

"You know what I need from you," I tell her. "Be good."

"Don't worry. We'll be fine."

She goes to stand with Grandma. When I look back from the street, they're still standing on the porch, arms around each other's waist now. I find myself wondering what Donalita really wants more: vengeance on Vincenzo, or a new family she can call her own. I give them a wave and drive off.

I only go as far as the next block before I pull over to the curb. Leaving the engine idling, I take out my phone.

JOSH

There are no hawks following me as I head into East Riversea—
or at least, not that I can see, and I can see with more than my
eyes now. I'm getting the hang of dialling down this weird info
overload in my head. It's a sweet relief, but now that I know how
to use it, I decide to let it hang in the periphery because it's pretty
useful. It lets me know there aren't any Kings around. I don't
"see" any of the Black Key Securities guys that Solana warned
me about, either. No ambushes. No hidden snipers.

I already know that Ampora's in the park with her sisters
when I'm a block or so away. As I come into sight, Suelo notices
me and jumps down from her swing. A moment later she and
Ria are running toward me, waving and calling my name. I don't
need my Wildling sight to tell me that Ampora's reaction to my
showing up is the opposite of theirs.

The girls hang off me, each taking an arm as they chatter
away. Ampora gives them a few moments before she calls them
back.

"Okay, brats! Time to go home."

They won't let go of my hands, so I follow along with them.
Ampora frowns at me, but she doesn't say anything as she leads

the way back to their house. The girls make up for their older sister's bad mood by keeping up a constant stream of conversation until Ampora ushers them inside to wash up before dinner. Not until they're out of hearing does she turn to me, arms folded across her chest.

"What now?" she asks.

"I know you don't like me," I tell her, "and that's okay. I just wanted you to know that I had a talk with Fat Boy. You and your family are off limits—and so is the park. If one of them so much as gives you a wrong look, tell me and I'll deal with it."

"I don't need the protection of one gang to save me from another."

"I'm not in a gang."

"Bullshit. Everybody knows you're tight with Chaingang."

"That's not a gang thing," I say.

She gives me a mocking look. "Oh yeah? Then what kind of a *thing* is it? Is it a *bromance* like some people say?"

I don't give her the satisfaction of seeing any reaction, but she really pisses me off. How would *she* react if she knew what I really am? And besides, is there really any point now in pretending otherwise?

"No," I tell her. "I guess Chaingang likes the idea of knowing a Wildling."

She starts to laugh, but then she sees how serious I am. Her eyes go cold.

"So you're with the government," she says.

"What?"

"Come on. You don't expect anybody to really believe people are turning into animals, do you? I'm not stupid. I know it's all some weird-ass scam they're running."

I almost laugh. Here I'm thinking that she's going to be all freaked out, and instead, she doesn't even believe me. So I lift my index finger until it's right in front of her eyes, then I let the change come over that one finger. The mountain lion's big claw pops out of its furry sheath and I wiggle it at her before I make it go away.

She jumps back, banging into the door frame.

"*Madre de Dios*," she says.

"Do you still think the government's faking it?"

She grabs my hand and turns it back and forth, studying my finger. While she's doing that, I let the claw pop out again—just for a moment. She drops my hand like it's a hot coal.

We look at each other for a long moment. I expect her to freak now, but she doesn't.

"So you really took care of the Kings on your own?" she asks, her voice soft for the first time since I met her. "There's no gang—I mean, you're not in one or anything?"

I shake my head. "I'm just a kid who woke up one day and he's a Wildling. It was the luck of the draw, nothing more. I could have just as easily gotten some really horrible disease and be on my deathbed right now. Why either might happen is something that nobody can really explain. It just does."

She gives a slow nod.

"It just does," she repeats. She looks mesmerized.

"Well, it's sure not something I chose."

"Okay," she says. She waits a beat, then asks, "Why are you telling *me* all of this?"

I shrug. "I honestly don't know. I suppose I was interested in your reaction. You already don't like me, so I guess you could say this is a trial run for when I tell all the other people who feel the same way you do."

"That's messed up."

I give her another shrug.

"So who else knows?" she asks.

"My mother. Your sister. Des. A couple of FBI agents suspect. Oh, and Chaingang."

"What about your girlfriend—the one you were running with a few weeks ago?"

How would she even know that? And why would she care? I hate how this town just runs on gossip.

But all I say is, "You mean Elzie? Yeah, she knows, too."

"Whatever happened to her?"

"She went away."

"Is she coming back?"

"To me, or to Santa Feliz?"

"Either, I guess."

"I don't know."

Ampora gives me a considering look. She looks soft, more like Marina.

"Huh," she finally says. "And you don't have a thing for my sister?"

"She's my friend. Why?"

"Maybe I'm curious about how upfront you're going to be with me."

I'm confused. A minute ago she was dissing me.

"Why would that even matter to you?" I ask.

She smiles. "I don't know. You could call me sometime and maybe we can find out."

She leans forward and gives me a quick kiss—right on the lips—then steps back inside the house and closes the door, leaving me standing there on her porch feeling like a complete idiot. Because now I know why she had all those questions.

I so don't need *this* complication. She hates Marina, who's my best friend, and Marina hates her. I've got a million things on my mind, all kinds of things I have to figure out and do. But right now, all I can think of is the touch of her lips on mine.

MARINA

My phone pings with a text while I'm composing a comment to the post about the upcoming anti-Wildlings rally. I grab it, my heart lifting. My pulse drops just as fast when I see it's a message from Des, not Theo. Des is updating me on what just went down at the skatepark. I send him a brief thanks and breathe a sigh of relief.

I think about how Josh never wanted to be a leader, yet there he went and somehow convinced the Kings to leave my family alone. I'm grateful, but it also makes me realize how much everything has changed. And it reminds me he's still in danger from that elder.

I consider sending Theo a text, but decide to resist. I don't want to come across as needy. If he wanted to talk to me, he'd call me himself. It sucks, waiting like this.

I sigh, put my phone down and turn back to the computer screen. The problem in trying to compose a proper response to this Humanity for Humans rally is that I can't dial back my anger. I've started it a half-dozen times now, but no matter how calmly and rationally I begin, within paragraphs I'm reduced to name-calling and typing in all caps.

Then it's delete delete delete and start over again.

I think it's the unfairness that's making me inarticulate with rage. If any other minority group were the target, the rally's webpage servers would be shut down in minutes from the sheer volume of people protesting the bigotry of it all. Quarantine blacks? Jews? Native Americans? Gays?

Sure, there are whack-jobs out there who'd think any of those options would be perfect, but thankfully, they're in the minority these days. The public outcry would be deafening. But when it comes to kids who—through no fault of their own—turn into animals? Not much outrage about putting *us* into camps.

It's not that the general public agrees, so much as that they seem to be indifferent. They'd much rather weigh in on some celebrity scandal.

It makes me furious.

Except maybe that's not it—or at least, not entirely. Maybe it's this quick temper I seem to have developed. Because all I want to do is take the people behind this rally and slap some sense into them.

My phone pings again, and again it's Des texting, not Theo. This time he's letting me know that they're trying to set up a meeting between Josh and Auntie Min. He says he'll get back to me as soon as he knows the when and where.

Now, why can't everybody be like Des, I think, as I set my phone aside. Sure, he's a bit gaga over the Wildling coolness factor, but otherwise, he doesn't treat either Josh or me any differently than he ever has.

And that's all anybody wants. Nobody wants to be defined *only* by things they can't control, like their physical appearance or their race. When someone looks at me, I just want them to see a girl. Not a Mexican. Not a Wildling. An ordinary girl.

Is that too much to ask?

Apparently so, for the Humanity for Humans people.

I decide that's the tack I'll take in my comment. Dial back the outrage and just try to be reasonable.

I clear the comment box for the umpteenth time and start to type again when this time my phone rings. I know who it is. Des is obviously loving being call central on setting up this meet and is dying to talk about it. I press Talk.

"I got the text, Des," I say, "but I don't know if I can sneak out. It all depends on how late the meeting is, and if my mother's asleep."

There's a moment's silence, then the voice I've been waiting to hear all day says, "Hey, sweetcheeks."

A sudden heat comes up the back of my neck and my heart begins to race. But I manage to squeak out an automatic, "Don't call me that."

Theo chuckles.

"I guess you've had a busy day," I hear myself saying. God, why don't I just get over it already?

"Babe, you don't know the half of it."

"Me too. It's been crazy."

"I wish I could see you."

I don't want to read too much into it, but that doesn't sound like "business." An unstoppable grin takes over my face.

"Really?" I say.

There's a moment's hesitation. "Let me know if I'm getting out of line."

"You're not. I—you know what? Meet me at my surfing spot in about half an hour."

"I'll be there."

I put the phone down, jump out of my chair and do a happy dance around my room. Then I sit back down, make myself finish my comment, hit Post and shut down the computer. I get back up, look in the mirror, wipe the silly smile off my face and go looking for my mother. I find her in the kitchen.

"Am I still grounded?" I ask.

We both know I've still got a few days left. But I'm betting our earlier conversation is still going through her head.

"Where did you want to go?" she asks.

"Surfing. I need to do something before I go crazy."

"Will Josh be there?"

I can tell by the way she asks that she's re-evaluating how she feels about him. It was one thing when he was just my friend, but now that she's learned that he was able to shut down the Riverside Kings, she's worried about what else she doesn't know about him.

I don't even want to think about how she'd feel if she learned he's a Wildling.

"I doubt it" is all I tell her.

She nods. "Go. But be careful."

"I'm always careful. Thanks, Mamá."

I see Theo as soon as I turn down the street that leads to the beach. His big Harley is parked along the side of the road and he's standing on the beach with his back to me, looking out at the waves. He turns as I approach. I feel a little self-conscious in my wetsuit, wheeling my board behind me. The suit clings to every contour of my body, and the way Theo's smile gets bigger as I close the distance between us makes me even more self-conscious.

And of course he has to come out with, "Anybody ever tell you how hot you look in that suit?"

I try to laugh it off. "Oh, please. Is that the best opening line you've got?"

"Nope."

Before it entirely registers what he's doing, he steps in close, puts a hand behind my head and draws me in for a long kiss. I don't bother to ask if it's for real or just more of the show we're supposed to be putting on for Vincenzo. I don't really care. I've been wanting to do this ever since the first time we kissed.

I let my board drop and put my arms around him, and it's a long time before we come up for air.

"Wow," I manage when I've got my breath.

"More than wow," he says.

It's so comfortable in his arms. We're a perfect fit. I look up and smile, pull his face back down to mine.

We revel in the deliciousness of the kiss for a long time. When our lips part, I take a step back, but catch hold of his hand so that we're still connected.

"What are we doing?" I ask him.

"I know it doesn't make sense," he says, "but I can't stop thinking about you. Maybe we come from different worlds, but it feels too right to just let it go. We're smart. We can figure this out if you want to." He pauses to study me for a moment. "I'm not saying it'll be easy, but we could do it. If you want to."

"I do."

There's a bench beyond the tumble of rocks that marks the end of the public beach. I discovered it by accident one day when I was looking for shells with my little stepsisters. It's the only secluded place around, so I reach down for my board and pull it and Theo over there. When we sit down, I lean my head against his shoulder. He puts his arm around me and I snuggle closer.

"It's going to be complicated," I say.

"I know. The whole gang thing for starters."

I nod. "But I don't want to be the girl who makes a guy change who he is just so he can be with her."

"But you don't want to be the girl going out with a guy in a gang, either."

I nod again. "Complicated."

"Well, I don't want to be the guy in a gang," he says.

I pull away so that I can look at him.

"Really?"

"I always had a plan," he says. "I've been putting money away for years. I'm only with them for the short term because they're not my style. I've never been into the gang life. I don't do the parties or the dope and crap."

"Then why are you even in one?"

"Two reasons. To get myself a stake—the only way a guy like me can—and to keep an eye on my brother, so that he doesn't do something monumentally stupid."

"Is that why you went to jail for him?"

Theo nods. "J-Dog's got a juvie record and a file on him that's probably a mile thick. Next time he goes down, it's to adult jail, and when that happens, we'll have lost him for good."

"No offence," I say, "but by all accounts, your brother's never been a good guy."

"I know. But he's still family, and it'll kill my grandma if either of us ends up in federal prison."

I think of Ampora. She's not in J-Dog's league, but she's not particularly endearing, either. But if anyone ever tried to hurt her, I'd do everything in my power to protect her.

"I understand," I tell Theo. "And it's sweet that you love your grandmother so much."

He puts his arm around me again and pulls me in closer.

"Yeah, I know you get it," he says into my hair. "You're a smart little chica."

I like this. I could get so used to just hanging here on the beach with him, watching the waves and the sun as it makes its steady descent toward the horizon. But there's a world of crap out there that we still have to deal with.

"Catch me up on your day," I say. "Des said something about Josh dying and then coming back from the dead, but his typing is so bad I'm not sure I got it all straight."

"Oh, that happened all right," Theo tells me. "We've got a whole new Josh on our hands. Assertive, and he's got the chops to back it up."

"No kidding," I say. "You should have seen him take out the guys who were waiting for Ampora and me after school."

"*What?*"

He turns to look at me, fury written all over his face.

"Obviously, I came out of it okay. You go first and then I'll fill you in on my day."

JOSH

I can "see" Des coming while he's still around a corner and a couple of blocks away. There's no actual image of him, not even a pulsing dot like the GPS on my phone. It's just that I *know* it's him—his essence, I guess I have to call it, setting him apart from all the others I can sense around me. Human and animal. Birds in the sky, ground squirrels in an empty lot, a lizard sunning itself on a stone. People in their homes, driving their cars, walking side streets, sitting in deck chairs in their backyards.

If I were to let it, my awareness could probably spread out to include not only my immediate vicinity, but for blocks and blocks further. Maybe all of Santa Feliz. Maybe the whole world.

That freaks me out, and so I dial it way back down.

When Des actually comes into sight, I raise a hand and he waves back. Moments later, we're walking side by side, back the way he came.

"Everything okay, dude?" he asks.

"Sure."

"Because you're looking awfully pale—and that's a new look for you."

When we were still little kids, Des had the hardest time

accepting that black people tan and blush or even go pale from shock or blood loss, just like anybody else. I'm already fairly light because of having a white father, and I guess I'm even lighter than usual right now.

"It's just been one of those days," I tell him.

"No kidding. Still," he adds. "I don't know why you took off like you did. Sandy was really into you."

"Yeah, but for the wrong reasons."

Des's eyebrows go up. "There's a wrong reason for a cute girl to be into you?"

"She's only interested because I stood up to the Kings."

"So what?"

"So it's not what I'm looking for in a girl."

"Oh, come on, dude. She doesn't want to have your babies— or at least I don't think she does."

I aim a punch at his shoulder but he dances out of range.

"Dude. She only wants to hang out and have some fun. Where's the harm in that?"

"It's not only her."

So then I have to tell him about the weird conversation I had with Ampora.

Des shakes his head. "Okay, first off, dude—what the hell were you thinking? Are you nuts?"

"Hey, I didn't kiss her back or anything."

"Except you actually sound kind of interested, which is not cool. Yeah, she's hot, but you know how she treats Marina."

"You think I don't know that?"

He shakes his head. "Dude, I don't know what's what anymore. I still can't believe you went and took on a whole gang of the Kings on their own turf."

"Yeah, probably not my brightest idea."

"But seriously?" he says. "I'd rather face them than have to tell Marina I was going out with her sister."

"I'm *not* going out with her."

"That's what you say now."

"That's what I'll say whenever you ask me."

"Still, she's pretty hot," he says. "A dead ringer for Marina, too, but Ampora's the bad-girl version."

"Marina would kill you if she heard you say that."

"Yeah, but you know it's true. They're both hot. I just never knew you liked the bad girls," he says with a smirk.

I roll my eyes.

"Keep it in your pants," I tell him.

"Dude. Like you're the one to talk."

"I'm not doing anything," I say. "Do I look like I'm doing anything? How come all these girls are suddenly into me? I mean—Ampora? *Really?*"

"It's got to be pheromones."

I give him a blank look.

"You know," he says. "Like a smell or something that animals give off when they're mating or whatever."

"I know what pheromones are. Why would you think *I'm* doing that?"

He shrugs. "Maybe it's a new Wildling thing."

I think of all the weird new sensory stuff that's now in my head and wonder what else is going to happen to me.

"No-o-body can resis-s-st you now," Des says in a bad spooky voice while he wiggles his fingers in my face.

I push him away. For a moment we're both laughing like old times, then his face goes serious.

"Dude," he says, "I forgot to tell you. You *have* to talk to Auntie Min."

I shake my head. "I will. But only when I've figured things out first. I don't trust her or any of the older cousins."

"Not even Cory? Because he thinks you should talk to her and you promised him you would."

"Why are *you* so keen on me doing this?"

"You don't want to talk to her, dude, I'll back you up. But like I told you before, she's pretty cool."

I raise my eyebrows.

"Seriously, dude. She's a big deal."

"You mean versus you lowly humans?" I ask with a grin.

He whacks my arm, then dances back, jabbing at the air, pretending to be a boxer.

"Come on," he says. Jab. Jab. "Think you can take me?"

I laugh. "I could take you before I changed. Now I ..."

My words trail off as the GPS in my head registers an anomaly. Something around us isn't right.

Des takes a couple more air jabs in my direction.

"Hold on," I tell him.

"Yeah, dude. Now I've got you scared."

"Seriously. Hold on."

He rolls his eyes, but falls silent.

I let my Wildling gaze focus on the spot where something's out of place. It's an old adobe building. There's a yard with some brush and scraggly trees. I don't see anybody. As I let my gaze go up the side of the building, I catch a glimpse of the top of some guy's head. Metal winks.

My body seems to know what to do before my brain can react.

I tackle Des and we both go down behind a parked car. Something pings sharply off the pavement, right where we were just standing. If we hadn't moved, one of us would have been hit.

"Dude!" Des says. "Did somebody just shoot at us?"

He starts to sit up, but I push his head down.

"Seems like it," I tell him.

"I didn't even hear the shot."

"Me neither."

Which means two things: that the sniper has a silencer, and that Solana was right when he warned me that the guys from Black Key Securities might be coming after me. Danny said they were in protective custody, but that was obviously a lie or they wouldn't be out here shooting at me.

Another bullet pings off the hood of the car behind us before ricocheting away into the distance.

"Dude, how did you even know that guy was there?"

I tap my head. "New tracking device," I say. "Somehow I've got, like, a GPS in my head. I'm still getting used to it."

"As if your other superpowers weren't enough. Dude, I am so jealous."

"Can I borrow your phone?" I ask.

"Who're you going to call?" he asks as he hands it over. Before I can answer, he goes right on with, "Man, does this have to do with the Kings?"

"I doubt it."

I close my eyes so that I can recall the business card Solana gave me the first time we met at the end of the pier. I never could have done this before I became a Wildling. Imagine if I could put this souped-up memory bank to use in school. I'd ace every course.

Once I have the digits, I thumb them into Des's phone. Solana answers on the first ring.

"Yes, Mr. Wilson?" he says, which throws me for a loop until I realize he's got call display and thinks it's Des.

"It's me," I say. "You need to get here right away. Some guy's shooting at us and he's got a silencer on his rifle."

"Where are you?"

"Are you really telling me that you don't have a tracker on this phone as well?"

I hear a siren start up in the background.

"We'll be right there," he says.

I close Des's phone and hand it back to him.

He looks incredulous. "Somebody's got a tracker on my phone?" he says.

"Don't look so surprised. Every phone's got GPS now. The police can trace any one of them, so long as they're turned on."

"You called the police?"

"No, the FBI."

Des nods like it's an everyday occurrence.

"I wonder if the guy's still there," he says as he starts to have a look.

I pull him down and a bullet cuts the air where his head just was. It bounces off the grille of the car behind and whizzes between us. We both wince at the ugly sound.

"Remember my GPS?" I say, putting a finger to my temple.

Des just nods and stays down.

My senses tell me the guy's still in place. I can pinpoint precisely where he is.

"Give me your phone again," I say.

When Solana picks up, I describe exactly where they'll find the shooter.

"Stay on the line," I say when I hear the approach of a siren. "Okay," I add. "He hears you coming and he's on the move."

"Jesus!" Solana says. "Just stay put and let us deal with this. Don't start following him."

"I'm not. It's—like an uncle thing. *Los tíos*, right?"

"Huh?"

"He's off the roof, but he's still on the move. So, unless he can fly, he's made his way down to the lane that runs behind the building."

"You don't move," Solana tells me.

"Wouldn't dream of it. He's heading north now. Moving fast. I think he must be in a car."

"What make?"

"I can't actually *see* him."

I hear Agent Matteson curse in the background and I know why. The shooter's car has merged with other traffic. There's no way they're going to find him now.

Solana's alone in the car when it pulls up to where Des and I are now standing on the sidewalk. Even though I know the shooter's long gone, I can't get rid of the little warning prickles in the back of my neck.

"Where's Agent Matteson?" Des asks. "I thought you two were joined at the hip."

"I'll be sure to tell him you said that."

"He's on the rooftop," I say. "Where the guy with the gun was."

Solana nods, staring at me like I've got a third eye or something. "That's right. He's looking for shell casings. You're both okay?"

"We're fine."

"*Now* can I convince you to get off the street and go somewhere safe?"

I shake my head. Solana's cell rings before I can say anything.

"There's nothing." My Wildling hearing lets me pick up Matteson's voice. "Some scuff marks, but no casings."

"If he's from Black Key, he's a pro."

"The kid all right?" Matteson asks.

"Yeah, but he's still being stubborn," Solana says. "Want me to come pick you up?"

"Nah, I'm good."

Solana turns his attention back to us. "Will you at least let us drive you somewhere?"

"Can we use the siren?" Des asks.

Solana shakes his head. "What are you, twelve? Not a chance."

"I've met some more of your uncles," I tell Solana. "They don't seem to like giving straight answers."

"That sounds about right."

"I also ran into Danny Reed. He told me what your Bureau Chief's planning."

"I know. It's unfortunate. But he doesn't have any choice. Not with Congressman Householder coming to speak at that rally. By going with the registration idea, the Chief thinks he might be able to forestall the quarantine that Householder and his people are demanding."

"What rally?" Des asks.

"Humanity for Humans."

"I never heard of it," I say.

"It's happening this weekend," Solana tells us. "In the parking lot of the mall."

"What's happening?"

I turn to see that Matteson has joined us. It's interesting that he didn't set off any little warning *pings* in my head. I guess I really do trust him.

"The rally," Solana tells him.

Matteson snorts. "You mean the crapfest."

"This registration thing that your boss is rolling out," I say. "Is it even legal?"

"That's for Congress to decide," Matteson says. "Personally, I don't think they can make it stick. If they could, every gang member and mobster would be in custody by now."

"I thought the Black Key guys were already locked up," I say.

"Some are, but not all—the operative word being 'some.' As you just found out, that means it's dangerous for you to be out in the open."

"I'm not hiding."

Solana nods. "Will you at least start carrying your phone again?"

I give him a look of mock surprise.

"What?" I say. "The uncles won't tell you where I am anymore?"

"What uncles?" Matteson asks.

Solana gives me a pissed-off look and sighs.

"I'll tell you later," he says to his partner before returning his attention to me: "Carry your phone."

"I will. I just haven't been home yet to get it."

"So go. Now."

I nod.

Speaking of phones, Des's starts to ring in his pocket. He pulls it out and checks the call display.

"We're gonna have to motor," he says as he brings the phone to his ear.

I hear Cory giving him the time and place where we're meeting with Auntie Min.

"We'll be there," Des tells him, though he's looking at me with a question in his eyes.

"I'll go," I tell him.

"Go where?" Solana asks.

I smile. "It's private. You've got a tracker on Des's phone, so you'll figure it out. But you won't be welcome."

"Kid," Matteson says. "These gangs are just going to bring you more trouble. Your buddy Chaingang is only going to keep you around until he gets whatever it is that he wants from you."

"Tell me something I don't know," I say.

But I don't agree.

"Come on, Des," I say. As we start walking away, I call over my shoulder, "Thanks for chasing off that guy."

Solana is still frowning. Matteson just shakes his head.

"Who are these uncles the kid was talking about?" I hear Matteson say.

Des and I keep walking.

CHAINGANG

J-Dog would laugh his ass off if he could see me right now, and I don't want to even think about the guys back in juvie. But I don't care. Sitting here on this bench with my arm around Marina is pretty much the best thing that's happened to me since we first kissed. Better. Because neither of us are pretending this time.

Not that I ever was.

I know it's not going to be easy, but I don't care about that, either. We can work this out. I'll do whatever I can to make it work.

But first we have to deal with all the crap the rest of the world is throwing at us.

"Sounds like Donalita has a crush on you," Marina says when we finish up telling each other about our days. "Should I be jealous?"

Oh, crap. Why did I have to bring up Donalita's flirting?

"It's not like that," I start, but then I see her smile and I let it go.

I know exactly what that smile means. She's getting a kick out of seeing me flustered because I'm the big bad Chaingang who never loses his cool.

"Relax," she says. "I'm kidding. What we really have to do is figure out how to handle *this*. Us."

I nod. "What's your take?"

"Well, no public displays that could get back to Mamá—this'd kill her, and I'd never get out of the house again."

"Okay."

"What about your brother and the other Avers?"

"It's none of their business, but I suppose if they found out, it could get back to, you know, school, and your sister, which would get it to your mother."

She nods. "Except she doesn't talk to my mother, but I get your point. She'd definitely tell my dad.

"What about Josh and Des?" she adds. "I'm not so into keeping secrets from them, especially Josh, but Des isn't exactly known for being discreet."

"Your call. I've got no problem with them knowing, so long as Des can keep a lid on it."

"How about my friend Julie?"

"I'm okay with that. I'd like to introduce you to my grandmother, but you've got to promise me no joking about how I'm trying to jump you into the gang or anything like that when we see her."

She smiles. "Like I'd do that."

My phone rings. I'd prefer to ignore it, but I know I probably can't. I check the call display and see that it's Cory.

"Go ahead and take it," Marina says.

I nod, but I have to make sure she knows what this means.

"If we get any deeper into this," I tell her, "we could lose control over everything and things will never be the same again. Your mother finding out about us will be the least of your worries."

"I know. But it's Josh. We can't just abandon him."

"He's already outted himself to the Kings. We're not far off from the whole world knowing what he is. When that happens, it won't be long before they know who we are, too. Guilt by association."

She pulls back and looks at me. "Are you saying we shouldn't get involved?"

I shake my head. "I just want to remind you what's at stake. There's no turning back after this."

She swallows hard and says, "Do it. Answer."

I press Talk.

"What's up, bro?" I ask Cory.

"You know where that is?" I ask as I stow the phone back in my pocket.

Marina shakes her head.

"It's just south of Tiki Bay—you've surfed there, right?"

"But there's nothing on that headland."

"Kinda the point," I say. "Private. No one's going to drop in uninvited. Can you come?"

I like the way her face goes when she's thinking. Hell, I like everything about her.

"It's early to be sneaking out," she says.

"Maybe you could say you're going to your father's? Get Ampora to cover for you."

"Like that'd ever happen."

"Tell her she owes you."

"She'll just laugh."

I shake my head. "No, she won't. Tell her like it's already a done deal. The only reason she gets away with the crap she does is because she plays on your guilt. She disses you, threatens you, just give her the hard stare, no budging. The only tough part is, you've got to be prepared to back it up."

"And if that doesn't work?"

"It'll work. You've already shown her today that you can play hardball. Just lay it down like you mean it and she'll cave."

"But I do feel guilty. She didn't deserve the heavy treatment I gave her today. I totally blew it."

"But look at how she treats you. No wonder you misread her. She's always playing the tough little gangsta chick. The best thing you could do for Ampora is to give her a dose of her own medicine. Talk her own language and maybe she'll finally start listening to you."

Marina shrugs. "You make it sound so easy."

"It's not so much easy, as looking at the world in a different way. Act like you're in charge, and nine times out of ten, people just accept it. Why do you think I get to sit on my ass on a picnic table outside the school every day, but I don't get expelled? Part of it's that I'm not making trouble and they know I could— especially if I call in my brother. But most of it's because I'm not entertaining any other options. I put out a 'this is the way it is' vibe, and they let it ride."

She smiles. "Yeah, but that's *you*."

"Don't kid yourself," I tell her. "Ampora knows she owes you, and I'll bet under that hard-ass mask of hers she feels just as guilty as you do. For some people, being pissed off is the way they deal with their guilt."

"Okay," she says. "I'll give it a shot. But first I have to jump in the surf so that Mamá knows I actually came down here."

"We've still got some time before we have to meet the others," I tell her. "Ride a few waves. After the day you've had, I'll bet you need it."

"You're something, you know that?"

"Something good or something bad?"

Her smile gets bigger. "Probably a bit of both." She waits a beat then adds, "So will you ever come surfing with me?"

I smile right back at her. "Will you ride on my bike?"

"I've already done that."

"True."

"So will you?"

"We get through all of this," I tell her, "and there's no end to the things I'd like to try with you."

She ducks her head, but I can see the blush. Grabbing her board, she pops it free from its wheels and runs around the rocks toward the surf.

I stand and move to the far side of the rocks to watch the poetry in motion.

Man, I can't stop smiling. Her, me. Nobody else around. It doesn't get much better than this.

JOSH

"Want to stop and grab your phone?" Des asks.

We've been walking in the direction of the beach to catch Ocean Avenue, which we'll then take out to the Pacific Coast Highway. The route takes us right through the east side of our own neighbourhood.

I shake my head. "That'd mean I'd have to talk to my mother. She's been pretty cool with all of this, but if I stop in now, she's going to want to know what I've been up to and where I'm going, and I wouldn't know what to tell her."

"There's that."

"Do *you* need to check in?"

"Nah. I already told Mom I was hanging with you and I might be late getting home."

"And what are we supposed to be doing?" I ask in case his mother asks me. It's always good to get the stories straight.

Des shrugs. "No specifics. Just hanging out."

We walk a couple more blocks before he adds, "Maybe we should have taken the Feds up on their offer of a ride, dude. It's at least a twenty-mile hike out to Tiki Bay. It's going to take us forever."

"We're not walking."

"I'm not riding you as a mountain lion," he tells me.

I have to laugh out loud at the image. "Like I could carry you."

But I know I'm strong enough to carry him in human shape and I could run the distance easily.

"Let's try hitchhiking," I say. "We haven't done that in a while."

"There's a good reason for that, dude. Nobody picks up hitchhikers anymore except for the surfers, and they're all out on the waves by now."

"Do you have money for a cab?" I ask.

"Dude. You're not seriously asking me that, are you?"

Des never has money. Soon as he gets any, he spends it.

"Then it's hitch or walk," I tell him.

"Hitchhiking it is."

There's still lots of traffic on the Pacific Coast Highway as we follow it south, but no Good Samaritans. We keep to the side of the road, sticking out our thumbs as we walk along. When we get near the Ocean Avers clubhouse I consider stopping in to get my bicycle, but I put the idea right out of my head as soon as it comes. If Chaingang's not there we'll just be walking into a whole new mess of trouble.

The sun is starting to lower onto the horizon. I figure we've got about another hour of light and there's still a long way to go. Des isn't going to like it, but if we're going to get to where the others are before the night's over, I really might have to piggyback him the rest of the way.

"Dude, we are never getting a ride," he says as another car goes whipping by.

There's just the driver, alone in a big Buick with lots of room. I watch him until a curve takes the vehicle out of sight and then give Des a glum nod.

When a white Dodge van stops for us around ten minutes later, it doesn't even register that they're offering us a ride until the driver beeps his horn. Des and I give each other a grin and sprint for the vehicle. The side door slides open and a big Latino guy smiles down at us.

"Come on in," he says.

But Des and I just stand there with our mouths open.

There are six people in the van—and all of them are Wildlings. One of them gives off the powerful vibe of one of the older cousins, the rest are like me. Newly minted. But that's not what has us staring.

I don't recognize the guy driving, or the guy giving off the old cousin vibe in the shotgun seat, but the other four I've seen a million times. On the sleeves of CDs and seven-inch vinyl singles. On YouTube and their website.

It's The Wild Surf.

Only our favourite band of all time.

Chuy Martinez, the drummer, is the one who told us to get in. Beside him is Eddie Myers, the bass player, looking thinner than ever next to Chuy's towering bulk. Behind them are La Bamba, the lead guitarist who looks like a young Mexican Elvis, but plays like Dick Dale on speed, and Joanie Jones, the singer, just as hot in person as she is on a computer screen. When she smiles at us, I feel something melt inside.

La Bamba waves a hand in front of her face.

"Jesus, Joanie," he says. "Will you tone it down?"

"But they're cute."

Joanie Jones thinks *we're* cute.

"Especially the surfer," she adds.

Okay, so she likes Des better, but she still thinks I'm cute.

"Joanie," the older man in the front seat says with a warning in his voice.

"Okay, okay."

And just like that, the melting feeling is gone. I shake my head. Joanie's still hot, but where a moment ago awareness of her seemed to fill my every nook and cranny, now I can just admire her and still think straight.

"Pheromones," Des whispers beside me.

I cringe a little. Des thinks he's being subtle, but everybody here except him is a Wildling. They all heard him. But if he's right, if that's what pheromones can do, no wonder Ampora and Sandy were so into me.

"Hey, I know you," Des says to the older guy. "You're Tomás— the L.A. Wildling godfather or whatever."

Everybody in the van laughs.

"Oh, yeah," La Bamba drawls. "The Big Kahuna himself."

"Or at least he thinks he is," Joanie adds.

They all laugh some more, then Chuy repeats his invitation: "Get in, get in."

Joanie hooks a finger at Des and pats the seat beside her. He looks at me. When I shrug, he squeezes past Chuy to sit beside her. Eddie and Chuy move over to make room for me. I close the door and the driver pulls back out onto the highway.

"We're just going up as far as Tiki Bay," I say.

"Yeah, we know, Josh," Chuy tells me.

I turn to look at him. This is too weird.

"*How* would you know?" I have to ask. "How do you even know my name?"

Eddie starts to hum the theme from *The Twilight Zone* until Chuy elbows him.

"I told them to stop," the guy in the shotgun seat says. He turns to face me. "We're going to the same meeting."

"Meeting? I thought I was just going to talk to Auntie Min. I didn't know there was going to be a whole crowd."

"We're with Tomás," Chuy says. "But we're not taking part in any meeting."

"Because it would be bor-ring," Joanie says from behind me.

"This isn't making any sense," I say. "Why's the band here? How'd you know I'd be on the highway?"

"He's our manager," Chuy says.

"Yeah," Eddie adds, "and we've got a gig in San Diego tomorrow night. Our sound crew's already gone ahead with the gear."

"Okay, but—"

"I didn't expect to see you until the meeting," Tomás says. "But when I saw you and your friend walking along the side of the road, I had Brian stop for you." He cocks his head. "Are you always this suspicious?"

"Hey, dude," Des says. "It's not paranoia when everybody *is* out to get you."

Joanie giggles. I'm fast losing any excitement I had in meeting her. She may be cool on stage and have a great voice, but here—away from the stage lights where she fronts a kick-ass band—she could be any one of a dozen or so interchangeable airheads at school.

"Who's out to get you?" La Bamba asks.

"*Every*-freaking-body, dude," Des says before I can reply. "We just had a guy with a sniper rifle taking pot shots at us."

That shuts them up for a moment. Then they all start talking at once.

"Seriously?"

"Did you get the guy?"

"Did you beat the crap out of him?"

"Either of you get hit?"

"Where was this?" Tomás says and everybody falls quiet again.

"We were just coming out of Riversea," I tell him. "On the west side of the barrio. We think it was one of the guys from Black Key Securities."

Tomás looks confused. "Okay, I know that you have some history with them, but why would they want to shoot you?"

"Someone's been killing the guys who kidnapped me. And they're making it look like it was done by a Wildling." I shake my head. "Maybe it *was* done by some Wildling, but I can't begin to figure out why."

"I hadn't heard that particular detail," Tomás says, looking a little peeved at being left out of the loop. "And it makes even less sense."

"Come on," Eddie says. "It makes perfect sense. Someone's trying to frame Josh."

Chuy nods sagely.

"Where did you hear about the Wildling connection?" Tomás asks.

"From the cops," I tell him. He gets that puzzled look again, so I add, "The Feds."

"Of course. You mean Agent Solana—the little pet of *los tíos*."

I feel the need to defend Solana.

"You shouldn't call him that," I say. "He's a good guy."

"And you know this because?"

I look Tomás straight in the eye. "Because I know him a hell of a lot better than I know you."

"Yet I was there to help with your rescue from ValentiCorp. Where was Agent Solana then?"

"Dude!" Des says. "You so bailed. You never even went into the building."

Tomás glares at him.

"And Solana was doing his job," I say. "With the limited information he had. Plus he's saved my ass any number of times since then."

"Yeah," Des says. "Who do you think chased off the sniper?"

Tomás nods. "I stand corrected. Brian," he adds, talking to the driver. "When we get to the parking lot at Tiki Bay, slow down, but don't pull in. We'll go a little farther down the road and work our way back on foot to make sure there aren't any more of these Black Key snipers lying in wait for us."

"How would they even know I'm going there?" I ask. "I just found out myself, an hour or so ago."

"How did they know to find you in the barrio?" Tomás asks.

Then he turns around to look out the windshield. Someone taps my shoulder and I turn to see it's La Bamba.

"So I hear you've got a surf band," he says.

I nod. "Yeah, we do surf and spy music. A few hot rod tunes."

"Cool. We should jam sometime."

I glance at Des and notice that Joanie's got a hand on his

thigh. This whole experience might be the most surreal thing that's happened to me yet. We're riding in a freaking van with The Wild Surf. La Bamba wants to jam with us.

"So these pheromones," I say to Joanie. "How do they work?"

"You mean the ones like you're kicking out right now?"

"I am? I mean, I don't even know that I'm doing it."

She licks her lips and smiles. "Well, they sure taste sweet."

"How do I stop doing it? Is it the same as our other heightened senses?"

She shrugs.

Chuy nods. "Yeah, you just tone it down like you do with your other senses."

"So you all do it?"

Maybe that's contributed to why they're so popular—at least along the southern coast. Pheromones aren't something that would translate well on recordings or videos. But live and on stage? That'd be a whole different story. Except Chuy shakes his head.

"No, it's only Joanie."

"Do any of you have this kind of GPS tracker thing in your head?"

"What do you mean?"

"You sort of have a mental map of everything around you and you can tell where various people and animals and things are."

Chuy's shaking his head as Tomás turns around again.

"When did this start?" he asks. His voice is a little sharp.

"This afternoon."

"That sounds handy," Eddie says. "Hey, Tomás, when do we get ours?"

Tomás shakes his head. "That's only reserved for ..." His voice trails off, then he quickly adds, "I don't know. It's different for everybody."

Except I can tell he doesn't think so.

"You ever cover any of our songs?" La Bamba asks.

As I turn in my seat to answer, Des's phone rings. He starts to reach for it, but Joanie lays her hand over his.

"You're going to talk on the phone," she says, "when you should be concentrating on me?"

It's obviously no contest. Des presses the button to kill the ring.

"Because," La Bamba goes on, as if there was no interruption, "I've always wanted to do the twin guitar thing live on tracks like 'Poppin' or 'Gimme Gimme.'"

Neither Des nor I have a chance to comment because just then we come up on the Tiki Bay parking lot. Brian slows the van down and we all look out the window. There's only a few cars there, including a Woodie like the one I saw that night when Elzie and I were down this way.

I feel a little guilty pang when I think of her and how I was drooling all over Joanie just before we got into the van. Sure, we split up a couple of weeks ago, but still. And then there's this odd thing I felt after Ampora kissed me. That's even weirder.

"Looks normal," Chuy says. "You can't expect the lot to be totally deserted."

"Yeah, it's probably just some surfers," Brian says.

Tomás nods. "But let's be safe. Keep driving until we get around that headland. You can let Josh and me off and then make your turn. The rest of you can wait for us in the parking lot."

"Des is coming with us," I say.

Tomás frowns and shakes his head. "This is cousin business."

"Then you're doing it on your own."

He gives me a hard look, but I hold his gaze until he's the one who looks away.

"Fine," he says. "Pull over here, Brian."

"You're really going to leave?" Joanie whines, looking all doe-eyed at Des. "We're just starting to get to know each other."

"Hold that thought," Des says, as he lifts her hand from his thigh and kisses it.

Brian pulls over to the shoulder and the three of us get out. I look back into the van before I slide the door closed. Chuy gives me a thumbs-up. Eddie nods. La Bamba makes a gun with his hand and pretends to shoot it.

"Give 'em hell, kid," he says.

Joanie pouts.

Then the door slides closed and the van pulls back onto the highway.

MARINA

I take a shower as soon as I get back home, then go find Mamá.
She's still in the kitchen making dinner. My stepdad, Jim, is in
the dining room reading the news on his iPad while waiting for
supper to be ready.

"Did the surfing help?" Mamá asks.

I nod. "A little."

I talk about the waves—the ones I missed, the couple I
caught. She doesn't really know anything about surfing, but she
likes to listen to my enthusiasm. When my cell rings, I pretend
it's my stepmother, Elena, instead of who it really is: Theo.

"It's Elena," I tell Mamá. "Is it okay if I go over and babysit
the girls?"

"Right now?"

I nod.

"It seems very short notice."

"Something came up. It's only until Ampora gets home."

Mamá gives me a worried look. "Is that really such a good
idea?"

I know she's thinking about the conversation we had earlier,
and it's obvious she doesn't think Ampora and I should be

together with no one else around to referee, except for our little stepsisters.

"It'll be okay," I say.

"Have you done your homework?" Jim calls from the dining room.

"Of course."

"Then let her go, Nita."

Mamá nods. "All right. How late will you be?"

I repeat the question into the phone.

"She says not long," I lie. Then I add into the phone, "I'll be right over."

Five minutes later, Jim is driving me over to Papá's house. I get him to let me off at the corner store to buy some treats for the girls and tell him he doesn't have to wait. He hesitates, but we're close to Papá's house. I know he gets uncomfortable around Papá and Elena, so he's probably happy for the excuse not to run into either of them.

"Be careful," he says.

He thinks the barrio is a scary place, but it's not even dark yet. I may live on the other side of town, but this neighbourhood will always be my home. But I keep that thought to myself.

"I will," I say. "Thanks for the ride, Jim."

I give him a kiss on the cheek and I'm out the door before he can change his mind. He watches me go into the store, where I buy each of the girls a package of gummi bears. I watch him from inside as I'm paying. I wait until he turns the car around and heads back home before I step back outside and call Ampora.

Theo told me: you don't do this over the phone. You do it in her face and you don't give her the chance to say no.

I practice with this phone call.

"Meet me in the park," I tell her when she answers. "Right now."

"Why the hell would I—"

"Just do it," I say and I hang up.

I'm sitting on a swing when she comes storming into the playground area, her face dark with anger.

"Here's how it's going to work," I say before she gets a chance to talk.

But she barrels right over what I'm about to say. "Give me one good reason why I shouldn't punch you in the face."

The unfamiliar temper that's been plaguing me all day has me on my feet and I'm about to take a swing at her myself before I manage to rein it in. I take a steadying breath.

"I need you to cover for me in case Mamá calls," I tell her.

She laughs. "Like that's ever going to happen."

"And if she does call," I go on, "just tell her that we're talking things out and I'll be home later."

"Seriously, have you been smoking loco weed?"

"If you don't," I tell her. "If you screw me over, Papá's going to find out just how sweet a daughter you really are, starting with everything that happened today."

"You wouldn't."

"I will if you don't cover for me."

Her eyes are still flashing with anger, but now her curiosity wins over.

"What are you planning to do?"

"It's none of your business."

She smiles—that mean smile of hers that she has down to an art and throws at me every day at school.

"Either you tell me," she says, "or I won't cover for you."

I hesitate. Theo told me that if I try to explain myself it'll just show weakness, but as crappy as she treats me, she's still my sister. Once upon a time, we were best friends and I'd love to get that back again. But it's not going to happen if I stoop down to her level of meanness.

"It's just to clean up a few loose ends from what happened today," I tell her.

"You mean gang stuff."

My good intentions wash away and I feel like hitting her again.

"Gang stuff that *you* put in motion."

"Hey, those losers think they can waltz into this park and set up shop, they—"

I stop her with a raised hand. I take another breath and let it out while I try to ignore the way she's glaring at me.

"I get it," I tell her. "I agree. I think you were brave to do what you did." Stupid, but brave, but I don't say that out loud. "There aren't many people who would step up like that. I'm so sorry I doubted you."

That seems to take her off guard.

"You really think that?" she says.

I nod. "I really do."

"So this has to do with Josh and what happened today?"

I nod again.

"Then I'm coming," she says.

"What? Why would you come?"

And then she actually looks away and blushes. I don't think I've ever seen Ampora blush.

"It's just," she says, "you know ... after he helped me ..."

Oh my God.

"You're *interested* in him?" I say.

She tries to shrug it off. "He's a nice guy. Why are you so surprised? You pined over him for years."

"I guess I did."

"But not anymore, right? That's what you said."

I'm having so much trouble processing this. My sister and *Josh*?

"Does he—know that you're interested in him?"

"I think so. That's why I have to come."

"Will you just trust me in this?" I ask. "The most help you can be right now is to cover for me."

"What can you do that I can't?"

"I'm going to a ... meeting, I guess you could call it. But it's private. You're not invited and if I show up with you, the whole thing could get called off. We can't let that happen because it took a long time to set it up."

She studies me for a long moment.

"Just what are you really into?" she finally asks.

"Maybe I can tell you all about it one day. But not now."

Except she's not ready to let it go. "Does this have anything to do with Wildlings?"

I can't hide my shock. What does she know?

"Why—why would you ask that?" I manage to say. "You don't even believe they're real."

"I do now. Josh showed me."

Can this day get any stranger? Ampora crushing on Josh. Josh telling her—showing her?—he's a Wildling. Is there anybody he hasn't told?

"And just like that, you're okay with it?"

I see a moment of vulnerability in her eyes.

"I don't know. All I know is what I saw."

"But what about the government conspiracies and all that stuff you're always on about?"

"I guess I was wrong," she says.

"Do I even *know* you anymore?"

"I could ask you the same thing. What secrets are *you* hiding?"

"They're not mine to share."

"But Josh already told me he's a Wildling."

I nod. "Okay then, since he's your big confidant, ask *him* about secrets." Then, before she asks me anything else, I pull the packages of gummi bears from my pocket and add, "These are for the girls."

"Okay."

"So you'll cover for me?"

"Sure. But this doesn't mean I like you any better."

I smile. "You're going to need to work on that if you plan to be hanging with Josh."

I walk away as she thinks about that. As soon as I turn the corner I call Theo.

"So how did it go?" he asks me a short while later, as I get onto the back of his bike.

"Fine. It was ... interesting."

He turns to look at me. "Interesting how?"

"I think she's crushing on Josh."

Theo's brows go up. "Well, I can understand the basic attraction. That is, if he's crushing on her."

"Oh, *really?*"

"Sure. There's good genes in your family."

I smile. "Good recovery."

"Nothing to recover from," he says, his eyes earnest. "You need to understand that you're the one for me, nobody else."

I wish we could just stay in this moment, but I have to tell him the rest.

"Plus she knows he's a Wildling," I say. "Josh told her."

"Tell me you're joking."

"I wish. She says he *showed* her."

Theo starts to say something, then shakes his head.

"I'm going to assume he knows what he's doing," he says.

He gives me a kiss, then turns around and starts the bike. I wrap my arms around his waist and press my cheek into his back.

The world's turning upside down, but at least I've got this. *We've* got this.

Halfway to Tiki Bay Theo suddenly pulls over to the side of the road.

"Why are we stopping?" I ask.

Theo shakes his head. "I'm so stupid."

"What? Why are you stupid?"

I get off the bike so I can see his face.

"I didn't put it together," he says.

He looks so fierce I could be afraid of him, except I know in my heart that he'd never hurt me. I put my hand on his arm.

"Theo, tell me what's wrong."

"Tiki Bay is what's wrong. That's where Vincenzo killed Lenny."

A chill runs up my spine.

"Exactly," Theo says, reading my face. "This feels like a set-up. I'm already jumpy because there's been no sign of Vincenzo for a while."

"But I thought it was Auntie Min and Cory who picked the location. I can't see either of them betraying Josh."

"What do we really know about them?" he says. "All I know for sure is that they've been keeping things from us. That's a given."

I find myself nodding. What little interaction I've had with either has been frustrating. They only ever tell us so much.

"Do you think Vincenzo's working *with* the elders?" I ask.

"Honestly? I don't know my ass from a hole in the ground anymore."

I can't help it. That makes me laugh. Theo smiles and I can feel his tension ebb.

"But we have to keep going," I say. "If it *is* a trap, Josh is already on his way."

He nods. "I'll call Des. Josh hasn't got his phone with him. But we have to be careful. I ..."

He lets the word just hang there.

"You what?" I ask.

"Okay, you can get mad at me, but I wish you weren't here. If anything happens to you ..."

I smile. "Actually, I find that sweet. But I'm a tough surfer chick. You don't have to worry about me."

"I know you're tough. But I'm still going to worry."

JOSH

"Okay, that was weird," Des says once the van pulls away.

"You mean getting a ride from The Wild Surf," I say, "or having Joanie Jones fawning all over you?"

"Both. Dude, what is wrong with that woman?"

"I would have thought you'd be loving it."

He nods. "So would I—if you'd asked me any time before today. Now? Not so much. And I don't get it. Why is she into *me*? I'm not putting out the pheromones or anything."

"I get the feeling she just likes to hook guys in for the fun of it."

"So why wasn't she affected by yours?"

"Beats me. Maybe she knows how to filter them out. It's all just one more complication I don't need."

Des grins. "Still, dude. It's not the worst superpower to have."

Tomás shushes us. "Keep it down. We need to make sure none of those Black Key operatives are nearby."

"Relax," I tell him. I've already had my internal radar turned up, surveying the area around us. "There are a couple of people up on the headland—Cory, and someone I don't recognize, but I'm guessing it's Auntie Min since I'm getting the big-cousin vibe from her. Besides them, there are a half-dozen kids building a fire on the beach and a couple making out in one of the cars in the parking lot."

"Cool," Des says, and I don't know if he means the couple going hot and heavy or the fact that I'm aware of all of this.

"We still need to be careful," Tomás says.

I give him a curious look.

He doesn't have it, I realize. This radar thing I have in my head, that's not in his particular repertoire.

I start thinking about everything Des told me about this guy when he showed up at ValentiCorp. What stands out the most is how Chaingang was always in his face. Now that I've met him myself, I can see why. There's something about him that rubs me the wrong way, too.

"Come on," I say to Des. "Let's get this over with."

I turn away from the highway and start up the incline of the headland instead of going around by the parking lot. Des is right behind me. Tomás watches us for a moment, then mutters something under his breath and follows as well.

The tall grass is brown and stiff, but easy to push through. The incline is steep, loose dirt sliding under our feet. I keep scanning the area as we climb. Nothing much seems to have changed, except that The Wild Surf's van has pulled into the parking lot. The band and their driver are sitting in their van. Everything else is the way it should be. There aren't any surprises. No snipers sneaking up on us. No hawk uncles hanging around nearby. No FBI agents.

But then I do get a surprise. Through the sporadic traffic on the highway, I home in on a motorcycle with two very familiar people on it.

"Huh," I say.

I don't realize I've made the sound aloud until Des says, "Dude?"

"Did you know that Chaingang and Marina are an item?" I ask him.

"What are you talking about?"

"Chaingang told me he had a girlfriend, but he didn't say who it was. Now I'm guessing it's Marina. You should see the way their auras entwine."

"Marina and Chaingang hooking up?" Des says. "No. Way."

I tap my temple. "The system doesn't lie."

"And since when do you say 'auras'?" He waits a beat, then adds, "Are you okay with this, dude?"

Actually, I do have a weird twinge in my stomach, but I decide to ignore it.

"Why would I have a problem?" I say.

"Well, it's Marina. And Chaingang's brother runs the Ocean Avers. Do you really want Marina mixed up in that?"

"They're both friends of mine," I say. "I'm—I'm happy for them."

"Dude! Did you not hear what I said? I don't care how much you like Chaingang, he's still all heavy into drugs and guns and who knows what kind of crap."

"I know," I say, but I'm only half-listening to him.

My radar lets me watch the bike pulling into the parking lot, Chaingang and Marina getting off. When they stay in the lot, I realize that Chaingang's checking things out for an ambush. I do another sweep myself. Still nothing. Finally they start climbing up to the headland where we're headed.

"We have a meeting to attend to," Tomás says.

I nod. "I haven't forgotten. We're just going to wait on my friends. Safety in numbers, right?"

"Safety from what?"

"You tell me."

"We aren't the enemy," Tomás says.

"That's easy to say—harder to prove. You go on ahead. We'll catch up to you when Chaingang and Marina get here."

"No, I'll wait with you."

"Suit yourself."

I turn away and start climbing again, angling my ascent so that we meet up with Chaingang and Marina before they reach the top. They're holding hands, but let go when they see us. I lift my eyebrows and meet Chaingang's gaze. I don't know what he's looking for—a challenge? approval?—but after a moment he takes Marina's hand again. In his free hand he's carrying a tire iron.

"Hey," I say.

Marina's searching my face as well with a worried, guilty look.

"Really?" I say. "What makes you think I wouldn't be happy for you guys?"

I see her visibly relax. She returns my smile, then looks to Des, who shrugs.

"Whatever, dude," he says. "Just don't start dealing drugs or beating me up."

"Asshole," she says and we laugh.

Even Chaingang cracks a smile. But then he points his tire iron at Tomás.

"What the hell are *you* doing here?" he says.

"What's wrong with you kids?" Tomás says. "Can't you see we're just trying to help you?"

"Yeah, you were a big help the last time we got together. Tell me, did *you* pick this spot for us to meet?"

He shakes his head. "Señora Catalina thought it best that we get together away from prying eyes. Why do you ask?"

Chaingang shrugs. "No reason. Let's go see what she's got to say."

He gives me a nod and I lead the rest of the way to the top.

As soon as I crest the headland, I stop dead in my tracks, caught by the wonder of the last of the sun going down on the Pacific horizon. I don't often get to see it so far from Santa Feliz's light pollution, so I forget just how killer the sunsets are around here.

"You were right," Des says. "There's just the two of them up here."

I tear my gaze away from the horizon to focus on the pair waiting for us.

Auntie Min's pretty much what I expected from Des and Marina's descriptions of her. She's an old Indian woman with sloped shoulders. Her skin is brown and her black hair hangs in a long single braid upon her red shawl. Her face is broad, nose flat, eyes dark and wide-set. Under the shawl she wears a white blouse, and a blue cotton skirt falls to the ground, hiding her feet.

I head for where she and Cory are standing, my companions trailing along behind me as we walk through the tall grass to the big flat outcrop where they're waiting for us. I hear the waves crashing on the rocks below. The air's thick with the smell of salt and beach debris. When I get close, Auntie Min puts her hands together like she's about to pray and smiles at me.

"Welcome, young lion," she says. "I am Señora Catalina Mariposa, of the Black Witch Moth Clan. It is my great pleasure to meet you."

"I thought your name was Auntie Min."

She shrugs. "Some of us have more than one. We gather names through the years the way a cholla attaches itself to the unwary."

I hold up a hand before she can go on.

"I'm sure you're a perfectly nice person," I tell her, "and I mean no disrespect, but you need to know that I didn't really want to come here. And I'm not interested in flowery language or vague explanations. If we're going to do this, you need to talk straight or I'm gone."

"Easy there, Josh," Cory says. "Show a little—"

But Auntie Min cuts him off.

"It's all right," she says. "Josh has merely stated his wishes and he has done so without rudeness. I appreciate his honesty. I'm glad you all could come," she adds, welcoming the others.

"Why'd you pick this spot?" Chaingang asks.

If she's noticed the tire iron dangling from his hand, she makes no mention of it.

"This was a sacred place in the long ago," she tells him, "and it still holds echoes of that time. The veils are thinner here. If you listen closely, sometimes you can hear the waves of the otherworld harmonize with those that break against the rocks below."

Tomás makes a protesting noise and Auntie Min turns to him.

"What?" she asks.

"We aren't all cousins here."

"True," she says. "But Desmond is Josh's blood brother. They will have no secrets from each other." She looks at me with a smile. "Is that not so?"

I nod. "Yeah, Des is cool."

Des grins and punches me lightly on the shoulder.

Auntie Min returns her attention to Chaingang. "Why are you so uncomfortable in this place?"

"Vincenzo killed Lenny here," Chaingang tells her. He points with the tire iron. "Down there—on the beach."

The easy friendliness of her features goes hard.

"You're sure it was him?"

"I know the face of the guy who did it. Donalita confirmed his name for me."

"Who's Vincenzo?" I ask.

Chaingang turns to me. "One of the older cousins. He wants me to kill you. If I don't, he'll start getting rid of the people I care about the most, starting with my grandmother. You saw him outside the taquería earlier today."

"The homeless guy? And he's still in one piece?"

"Believe me, I tried. I couldn't lay a hand on him."

"And you're only telling me this *now*?"

He shrugs. "Maybe it was a bad call, bro. But I didn't want you going off half-cocked and have him take you out. The smart thing seemed to be to get some background first—see what his weaknesses are, figure out how to take him down without any collateral damage. Are you feeling me?"

I look at Marina.

"Yeah, she knew," Chaingang says before she can speak. "It's on me that she didn't tell you. She wanted to."

They're both watching me now, waiting. Marina is hugging

herself, clearly anxious—probably because of what happened the last time she kept a big secret from me. I can't read Chaingang's expression.

I think about the past couple of days. How I've been right in everybody's face as soon as I felt threatened. I suppose I should feel shocked with this news, but the truth is, I'm exhausted. At this point, it would be unusual if someone out there *didn't* want to kill or use me.

"You made the right call," I tell them. "I've had enough on my plate."

"So we're good?" Chaingang asks.

I nod and offer him my fist. He gives it a bump.

"I find this very troubling," Auntie Min says. "Vincenzo threatened your family?"

Chaingang nods.

"What can he possibly expect to gain by this?" she says. "Josh is our hope for going into the future."

I want to interject here, but Chaingang responds before I can.

"I think he figures that with Josh gone things can get back to how they were before we Wildlings started showing up. He made it clear he wanted Josh's death to look like it had been done by a human—maybe that's so he doesn't get any blowback from the other older cousins—but I'm pretty sure he plans to kill off the rest of the Wildlings himself."

"That doesn't make any sense," Auntie Min says.

Chaingang shrugs. "All I know is he's hardcore. He's super pissed off that Wildlings even exist and that they're not keeping a low enough profile. Donalita told me that he killed her sister just because she brought a human over to that otherworld. I guess he figures if there aren't any more Wildlings, all of this will just fade away. You know, like an urban legend. Never real in the first place."

Auntie Min shakes her head and turns to Tomás. "Is Vincenzo capable of this?"

"Why not? He's Condor Clan. All the carrion eaters thrive on chaos—they eat better in times of war."

"Hey!" Cory says.

"Present company excluded," Tomás adds, but it's easy to tell he doesn't mean it.

Auntie Min looks pointedly at him. "You might remember, Tomás, that the carrion eaters are an essential part of the cycle of life."

"Sure. But that doesn't mean I have to like—"

Auntie Min cuts him off. "Perhaps you should be having this conversation with Raven."

That shuts Tomás up, but I don't know why.

"Who's Raven?" I ask.

"He was here before the world was made," Cory says. "Back then, there was only Raven and a couple of crows hanging around until he stirred the world into being out of that big old cauldron of his."

"Yeah, right," Chaingang says.

He looks at me and rolls his eyes.

I get it. Things are strange enough without buying into the idea that the whole world came into being because some raven was brewing stuff up in a pot. So much for them dropping the flowery talk.

"Is this war?" Auntie Min asks, bringing everything back to the here and now.

Tomás shrugs.

"It is, so far as I'm concerned," Chaingang says.

Auntie Min turns to him. "I need to hear everything that has happened—from the beginning."

She's an old woman, but she seems to just float as she grace-fully settles down into a half-lotus. Her gaze stays on Chaingang, expectant, until we all sit down and tell her what we know.

It takes a while. When it's my turn, I don't hold anything back. If I'm going to figure out why this is happening to me, I have to give them all the information I've got. When I get to the part about meeting the uncles in the skatepark, and the internal radar system in my head, Auntie Min and Cory study me with renewed interest. Tomás looks away, a sour look on his face. But no one says anything. They just let me continue.

After talking about the park, and how a hawk stopped me from following the guy I now know was Vincenzo, I start to run out of steam. I let Des pick the story up. He tells the part about the sniper attack, talking to the FBI, the weird business with pheromones and getting here.

As Des is finishing his part of the story, I notice that Chaingang keeps looking around like he still thinks it's a trap.

"It's cool," I tell him softly, so as not to interrupt Des. "There's no one around who shouldn't be."

"Yeah?"

"Yeah. This GPS thing in my head's pretty damn accurate. I knew you two were coming long before you pulled into the parking lot."

"What kind of range do you have?"

"Honestly, I have no idea. It feels like it could go on forever if I don't keep a lid on it."

"What did you say?" Auntie Min asks.

Everybody's looking at me.

I repeat what I just told Chaingang.

"This changes everything," Auntie Min says.

I don't like the sound of that.

"Changes everything how?" I ask.

For a moment it seems as though a big black moth fills the air behind her. Her skin seems to glow and grow tight, as though it's too small to contain her. Then the moment passes and she's just an old Indian woman again, though she's still got that big-time Wildling vibe.

"I thought the Thunders had sent you to take my place," she says. "But now I see they have larger plans for you."

Crap. Could this get any worse?

"The Thunders?" I repeat slowly, looking at Chaingang and Marina, then back to the older cousins. This is so not computing. "What does that even mean? I asked you to talk straight with me."

"I am," Auntie Min says. "You understand that everything's connected?"

"In theory, I guess. But how does any of this relate to what's happening to me?"

"We are all here as caretakers," she says. "We are here to look after each other and the land upon which we live. As individuals, we care for those directly around us and the acres upon which we tread. But some of us have more responsibilities. Tomás and I—and others like us—look after the well-being of *all* the individuals and all of the land under our protection. We are given to see a larger picture. The canvas upon which we do our work is broader than it is for others. And the Thunders—the great spirits—they look after us all."

"You say you're looking after the land," Chaingang says while I'm trying to digest all of this. "So why are there buildings and streets and pavement and crap everywhere?"

"The land is still there—underneath. The earth spirits are patient. They know that what the humans lay upon them will all pass away in time."

Chaingang shakes his head. "So you do—what, nothing? Just sit back and watch?"

"I remember them," Auntie Min says. "I talk to them. Sing them their songs. Tell them their histories. I let them know that they are not forgotten and remind them that the time will come again when they will be freed of the burden they carry now."

"And you're doing a good job of that?" Chaingang asks.

"I do my best. I have been the caretaker of this land for longer than even I can remember," she says. "But I grow old. My stamina is not what it was. And I'm beginning to forget the stories—the histories of the spirits under my care. I believed that was why the young lion has been sent. To replace me."

I want to puke. This was so not my life plan. I get this insane mental image of strapping on my guitar, turning my amp to full volume and wailing out my frustration through music. But playing guitar seems like a distant memory now.

"Okay," Chaingang says. "Now I get it." He jerks a thumb in Tomás's direction. "L.A.'s here because he's hoping to grab your territory."

Tomás bristles. "Don't presume to—"

Auntie Min holds up a hand to stop him.

"You're partly right," she tells Chaingang. "But Tomás is here at my request. He is younger and stronger than me. If I should fail before a replacement can be found, he will have to step in.

The connection he has to Los Angeles will also embrace Santa Feliz."

Marina is shaking her head, maybe having the same thoughts as me about giving up on the band, school, hanging out at the skatepark and stuff.

"You thought Josh was your *replacement*?" Marina asks.

"I didn't think so at first. At first I thought he was to be the bridge between our worlds: that of the cousins and the humans. Then, when I sensed his affinity to the land under my care, I realized perhaps the Thunders had sent him to take my place. To be my apprentice."

"Do you still think that?" Chaingang asks.

Auntie Min shakes her head. "I'm not sure. I only know the Thunders sent him to us, and that they have a purpose. Just as all of you children becoming cousins has a purpose."

"So someone's been waking up the Wildlings in us," Chaingang says, "until they got Josh."

"Or someone like him. Someone from the old clans."

"I've been saying that all along," Cory puts in.

It's weird listening to them talk about me as though I'm not even here, but I don't want to participate in this conversation anyway. I just want my old life back.

"Okay," Chaingang says, "so then maybe you can tell us this: why does Vincenzo want Josh dead?"

"I don't know," Cory says.

Auntie Min shakes her head as well.

"Maybe *los tíos* can tell us," Tomás says. "They seem to have been watching Josh for a while."

This could go on all night.

"Look," I say. "I appreciate everybody putting in their two

cents, but I don't know any more now than I did before I arrived. Nobody actually *knows* anything. But we've got a lot to think about—which is what I'm going to do after I get a good night's sleep. I'll tell you this much. I'm not going to be anybody's leader. I've got enough crap going on in my life without taking on responsibilities that I don't even understand."

"But if the Thunders have a plan for you …" Cory begins.

"Then they're going to have to spell it out for me," I tell him. "And then I'll decide what I'm going to do."

Cory's shaking his head. "Sometimes you just have to step up and learn as you go. You don't get to make the choice—the choice picks you."

"I'm only here because I promised you I'd come, after you did me that favour by dealing with Erik."

"Favour?" Auntie Min says. "The little cousins won't stop gossiping about it. He did you no favour dealing with that boy the way he did. Everything is sacred in the eyes of the Thunders—even the humans."

"The kid got what he deserved," Chaingang says. "He's lucky it was Cory who paid him a visit instead of me."

"I just want to know, what *did* you do to him?" Des asks.

"He dropped him off in the otherworld," Marina says before Cory can answer. "On top of some mountain. I saw Erik just before school was over and he was a total mess." She waits a beat before adding, "But he was humble."

"Otherworld, huh? You'd better watch your ass," Chaingang tells Cory. "If Vincenzo finds out, he'll be gunning for you like he did with Donalita's sister."

"Perhaps the boy was humbled," Auntie Min says, "but was it still such a wise thing to do?"

"You didn't see Josh's face," Chaingang says.

"There are secrets we cannot share with the five-fingered beings."

Yeah, I think. Like that whole other pristine world, ready to be plundered.

"If the boy talks about his experience ..." Auntie Min goes on.

"Erik thinks he was drugged," Marina says.

"And if anyone digs a little," Chaingang adds, "they'll find that his squeaky-clean Purity Club image is just a mask to hide one more dumb-ass doper. Nobody's going to believe a thing he says."

Tomás gives Cory a warning look. "So maybe we got lucky, but this is still exactly the kind of thing that could blow up in our faces."

"As I was saying," I say, and this time I stand up, "I'm heading home. The Thunders or anybody else wants to find me, that's where I'll be."

But before I can leave, the GPS in my head goes haywire. I'm looking right at a spot between where Auntie Min is sitting and the drop to the rocks below. I don't see anything, but the GPS tells me that there's a big-time cousin standing there.

Then he steps through out of nowhere—that same tall, dark-skinned guy I saw in the barrio. The one Chaingang says wants to see me dead.

"Oh, fuck," Chaingang says.

CHAINGANG

I'm on my feet before Vincenzo has stepped all the way through. He's moving fast, but not fast enough to stop me from getting a glimpse of the otherworld. Then it's gone and he's standing there, cocky and tall, with the cliff behind him, like he owns the world.

I'm so pissed off at myself.

I *knew* this was a trap. I *knew* we were being played.

Why did I have to be right? I don't know which of them set us up—Auntie Min, Cory or Tomás—but at least one of them did.

And why the hell didn't I bring a gun? Vincenzo might be fast, but no one outruns a bullet. One shot to the head and he wouldn't be playing Josh's resurrection trick. You'd need a brain to pull off the switch from human to animal shape and back again.

But all I'm carrying is my tire iron and he's got us all dead to rights.

Maybe he thinks that means I'm going to roll over. Someone should have told him that's not going to happen. When I go down, I'll go fighting.

I'm on my feet and standing between him and Marina without even having to think about it.

Vincenzo shakes his head. "I see that family ties don't mean so much to you after all."

"If you lay so much as a hand on my—"

He talks right over me. "Too late. As soon as we're finished here, the old woman dies next."

I know he's just pushing my buttons. I know I've got to be smart about this. But knowing doesn't help. Soon as he threatens Grandma, I see red and charge him.

The only thing I've got going for me is that Cory and Tomás are also coming at him.

Okay. Maybe I've got a chance. Maybe *we've* got a chance.

I lift the tire iron, moving as fast as I can. Anybody human seeing this, I'd be just a blur. But it's not enough.

He hits me with a backhand and it's like I got clipped by a speeding car. It rocks my head and I literally see stars. The force of the blow actually sends me airborne.

But I'm already planning my next move. Tuck in and hit the grass, then roll back to my feet and throw the tire iron as hard and fast as I can. With any luck he'll be too busy with Cory and Tomás to even see it coming.

Except I don't hit the grass.

I land on my back on the edge of the outcrop and I hear something go *crack*. Then my head hits the stone right after. The tire iron drops from my suddenly limp fingers. I try to get up but nothing seems to work. I can't move my arms or legs. I can't even lift my head. I—

Fuck me. I think he broke my back.

Then everything goes black.

JOSH

Vincenzo's sudden appearance catches me completely off guard. I don't even have a chance to react before Chaingang is already down. Then Cory and Tomás are on the guy. I know how fast and strong Wildlings are. Tough as Vincenzo is, they still should have been able to take him. I mean—come on. It's two to one. But Vincenzo plucks Cory from the air like he's nothing more than a child's toy and flings him over the edge of the headland to fall on the rocks below. Then he grabs Tomás by the head, a hand on either side of his face. One twist and he snaps Tomás's neck.

Only seconds have passed. I'm just starting to lunge forward when Vincenzo heaves Tomás's body at me. It knocks me to the ground, but I'm only down for a moment. I push the body off and jump to my feet.

I see Marina running for where Chaingang's lying so still. Cory's gone. Auntie Min's staring in shock. I feel Des moving beside me.

"Don't," I tell him. "This guy's mine."

But before I can attack, Vincenzo says one word that stops me in my tracks:

"Elzie."

He smiles at my hesitation.

"I thought that might get your attention," he says. "She's such a free spirit, don't you think? Or at least she was."

"What have you done to her?"

"Nothing—at least not yet. I have a little task for you. Do a good job and she goes free. Fail and you'll get to watch everyone you love die before I kill you."

"Why are you *doing* this?"

"*We* don't believe in messiahs."

"What's that supposed to mean?"

His gaze is locked on me. Without looking, he points a finger at Auntie Min as she comes to her feet.

"Don't make me kill you, old woman," he says. "L.A. can stand to lose its caretaker—the city's been a lost cause for years—but Santa Feliz needs you. Once these children are gone, the spirits of the land will be in turmoil. You will have much mending to do."

"When the other elders—"

"The elders will do nothing," Vincenzo says. "I insult the honour of no clan. All I have in mind is to rid the world of these five-fingered children pretending to be cousins."

"You interfere with the will of the Thunders."

Vincenzo shakes his head. "I doubt that. Do you really think they want our existence revealed so that the five-fingered beings can hunt us down for their pleasure? That we give up the secret of the otherworld so it can be pillaged the way this world has been? If I am offending the Thunders, they will deal with me, but I think you will have to wait a long time for that to come about.

"Now, boy," he adds, turning back to me. "There is a rally protesting the existence of you Wildlings this weekend. You will go to the rally. You will work yourself close to the stage. You will leap up onto it and change in front of all the people and their cameras. Then you will kill Clayton Householder."

"How's that supposed to stop people from knowing about Wildlings?" I say. "You're just making it worse for us—and yourselves."

"Everyone has already heard about Wildlings. They aren't my concern. The cousins are. I want them to see you as dangerous, so that when your bodies start showing up they will be relieved that the problem has been solved for them. Let the five-fingered beings have your bodies to cut up in their laboratories. They won't find anything because their parameters could never envision the existence of the Thunders. But we will not allow our own people to be further compromised by you pretenders. We must clean up the mess you've made.

"And don't make the mistake of thinking I'm alone in this. We're not all content to live on the fringes of your poisoning cities, begging for scraps."

"'We'?" Auntie Min says. "Who makes up this 'we'? Give me their names."

"Old woman, be still." His dark eyes fix on me. "Well, boy. Does your Elzie and everyone you care for die, or will you do this little thing for me?"

"You'll just kill us all anyway."

"That's true. But your deaths will be quick and I promise not to harm any of the five-fingered beings in your life."

"There'll be Secret Service there. They'll shoot me down before I ever get close to the congressman."

"Then you'll have to be quicker than them, won't you?"

"I don't get it. Why kill Householder?"

"He annoys me. He's a public figure. But more to the point, he's far too tenacious. When the pretenders are all dead, he'll still be out there looking for more, and it won't be long before he stumbles over the cousins."

"This is madness," Auntie Min says. "Householder's death will have the exact opposite result. All you will accomplish is to turn him into a martyr and the five-fingered beings will never stop hunting us."

"No, with Householder and the pretenders gone it will all dissipate. Humans would rather not believe in our existence."

"They've got hours of video," I say. "It's not going away."

His dark gaze settles on me again.

"Just do what I tell you," he says. "Let me worry about what comes after."

"Because I won't be here to see it."

"But your girlfriend and your friends and family will be. You won't see me again unless you fail. If that happens, we'll meet again with the bodies of all you love scattered around us."

Except Chaingang's already down. Marina's on his target list. And no matter what he says, Elzie will die, too, because she's a Wildling. She might already be dead. I have no way of knowing what is a lie and what's not.

And then there are all the Wildling kids I don't know. None of us asked for this. We shouldn't have to die just because we're an inconvenience to Vincenzo and his friends.

I'm not going to let that happen.

I need to end this before anybody else dies or gets hurt.

And I'm not going to make the mistake everybody else has of taking him on in my human form. Not when I've got the advantage of the sheer ferocity, speed and strength that the mountain lion can bring to a fight.

Vincenzo turns away, stepping back into the passageway that will take him away to the otherworld. Auntie Min looks stunned. Tomás is dead. Cory went over the cliff. He's probably dead, too. Marina's on her knees beside Chaingang, trying to bring him around. Des is crouched beside her, but he's white as a sheet and looking at me. He starts to shake his head as I change into the mountain lion.

Vincenzo is almost all the way to the other side.

Before the passageway between the worlds can close, I leap through it after him.

MARINA

Theo is limp and unresponsive no matter how many times I've stroked his face and called his name. Des is over here trying to help, but suddenly he jerks his head toward where the others are. I follow Des's stare just in time to see Vincenzo disappear and Josh switch to his mountain lion form, then leap after Vincenzo into the otherworld.

"Josh, no!" I cry.

I race from Theo's side and throw myself at the disappearing passageway. But fast as I can move, I'm still too late. The passageway vanishes and I skid right to the edge of the headland. Rocks and rubble roll down from the rim, bouncing off the cliff face to the waves below. My balance is all wrong and I'm about to fall over myself, except Auntie Min grabs me by the scruff of my shirt and hauls me back.

I sit there at the edge when she lets me go, unable to trust my legs. For a long moment, I stare out across the darkening ocean. I can't believe it all went bad so fast. Finally I turn around to look at Auntie Min.

"We have to go after him," I say.

I think of how easily Vincenzo handled Theo—Theo!—and the others. What chance does Josh have on his own?

Auntie Min shakes her head. "Josh has made his decision and we should respect it. We have enough to deal with here."

"But—"

"Either the Thunders have given him the strength to deal with Vincenzo, or they haven't. Our being there with him will not make a difference either way." She lays a hand on my head, fingers smoothing my hair. "See to Theo, little otter. He is the one you can help today. I will go to Cory."

Huge moth wings unfold from her back with a sudden snap. She steps off the edge of the headland and glides downward, out of sight.

I turn back to where Theo's lying. Des is still crouched beside him, but he's staring open-mouthed at where Auntie Min was standing. When he sees me looking at him, he gives a little shake of his head as though to clear it, then returns his attention to Theo. I hurry over.

"You're not supposed to move somebody with a back injury!" I tell him when I see what he's doing.

He's shaking Theo's shoulder, trying to rouse him.

I push him away and take out my phone. "We need to get him to a hospital."

"No," Des says, "we need to get him to wake up so that he can pull that trick of Josh's."

"He's not dead," I say.

At least, not yet. Please, not ever. But everything's gone so horribly wrong. It's all I can do to keep a lid on my feelings and not dissolve into panic.

"And I don't think that trick works for everyone," I add. "If it did, Tomás would already be up and about."

"That dude is dead. I'm not talking about resurrection. I'm talking about the healing factor you Wildlings have. Remember how beat-up Josh was? Or how about the guy who was with him in the ValentiCorp lab?"

"You mean Rico."

Des nods. "They cut off his leg, right? But he switched to his animal shape and when he returned to his human shape, that leg was back like he'd never lost it."

Now I understand and put my phone away.

"Except you have to be awake to do it," I say.

It all feels so hopeless. Josh is gone. Tomás is dead. Cory's probably dead. And Theo ...

I can't get it out of my head, the horrible cracking sound of him hitting the rock. It makes me sick just thinking about it.

Auntie Min comes back, those big wings carrying her up from the rocks below. I get a shiver looking at her, remembering the stories Mamá used to tell Ampora and me about *Mariposa de la Muerte*. At this moment, Auntie Min looks just like some harbinger of death.

She lands lightly on the rock. Her wings disappear when her feet touch the stone.

"Cory's making his way back up," she says. "He managed to hit the water." Her gaze goes to Tomás, then Theo. "At least your Theo's still breathing."

"Except we can't rouse him so that he can heal himself."

"Just keep trying."

"Why didn't you do anything?" I ask. "When the others attacked Vincenzo."

"None of us should have done anything," she says. "It was obvious at that moment that he was too strong for any of us. What we should have done was let him go so that we could use the new information he gave us to plan a better course of action."

"Except Vincenzo was going to kill Theo's grandmother," I say.

Auntie Min nods. "I still can barely believe that he's doing any of this."

"Believe it," Cory says from below.

I look up to see him approaching through the grass. He doesn't look any the worse for wear—he's not even wet—but one look in his eyes and I'm glad it's not me he's mad at.

"Next time I see him," Cory goes on, "I'm taking him down with a Taser and we'll really give him a reason to hate humans."

"We need to confer with some of the other elders," Auntie Min says.

Cory stops by Tomás's body.

"I'm done with talk," he says, looking down at the dead cousin. "We tried it your way, Señora, and it didn't work. What we're going to do is find Vincenzo and remove him from the equation before he does any more damage."

"Violence isn't always the answer," Auntie Min begins.

Cory cuts her off. "It is this time."

His gaze settles on me. "How's Chaingang?"

"Alive," I tell him, "but unconscious. I'm not sure, but it sounded like his back ... broke."

I realize I'm in shock, otherwise I'd be too messed up to even speak, but I feel the shakes threatening to come on. I need to hold it together for as long as it takes to help Theo.

Cory nods. His gaze goes to Des, who looks paler than I've ever seen him, then he looks around the headland.

"Where's Josh?"

"He went after Vincenzo," I manage. "Into the otherworld."

"And no one stopped him?"

"Dude," Des says, "it all happened so fast. They were both gone before we even knew what was happening."

"Why would he do something so stupid?"

"Vincenzo threatened to kill Elzie," Des tells him. "Along with everybody else Josh cares about. Unless Josh kills Congressman Householder."

Cory shakes his head. "That doesn't even begin to make sense."

Des tells him everything else Vincenzo said.

Cory rubs at his face. "Crap. This is worse than I thought." He looks to Auntie Min. "You have any thoughts on who else is behind this?"

She shakes her head.

"Okay," he says. "We've got our work cut out for us. We need to clean this place up as though we were never here."

I know he means we have to do something with Tomás's body, but I don't know what it means for Theo.

"You should know," Des says, "that The Wild Surf are waiting for Tomás in the parking lot below—along with their driver."

Cory nods. "But first things first. Let's get Chaingang fixed up."

"What are you going to do?" Auntie Min asks as he leaves Tomás's side and walks over to where Des and I are with Theo.

There's a worried tone in her voice, which makes me wonder if I should be feeling even more freaked out than I already am.

"Relax," he tells us. "I'm Coyote Clan. We've got lots of tricks up our sleeve."

"I know," Auntie Min says. "*That's* what worries me."

He waves her off with a casual motion of his hand. "I've done this a thousand times."

"Done what?"

He grins at me. "Taken a walk into somebody else's head."

"Oh, come on, seriously, dude?" Des says. "You expect us to believe you're going to just walk into Chaingang's brain?"

"After all you've seen, *this* you can't accept?"

"So anything can happen?" Des says. "Is that what I'm supposed to believe?"

"I don't go inside him physically," Cory explains. "We call it dreamwalking, which means I can visit his spirit in the place he goes when his body's asleep. The dreamlands are part of the otherworld, and everybody goes there at some point or another. You just don't usually remember your visits. Time spent there gets all messed up with the actual dreams you have. But when a cousin like me is a character in one of your dreams, you're usually not dreaming. You're in the shifting part of the otherworld, where anything can happen, and you're actually talking to a cousin."

I guess the fact that neither Des nor I look like we really get it makes him continue.

"Okay, it's like with your friend Erik. You don't think I *really* took him into the otherworld, do you?"

"Didn't you?" I say.

"Of course not. I took him into a dream of the otherworld. He only thought he was having all those experiences."

"But he was all messed up when I saw him in school—caked in dust, his clothes all dirty and torn."

Cory gives that coyote grin of his. "Oh, that. I just had him roll around in the service lane behind his place until I thought he looked like somebody who'd been having a rough time out in the mountains. The whole time he was rolling around out there, he was dreaming that he was scrabbling around in the mountain dirt and rocks."

"Theo's not going to get hurt," I start.

"Of course not," Cory breaks in. "He's one of us. I'd never treat him like that. I'm just going into his head to have a conversation with him. Tell him it's time to wake up so we can get this show on the road."

"You be careful," Auntie Min warns as Cory kneels down beside Des and me.

"Careful's my middle name," Cory says.

He winks at me as he reaches out with a finger to touch the spot between Theo's eyebrows. Maybe it's my imagination, but I swear there's a little spark of light when the pad of his finger makes contact. Then Cory's eyes roll up in his head, showing their whites.

I'm thinking that his wide-open blank gaze is pretty much the creepiest thing I've seen when the coyote head takes the place of his human features and he vanishes from sight.

"Dude," Des breathes from beside me.

I look to Auntie Min. "This is safe, right? Nobody's going to get hurt?"

"It should be fine," she says, but she doesn't look entirely convinced.

JOSH

I land on Vincenzo's back when I come out of the passageway into the otherworld, ready to tear him to shreds. But he shrugs me off before my claws can dig in, flipping me over his head like I'm still a kid, not a hundred and eighty pounds of mountain lion. There's no grass to land on. There's just the empty space on the other side of the cliff edge. The waves pounding on the rocks below.

Vincenzo snatches me out of the air, one hand grabbing me by the nape of the neck, the other backhanding me along the side of my head. He's so strong that my ears ring from the blow. My gaze fills with stars and I can't think. I can't do much of anything, except hang limp in his iron grip.

"Didn't think you'd have the balls, kid," he says. "Not that you ever had a chance."

I'm still stunned, but the mountain lion has me growling deep in my chest as I start to recover from the blow.

Vincenzo gives me a shake. It feels like my brain is being rattled around in my skull, bouncing off the bone. When he's done I hang limp once more, dangling from his hand. The mountain lion takes a weak swipe at him. He gives me another hard shake.

"You see?" he says. "You're nothing special. The Thunders never sent you—I don't care what anybody says. All you are is some freak of nature."

He's right. It's what I've been trying to tell anyone who'll listen, ever since all of this began.

"I can see in your eyes that you agree." He gives me another shake when he doesn't get a response. "Don't you?"

It's hard with his hand holding me up over the edge of the cliff by the scruff of my neck, but I give him an awkward nod.

"I thought I could use your death to send a message," Vincenzo says, "but you're not even useful for that, are you?"

I move my head to let him know I'm listening before he gives me another rattling shake.

This seriously sucks, but I've no one to blame but myself.

What the hell was I thinking?

Chaingang couldn't take him. Cory and Tomás couldn't do it together. Sure, I have the benefit of a more powerful Wildling shape than any of them, but that's turning out to not be so much of an advantage.

I'm such an idiot. All I was trying to do was stop him from hurting Elzie and Mom. Instead I just threw away any chance I might have had to stop him. Vincenzo's had me so outclassed from the beginning, it's pathetic. My going after him was like a heavyweight being attacked by a lightweight. David going hand-to-hand with Goliath instead of doing the smart thing and taking the giant out from a distance with his trusty slingshot.

I blew it and now everybody's going to die, starting with me.

CHAINGANG

There weren't a lot of things Grandma could afford, but one bill she always paid right smack on time was the cable bill. She had her favourites, but there was plenty of time between soaps and game shows for J-Dog and me to watch the stuff we liked. The pair of us grew up watching a lot of TV—old and new.

One of our favourites was *The Fresh Prince of Bel-Air*—back when Will Smith was still an up-and-comer and hadn't yet made any movies or albums. The idea that some black kid from the 'hood could end up living in a Beverly Hills mansion was a real kick to me and my brother, considering how we had to make do growing up in the Orchards with our grandma. Her place was a long way from the crack house that we'd be stuck in if our mother were still alive, but it couldn't hold a candle to the Fresh Prince's crib.

The thing that's got me thinking about all of this is that I'm standing in the vast marbled foyer of a mansion. I swear the ceiling goes up thirty feet. Suspended from it is a huge chandelier made up of thousands of sparkling crystals. A big stairway comes curving down to meet the marble. Everything smells fresh and clean, like somebody just washed the floor.

I've no idea what I'm doing here, how I got here or who this place belongs to. I glance behind me at a pair of tall oak doors, which I guess I must have walked through to get inside.

Any minute, somebody's going to come along and throw me out.

Or call the cops.

Or both.

But the place is silent except for the ticking of a big wooden grandfather clock standing against the wall to my right. There's a small table beside it with envelopes scattered across its polished surface.

The owner's mail, I guess.

I walk over and pick up an envelope. It's addressed to Mr. & Mrs. T. Washington.

I stare at it for a long moment before I pick up the next one. This one's a bill, and it's addressed to Theodore Washington.

I look around the foyer again.

You have got to be shitting me. This is *my* place?

I rub a hand across my head, looking for the bump I must have gotten when I banged my head and lost my memory.

There's nothing there. Just my head, the stubble telling me it's due for a shave.

So I didn't smash my head. But this doesn't make a lick of sense. I know I'm a member of the Ocean Avers. That my brother runs the gang. That my grandma lives in the Orchards, in a little clapboard house with next to no yard, and an asshole next door whose lane is so full of car parts you have to walk across the dirt of his front yard to reach the door.

So where does this place fit in? How did I get here?

And who the hell is Mrs. Washington?

Besides the stairs going up to a second floor, a large archway on my right leads into a fancy living room that's just as unfamiliar as everything else. Past the stairway and the grandfather clock, a corridor runs off deeper into the house. On the other side of the archway is a closed wooden door, beautifully carved with mythical creatures.

I walk over and try the knob. The door opens into a movie geek's wet dream. It's like a miniature movie theatre with a couple of rows of big plush chairs facing a screen that takes up almost the entire wall. There's a wet bar in the corner with a phone on the gleaming bar top. An answering machine sits beside the phone with a blinking red light.

When I push Play, a familiar voice comes from the little speaker.

"Hey, honey," Marina says. "I'm running a little late. If I'm not back by five, could you heat the oven to three-fifty and put in the enchiladas that Rosa Maria said she'd leave in the fridge? Love ya."

Click. The message is over.

I push Play and listen to it again while I look behind the bar at the rows of liquor bottles. I just might have to break my own rules and have a stiff drink because this is starting to freak me out now.

Marina Lopez is Mrs. Washington?

Why don't *I* know that?

I turn away from the bar and that's when I see the guy sitting in the front row of those big plush chairs, head back on the seat, staring up at the blank screen like he's watching a movie. He wasn't there when I first came in, and he doesn't turn around as I walk down to the front of the chairs. I get an uneasy prickle in the nape of my neck when I can finally see his face. He waits until I'm standing right in front of him before he winks and tips a finger against his brow.

"I know you," I say.

And I do. I just can't remember from where, or even what his name is.

"Of course you do," he says.

I wait, but he doesn't go on. He just sits there, checking me out with this mild gaze that doesn't fool me for a minute. He's not big and he's at a disadvantage, sitting while I'm standing up. Under normal circumstances, I'm pretty sure I could take him, no problem. But there's an intensity about him like a coiled spring that, when it snaps, snaps hard.

I need to know more about him. Who he is, why he's here.

And more important, if he can explain how *I* got here.

"I can't remember your name," I say.

"That happens."

"Or how we met."

He nods. "That, too."

He's not going to make this easy. I feel like pulling him up by the front of his shirt and slapping some answers out of him. Except that's what J-Dog would do. Me, I can be reasonable for as long as it takes. Unless he pulls a gun or takes a swing at me. Then all bets are off.

So I smile and nod right back at him.

"I was hoping maybe you could help me out with that," I say.

His gaze settles on mine.

"What's the last thing you *do* remember?" he asks.

"That's easy. I ..."

My voice trails off because I've got nothing. I know all kinds of things. I know my own name. Where I came from, how I grew up, the school I go to, though I don't so much attend classes as sit outside on a picnic table and let the days go by.

But an actual incident? A real memory of something I did?

I guess it shows on my face.

"Yeah," he says. "I thought as much."

I take a breath to steady the unfamiliar jolt of anxiety that's flooding me.

"You know what's going on, right?" I say.

"I do."

"So tell me."

He nods, but he doesn't say anything for a long moment. I keep studying his face. I'm sure I know him, but I still can't figure out from where.

"Normally," he says finally, "we're supposed to ease into this kind of thing. Go too fast and the mind can get so messed up it might never come back. But we're already a couple of steps behind as it is. We don't have the luxury of taking our time to work this through."

"I have no idea what you're talking about."

"I know. And maybe you never will. But let's give it a shot anyway."

"Any chance you could start talking English?"

"Do you trust me?" he asks.

I shake my head, but the thing is, I kind of do. I don't know why.

He stands up and waves to the chairs. "Grab yourself a seat."

"I'll just stand, if it's all the same to you."

"If you want my help, you'll sit."

With him on his feet, I still tower over him. My sitting will put him at the advantage and that's not how I roll. The first thing you learn on the street, in school, in juvie: never give up an advantage, no matter how small.

He folds his arms and waits.

"Just tell me what's going on," I say.

He shakes his head. "It doesn't work that way."

I want to argue, but I can tell he's got no give in this. If I want answers, I have to play it his way.

So I sit. Reluctantly—and I make sure he knows it—but I sit.

"Now what?" I ask.

He leans a hand on my armrest so that his head's close to mine.

"This is either going to hurt for a moment," he says, "or it'll hurt forever."

"What are you—"

I don't even see where the knife comes from before it's in his free hand. I start to ward off the blow, but I'm way too slow.

The blade punches into my skull, right between my eyes.

My head explodes with white light and pain.

When the black wave comes rolling over me I sink into it with relief.

JOSH

It's funny, the things that go through your head when the guy who's going to kill you is looking you right in the eye. Vincenzo's about to snap my neck like he did with Tomás, and all I can think about is hanging in Des's garage one afternoon and him insisting we should each make out a bucket list—write down all the things we want to do before we die.

"Yeah, yeah, dude," he said. "I get it. All things considered, we've got years to go. But you see all those guys at school with no direction and we know where they're going to end up. That's not going to be us. If we've got something to shoot for, we've got a shot at making something out of our lives." He grinned. "Or at least we'll have a damn good time trying."

So we made out our lists. Goofy, typical stuff.

Lose my virginity. Check.

Jam with The Wild Surf. A half-check there, because at least I did get to meet them.

Win the X Games in L.A. and get a bunch of product endorsements. Des has at least come close, winning a few local comps, though no one's throwing money at him yet.

But most things are still sitting there on those lists.

The headline tour. Except we still haven't even had our first gig. The band doesn't even have a name yet.

Backpack through Europe.

Go to Hawaii and surf with Marina—or at least, go along to lend her moral support because those waves would kill me.

Make it to the Olympics like Shaun White.

Wrestle a kangaroo in Australia. Okay, that was Des's, but he made me put it on my list, too.

It went on, some serious, some just a couple of guys taking the piss out of each other. The wilder those lists got, the harder we laughed.

We managed to fill a couple of pages. A lot of the stuff was never going to happen, but the possibility was always there.

Except not anymore. Not for me.

Vincenzo is saying something to me, but I can't even hear him. I just want this to be over with. I look anywhere but at him. Movement catches my eye overhead and I track a red-tailed hawk until it's out of sight. It makes me think of *los tíos*.

Boy, did they make the wrong call about me.

If that hawk's one of *los tíos*, he's probably flying back to the others to tell them that whatever they thought they'd seen in me wasn't there, and they'd better get back to looking for someone else.

Vincenzo gives me another shake and I realize he's been telling me to change back to my human shape. That suits me just fine. I'd rather die the way I came into this world. The only thing being a Wildling has ever done is bring me grief.

As soon as I change, he throws me onto the ground. I can hardly think straight—but even if I'd had plans to get away, I'd never pull one of them off because he's on me as soon as

I'm down. His bare foot presses down on my chest—not hard enough to crush it, but hard enough so that I can't grab a real breath or get out from under it.

"This is better," Vincenzo says. "It will be so much more satisfying to kill you when you look like what you really are: a five-fingered *pretender*."

Past his face I see that damn hawk is back, circling directly above us like a vulture waiting on his dinner. I wish it would either fly down and save the day or screw off and leave me alone. The way it is, it looks too much like a big fat "I told you so." Because I can remember another hawk in the barrio, warning me off when I went to follow Vincenzo—back before I even knew who he was.

So yeah. I get it already. I'm an idiot.

The stupid bird doesn't have to hang around up there to keep reminding me.

Vincenzo bends down closer to me.

"I could lie," he says, his hands reaching to grab either side of my head, "but we both know I'm going to enjoy this."

If he wasn't so damn strong. If I wasn't so helpless ...

That hawk up there reminds me of something Tío Goyo told me the first time we met.

You are only as weak as you think you are. Expect to be defeated and you will be.

It just pops into my head and I think, what the hell. Sure, it sounds like what Chaingang said it was—fortune cookie advice—but that doesn't mean it's wrong. I may not be what everybody thinks I am, but I'm better than the loser who just gives up. I'm fast and I'm strong. These Thunders—whoever they are—made me what I am for a reason. I'm guessing that reason isn't to simply die here.

I catch hold of Vincenzo's hands before they can grab me.

He laughs and pushes down harder with his foot. I can feel my ribs cracking under the pressure.

But then I let the mountain lion free.

MARINA

It seems like we've been here forever, Des and I, sitting on either side of Theo, too scared to even lift his head to pillow it in case it makes things worse. Auntie Min stands with her back to us, arms folded, her gaze on the far horizon of the Pacific. Tomás's body lies where it fell, unchanged except that Auntie Min laid her scarf over his face after she talked to us.

I turn to Des. "How long has Cory been gone?"

I can't get my head around the fact that Cory's supposed to be literally inside Theo's head—or at least inside his dreams. Except how is that even possible? I know we saw him touch Theo's brow and then disappear, but it doesn't make any sense. Cory's not a big guy, but how can *anything* physical go into a person's head without, you know, severe physical damage?

Des looks at his watch. "Since it's only been a minute since the last time you asked, it's now sixteen minutes."

"Thanks."

I smooth my hand across Theo's brow.

"If he's not back in another ten minutes," I say, "I don't care what anybody thinks. I'm calling an ambulance. They can airlift him out of here and have him in the hospital in about—"

"No." It's loud enough to echo off the rocks.

Auntie Min has turned around to fix us with her gaze. Something changed in her after Tomás died and everything else that's happened. That calm, wise energy she's always given off seems really tired now, and there's a deep anger inside that's a little scary. But I'm too worried about Theo to let it intimidate me.

"This is serious," I tell her. "It's not something that can be fixed with hocus-pocus."

"I understand your concern," she says, "but if you move Theo before Cory returns, we might not get either of them back."

"I don't understand. *How* can he be inside Theo's head?"

"He's not. Cory's walking with him in the dreamlands."

"In his head."

Auntie Min sighs and shakes her head. Then she comes over to where we are and sits on her haunches near Theo's feet.

"The dreamlands are a physical place," she says. "The five-fingered beings usually access it only with their spirits—when they dream. We cousins can access it more freely, though some of us—like Cory—can do it with greater ease."

"You mean it's in the otherworld?"

She nods. "But they lie much deeper. The otherworld you visited can be accessed by anyone, once they've been shown how to make their way through to it. The dreamlands are far more dangerous. The landscape, the weather, the time of day, even the points of the compass change randomly from one moment to the next."

"Like in a dream," Des says.

"Exactly," Auntie Min says. "So Theo's position here on this headland is the only anchor that will allow Cory to bring him back."

"But how long does it take?" I ask.

"That, I can't say. The dreamlands—by their very nature—invariably present complications to even the simplest task."

"So, it might be a while."

She hesitates, then finds a smile that I don't believe.

"Yes," she says. "But not too long, I hope."

She doesn't say it, but in her eyes I can see what she's not telling us: if they *ever* come back.

I feel like crying, but I try not to let it show. If I give in to it now, I might never stop.

I can't lose both Josh and Theo in the same day.

Des reaches over Theo's still body and pats me awkwardly on the shoulder.

"It'll be all right," he says. "I mean, dude. We're talking Josh and Chaingang here. They've been in worse situations."

He doesn't believe it any more than I do. But he means well, and I know what he's trying to do, so I just take a deep breath and nod.

CHAINGANG

When I come to, I'm lying on my back, staring up into a deep blue sky. I reach up to touch the bridge of my nose, where the knife went in, but it feels normal. No wound, not even a scab. I push myself up into a sitting position and look around. I'm in a dry wash in the middle of I don't know where. There's just dusty scrub and desert for as far as I can see. The wash disappears in either direction, marked only by the scraggly mesquite and prickly pear that follow its banks.

Sitting on his haunches a few feet away is Cory. His forearms rest across his knees and there's no sign of the knife he rammed into my brain back in wherever it was that we were.

"That's a pretty good recovery," he says. "I know cousins twenty times your age who would never snap back so quickly."

"Let's see how quickly *you* snap back," I tell him.

I lumber to my feet and sway there, trying to stop the sudden vertigo.

Cory never moves. He just looks up at me, waiting.

"You're a dead man," I tell him.

I'll take him apart with my bare hands—just as soon as the world stops whirling around me. I think I'm going to hurl.

"I was never a man," he says. "And cousins in Coyote Clan are hard to kill."

"A bullet in the head'll take you down the same as anybody else."

He shrugs. "You need a gun for that."

I think I'm going to fall down.

"Maybe later," I manage to get out.

I drop to my knees, then lie down in the dirt again. The world settles down around me.

"As soon as I—can stand without falling down," I add.

Cory smiles. "I knew you were a fighter."

"That was no fight. You sucker-punched me with a knife."

He shakes his head. "No, I just woke you up from that stupid dream of yours. I mean, really? You've got the entire width and breadth of your imagination at your disposal and *that* was the best you could come up with?"

The dirt feels good against my cheek. Like it's grounding me.

"What the hell are you talking about?"

"What's the last thing you remember?" he says.

All the humour's gone out of his eyes. But I've got my own thousand-yard stare.

"You stabbing me in the head with a knife," I tell him.

He waves that off like it was nothing.

"Before that," he says. "Before you were walking around admiring your little Beverly Hills wet dream."

Dream? I guess maybe it was. That makes a lot more sense than me actually owning a place like that.

So—before that?

The memory floods in and I feel a twinge of phantom pain

that runs up my back, from the start of my spine to the nape of my neck.

"Vincenzo," I say. "He threw me onto the rock. I think he broke my back."

Cory nods. "Broke your neck, too, and put you in a coma. Comas are funny things. Sometimes you come right out of them. Sometimes you hang on for years until somebody comes along and pulls the plug."

"I'm in a hospital somewhere?"

"No. You're still lying on a headland overlooking Tiki Bay."

"Seems more like we're at the ass-end of nowhere."

He nods. "Yeah, maybe so, except the fact is, you're here while your body's still over on that headland. It's taking a little time, but we'll be working our way back. The condition you're in—we can't rush this." He flashes me that damn grin of his. "But I'm starting to feel we might be looking at a positive outcome now."

I roll over on my back so that I don't have to look at him.

"So that mansion," I say. "What was it?"

"A safe place. Somewhere your spirit could escape the trauma of what happened to your body. Do you dream about that place a lot?"

"Never saw it before."

"Interesting."

"No, it's not. It's just part and parcel of this freak show I seem to be stuck in." I turn my head to look at him. "Level with me for once. What the hell's going on?"

"Okay. Short version. You know that otherworld we were in a few weeks ago? Now we're in a deeper part of it—some of us call it the shifting lands, or the changing lands. Mostly, it's known as the dreamlands."

"So it's not real."

"It is and it isn't." He holds up a hand before I can speak. "I'm being straight with you. This is where we come when we dream—well, not exactly here in this desert. I chose this place because it's pretty stable and I need you to get yourself together for the next thing we have to do."

"Which is?"

"Get you conscious again so that you can shift from your broken body to your cousin shape and heal yourself."

"Just like that."

"It's easier to do when you're not fighting me," he says.

"So you're going to knife me in the head again."

He smiles and shakes his head. "But if we get out of this, you can take a swing at me if you think it'll make you feel better."

"Count on it."

"Look," he says, "I know you're a tough guy, but sustaining a shock like you did from your injuries, your body just shuts down and your spirit goes away. If we'd had the time, I could have talked you away from the mansion—but that method can take weeks. Nobody wants to believe the place isn't real—especially because deep down they know what's waiting for them when they get back. The knife was the fastest way to get your attention."

"To get my *attention*? If I could get up I'd—"

He cuts me off. "Exactly. To show you that the place you were in *wasn't* real. Now, as soon as we're sure you can handle returning to your body without going into shock again, we'll get everything fixed up."

"You still stuck a knife in my head."

"Like I said, it wasn't real."

"It sure as hell felt like it was real."

He glares at me. "Man, you're stubborn. If I thought it would help, I'd stick it in your head again."

"I'd like to see you—"

"Will you *listen* to me? If I wanted you dead—or even just incapacitated—I wouldn't have bothered to come looking for you. I'd just leave you on the headland and let whatever happens happen."

I can't deny the logic of that.

"Okay," I tell him. "Thanks for stabbing me and saving my life. What happens now?"

"Will you shut your mouth? Just for five seconds even?"

"I—"

But I see the look in his eyes and cut myself off.

Cory sighs, then takes a breath. "Thank you. Now try to stand up again."

I want to tell him, *But I like lying here in the dirt.*

You ever get so nauseous that the only way you feel even remotely okay is to lie down on the floor and not move? That's where I'm at.

"I need you on your feet," Cory says.

I realize I've closed my eyes. I snap them open, half-expecting to see him with that knife in his hand again.

But he's a few feet away, not looking any happier.

"I'm not sure I can," I have to admit.

"You need to try. I don't know how big a window of time we have here. If we take too long and they move you, we won't get a second chance."

Man, I hate this.

"Give me a hand up?" I ask him.

He nods. He hauls me to my feet without any problem—after all, he's got that Wildling strength. Keeping me upright is harder because the world is playing Tilt-a-Whirl on me again. He gets his shoulder under my arm and holds me up.

"Hang in there," he says.

My only response is to throw up on him. The goopy mess spills onto the side of his face and his shoulder before flowing down his neck and chest. He doesn't even flinch. I just feel sicker at the reek of it.

He wipes vomit from the side of his face with his free hand.

"Here's what you need to concentrate on," he says in a calm voice, like this kind of thing happens every day. "You need to be conscious when we get back. Shift right to your cousin shape and then back again."

I can hear him, but everything's spinning so hard that I can't really stay on my feet. Without him holding me up, I'd be down for the count. That wouldn't be so bad. I really really need to lie down again. I start to slump, but he hoists me up again and keeps me standing.

I think I hate him the most for that.

"Focus!" he tells me.

I throw up again. Mostly dry heaves because after the mess I made earlier, there's nothing left in my stomach.

"*Focus*, damn it!"

It's impossible. I don't seem to be aware of anything except the combination of vertigo and my nausea—made all the worse from the stench of the puke I've hurled all over him. His voice seems like it's a hundred miles away. The world spins. The ground feels like it's falling away from under my feet. I keep dry-heaving like I'm never going to stop.

That familiar black wave of unconsciousness comes rearing up over me once more and I welcome it like an old friend.

"Don't you *dare* go away again!" Cory yells.

He says something else, but it's just a mumble. The black wave's swallowing everything.

JOSH

I haven't even finished shifting to my Wildling shape before I'm using the mountain lion's claws to rip into Vincenzo's arms. I'm not getting great purchase, but any normal person would still be incapacitated. Vincenzo just grins at me. It's like he can't even feel the torn flesh.

"Found a little courage, did you?" he says.

He presses down with his foot and the ribs that were cracking snap. One of them pierces a lung and my mouth fills up with blood. I lose my concentration and realize that all I've managed to do so far is shift my arms into the mountain lion's front legs. The pain makes me lose my grip on Vincenzo.

"This is a man's business, boy," he says.

He lays his hands on either side of my head.

I know why he snapped Tomás's neck. Dead, there's no chance of coming back the way I did at the taquería. Dead, I'm not coming back this time.

"You should have done what I told you," he tells me. "Then you'd be the only casualty. Now I'll kill them all. This is on you."

Liar!

I want to scream the word at him, but I'm suffocating on

my own blood. I save the last of my energy to try to prove him wrong. I put away the burning pain that's spread through me because I can't get a breath. The crush of his foot. The hard grip of his hands.

I force it all out of my head to focus on triggering the shift.

Let's see Vincenzo not feel *this*.

MARINA

Theo makes a choking sound. Then his breath—weak as it is—catches. He gags.

"We have to move him," Des says. "Just onto his side."

"But—"

Des nods. "I know. We're not supposed to move him. But I think he's throwing up. He's going to choke to death if we don't do something."

Auntie Min quickly joins us beside Theo.

"He can heal himself when he gets back," she says, "but not if he's dead."

Auntie Min and Des put their hands under his body while I cradle his head. Between the three of us, we manage to turn him onto his side. He retches up spittle and some watery vomit.

Des pulls a face.

"I know," he says before I can speak. "It's not his fault. But dude, that reeks."

"What do we do now?" I ask Auntie Min.

"We can only wait."

I'm not good at waiting.

I lean close to Theo's face. Des is right. It really does reek. But I ignore the sour smell.

"You'd better get your ass back here," I tell him. "You hear me? Don't you dare think you can bail on us now."

CHAINGANG

It's so calm in this black wave that it takes me a moment to realize that the looping 50 Cent riff I'm hearing is a cellphone's ring. My cellphone's ring. Which is weird for all kinds of reasons. To start with, I have no sense of a body at all, so what am I hearing with? Followed up with another biggie: what the hell's a phone doing wherever this is? And how do I answer it?

While I'm still trying to figure that out it goes to voice mail. I can recognize Marina's voice, but not what she's saying. She seems to be coming from a million miles away. I strain to hear the words until I remember where I left her: on the headland near Tiki Bay, where Vincenzo put me down. He'll be going after her and the others. Then he'll go after Grandma. Yeah, Donalita's at Grandma's house, but she won't have a chance in hell of stopping him.

Whatever Marina's saying dissolves into Cory's voice—the words equally unintelligible—and that's when the black wave spits me out.

I open my eyes to find the coyote cousin right in my face. I'm still lying down in what feels like dirt. The blue sky from before has clouded over and the air's not as dry as it was the last time I opened my eyes.

"That's interesting," Cory says. "Usually people go a lot deeper into themselves when they have a setback like that."

He draws back, sitting on his heels. I have to turn my head to look at him. I remember throwing up all over him but there's no sign of the mess now. The dirt I'm lying on seems to be a rough road. There are fields around us, dotted with trees—I couldn't tell you what kind. But it doesn't look like So-Cal to me.

"We have to get back," I tell him.

"I know. Can you sit up?"

"Probably not."

"Are you at least going to try?"

I reach a hand up to him in response.

He pulls me up into a sitting position and we both wait for the world to go spinning on me again. It does—but this time it only leaves me with a mild queasiness. I can deal with this.

"Okay," I tell him. "So far, so good. Let's try standing."

Cory's eyebrows lift.

"Seriously," I tell him.

Cory stands up and gives me his hand again, pulling me up to my feet once more. I sway and begin to fall, but he gets his shoulder under my arm to brace me. I close my eyes.

For a moment, I'm back in that place where the black wave took me. No up, no down. My stomach has settled. A sense of calm floats through me.

But then I remember what's happening back in the world where my broken body lies.

Marina could already be dead.

That freak Vincenzo will be going after Grandma.

I snap my eyes open. My stomach lurches. I stiffen myself so that the weakness in my knees doesn't drop me back onto the ground, but it's Cory bearing my weight that really keeps me on my feet. A flicker of bile comes up my throat and I spit it out onto the dirt.

"How are you holding up?" Cory asks.

"Good," I lie.

"You sure? If you're too weak to regain consciousness, you won't be able to—"

I cut him off.

"Just do it," I tell him.

I think I'm ready for what's going to come next. Big laugh. I don't know what Cory does. One moment, I'm wherever the hell we are, trying to stay on my feet. The next, every nerve end I have is shrieking with a fierce, white-hot pain.

The black wave comes rearing up, but I won't let it take me this time. Instead I embrace the pain. I picture Vincenzo's face in my mind and imagine this is happening to him, not me. I'm just watching.

It doesn't help much. But it's enough.

JOSH

I focus on what Tío Goyo told me.

You are only as weak as you think you are.

Expect to be defeated and you will be.

I tell myself these are truths, not advice.

I keep repeating to myself: I'm not weak. I'm a Wildling mountain lion. Powerful and deadly. In my human shape, I'm stronger and faster than I ever was. Than any humans are. The Thunders changed me for a reason. I don't know who or what they are, why they picked me or what they've got in mind for me. But whatever the reason, I'm pretty sure it wasn't to die at Vincenzo's hands.

I *won't* be defeated by him. Sure, he's old and has been around forever, but you know what? Blah blah blah. I don't care how tough and strong he is. At the end of the day, he's only a condor. A bird. My mountain lion can take a bird.

I believe it. I believe it absolutely.

I snap into my Wildling shape so fast something pops in my ears. I get a momentary glimpse of the shock in Vincenzo's eyes. Then my hind legs come up and I tear him open. My claws scrape along his ribs until they can really dig in and scoop out his insides. Organs and intestines come spilling out all over me.

He doesn't even have time to fight back.

I twist around so that he's underneath. He starts to change into his own Wildling shape, but I'm faster. I'm not giving him a chance to heal himself. My jaws close onto his head, fangs puncturing the skull like it's made of cardboard before I rip his head from his torso.

Blood gushes from his neck like a geyser cutting loose, spraying me in the face. I toss his head away and back off. I have a moment where I tell myself to be patient, to watch for any sign that he's going to come back. But a red veil of rage envelops me, and before I know it, I've shredded his body until the pieces are scattered all over the ground around us.

When it's over, when the adrenaline finally fades and the red haze falls away, I stand there looking at what I've done.

A few weeks ago, I killed that researcher at ValentiCorp and I couldn't get it out of my head. She was despicable, but I still felt guilty.

Now, I only feel satisfaction.

I think the only guilt I have is that I don't feel guilty.

I could worry at that forever, I suppose. Instead I bound away. I make my way down from the headland to where Tiki Beach would be in the world I left behind. At the water's edge I shift back to my human shape and plunge into the waves, washing off the blood and gore.

When I come out again there's a figure waiting for me on the beach. I reach out with that detection system in my head, but it doesn't seem to be working anymore. Maybe it's gone away.

Maybe it just doesn't work in this world. I don't have time to puzzle it out right now.

I'm about to shift again and tear into him until I realize that it's not Vincenzo, impossibly resurrected. It's Tío Goyo.

I close the distance between us until I'm only a few feet away.

"Was that you up there," I ask, "watching while Vincenzo tried to kill me?"

"I was nearby," he says, which isn't an answer at all.

"Well, thanks for the big assist."

He shrugs. "You never needed my help."

"Then why did the hawk stop me from confronting him in the barrio?"

"It wasn't time. Back there," he says, "you can borrow strength from the land under your feet. You don't have that connection here—at least, you don't have it yet. We needed you to understand that everything you require to prevail is already inside you."

"*Seriously?* I almost died."

"But you didn't."

"So it was—what? All some test? Did you sic Vincenzo on us in the first place?"

"Absolutely not."

I find myself believing him. I don't particularly like him right now, but I believe him.

"But," he adds, "we did take advantage of the situation. We had to know that you will be strong enough for the challenges to come."

While I don't know what he thinks is going to happen next, I do know I'm not going to be a part of it.

I shake my head. "Good luck with your problems," I tell

him, "but the only challenge I've got in front of me right now is finding Elzie."

"This is larger than your girlfriend."

"First off, she's not my girlfriend—not anymore. But that doesn't matter. I don't know what it's like where you come from, but me? I think everybody's important—it doesn't matter who. Whatever you've got going on that's such a big deal for you, it's not my problem. My problem is tracking down my friend. I don't know what he did to her."

"I understand. But—"

"The only thing she did wrong was knowing me. If we'd never met, Vincenzo would never have grabbed her."

"What's going on is a 'big deal' for everyone," Tío Goyo says, "including your friend. There's a monster waking up in the heart of the world and you're here to stop it before it destroys everything."

I remember Agent Solana telling me something along these lines. Not that it was up to me to deal with it, but that *los tíos* are fighting some kind of giant parasite thing. The idea that I'm their go-to guy is ridiculous.

"Really?" I say. "You think I got changed into a Wildling to save the world from monsters? I don't know which of you is worse. The elder cousins have another theory or two. That some bunch of guys called the Thunders changed me because—well, nobody seems to know exactly why. It's a guessing game. Now you've got some *other* agenda all laid out for me.

"The problem for all of you is, I'm not your chosen one. What happened to me was random. I'm just a guy with a friend who's in trouble. So you and the elders need to go solve your own problems."

Tío Goyo studies me for a moment before he asks, "And how will you find your friend?"

"I don't know. I'll track her, I guess. How hard can it be?"

Hard enough, I suppose, since I can't get the radar in my head to turn on, but I don't feel like admitting that at the moment. I'll figure it out.

He smiles.

"What?"

"You have no idea what this world is like, do you?" he says.

I shrug. "I know it's just like our world before everything got all messed up."

"Here," he agrees, "where we're standing, that's close enough. But go deeper into it and it isn't anything like the one you know— and not for the obvious reasons. You'll soon find it's layered like an onion and structured like a maze. The deeper you go, the more complex and confusing it becomes. Time passes faster or slower, the very land under your feet changes climate and terrain in the blink of an eye."

We're standing on a beach. The night sky holds stars, their light glinting on the whitecaps as they roll in to shore. I smell brine and seaweed. I can hear the waves close at hand and the wind up in the hills. But there's nothing else. There are no cars, no highway, no cities.

"It doesn't seem that complex to me," I tell him.

"If I were the man you think me to be," he says, "only concerned with how I could use you, I would leave you to your own devices until you understood the enormity of the task before you. Instead, I will help you find your friend."

"In exchange for what?"

"I don't make bargains," he tells me. "But if we find your friend, and if we can return her to safety, we can have this conversation again and perhaps you'll consider helping me."

"And if I still say no?"

He shrugs. "Then I'll go on alone."

I figure there's got to be a trick—something I'm not getting—but I can't for the life of me figure out what it is.

I reach out again with the radar system in my head. It still won't come on board. It's there—I can feel it trying to focus—but I can't seem to make it work. That's going to suck if I have to find Elzie on my own.

"I should remind you," Tío Goyo says when the silence stretches out between us, "that Vincenzo's allies won't take kindly to what you've done."

"He was trying to kill me," I say. "He threatened to kill my mom and friends. What was I supposed to do?"

"That will be irrelevant to them. What we need to do is get away from here and find your friend before they discover that you killed Vincenzo."

He's right.

I look at my hands. The ocean washed away the blood that covered them.

I nod to where the headland rears above us. "Why don't I feel bad about what happened up there?"

"He was a mad dog," Tío Goyo says. "Someone had to put him down."

"Okay. But the *way* I did it ..."

"I have noticed," Tío Goyo says, "that those who *become* animal people—rather than those who are born into the clans—

undergo a period of change as their human and animal natures adjust to one another. The temporary appearance of a quick temper is the most common."

I think of the mess I left up there on the headland.

"What I did was way more than just the result of a quick temper," I say.

"You don't know your own strength."

Maybe. Except Vincenzo was already dead when I tore him apart. What does *that* say about me?

Tío Goyo cocks his head suddenly.

"We need to go," he says.

"Go where?"

"To look for your friend."

"I have to tell Mom and my friends first," I say. "They'll freak if I just disappear."

He shakes his head. "We need to leave *now*. Someone's coming and we don't want to be here if they expect to be meeting Vincenzo."

"But—"

"Won't your friends and your mother be more upset if you're dead?" he asks.

"Well, sure, but—"

"Then we have to go. Now."

He grabs my shoulder and takes a step, pulling me with him. There's a sensation like cobwebs brushing all over me—my face, under my clothes—then the ocean and the shore are gone and we're someplace else.

MARINA

Auntie Min is telling us about the old days—before there even was a Santa Feliz. She's relating a story about a pair of crow girls getting into mischief. She and Des are sitting on either side of Theo, keeping him propped up, while I've got his head cradled in my lap. His breathing is even now. I hear singing come up from the beach below. I guess The Wild Surf are hanging out with the surfers, jamming. They sound like they're having fun. It must be nice not having a clue about what happened up here. They don't even know yet that Tomás is dead.

I wish I didn't have a clue.

I can tell that the story Auntie Min's in the middle of right now is supposed to be funny—I guess she's trying to cheer us up—but I'm not feeling it. How can I, with Josh still missing and Theo as unresponsive as he is? But I'm trying to pay attention. For long stretches of time—like five or ten seconds—it takes my mind away from why we're here and my worries about Theo and Josh.

But then I immediately come back. I hate this waiting.

I'm about to ask Des what time it is again when two things suddenly happen:

Cory appears out of nowhere. He falls in a tumble of limbs across the big flat stone where we're sitting, like something just spit him out.

And Theo disappears.

I immediately begin to shriek.

"Dude!" Des yells and jumps to his feet.

"Nobody move!" Auntie Min says in a voice that freezes everybody in place.

"Yeah," Cory says. He's sitting up, rubbing his shoulder. "Wait for it."

"Wait for what?" Des asks.

But suddenly I get it. Theo shifted to his Wildling shape, which is so small it only looks like he vanished. I spy the mouse he became just before he shifts again, and then he's back in his normal body. I forget that he might still be injured and throw myself on him. When I realize what I'm doing, I pull back.

"Are you here for real?" he asks.

There's a weird haunted look in his eyes. I'm so relieved he's okay that I get mad at him.

"Don't you *ever* scare us like that again!" I tell him, tears finally rolling down my face.

He smiles and reaches up. "Yeah, you're for real, sweetcheeks," he says, pushing my tears aside with his thumb. "Did Cory make it back?"

"Over here," Cory calls to him. "Are you going to punch me now?"

Theo sits up. "Depends. Are you going to stick a knife in my head again?"

I wipe my eyes and look from one to the other. "*What* are you talking about?"

"Nothing," Theo says. "It's just good to get back and be mobile again."

When he gets to his feet, he sees Tomás's body.

"What happened to him?" he asks.

"Same thing as happened to us," Cory says. "He took on Vincenzo, except he didn't survive."

Theo sighs. "Crap. So he really was one of the good guys."

Then he looks around.

"Where's Josh?" he asks.

For a long moment, nobody knows what to say.

"He went through the portal thingy," Des finally says. "After Vincenzo."

"And nobody stopped him?" Theo asks, echoing Cory's earlier reaction.

Des takes a step back at the glare in Theo's eyes. "Dude, he was through before anybody even knew it."

Theo's gaze tracks across us until it lands on me again.

"It's true," I tell him.

And then we had to look after you, I want to add, but I can tell from the look on his face that's not something he's going to want to hear about.

He picks up his tire iron.

"So what are we waiting for?" he asks. He points to Auntie Min. "Get us over there."

"I don't know if that's exactly what we should be—"

"I'm not asking," Theo tells her with a growl in his voice.

Cory gets up. He brushes dirt from his jeans.

"I can take you over," he says.

Auntie Min shoots Cory a warning look, which he just

ignores. When Theo and I walk over to him, Auntie Min sighs and comes over as well.

"I'm not saying it's the smart thing we're doing," Theo tells Auntie Min. "But it's the right thing—you see the difference?"

She nods.

When Des starts to join us, I shake my head.

"You stay," I tell him.

"You're kidding me, right? Dude, I've known Josh longer than anybody here. There's no way I'm sitting this one out."

"But it's too dangerous."

"Why? Because I'm human? I hate to break it to you, but I didn't see the Wildling contingent doing all that great earlier."

"He's right," Theo says to me. "Let him come." Then he turns to Des and adds, "But once we're there, hang back a little, bro—just till we get the lay of the land."

Des nods.

"Any time," Theo tells Cory.

Cory doesn't seem to do anything special. No chants, no intricate movements of his hands. One moment, we're looking out over the ocean with the lights of the oil rigs and a freighter in the distance, the next, there's a hole in the world and we're stepping back into that amazing otherworld. I remember the air being so heady the last time we were here and take a deep breath only to gag on the stench of blood and gore.

It's the most horrific thing I've ever seen. There are body parts littered all over the ground.

"Ah, Jesus," Theo says.

It takes me a moment longer to process what Theo's already figured out.

Josh.

This ... this horrible butchery ... it's all that's left of him.

I turn away and press my face against Theo's shoulder. His arms around me can't even begin to comfort the awful grief that floods me.

"I was supposed to have his back," Theo says, his voice a bare murmur.

"Hold up," Des says. "If you're thinking this is Josh, you're so jumping the gun."

I swallow hard and pull away from Theo to look. Des is standing a few yards away from the worst of the gore, pointing with his shoe at a head that's lying on its side. I can't really focus on anything except that it's not Josh's.

"Vincenzo," Cory says.

Theo nods slowly. "So that means ..."

"That this is Josh's handiwork," Auntie Min finishes for him.

"But if all of—this—is what's left of Vincenzo," I say, "where's Josh?"

Cory's walking around the edges of the awful mess of blood and body parts.

"Here," he says. "I've got a scent."

He shifts to his coyote shape and trots off down the slope toward the beach, nose to the ground. I can't get away from here fast enough.

"Dude, that is so cool," Des says as we follow Cory.

I shoot him a look.

"Well, it is," he says. "You need to embrace the awesomeness of what you guys can do."

"I don't know about the rest of us," Theo says, "but if Josh can take out Vincenzo like that, there's probably not much he can't do."

"Then why would he just take off?" I say.

"Perhaps," Auntie Min says, "he is troubled to learn just what he is capable of. Or perhaps he ran into Vincenzo's associates. Vincenzo said he wasn't working alone."

"Dudes," Des says. "Think about what else Vincenzo said. Josh has gone to look for Elzie."

Cory is waiting for us in human form at the edge of the water.

"He met someone here," he says when we reach him. "A man. They left together."

"Left to go where?" I ask.

"Deeper into the otherworld."

"Did he go by choice," Theo asks, "or was he forced?"

Cory points to the wet sand, where there are two sets of footprints. You can see where they were standing around, talking, then they just step away into nothing. What's stranger is that, while we can work out Josh's approach—the mountain lion's paw prints are pretty obvious even for me—the other man's prints show that he came out of the same nowhere into which they disappeared. He didn't walk onto the sand. He simply appeared.

"There's no sign of a struggle," Cory says.

"So what do we do now?" Des asks.

He looks to Theo rather than Auntie Min for the decision. Oddly, so does Cory.

"I don't know," Theo says. "This is messed up. If Vincenzo wasn't working alone, what are his pals up to? What's their next move?"

"Vincenzo spoke of assassinating Congressman House-holder," Auntie Min says.

"Dude, who cares about that freakin' bigot."

I nod in agreement.

"You *should*," Cory says. He enumerates on his fingers. "He dies at that rally, and he becomes a martyr. That gives his cause more credence. Wildlings will be blamed and the hunt will really be on."

Des nods. "Yeah, that Danny dude who was friends with Elzie told Josh the Feds are already planning to up their game."

"Maybe we should have a word with Josh's pet agents," Theo says. "Get the real lowdown on where that's going."

"But Vincenzo wanted *Josh* to kill the congressman," I say. "If Vincenzo's dead and Josh is gone, that's over, isn't it?"

"Don't kid yourself," Theo says. "All they wanted was a Wildling to do it. There's lots of kids who got changed, and I'll bet there's more than a few who don't have Josh's backbone. They'd be easy targets for Vincenzo's friends."

Auntie Min nods. "We need to find out exactly who we're up against."

"Plus we've got those guys from Black Key who were gunning for Josh," Des says. "They're still running around. What if *they* decide to go after his mom? Or one of us?"

Theo's nodding slowly. "It's obvious Josh can handle himself. That leaves it up to us to head back and take care of all this other crap."

"And we should do it soon," Cory says. "Someone's going to come looking for Vincenzo, and I don't think we want to be here when they find what's left of him."

"Yeah," Theo says. "I don't know what Josh's got running under his hood, but I don't have that kind of horsepower and I'm not ready to get my ass handed to me again. Next time I go up against any of these guys I want to be standing with a rocket launcher in my hands, pointed right at their heads."

Des looks dumbstruck. "Dude, you've *got* one of those?"

Theo looks at me and rolls his eyes.

"Yeah," he tells Des, "but it's in my other jacket."

"Ha ha," Des says.

"Seriously," Theo says to us. "We've got our work cut out for us and we need to get moving."

He nods at Cory, but it's Auntie Min who opens the way back for us. We just about give one of the surfers on Tiki Beach a heart attack when we appear right beside him. He takes a couple of steps back and runs a hand through his blond hair. He's unsteady on his feet—a little drunk, or a little stoned. Maybe both.

"Whoa," he says. "Where the hell did you guys come from?"

Theo bristles at my side and I lay a hand on his arm.

"I'm cool," he mutters.

Des steps in between us and the surfer with his hands spread out in front of him.

"Dude," he says, "we were here all along. How did you not see us?"

The surfer gives Des a closer look.

"I know you," he says. "You're Cindy's skateboarder friend."

"That's me."

Des puts an arm around the surfer's shoulders and steers him back toward the fire.

"You should go," Cory says to Theo and me. "We'll deal with Tomás's body and get Des back to town."

Before we can respond, he and Auntie Min are walking toward the van, which I assume belongs to The Wild Surf. There's an older guy giving off a Wildling buzz leaning against the front of the van, arms folded across his chest. Since I know he's not a member of the band, I assume he's the driver. He straightens up at their approach.

I look over at the campfire and see that Josh and Des weren't exaggerating. Joanie Jones is all over Des. He mouths "Help me" when he sees me looking. I shake my head and give him a wave. The look he gives me back is the first thing to make me smile in hours.

"I really need to get to my papá's house," I tell Theo.

"You're actually going to leave Des hanging?" Theo says.

"Do you have room for three of us on your bike?"

"Well, no."

"So you see ..."

He nods. "Yeah. I guess he's a big boy. He can handle it. Besides, as soon as the band finds out what happened to their manager, Joanie's going to have other things on her mind."

Cory nods at us as we pass the van. When we get to the Harley, Theo swings his leg over the seat. I get on behind him and a moment later we're on the highway heading back to Santa Feliz.

I lean my head against Theo's back, trying to remember what it was like before I got changed into a Wildling.

It seems like a lifetime ago.

Back then, drama was an argument with my sister, or Julie breaking up with yet another guy. I thought the world was ending if I got a bad mark in a test or took a spill at a meet with the surf club.

I had no idea.

Six months ago, I was trying to survive being a teenager.

Now I'm just trying to survive.

ACKNOWLEDGMENTS

My deep appreciation and thanks go to those who helped carry the Wildlings story a little further: my wife and first editor, MaryAnn, who offers encouragement and assistance at every step along the way (and gives up some of her own creative life in the process); my editor, Lynne Missen, and the team at Penguin Canada, for all of their excellent help and support; my agents, Heather Baror and Russ Galen, who offer sound advice whenever I need it; my webmaster, Rodger Turner, who is that, but also a treasured friend; MaryAnn's and my family members who put up with our busy lives and help us out; and last but not least, my readers, young and not so young, who buy my books and thereby let me continue to do what I love. I am grateful to each and every one of you.